TREACY

FIRE FORCE

By Matt Lynn and available from Headline

DEATH FORCE
FIRE FORCE

MATT LYNN
FIRE FORCE

headline

First published in 2010
by HEADLINE PUBLISHING GROUP

1

Cataloguing in Publication Data is available from the British Library

ISBN 978 0 7553 4496 3 (Hardback)
ISBN 978 0 7553 4497 0 (Trade paperback)

Typeset in Hoefler by Avon DataSet Ltd,
Bidford on Avon, Warwickshire

Printed in the UK by CPI Mackays, Chatham, ME5 8TD

Headline's policy is to use papers that are natural, renewable and
recyclable products and made from wood grown in sustainable forests.
The logging and manufacturing processes are expected to conform
to the environmental regulations of the country of origin.

HEADLINE PUBLISHING GROUP
An Hachette UK Company
338 Euston Road
London NW1 3BH

www.headline.co.uk
www.hachette.co.uk

To Claudia

Acknowledgements

Most of all, I'd like to thank the four different mercenaries who shared their experiences with me: descriptions of all the weapons, based on their experience, can be found in the Appendix. Without first-hand accounts of fighting in Africa, this book wouldn't have been possible. You know who you are, boys. Thanks to Martin Fletcher at Headline and Bill Hamilton at A.M. Heath for their advice and encouragement. And, of course, to my wife Angharad and my three daughters Isabella, Leonora and Claudia, who did their best not to disturb me too much whilst the book was being hammered into shape.

Matt Lynn

The Unit

Steve West A South Londoner, Steve served in the SAS for five years, fighting in Bosnia and behind the lines in the second Iraq War. After leaving the Army, Steve started freelancing for Bruce Dudley's Private Military Corporation, Dudley Emergency Forces – an outfit known in the trade as Death Inc. for the high-risk, high-stakes jobs it is willing to take on. With the money he made in Afghanistan – a mission described in *Death Force** – Steve has bought out his Uncle Ken's half-share in a vintage car dealership in Leicestershire.

Ollie Hall Once an officer in the Household Cavalry, the most blue-blooded of British regiments, Ollie was trained at Sandhurst and was, for a time, one of the fastest-rising young stars in the armed forces. But he had a problem with drinking and gambling, and eventually left the Army to make a career in the City. When that failed as well, he started trying to form his own PMC, before joining up with Steve for the mission in Afghanistan. He is engaged to Katie, a London public relations girl.

David Mallet With twenty years' experience as an officer in the Irish Guards behind him, David is an experienced, battle-hardened soldier, an expert in logistics and military strategy and planning. He is divorced from his first wife, with two grown-up children at private

* Headline, 2008

I

schools to pay for, and his second wife has just given birth to twins.

Nick Thomas From Swansea, Nick spent two years in the Territorial Army before joining Steve on the Afghanistan mission. An only child, he was brought up by his mother Sandra, and never knew who his father was. He is the man with the least military experience on the team. But he is also the best marksman any of them have ever met, with an uncanny ability to hit a target with any kind of weapon.

Ian 'The Bomber' Murphy A Catholic Ulsterman, Ian grew up in Belfast and spent ten years working as a bomb-maker for the IRA. He was responsible for several explosions that killed both soldiers and civilians, and was sentenced to life imprisonment. After spending years in the Maze prison, he was released as part of the Good Friday agreement. He is no longer a member of the IRA, and has severed his connections with his old life. But he is still an expert bomb-maker, able to fashion an explosive device out of the most basic components.

Dan Coleman A former member of the Australian Special Air Service Regiment (SASR), a unit closely modelled on the British SAS, Dan fought in Afghanistan as part of an SASR-unit deployed to fight the Taliban. Wrongly accused of killing two children during a patrol in Helmand, he spent a year in a military jail. Haunted by the incident, he has left the Australian Army and has taken up freelancing for PMCs. Dan is an expert on weaponry, always aware of the latest military technology, and desperate to try it out.

Ganju Rai A former Gurkha, Ganju served for eight years in C Company, in the 2nd Battalion of the Parachute Regiment, primarily staffed by Gurkhas. He comes from a small Nepalese village, and is fiercely loyal to the traditions of the Gurkha Regiments. Rai's brother, also a Gurkha, was killed in Kosovo, and his wife and children are not getting a pension. Ganju has become a mercenary in order to earn enough money to help support his extended family back home. He is an expert in stealth warfare.

Chris Reynolds A veteran of South Africa's Special Forces Brigade, known as the 'Recce' unit, Chris spent fifteen years in the South African Defence Force, and regards the Recces as the finest fighting unit in the world. But he left the armed forces after he became disillusioned with the post-apartheid regime. He bought himself a farm in South Africa, but when that went bust, he was forced to work as a mercenary to pay off his debts, even though it is illegal for South Africans to work for PMCs. Of all the men in the unit, he is the most battle-hardened, his combat skills sharpened by years of fighting in Southern Africa's vicious border wars.

Maksim Perova A former member of the Russian special forces, the Spetznaz, Maksim is a suicidally brave soldier. His father was killed in Afghanistan in the early 1980s, and he has a bad vodka habit. During the mission in Afghanistan described in *Death Force* he was tricked into betraying the unit, but was forgiven because he proved himself the most ferocious fighter any of the men had ever seen. Fit, strong and courageous, Masksim is always ready for a fight.

Bruce Dudley A gruff Scotsman, Dudley is the founder and chief shareholder in Dudley Emergency Forces. A former SAS Sergeant, he left the Regiment ten years ago, and soon realised there was money to be made from running a private army. He was a legendarily tough soldier himself, and doesn't see why anyone else should complain about terrifying conditions. He has a great understanding of what makes his mercenaries tick, and knows how to manipulate them.

Jeff Campbell, deceased A former soldier, Campbell came from South London, and grew up with Steve. The two men were best mates. He was the man in the unit with the greatest sense of camaraderie, always organising a party, and making sure everyone had enough to drink. Despite the best efforts of his comrades to save him, Jeff died from his wounds on the mission in Afghanistan described in *Death Force*.

One

UNTIL YOU'VE SAT DOWN TO a game of poker inside Africa's most brutal jail you don't really know what it's like to sweat, decided Steve West. He could feel a drop of perspiration snake down his neck, then drip down his back. It was cold – the sweat of fear. He glanced down at his cards. Two eights. 'Christ,' he muttered under his breath. With a life at stake, you'd be hoping for something better than a couple of eights to bet on.

But those were the cards.

And sometimes there was no choice but to play the hand fate dealt you.

'Raise you,' he said, pushing a fifty-dollar bill onto the table.

The man opposite chuckled, took a deep, thoughtful drag on his cigarette, then glanced furtively at his own cards. Felipe Abago was a big, angry beast of a man, weighing at least 300 pounds and, from the way he sweated in the early-evening warmth, a lot more of it was fat than muscle. He was wearing a cream linen suit, though it looked to be years since he'd last put on the jacket. But then, reflected Steve, when you ran one of the biggest, most terrifying jails in Africa, you didn't have to dress for the office.

On Bioko, a small tropical island off the main coast of the oil-rich African state of Equatorial Guinea, Broken Ridge jail held more than 5,000 men and women, often for years at a time, cramped sometimes as many as 100 to a cell. According to the taxi drivers, the screams of the women being raped could be heard as far away as the capital Malabo. And Abago was the Commandant. His own private hell, thought Steve. And he seemed to revel in it.

'I said I'd raise you,' repeated Steve, a note of quiet determination running through his voice.

'I like to think about my cards, Mr West,' said Abago.

Steve just shrugged. 'Play it your way,' he replied casually.

'Some beer,' shouted Abago loudly.

One of the prisoners quickly brought across a tray, with two bottles of Ghanaian-brewed Stone Strong Lager. The man was six foot, noted Steve as he grabbed a bottle of the chilled lager, but he had thick iron manacles clamped to his feet and hands, and there was a metal ring around his neck so that he could be hooked and unhooked from his cell with ease. He walked with a limp, and there were raw, bloody welt-marks down his back where he'd taken a whipping. He was dressed only in a pair of dirty denim shorts and smelled of blood and rotting flesh. 'Thanks, mate,' said Steve as he grabbed the bottle, watching the man scurry away like a frightened animal.

Steve took a hit of the beer, and looked around the bar.

The main block of Broken Ridge was on the seafront, its forbidding exterior ringed by a barbed-wire fence that rose eight feet into the air. It was patrolled constantly by heavily armed guards, whilst four watchtowers, one at each corner of the compound, were manned by sullen-looking soldiers with machine guns. The bar was just outside the main jail, next to the dusty road that led up from Malabo. Men from the jail were made to work at the bar, while a dozen or so women were dragged from the cells each night and forced to service the guards and customers in the few bedrooms out the back. Like many African jails, the staff were paid a pittance, and running the makeshift bar and brothel was the only way they could earn a proper living. The oil workers from the rigs would come up here at the weekends and spend their cash on beer and girls, but this was a Tuesday night, and the place was quiet.

Maybe it will warm up later on, wondered Steve. But let's hope not. This place is bad enough on a quiet night.

I'd hate to see it when it gets rough.

Steve had landed in Malabo this afternoon, after catching an Air France flight from Heathrow to Paris, then connecting onto the French airline's service to Equatorial Guinea. He'd spent most of the ten hours in the air cursing the fact that he was here at all. A mate of his called Ollie Hall, who also worked for Dudley Emergency Forces, had taken on a contract to break a man out of the jail. Why Ollie had accepted the job, Steve couldn't begin to understand. Nobody broke out of Broken Ridge. Once you were locked up here, you were already as good as dead. You were just waiting to be buried.

That was true of the five thousand miserable souls locked up here.

And now it was true of Ollie as well.

And it was Steve's job to get him out.

Two days ago, Ollie's fiancée Katie had come to see him. There were tears streaming down the woman's face. Their wedding was in less than four weeks' time. The Embassy had promised to do all they could, but they couldn't even guarantee to get a meeting with the Interior Minister in four weeks. If they were to negotiate Ollie's release, it would take six months at least.

And even then they weren't exactly optimistic.

The government of Equatorial Guinea didn't have much sympathy for white mercenaries. And neither did the Foreign Office.

'You have to get him out, Steve,' Katie had said, weeping on his shoulder. 'You're my only hope.'

So, reluctantly, Steve had agreed to try. It was either that, or else go back and tell Katie to put her wedding dress in mothballs. Because Broken Ridge didn't look like the kind of place that had a parole board.

'I'm folding,' grumbled Abago. He slammed his cards down on the table.

Steve reached across and collected the pot. It came to $120, a fortune in a country where most people earned less than that in a year.

'Another round?' he suggested.

He was keeping his voice as casual as possible but that wasn't the way he felt. After checking into the Sofitel downtown, he'd scoured the street market and bought the first handgun he could find, a Raven-25, and then he'd caught a taxi right up here. Ollie had accepted a $100,000 contract to break out a man called Newton Bunjira who'd already spent ten years locked up here. Now it was costing the same guys another $250,000 to break him out: even with that kind of money on the table Steve wouldn't have taken the job unless Katie had begged him. He had kitted himself out with $1,000 in cash, and ten South African minted gold Krugerrands, each one weighing a single troy ounce, then come straight up to the bar. There was only one way into Broken Ridge, and that was through the front door.

I just have to get the Commandant to let me in, he thought. And the only way to do *that* is over a card table.

Abago clicked his fingers and one of the four girls sitting at the bar walked across to the table, draping her arms across the man's sweaty chest. She didn't look any older than fifteen. Her skin was smooth and supple, and she was wearing a white cotton dress that did little to disguise her figure. 'Deal us some cards, you bitches,' he growled.

Another girl had already placed her hands across Steve's shoulders. He looked up into her huge, dark eyes. She remained silent, massaging the back of his neck, then reached down for the deck and shuffled the cards with her long red fingernails.

'What's your business in my country, Mr West?' asked Abago.

'Import, export.'

'In the oil trade?'

Steve nodded. Keep it simple, he told himself. Just play the part of an innocent businessman dealing with the local oil companies. A guy who's stumbled into this bar for some relaxation.

'I hope you make plenty of money, Mr West . . .' the Commandant took a hit from his beer bottle and squeezed the girl around the waist, his fat fingers digging into her skin until she squealed in pain '. . . because then I can win it from you at poker.'

Steve turned up the two cards lying face down on the table.

A pair of eights.

He felt another bead of cold sweat edge down his spine.

'Sodding eights,' he muttered under his breath. 'It's going to take more than that to break my mate Ollie out of this Hell's Butlins.'

TWO

'IS THIS A PRIVATE GAME, OR can anyone play?'

Ian Murphy had already pulled up a chair and helped himself to a bottle of beer. He was a small man, with a build that was half-footballer, half-bricklayer: short and round, with a low centre of gravity, and thick, bruising muscles. His cropped brown hair looked like it might turn orange if it was left out in the sun, and his cheeks were marked with freckles. A pair of thick dark glasses were wrapped around his face, obscuring his eyes completely. 'The Bomber', thought Steve. The man wasn't much to look at, but give him some fuse wire and some Semtex and there wasn't any kind of chaos he couldn't unleash.

'Another white man,' said Abago, grinning. He took a long, hard swig of his beer. 'If there's one thing I enjoy more than taking a woman off a white man . . . it's taking his money.'

'Make yourself at home, pal,' said Steve tersely, looking up towards Ian.

Ian had taken a different route into Malabo from Steve. He'd caught a British Airways flight to Casablanca, then connected onto a Royal Air Maroc plane down to Equatorial Guinea. The two men were staying at the same hotel, but they had checked in at different times and hadn't said a single word to each other. They were planning to keep it that way. If they were to have any chance of pulling this off, then it was absolutely vital that nobody realised they were working together.

We don't want to find ourselves locked up in this rat hole, Steve thought. Saving Ollie's miserable skin isn't worth twenty years in this place.

'Five card?' said Ian.

Steve nodded. 'Deal yourself in, mate.'

The plan was a simple one. They knew Abago liked to gamble. Ian and Steve would make their separate ways to the bar, then get Abago into a game of poker. Working as a team, they'd force the Commandant into big losses. They'd then offer to settle the debt off the books. Let Ollie go, and Abago could keep the money he'd lost.

It had sounded fine when Bruce Dudley, the man in charge of Dudley Emergency Forces, or Death Inc. as it was known in the trade, sketched it out for them back in London. But out here, reflected Steve as he looked up across the table at Abago, it didn't feel quite so easy.

The Commandant was fat, cruel and malevolent, his brain rotted by years of sycophancy and torture. The trouble was, none of that meant he couldn't play cards.

'Deal him in,' instructed Abago.

The girl unwrapped the arms that were draped over his chest, and laid out a couple of cards in front of Ian. Steve checked his own deck again. Two eights, same as before. Ian took a hit of beer, then pushed a twenty-dollar bill into the pot. 'Raise you . . .' he said.

Steve chipped in twenty, so did Abago, then they laid their cards on the table.

The Commandant had a full-house.

An easy win.

Steve smiled to himself. Lose a couple of rounds, that was the plan. Get the man hooked on the game. Then start to toy with him, the same way you'd toy with a fish at the end of a line. Let him wriggle and gasp for air, give him a bit more line, then when you're ready, land the bastard on the deck of the boat.

Abago scooped up the money, handing five dollars to the girl and tucking the rest into the breast-pocket of his shirt. A prisoner was bringing across a bowl of fresh pumpkin seeds. Steve noticed that he only had a left hand: the right had been severed just below the elbow, replaced by a stump where the wound had slowly and messily closed up. 'Deal again,' snapped Abago. 'We're just getting started.'

He took a mouthful of the seeds, chewed, then spat a few on the floor, while the girl dealt out three hands of cards. Steve glanced down. A Queen and a Jack. The start of a flush maybe? He asked for more cards, but ended up with nothing better than a pair of Jacks. That's OK, he decided. We're still planning to lose this round. Which is lucky, given the kind of cards I'm getting.

'Raise you,' said Ian.

Steve glanced across at him, but through the Irishman's dark glasses it was impossible to see what he was thinking.

Abago pushed fifty dollars onto the table.

Steve laid down three tens.

Ian tapped the table twice, chewed a couple of seeds, then put down two aces.

Abago laughed, scooping up the money, folding the bills into his pocket. 'The gods are with me tonight, I can feel it'.

'Just play,' said Ian. His voice was tense and strained.

Just the way it should be, thought decide Steve. They had already decided on their roles. Ian was the serious, strung-out card player, while Steve would play the businessman just looking for a few laughs, some beers and some women.

Another hand. And again, Abago won. The Commandant was a couple of hundred dollars up already, more money than he usually made in a month. 'I can read you white boys like a book.'

'At least there aren't any of us in your jail,' said Steve.

Abago threw back his head, roaring with laughter. 'That's where you are wrong, my friend. We arrested one last week,' he said, in high good humour. 'He's down in the cells right now.'

'A white man in a hell-hole like this?'

'We don't discriminate on the grounds of a man's colour,' Abago rapped out. 'A criminal is a criminal . . . we treat them all the same.'

'What's his crime?' asked Ian. For a brief moment, he'd lifted the dark glasses over his head and was looking straight at the Commandant.

'A mercenary,' Abago told him. 'There's oil in this country, and sometimes the white men think they can steal it from us. The fools end up here. We had five of them in this jail until recently – three British and two Germans. They'd been here for ten years, but the last of them died last year.'

Steve was draining his beer bottle. 'A white man in a place like this . . . I hate to think of that.' From his pocket, he took five gold Krugerrands, each of them worth $1,000. He placed them on the table. 'I'll play you for his freedom.'

'You don't even know his name . . .'

Steve shrugged. 'I don't need to.'

Abago's eyes narrowed, the sweat running in tiny rivers in the folds of flesh around his mouth and nose. He was looking at the gold coins. It was dark outside now, and the bar had only a couple of light bulbs to illuminate it. A wind was starting to blow in off the nearby beach, and you could hear the palm trees that lined the road start to creak. Yet even in the pale light, the gold still glittered: each lump of metal shimmering with the promise of pure wealth.

He reached down and picked one up, assessing its weight. In Africa, there were only three currencies that mattered: dollars and gold and bullets. You could fake any of them, but a man such as the Commandant would know the weight and feel of real gold, and could tell it instantly from tin plate.

'Like I said, I'll play you for his freedom,' Steve repeated. 'You win, you keep the coins. I win, the white man goes free . . . *tonight*.'

'I'll play for that,' said Ian.

'For the white man as well?'

Ian shook his head. 'I play only for myself,' he said. He'd pulled out

$1,000 in crisp new notes and placed them on the table in front of him. 'But I like to see some real stakes,' he continued. 'If I win, I get the gold as well.'

'Sounds fair to me,' said Steve. He glanced towards the Commandant.

Abago's eyes were darting from the gold to the money, and back again. The bar had fallen silent. One of the prisoners was backing away, his chains clanking as he did so. He's expecting a fight, decided Steve. And he might well be right.

Suddenly Abago shook with laughter. 'You've got a game,' he said, flashing a huge grin.

The cards were dealt.

This time, Steve folded with a pair of sixes, but Ian collected the pot with a straight flush. The next hand went to Steve, the hand after that to Abago. Over the next hour, the game ebbed and flowed, the gold coins and the dollar bills pushed slowly around the table. Ian and Steve were working as a team, playing off one another. Ian was a skilful poker player, noted Steve. He'd grown up in Belfast, turned himself into the IRA's most skilful bomb-maker, then done ten years in the Maze before being released under the Good Friday agreement and reinventing himself as a mercenary working for the same private military corporation as Steve. All those years in jail had turned him into an expert in just about every card game. But Abago was just as skilful. He knew the cards, and the odds on every possible combination – and in poker that kind of experience gave you the edge.

But it was two against one. And in any kind of battle, whether it is fought with guns or playing cards, numbers are usually enough to ensure victory.

And after an hour, the money in the Commandant's pocket had been emptied.

'A bet's a bet,' said Steve flatly.

Abago reached out for a cigarette. One of the prisoners stumbled forwards, torching up a greasy flame, allowing the fat man to take a long, thoughtful drag of nicotine before he blew some smoke back into the air.

'The white man goes free,' Steve told him.

Abago closed his eyes briefly, as if deep in thought, while the smoke curled up around his face. 'Let's up the stakes,' he said finally, and clapped his hands together.

One of the soldiers scurried behind the bar. He returned a minute later, carrying a jar which he placed carefully down on the table. There was a dark, murky liquid inside. Then, as Steve looked closely, a shape.

A shape that looked suspiciously like a human hand.

'Christ,' muttered Steve under his breath.

'From the last man who lost a hand of poker in this bar,' Abago chuckled, a pair of pumpkin seeds spitting out of his mouth as he did so. Then: 'We deal one more round,' he continued, the laughter suddenly stopping. 'If you win, you can have your white man. If I win, I get to keep your gold – *and* I'll put your right hand in the jar next to this one.'

Steve paused. He glanced across at Ian but, as before, could see nothing behind the other man's dark glasses.

His gaze flicked back towards Abago. The Commandant's eyes were taunting him, daring him to take the bet. We figured he might be a hard rough bastard, recalled Steve – but a madman? That wasn't part of the plan.

'Take the bet,' ordered Abago. He was shuffling the pack of cards in his hand, impatient to start dealing.

Steve felt cornered; how should he play this?

'Piss off,' he said finally, his tone flat.

For a moment, Abago remained motionless. Then he picked up one pumpkin seed and snapped it between his fingers.

'I said: take the bet.'

'Maybe the three of us could play another round?' interrupted Ian.

'Silence,' rapped out Abago.

Steve looked straight into the man's eyes. 'I told you, forget it.'

In the next instant, five soldiers stepped forward. All of them were carrying AK-47s, and from the smell of grease and oil on their barrels, Steve could tell they were loaded and ready for use.

They lowered the guns into position, pointing straight at Steve's chest.

'We deal the cards right now,' said Abago, his smile gone. 'Like it or not, you're taking the bet.'

Three

STEVE LOOKED DOWN AT THE first two cards.

Tens. At least they aren't sodding eights, he told himself. Abago had set the rules very clearly. One hand each. Five cards. The best hand won. You couldn't discard any cards, you couldn't ask for any more – and Ian was out of the game.

It would just come down to the cards fate dealt them.

Steve glanced up at the girl with the deck in her hands. Her fingers were delicate and nimble as she caressed the pack, flicked it open, and shuffled. A smile played in her soft dark eyes: they were as fresh and innocent as the sand on the beach a few hundred yards from here. She had yet to be brutalised by her surroundings. She placed one more card on the table next to each man. Steve looked up at Abago. The man wiped the sweat from his brow then smiled, baring his teeth in the wild grin of a born predator.

Steve looked at his card.

A seven. *Sod it*. Two tens and a seven. It wasn't much of a hand so far.

'Another card,' he said to the girl.

She placed one carefully in front of Abago, then tossed one towards Steve. He could see one of the soldiers, his fingers twitching on the trigger of his AK-47, glance from man to man.

A Queen.

Two tens, a seven and a Queen.

Abago wiped his mouth with the back of his hand. 'The last card,' he said roughly.

The cards were placed on the table, face down. Three of the soldiers had jabbed cigarettes into their mouths, creating a dense cloud of smoke around the table that was filling Steve's eyes and lungs. He waited a moment before picking up the card. Sod you, Ollie Hall, he thought to himself. Why the hell did you have to accept a suicidal contract to break a man out of Broken Ridge? And why the hell did you have to screw it up so badly that your mates had to come and break you out? If it costs me a hand, I'll kill you with the one I've got left.

Abago had already picked up his card, holding the full deck in front of him.

Steve picked up his card, slotting it carefully next to the other four. Then he permitted himself a brief tense smile.

'Let's see what you've got,' he said, looking straight at Abago.

The Commandant laid his hand flat on the table. Two Kings, a six, a four and a nine.

Steve paused for a fraction of a second, then put his hand down. 'Three tens,' he said firmly. He watched the Commandant's eyes flick down to the cards. 'I'll go and collect the bloke you've got locked up now . . .'

'Not so fast,' grunted Abago.

The soldiers stepped an inch forwards. You could see the sweat on their fingers as they held on tight to the triggers. One of them was spitting his still-burning cigarette onto the floor.

'A bet's a bet,' said Ian, an edge to his voice.

Abago grabbed the gold coins and thrust them greedily into his pocket. 'You can have your white man,' he said. 'He's too ugly even for this jail.'

Steve stood straight up. 'Then let's get him.'

Abago led the way. From the front of the bar, they walked a few yards along the dusty track, then straight through the front gate that led into the heart of the jail. Broken Ridge consisted of a single, crumbling block of concrete, two storeys high but with another two floors of cells sunk into the foundations. There were only a few windows, and they were blocked by thick metal bars. Beyond the building, thirty metres of scrubland reached up towards the high barbed-wire fence. Behind were two buildings made of corrugated iron: a barracks for the guards and soldiers and a cookhouse, from which a foul smell of boiled maize and gristle drifted on the night air. Two soldiers saluted as Abago stumped past them, glancing only cursorily at the two white men walking behind him.

'Ready?' whispered Steve.

'Ready,' said Ian, his voice terse.

They stepped through the gates. Steve didn't like jails, never had done. There was a guy he knew from his time in the SAS who'd got involved with a bunch of bank robbers and ended up spending eight years in Wandsworth nick. Steve had been to see him a couple of times and his blood had chilled every time he stepped through the doors. There was something about being caged up year after year that struck him as more punishing than any torture he could imagine. And that was a British jail. This place was like a slice of hell itself, dug up from out of the ground and delivered to the surface. You could hear the wind whistling in off the Atlantic, and the trees creaking down on the beach, and as you stepped towards it, it seemed as if the building itself was groaning in pain. There was a terrible stench drifting out of the place, the smell of bodies packed together, and you could hear the piercing howl of a man dying coming from somewhere deep inside. As you stepped into the main building, there was a long corridor, and in a couple of places, weak light bulbs. Along it was a series of locked doors. If there were people inside, it was impossible to tell. The doors were made from steel, with no windows. At the end of the corridor, one staircase led upwards, another down.

'You want the guided tour?' chuckled Abago.

'The one you give to Amnesty International?' Steve said coolly.

Abago chuckled. 'No – not the whitewash we give those fools. The real Broken Ridge.'

'Somehow I'm not in the mood,' answered Steve.

They followed the Commandant down a single staircase. With each step the smell got worse: excrement, mixed with rotting flesh. At the bottom was a set of steel gates, left open. Abago stepped right through. Two long corridors stretched into the distance, with just one light bulb in each. On either side were rough cages, each one containing ten to fifteen men. It was late at night now, and most of them were sleeping, but the cells were so cramped it was impossible for everyone to lie down at the same time, so some of them were standing against the walls, or hanging onto the bars, waiting their turn to kip down for a few hours. Each cell had a single bucket to crap in, but there was no sign of any water. The floors were matted with piss and straw. In one cell, a man was groaning in pain, bucking while he was consumed by a fever, but his cellmates were ignoring him as he sweated and writhed in agony. It looked like the end was close, judged Steve. But not tonight. The poor bastard still had a couple of days to get through before he could start to rest in his grave.

As they walked, Steve could feel dark, suspicious eyes tracking them. He glanced into some of the cages but, like animals, the men would instantly look away. The mere presence of the Commandant among them had cowed their curiosity, and they backed anxiously into the shadows, taking care not to draw any attention to themselves. Only the dying man was oblivious to what was happening, grunting like a pig as the fever chewed him up from the inside.

'This is what happens to white men who try to steal our oil,' said Abago, stopping in front of a cage. He turned round, switching on a flashlight and beaming it straight into Steve's face. 'You'd like to join them, maybe?'

'Some other time. You've been paid,' Steve said harshly. 'If you're not happy with the deal, I'll take my gold back.'

He then took five paces forward, making sure there was some safe distance between him and Abago, and peered through the bars. It took a moment before he recognised his friend. There were several days of stubble across his face, and his black hair was sweaty and matted with blood. His sweatshirt was ripped in two places, and there were streaks of dark mud down the side of his chinos. Bruises were visible on his neck and arms, and a scab had started to form where his cheek had been cut.

But the eyes were alive with grim defiance.

I'd recognise the man in hell itself.

Oliver Hall.

Once the fastest-rising young officer in the Household Cavalry – before the gaming table and the whisky bottle wrapped him in their deadly embrace. And now languishing in Broken Ridge. Jesus, mate, thought Steve. One day we're going to straighten your life out.

'Christ, man, you're meant to be getting married in four weeks,' hissed Steve, walking up to the cell and making sure the Commandant couldn't hear him. 'The way you look, even Katie might draw the line at shagging you – and the way I hear it, that bird has never been too fussy before.'

Ollie flashed a rough smile. Behind him, there was one other man in the cell – a slender, ghost-like figure who remained in the distance like a shadow. A single metal chain was slung around his wrist, attached to a metal hook on the wall, making it impossible for him to move more than a couple of yards.

'Well, I'll be damned – it's Steve West,' said Ollie. 'Now I really can abandon all hope.'

Stepping forwards, Abago pushed his key into the lock, then twisted the metal until the door slung open.

Steve pulled the dark glasses down over his eyes. The dim lights of the jail all but disappeared, and all he could make out through the murky light were figures and shapes.

Suddenly he could feel Abago's hands on his back. He was shoving Steve towards the cell.

'Two more white men!' he roared, his chest erupting into a mirthless laugh. 'I'm sure someone will pay some more gold coins to get you bastards out of here.'

Steve waited. They'd expected this from the start. At his side, he could sense Ian slipping his hand inside his sweatshirt. Beneath his vest, he'd taped two thunder-flash stun grenades to his chest: originally developed by the SAS, and used most famously during the Iranian Embassy siege in London in 1980, a thunder-flash was the most brutally effective way of temporarily neutralising your opponent. It produced a brilliant flash of light that blinded anyone not wearing protective glasses, and a high-pitched scream of white noise that stunned their senses and left them confused and disorientated. You couldn't take one onto a plane, it would never get through security, but Ian had placed all the ingredients inside some sandwiches and reassembled them in the hotel room. The grenade mixed potassium perchlorate and powdered magnesium: Ian had combined them in precise quantities, and placed them inside the shell of a mobile phone to create a rough and ready handmade device.

He smashed one into the ground, then another.

In an instant, the prison was illuminated by a flash of white light, and a noise that ripped through your ears like a hurricane. Even through his dark glasses Steve could feel his eyes blinking at the explosion. He'd practised with thunder-flashes plenty of times back at the killing house, the mocked-up building next to its Hereford headquarters where the SAS practised hostage rescues. But it didn't matter how many times you ran through the drill. You never got used to the dazzling light, so harsh it seemed to slit open your eyeballs, or the screaming noise that drilled into your brain. That's why they were so lethally effective. Even the best trained soldiers started to fall apart under the brutal assault on their senses. If you knew it was coming, you could steel yourself: their impact on anyone who wasn't prepared was devastating.

And to get out of here alive it would need to be, Steve told himself grimly.

He could feel Abago's grip loosening on his shoulder as he tried to adjust to the shock. Steve reached inside his sweatshirt, whipping out the snub-nosed Raven Arms M-25 pistol that he'd taped to his chest. Known as the Saturday Night Special in the US, the Raven was one of the smallest firearms ever produced. It didn't pack much punch and it didn't have much range, but none of that mattered when you were standing only a foot away from the man you were planning to kill. The tape ripped off his chest, taking a clump of hair with it, but Steve ignored the pain, balanced the handgun in his fist and squeezed hard on the trigger. A bullet tore into Abago's face, impacting just below the right eye, smashing through the skull, and chewing straight into the man's brain. He reeled backwards, his hand reaching up to his face, just in time for the second bullet to cut through the flesh and dig into his mouth.

'Bloody move, bloody move!' shouted Ian. He reached into the cell, grabbing hold of Ollie.

The man was shielding his eyes, blinded by the flash. Abago had just crashed to the floor, blood pouring out of his face, grunting with pain, but with the last remnants of life fast ebbing out of him.

'Bloody move, man!' bawled Ian, louder this time, struggling to make himself heard over the echoes from the flash grenade still reverberating around the cell block.

Through his dark glasses, Steve could see the two guards from the doorway running towards them. They were still blinded by the light, although its intensity was starting to fade now. All around them, the men in the cells were screaming. Steve fired at the first man, the bullet smashing into his shoulder. Steve cursed the miserable accuracy of the Raven: he'd aimed for the chest, and felt certain he'd take out the heart or the lungs. He fired again, this time slotting the

Matt Lynn

bullet neatly into the side of the man's chest, pushing him spluttering to the ground. Adjusting his sights, Steve then lined up a shot on the second man.

Two bullets left in the mag, thought Steve. I can't waste any.

He fired once, aiming at the chest. The bullet struck the soldier in the lungs, sending him flying backwards, blinded and bleeding heavily.

Normally, Steve would have stepped forward to put another bullet into him. The double tap was part of SAS training, drilled into you on the parade ground until you could never forget it. 'Your enemy is still your enemy until his last breath has been drawn,' he could remember his Sergeant yelling at him.

But not today. *There's not enough ammo left.*

'I'm not going without this bloke,' shouted Ollie, gesturing to the man chained up behind him.

'Jesus Christ, you mad fucker, there's no time,' screamed Ian.

'He's the bloke I came to rescue,' Ollie said hoarsely. 'The bastard's worth a hundred grand.'

Pulling out the gun he too had bought in the market before heading up to the jail, Ian shot once.

For a split second, Steve thought the Irishman had killed the other prisoner. He was certainly capable of it: Ian liked to settle arguments quickly and simply, and nobody was going to rescue a corpse.

But the bullet had sliced open the chain binding the man to the wall. His hand had been injured by the ricochet, cutting a wound that ran up to his elbow, but he bounced forwards like an animal that had suddenly been released from a trap.

'Now sodding *move!*' yelled Steve.

All four men started to run.

Both Ollie and the prisoner were still blinded by the flash grenade. The Commandant was lying dead on the ground, and so were the two soldiers. Steve bundled Ollie forwards, while Ian dragged the prisoner. They dashed up the stairs, leaving behind them the wails of hundreds of imprisoned men, then hurtled out into the courtyard. Steve was already running towards the exit, his Raven in his hand. One soldier was still standing guard, whilst the second man was rushing towards the barracks to stir the rest of the men. Up on the watchtowers, flashlights had been turned on, sending shafts of light scattering across the dusty surface of the ground. Bullets were starting to pepper the dirt around them. Steve had no idea how many men were firing on them. Three – maybe four, he guessed. He charged faster, his legs beating against the ground, yelling at Ollie to run even though he couldn't see where he was going. Raising the Raven in his right hand, he pointed it straight at the guard by the exit, loosening off the final bullet in the mag. It struck the man in the shoulder, spinning him around, making him clutch the wound in agony.

'*Now!*' Ian was shouting.

Steve lunged for the gate. Behind him, he could hear the barracks doors swing open, and the sound of shots being fired as the men poured out. Up on the watchtowers, two more flashlights had been switched on, flooding the courtyard and the gates with light, increasing the accuracy of the fire from the soldiers. Steve could feel one bullet fly past him, and saw another spit up a clump of earth two feet in front of him. He swerved violently, making himself as hard to hit as possible, and raced breathlessly onto the road.

To the left, he could see four soldiers advancing out of the bar, their assault rifles stretched out in front of them.

A Toyota Rav 4 was speeding towards them, a cloud of dust kicked up by its wheels. 'Jump, jump!' shouted Maksim.

The Russian former special forces – or Spetsnaz – man spoke in a rough, broken English. But Steve didn't even need the command. The door was already open and, as the Toyota slowed, he bundled Ollie towards it. Grabbing hold of the door, he levered them both inside. The engine was roaring as Maksim kept it revved up, with the gears in neutral. Ian climbed in, dragging the prisoner behind him, and

Maksim slammed his foot hard on the accelerator, spinning them away down the road. The sudden movement jerked Steve forwards. He rolled to the front seat, then quickly straightened himself. The Toyota was accelerating fast, climbing through sixty, then seventy miles an hour, even though the road was nothing more than a dirt track that twisted wildly as it made its way down to the sea.

'Christ, man, I can't bloody see anything,' wailed Ollie.

'You'll be fine in a couple of hours,' Ian said impatiently. 'It's the flash.'

'You don't want to sodding see this anyway,' interrupted Steve, looking behind them.

The four soldiers from the bar had climbed into a Nissan Navara pick-up truck and were giving chase. From inside the jail, another group of soldiers had climbed on board a Chinese-made Mengshi troop carrier. Both vehicles were hurtling down the road. Steve could hear the sound of assault rifles opening up as the night sky was lit up by flashes of co-ordinated gunfire. One bullet had already smashed into the back of the Toyota, narrowly missing the tyre. Another had torn out a chunk of its rear fender.

'Faster,' said Ian, his voice tense.

This is their territory, thought Steve grimly. If we get bogged down in a firefight we're done for.

'Where are the weapons?' he shouted.

When the plan had been put together, they'd decided that Maksim, as well as Nick, the young Welsh guy they'd taken along on their last job, should also be part of the rescue mission. Maksim would collect them in an SUV outside the jail: the Russian was the best driver they'd ever met, as well as the most fearless combatant, and if there was any man you wanted at the wheel during a getaway it was Maksie. Nick would rent them a boat, and lay up on one of the tiny coves that dotted the shore of the island: once they made their break from the jail they knew there was no way they were going to be able to get out via an airport.

But there should have been weapons, decided Steve. If it came to a fight, they needed something to level up the odds.

'They're on the boat,' Maksim replied.

'What the hell use are they there?' Steve said angrily.

'Get out and walk if you're not happy,' Maksim snapped back.

Steve was about to say something when the Toyota hit a massive boulder and leaped into the air, rising two feet, its frame shuddering. He could feel the impact of the blow rattling through him as it then crashed onto a sandy bank. The back window shattered, sending shards of glass showering through the cabin like confetti. For a moment, the engine stalled. Maksim had turned the key, but the machine was whining like an injured animal. Steve glanced anxiously around. He couldn't see the troop carrier or the Nissan through the darkness, but he could hear the roar of their engines.

In a moment, they'll be upon us, he thought. And without weapons we're done for.

Ian had ripped the last remaining thunder-flash from his chest. He slammed the detonator cord into place, then lobbed the incendiary device back along the track. It arced clean into the air, exploding five feet off the ground and, in an instant, its glorious white flash lit up the darkness of the African night, bathing the island in a neon, incendiary glow. A crack of noise fissured through the air, strong enough to make the trees around them groan.

There's no way a man can drive through that, decided Steve. You'd need nerves of hardened tungsten.

Then the engine roared into life again, and Maksim steered the Toyota back onto the track, kicking hard on the accelerator. They were rocking violently as they went down the narrow pathway, the metal of the machine scraping against the palm trees and rocks as they twisted through the dense foliage. Steve could feel his pulse quickening as he clung onto the dashboard, his eyes scanning forwards, desperate to see the first evidence that they had reached the shore.

'Sod you, Ollie Hall,' he murmured again. 'This is the last hole I dig you out of.'

Ahead, the track suddenly opened up, and Steve could feel his lungs flooding with relief as the Toyota broke out onto a sandy beach. It was lined with palm trees, swaying in the wind, and dotted with broken coconut shells. Paradise, thought Steve. That is, if you didn't have a truckload of soldiers fifty yards behind you trying to shoot your arse off.

'Drive straight to the boat,' he shouted.

You could see the small craft bobbing on the waves twenty yards or so out into the ocean. It was a 30-foot fishing vessel hired 150 miles down the coast in Libreville, with a metal hull, a wooden frame, and a 300 hp diesel engine. There were rough seas on the South Atlantic tonight, with a vicious wind blowing in from the north, and the waves were smashing onto the beach. The Toyota slowed as its tyres struggled to get a grip on the wet sand but it had enough momentum to keep going. Suddenly there was a bark of gunfire as the Nissan arrived at the end of the lane. The Toyota was already crashing into the water. Smoke was rising from the engine, and white, salty breakers were starting to wash over it.

'Bloody swim for it,' bellowed Steve. He flung the door open, pushing hard against the water. With his left hand, he grasped hold of Ollie, still blinded by the flash, and started to wade into the sea. At his side, he could see Ian dragging the prisoner. A wave slapped over him, soaking his clothes and knocking him backwards; he had to struggle to stay upright. Behind them, the troops were tumbling out of the Nissan. A rapid burst of fire peppered the waves with bullets.

Christ, thought Steve. We need some covering fire, otherwise there will be blood in this water.

'Get some fire down Nick,' he yelled.

His voice was carried eastwards on the wind, and he just hoped it would reach the ears of the boy on the deck. Nick Thomas was just twenty years old, his only training with the Territorials, and although he'd proved himself in Afghanistan, and was the best shot any of the men had ever seen, he was still only a kid. There was a reason why Steve insisted on only working with battle-seasoned soldiers: they'd seen every type of combat you could imagine and they knew precisely how to respond once they were in trouble.

'We're going under mate,' he said, his head swivelling towards Ollie. Then, taking a lungful of air, he grabbed Ollie's wrist and dived into the approaching wave. With the other hand tucked into Ollie's belt, he kicked his legs furiously, propelling them towards the blacked-out shape he assumed to be the hull of the boat.

Up on the deck, Nick had positioned an M40 sniper rifle, a weapon first issued to the US Marines during the Vietnam War and, as a result, one of the most widely available high-precision rifles in the world. It wasn't the best sniper rifle ever made, but it was cheap, you could always find fresh ammo, and it was plenty accurate enough to deal with the 200 yards that separated the boat from the soldiers swarming onto the beach.

Nick held the gun steady in his hand, and licked away a bead of sweat from his upper lip. He was a confident marksman, aware that he rarely if ever missed, but he'd never tried to make a shot from the stern of a storm-tossed boat before and, for the first time ever, he could hear a whisper of doubt inside his head. The boat was swaying under the swell, and as Nick lined up a target in his sights, it was instantly snatched away from him. *Aim and shoot, all in the same split second*, he told himself. *That's the only way*. He paused, then placed the chest of one of the soldiers firing on his mates within the cross hairs of his gun.

'*Kill*,' he whispered as he pulled the trigger.

The bullet bounced harmlessly off the skin of the Nissan.

The soldiers were growing more confident, advancing unhindered, unleashing a murderous barrage of fire. Steve and Ian had dived underwater, but pretty soon the lead skimming through the waves was going to catch them.

'*Kill*,' repeated Nick, firing again.

He slammed his fist hard against the metal of the boat. The bullet had struck a soldier clean in the chest, dropping him to the ground. Nick instantly readjusted his sights, lining up his next shot. Another soldier went down, writhing on the ground. Now the enemy were taking cover, diving behind rocks or their truck: they were still firing their weapons, but watching two of their mates get hit had slowed them down.

Below, Steve and Ollie suddenly burst out of the water, grabbing hold of the side of the boat. Nick reached down and hauled Steve on board. Within seconds, Steve, Ollie, Ian and the prisoner were gasping for breath on the deck. The wind was howling furiously around them, and the boat was swaying in the rising swell, but they had made it.

Just then, a bullet flew overhead, striking the prow of the vessel. Next, there was a vicious explosion as a mortar grenade exploded in the water fifteen yards ahead of them. It blew a huge jet of water up into the air, drenching everyone sprawled out on the deck with salt and seaweed.

'For Christ's sake start the engine, man,' coughed Steve. 'I'm in no sodding mood to take on the Equatorial Guinea Navy. And that's what they'll have on our arses next.'

Four

DAWN BROKE GENTLY OVER THE horizon.

Steve nestled a cup of instant coffee in his hand, and adjusted the wheel. He was steering using a compass and charts but mainly by keeping the West African coastland about a mile to his left.

It was just after six in the morning, and the winds had finally dropped. They had been sailing through most of the night. As they fled the coast, the troops had fired guns and mortars at them, but once the unit had got the diesel engine going, had switched out all the lights and steered straight out into the storm, it had been easy enough to make their escape. A couple of mortar rounds shook up the fish, but unless they managed to rouse the Equatorial Guinea Navy, assuming they even had one, there was no way they'd be able to continue the pursuit. They wouldn't even have to go back and explain themselves to Abago, reflected Steve with a half-smile. The fat bastard was already dead. 'That's the last game of poker I'll ever play,' he said to Ian as the latter emerged from the hold.

'Just as well,' said Ian. 'You were crap.'

Steve grinned, draining the dregs of his coffee cup. He'd steered the boat through the night, giving the rest of the guys a chance to get dry and enjoy a few hours' kip down in the hold. Now he could feel the nervous exhaustion of the battle starting to catch up with him. 'I was only playing for Ollie's life,' he said. 'If it was something I actually cared about I might have tried a bit harder . . .'

'Thanks, mate,' said Ollie, emerging from the cabin, scratching at the week's worth of stubble on his chin.

Steve glanced across at the man. A huge, orange sun was filling the sky, mixing with the dark blues of the Atlantic to create a vivid riot of colour. It was impossible to be angry with a bloke at daybreak, he decided. Something to do with the beginning of a new day. But later tonight he knew he'd be back to the opinion he'd formed of Ollie when he'd first fished him out of a brothel in Baghdad just before they'd started their first job together.

The man was a decent enough soldier, but he was also a loser. And in the end, that made him a waste of space.

'So where's your man?' he asked.

'Sleeping,' said Ollie, nodding in the direction of the cabin. 'I reckon it's a decade since the guy had a decent night's kip so we can hardly blame him for catching a bit of extra shut-eye, can we?'

'Who the hell is he?'

Ollie walked across to the pot of instant coffee Steve had brewed up on the ledge next to the wheel, pouring himself a large mug of the hot steaming liquid. 'How should I know?' he said. 'Bruce Dudley said there was a guy who'd pay a hundred grand to get the man broken out of Broken Ridge. For that kind of cash you get to keep your reasons to yourself.'

'And you—'

'Leave it,' Ollie said tersely.

Steve kept looking straight ahead. They were heading for Libreville on the coast of Gabon, a total of around 150 miles from Malabo. Nick and Maksim had hired the boat there, as well as picking up the weapons, and they'd steer it into the port, return it to the owner, and then head straight for the airport. With any luck, Steve thought, they'd be on a plane back to Britain by this afternoon. Dudley had got his man out, and the client, whoever the hell he was, would have to pay the hundred grand he'd promised Ollie, and the extra two hundred and fifty he was paying Steve to break Ollie out of the jail. Steve wouldn't say no to some spare cash: he'd sunk every penny he'd made out in Afghanistan into buying West & Hallam, a vintage car dealership his Uncle Ken had built up in Leicestershire, but with the City boys feeling the pinch, the market in old Jaguars, Aston Martins and Austin Healeys wasn't as profitable as he'd expected. Some money would help tide it over. But he wasn't about to take on any more mercenary jobs. He'd watched his best mate Jeff die last time around, and he wasn't going to put himself through that again.

My AK-47 is hung up on the wall, Steve reminded himself. *And that's exactly where it's staying.*

'Any chance of a beer?' said Ollie.

'Or a vodka?' added Maksim, emerging from the hold.

'The boat is dry,' said Steve. 'And considering the amount of trouble you boys have caused when drunk, it's staying that way.'

'In the Spetsnaz we found a way to distil tank fuel,' chuckled Maksim. 'Maybe we could take one of the spare barrels of diesel?'

It was after ten by the time they finally pulled in at the dock. Being early November, it had been wet and drizzly when they left Heathrow, but out here close to the Equator, there was hot and brilliant sunshine. The city was built on the delta of the Komo River. A former French colony, it remained one of the richest, best-organised and safest cities in Africa – a haven for tourists and businessmen travelling through the centre of the continent.

They handed the boat back to Hassan Ramzey, an Egyptian businessman who, for an extra $1,000 on the rental fee, politely ignored the two bullet-marks on its prow, and the fact that the M40 he'd supplied with it had used up most of its stock of ammo.

From the dock, Steve organised a taxi to take them straight up to

Libreville International Airport. Bruce Dudley had promised there would be tickets waiting for a plane to take them home.

The prisoner had been woken up, washed, and the wound to his arm where Ian's bullet had shot him free of the wall had been patched up. He'd introduced himself as Newton Bunjira, but apart from that he wasn't saying much. To Steve, he looked around fifty, but it was hard to tell. A guy could be thirty and come out of Broken Ridge looking like a grandfather. He was rake thin, with ribs that stuck out of his chest, and his skin was blotchy and covered in small scabs that could be wounds, could be fever, or could be malnutrition. Maybe three.

They bought him a sweatshirt and some new jeans and trainers from a market stall at the dock, then told him to get changed in a café. There was no way they wanted to take him to the airport in the bloodied rags he'd been wearing in the jail.

We'll deliver him to Dudley, collect our money, and then get rid of the guy, decided Steve. He smells like trouble.

The airport was clean and modern, but Air France was the only European airline that flew there, with a three-times-a week service from Charles de Gaulle in Paris. 'Your plane is ready, Mr West,' said the lady at check-in when Steve asked when the next flight was available and whether they could get a seat on it.

'Our plane?'

The girl nodded, and flashed him the kind of smile check-in staff reserve for the first-class passengers wielding triple platinum Amex cards.

'Mr Dudley has booked a private jet for you and . . .' She glanced slightly suspiciously at Ian, Maksim, Ollie, Nick and Newton standing behind Steve. Even after a wash they looked rougher than a landfill site after a bad storm '. . . your, er, colleagues.'

'We'll take it,' said Steve. He nodded to the others to follow him out onto the airstrip. Private plane, he thought to himself. Somebody must want this Newton guy pretty badly. But if he's so important, how come he's been languishing in Broken Ridge for the last ten years? And how come someone just paid three hundred and fifty grand to get him out?

Nothing about this job is making any sense.

The plane was a Cessna Citation 500 Series II, a small executive jet that was also used as light transport by armies around the world, including the Swiss, the South Africans and the Spanish. The first models had been flown in 1969, and the plane had been continuously updated since then: it was a rugged and reliable workhorse that had clocked up millions of flights with very few accidents. With a capacity for eight passengers it could cruise at 464 miles an hour and had a maximum range of 2,300 miles. The plane was configured with eight plush, black leather seats, a computer screen, a bar, and came complete with a hostess and a pilot. It was sitting in a side bay of the airport.

'We can take off when everyone is ready,' the Captain, a South African called Jim Stapleton, told them. 'Libreville only has about a dozen flights a day coming in and out. None of that stacking nonsense you get at Heathrow,' he added with a polite smile.

'Have you got the range to get us back to Britain?' asked Steve.

'Could do,' said Stapleton. 'But we're heading to Cape Town.'

'Cape Town? In South Africa?'

'It was, the last time I checked. Now, if you boys want to strap yourselves in, I'll get us out onto the tarmac.'

'What the hell are we doing in South Africa?'

Stapleton just shrugged, and walked back towards the cockpit. 'How should I know?' he said tersely. 'The guy who's paying the bill wants this crate flown to Cape Town so that's what we're doing.'

Before Steve could say anything, the hostess had secured the doors, and the Cessna was rolling onto the runway. Within seconds the tiny jet had lifted its nose into the air and was climbing steadily into the clear blue sky, then rolled as it twisted south to start what shouldn't be more than a two-hour flight.

'We just need to drop Newton off for Dudley,' said Ollie, glancing towards Steve. 'They've got BA flights from Cape Town every day – we can get home from there.'

As the Cessna steadied itself, hitting its normal cruising altitude of 43,000 feet, the hostess handed around some sandwiches and drinks. There was no alcohol on board, she explained to a disappointed-looking Maksim, just fruit juice and bottled water. The men ate hungrily: Ollie had spent a week in Broken Ridge and had eaten nothing except gruel, leaving him thin and famished. Only Newton picked at his food, removing the crusts and eating only tiny slithers of bread and the grated cheese inside.

'You must need some decent food by now,' said Ian, sitting next to the man. 'I spent a few years in the Maze, and the British prison grub was pretty bad, but nothing on that place.'

'I can't eat too much, too quickly,' answered Newton, in little more than a whisper. 'After ten years without any proper food and no natural light . . . it's going to take time to get my body back to normal. Eat too quickly, and I'll just make myself sick.'

'So where are you from, exactly?' asked Steve, sitting across the narrow aisle from the two men.

'Batota,' said Newton. His eyes flashed up to meet Steve's and you could see the intelligence and strength of the man in that single look. The name meant very little to Steve – just one more former colony in Africa now ruled by a brutal madman.

'So how in God's name did you end up in that hell-hole?'

'Different wars, man,' said Newton, with a nonchalant toss of his bony shoulder. 'I came out of Batota and I didn't know how to do anything other than fight. This is Africa, so there's always work for a soldier, as long as you don't complain about the food or the pay and you don't mind getting shot at. Angola, the Congo, Uganda, then Sierra Leone.' He chuckled softly to himself. 'You just point at the map, I've probably fought there.'

'Until Equatorial Guinea . . .' pressed Ian.

Newton moulded a fragment of cheese between his fingers then slipped it into his mouth. 'I don't suppose anyone's got any cigarettes, have they?'

'You've been in the nick too long, mate,' said Steve. 'No one smokes any more – and certainly not on a plane.'

Newton smiled, but remained silent.

'Tell us how you found your way to Broken Ridge and maybe we can find you some cigarettes,' said Ian.

'There was a coup attempt,' the man said carefully. 'The country is always a target. Small army, and lots of oil – that makes it vulnerable. A force was being put together to topple the government, and I was one of the scouts, going in ahead to assess the opposition. But we were poorly led, disorganised. I got captured, and the rest of the guys just melted away.'

'This is what, in ninety-eight, ninety-nine?'

'Ninety-nine,' Newton sighed.

'So why is someone paying all this money, after all this time, to get you out?' asked Ian.

Newton's eyes rolled up to look at him. 'I've been through a lot of wars, a lifetime of bloodshed,' he answered. 'You see things, you hear things. But I've no idea who you guys are, or why you've broken me out of jail. No one cared a damn about me before, and I don't know why they should do so now.'

Steve glanced out of the window of the Cessna. They were cruising at altitude over the arid wastelands that made up the Kalahari Desert. All you could see was sand for hundreds of miles in every direction.

No, nothing about this job made any sense, he thought once again. *And pretty soon I reckon we're going to find out why that is.*

Five

B RUCE DUDLEY SHOOK EACH MAN warmly by the hand. 'Well done, boys,' he said crisply. 'They said no man could ever get out of Broken Ridge. Not alive, anyway.'

'But when it comes to the impossible, Dudley Emergency Forces always gets the job done,' said Ollie.

'Good one,' said Bruce. 'I might even put it in the brochure.'

The Cessna had landed ten minutes earlier at Cape Town International. The pilot had taxied towards the private aircraft hangar, pulling up alongside a row of light aircraft flown by local amateurs. Dudley came on board to check everyone was OK, and to give Newton some temporary papers which, with the help of a generous bribe, would get him through immigration. Dudley was wearing the same cream chinos and green Ralph Lauren polo shirt he always wore, but his leathery Sergeant's skin was more tanned than usual and there was a glimmer in his eye that suggested to Steve that Newton was worth a lot more than he had even told Ollie.

A hundred grand?

Bruce Dudley didn't get excited about any number with only five zeros on the end of it. After a decade building one of the most formidable, fearless Private Military Corporations in the world it took at least seven figures for the man to start working up a sweat.

And he'd been sweating this week. You could see it on his face.

'We've got a couple of limos waiting, boys,' he continued. 'No point in hanging about.'

It was only a short, brisk walk across the tarmac, past an immigration official who'd already been shown their papers, and then towards a pair of black Mercedes limousines waiting for them right outside the terminal building. There were seven of them now: Steve, Ollie, Ian, Maksim, Nick, Newton and Bruce. Steve sat back in one of the limos, accompanied by Bruce, Ollie and Nick, whilst Ian led the rest of the guys into the second car. The chauffeur pulled away smoothly from the kerb, the engine purring, and steered the vehicle out onto the N2, the main highway that headed south out of the city. The seats were luxuriously upholstered, the wood and metal of the car all freshly polished, the air-conditioning kept at a constant eighteen degrees, and there were bottles of freshly chilled mineral water next to each seat.

'Private jets, limos – we're going up in the world,' Steve commented to Bruce. 'There's probably a tasty blonde tucked away in here somewhere.'

'DEF's latest client is seriously loaded,' answered Bruce with a wry smile. 'This is just the start.'

Steve nodded silently. Over time, he'd learned better than to question Bruce Dudley. The man told you what he wanted you to know and nothing more. Steve had worked for him for three years after quitting the SAS, but he wasn't on the payroll. Nobody was. Dudley Emergency Forces worked quietly behind the scenes, putting together small groups of men for each job, mixing the units to suit the task at hand. Steve respected and admired Bruce: the Scotsman had been one of the hardest Sergeants in the Regiment and was, without question, the finest judge of men that Steve had ever met.

But he was also a risk-taker, and didn't mind putting other men's lives on the line if there was a weighty-enough cheque at the end of it.

We'll find out who the client is soon enough, Steve told himself. And then I can scoot down to the BA ticket desk and get myself on the first plane out of here.

The drive took less than an hour. The N2 snaked down the coast, heading south through beautiful, lush countryside. The fertile lands around the Cape didn't look anything like anyone's idea of Africa. It was more like driving through Northern Spain. There were green, blossoming fields, covered in vines and fruit trees, with mountains rising up in the distance in one direction, and rocky, jagged cliffs tumbling away to the storm-tossed Atlantic coastline in the other. The countryside looked well-kept and prosperous: the land was so rich, you could hardly fail to make a good living from the wine and oranges.

After thirty miles, the limos turned sharply off the highway and drove more slowly along a winding road that led down to Hawston, a small, picture-postcard fishing town nestling on the shoreline. They entered a private driveway, flanked by a huge pair of iron gates and manned by two burly security guards. A strip of barbed wire ran along the perimeter, and a pair of mean-looking Alsatians kept watch. A long, curved drive lined with cedar trees, led then up to a neo-Georgian mansion. which, from the looks of it, had least twenty bedrooms. At the front of the house was a small, artificial lake, whilst the back looked out over the clifftops and across to the ocean beyond. It was set in fifty acres of parkland, Dudley told them, with two swimming pools, several ornamental fountains, and a set of five guest lodges, each with two bedrooms.

'So whose gaff is this?' asked Steve as the limo pulled up on the driveway. 'Nelson Mandela's?'

'Archie Sharratt's,' said Bruce crisply, climbing out of the car.

A cool breeze was blowing in off the Atlantic, taking the edge off the hot afternoon sun. Steve followed Bruce through the open door that led into the entrance hall. It was laid with creamy white marble, with a circular staircase descending into it, and, at the back, a huge pair of glass doors that led first onto a patio and pool, then down to a private beach. Out at sea, a 100-foot yacht was moored, its varnished wood and gleaming brass reflecting the light bouncing off the choppy blue sea.

'Nice place,' said Nick, a hint of awe in his voice.

'Isn't your mum's place a bit like this?' said Ollie, grinning.

From what Nick had told them on their last job together, he'd grown up on a council estate in Swansea, where his mum Sandra worked on the check-out at B&Q. 'Maybe with some money from the club,' said Nick.

'What club?' Ian asked, looking across at Nick.

The young lad had turned bright red. 'I . . . I . . .' he started to stammer, but was saved by the entrance of Archie Sharratt.

About forty-five, the man was wearing black jeans and a white open-necked shirt. He was slightly built, around five foot eight in height, with curly, sandy-coloured hair and a squashed face that looked like someone had sat on it. But there was an intelligence to his pale-blue eyes, noted Steve: a calculating, restless brain that was already scanning them for information. Steve didn't read the business pages much – he didn't usually get much past the sport and motoring sections if he picked up a paper – but he'd heard of Archie Sharratt. One of the richest hedge fund managers in the world, he'd made a fortune from a fund that traded in commodities, and had sold out in time to stop himself getting caught up in the crash of 2008. Last time he'd seen him written about, Sharratt was worth at least a billion pounds, and it looked like he'd dropped a few quid of that on building this place. Steve had never met a billionaire before, and so far, he was more impressed by what the money could buy than the man who'd made it.

'Thank you for joining us here, gentlemen,' said Sharratt. His voice was quiet but had authority in it.

'I know you've all been through a heck of an ordeal,' he continued, 'and I want to thank each one of you for that. So why don't you all go to your rooms, freshen up, relax for a bit, and I'll tell the cooks to start preparing some food.'

'First tell us why we are here,' said Steve.

Sharratt looked across at him, the smile on his face engaging, warm and open. 'I'll tell you over dinner.'

'Why not now?' Steve persisted.

'Because it's the kind of story for which a man needs a full stomach . . .'

Six

THE ROOM WAS SO LUXURIOUSLY decorated even a Hilton might have felt shabby in comparison. The lodges were to the side of the main house, along the clifftop overlooking the ocean. Each room had a full-length window, looking straight onto the sea with a splash pool outside. Inside, there was expensive art on the walls, a soft double bed with crisp clean sheets, and a plate of sandwiches, fruit and juice.

I could get used to this, thought Steve as he stepped out of the shower.

But I won't.

Whatever this Sharratt guy wants, I'm still getting the next flight home.

There were fresh clothes laid out on the bed: a pair of blue chinos, a polo shirt and a cream linen jacket, as well as swimming trunks and towels. Even though he'd spent most of the night steering the boat down the African coast, Steve didn't feel like sleeping. It was always like that after a job. It took a couple of days for all the adrenaline to work its way out of the system. Only some hard exercise would start to calm him.

Grabbing a towel and a cheese sandwich, Steve headed down to the pool, then decided the small private beach was a better place to swim. Maybe the waves would knock some of the nervous energy out of his system.

As he stepped off the wooden staircase that led down to the

beach, a woman was approaching from the other direction. Her long blond hair was dripping wet from the sea, but still looked neat and tidy. She was tall, with a supple strength to her body. Her face was delicate and intelligent, with a light even tan, and with big blue eyes that were as steady and warm as the sea behind them was rough and cold. She paused for a fraction of a second at the base of the steps, her eyes flashing up to meet Steve's, and he felt certain her gaze was lingering longer than was strictly necessary. He smiled, and she smiled back, but then she bowed her head, tightened the wet sarong that was fastened over her bikini and began to ascend the steps.

'Bloody gorgeous totty,' said Ollie, kicking a wave across Steve. 'I could get used to this place.'

We all could, thought Steve. He glanced back up the cliff, but the blonde had already vanished from view.

He lunged into the waves, kicking back with his legs and swimming hard out into the ocean. The water was cold, the way the Atlantic always was, and the waves were strong: the whiplash of the water, and the currents swirling around beneath it, reminded you why mariners had always feared the Cape. But it felt good to Steve all the same. He pushed up to the end of the cove, where the really big waves broke, and could feel the salty water washing him clean, putting the misery of Broken Ridge, and the danger of the escape, behind him.

By the time he swam back to the beach, Ollie was already drying himself off. Steve sat down next to him, letting the fresh air and the sunshine dry his skin.

'Thanks for getting me out of that crap hole, mate,' said Ollie. 'I owe you one.'

Steve nodded. 'What the hell were you doing there?'

'I told you, I needed the money.'

'You needed your sodding head examined, more like,' said Steve. 'Christ, man, Broken Ridge bloody Jail. Nobody except a complete nutter would go near the place, and certainly not a bloke who is meant to be getting married in four weeks.'

'It makes me feel alive,' said Ollie, his tone turning reflective. 'Only combat does that. It's the same for you, Steve. It's just that you haven't admitted it to yourself yet.'

'For me? Now you really are crazy, mate. I was well out of all this crap until your sodding bird started coming and weeping all over me. I only agreed to rescue you so I could shut the woman up.'

'Like I said, I owe you.'

'Then do me a favour.'

Ollie tossed a shell into the waves crashing up over the beach. 'What is it?'

'I don't know what this Sharratt guy wants, but if he's hiring Death Inc. and if it's got something to do with Africa, then you don't need to be Sherlock Holmes to work out that it's going to be bloody dangerous.'

'And . . .?'

'Just don't try and persuade me into anything,' continued Steve. 'I've risked my balls once this year, and that's enough.'

Ollie nodded.

'And don't expect to get rescued again.'

But Ollie had already turned around and was climbing the stairs back up towards the lodges.

By the time dinner was served, Steve had grabbed a couple of hours' kip, and changed into the clothes that had been left out in his room. A fierce sunset was streaking across the sky when he joined the rest of the party on the terrace of the main house. A selection of rock classics was playing in the background – the Stones, Queen, Guns 'n' Roses and Bruce Springsteen – and a waitress was handing out cocktails. All the boys had changed into the new clothes. Steve had never seen them looking so smart, and for a brief moment, he felt proud of them. They were rough and coarse, but they were also the finest group of men Steve had ever fought alongside. And although he never really missed the bombs and the bullets, there were plenty of days back at the dealership in Leicestershire when he missed the company of his mates.

Sharratt had laid on a massive spread. The table was piled high with food: different cuts of pork, beef and chicken, five different types of fish, salads and vegetables, plus a selection of wines, spirits and beers from around the world. Nick was sticking to the Stella, the only thing he liked to drink, but the rest of the guys were laying into the booze as if they might not see any more for weeks. Maksim was holding up a bottle of Red Army Vodka, a brand first distilled for the Russian Army's elite officers in the 1920s, and now made by a small company in Rostov on Dom and sold at huge prices in Moscow's nightclubs. He was teaching Ollie how to knock back neat glasses of the stuff and mix it with caviar in your mouth.

As they helped themselves to food, the blonde from the beach joined them, and introduced herself as Samantha Sharratt. She was wearing a short leather skirt, boots, and a white blouse with a couple of buttons open to display more than an inch of cleavage. I guess that's what a billion pounds buys you, decided Steve ruefully. The best-looking woman in the room. Mind you, he reflected, even the waitresses were pretty hot. There was probably more than enough talent to go round. Even Nick might score.

'I'm a rich man,' said Sharratt, standing up and looking around the room. 'But I'm also an angry one.'

The men fell silent. They'd all eaten, had a few drinks, and now they were about to find out what they were doing here. Even though Archie Sharratt was slightly built, when he spoke there was a natural authority to his manner. Steve had seen it in the Army. It was nothing to do with school or rank: it was a way of speaking man-to-man even when you were addressing a crowd, and you were as likely to find it in a Geordie squaddie as you were in a Sandhurst officer.

'I'll tell you guys a bit about myself, because later on I'll be asking you to do a job for me, and I reckon you've got a right to know what kind of bloke you're working for. I've made some money in the City – well, a lot of money if I'm being honest, probably a lot more than I'm worth – but that's not who I am. What makes a man is where he comes from, not where he chooses to go.' He paused, looking at Newton. 'I was born in a country that is now called Batota. It was a damned fine country – God's own land. After the war, thousands of Europeans moved there to make a better life for themselves and their families. They called it the Promised Land because that is what it is. The soil is rich, the rivers are deep, you can grow anything you care to put in the ground, it has every mineral underneath it you can think of, and the people . . . well, left to themselves they are the gentlest, kindest souls ever put on the planet.

'My father was a man called General Ritchie Sharratt, and I reckon you boys would have liked him because he was one of the finest soldiers who ever put on a uniform. He owned a big farm about a hundred miles north of a city that is now called Ibera, and grew mostly tobacco, which was where I learned about commodity prices. But he was a man who believed in his nation and didn't mind fighting for it if he had to. That was why he became a soldier, and he was bloody good at it, rising to become a General in the Batotean Army.

'Nearly thirty years ago, the country I grew up in was turned upside down. Like a lot of guys my age, I got out of there, I went to university in Britain, then found myself a job in the City. But Mum and Dad stayed behind, working their farmland and doing what they could for the nation. Dad had fought against the man who took over, the guerrilla leader Benjamin Kapembwa, but he was a soldier just like you and he wasn't going to hold a grudge. He decided he'd do everything he could to make the new country as good as the old one.'

He paused, his eyes scanning the men in front of him. 'And now I want to show you something.'

He walked briskly through the hallway towards the left wing of the house. Steve put his drink down and followed him. A pair of double doors led into a private cinema. There were eight rows of ten seats. The lights were dimmed, and Sharratt was standing right next to the screen as the men took their places. 'This is where I grew up,' he said.

A film flickered up on the screen. The first shots were black and white followed by colour sections shot on one of the Super 8 cameras that were popular in the 1970s. The house was made from red brick and white clapperboard, with flowers all around it. The gardens were lush and green, as were the fields. Some of the shots showed a couple of kids playing on a trampoline, followed by newsreel pictures of General Sharratt leading his troops from the Batotean Army into battle. Next, there were shots of Archie's father grown old, a distinguished-looking man in his seventies, still strong and proud, inspecting the work on his farm from the back of his favourite horse.

'And then this happened,' said Archie, his voice turning solemn.

The screen went dark, then sprang back to life. There was no sound, just a series of still pictures. There was blood on the finely polished oak floorboards of the hallway. And then in the next picture you could clearly see the bodies of an old man and woman. Their clothes had been torn from them, and there were cuts across their bodies where it looked as if they'd been whipped. The hands had been hacked off the old man. From the expression of agony on his face, it looked as if he'd still been alive when they'd amputated the limbs: it might well have been the shock that killed him.

But through the blood, their faces were still clearly recognisable.

'Mum and Dad,' said Archie, the emotion clearly audible in his voice. 'In 2000, the so-called war veterans came to the farm. That's what they called themselves anyway, but they were really just Kapembwa's thugs. All the white farmers were being driven off the land. My parents had always been excellent employers, providing homes and schools for all the families that worked the fields, and helping to pay for a doctor in the local town. That didn't make any difference to the thugs that Kapembwa sent up from Ibera. My parents were brutally murdered.'

There was a rasp in his voice, and his fists were grinding together.

'And now it's time for some payback.'

'You're talking about a coup?' asked Ollie.

Archie shook his head. 'An assassination,' he replied flatly. 'Kapembwa must die.'

Seven

STEVE ALLOWED A MOMENT FOR the words to sink in.

An assassination.

That wasn't what he'd expected.

'There's a group of ten of us boys – men who were born and grew up in Batota but went out into the world and did well for themselves. Most of them want to stay in the background, which is why it's me standing before you guys today. But there is plenty of money in the kitty so you don't need to worry about that.

'Here's the deal. You boys put together the unit you need to get the job done. I'll arrange for five million dollars to be paid into a bank account in Cyprus controlled by an independent law firm. When Reuters carries the story that Kapembwa has died, the money is yours. There will be a hundred thousand for each man to be getting on with. If you aren't successful, you can keep the cash. I don't care how you do it. All I ask is that Kapembwa dies . . . and that it happens in the next month.'

The image of his dead parents was still flickering on the screen, but Archie wasn't looking at that. He was looking straight at the men in front of him.

At his side, Bruce had stood up, pacing up and down the front of the auditorium.

'You'll be on your own,' he said. 'You'll have the kit, the money, and as for the balls . . . well, you already know you've got those. But apart from that, nothing. We have to have total deniability on this one. Nothing must be traced back to Archie's company, nor to DEF either. When this guy gets malleted, there will be shit flying all over the world – and we don't want any of it landing on us.'

He raised his left hand. 'No one should make a decision right now,' he added. 'Just think about it, and if you're up for it we'll discuss the details of the operation in the morning.'

There's nothing to think about, thought Steve. Assassinate the most brutal, longest-surviving politician in Africa?

They must be joking.

'Like Bruce said, no one has to take this job,' said Archie. 'And I for one wouldn't think any the less of a man for saying he doesn't want to take the risk. But Kapembwa is a mean bastard, and if you're up for it, you'll not just be making yourself a pretty hefty wage-packet, you'll be doing the world a favour as well.'

He grinned, and behind him the film was turned off. 'Now let's finish off that food and booze. No point in wasting it.'

By the time they got back to the hallway, Samantha had already slipped away, Steve noticed. So had Newton. He needed a lot of sleep on soft, clean sheets to get over ten years in Broken Ridge and wanted to start as soon as possible. Archie was handing out more drinks: Stella for Nick, Red Army vodka for Ollie and Maksie, Bushmills for Ian, while Bruce was getting stuck into a bottle of Moyet Antique, a Cognac considered by many people to be the finest in the world. It was certainly among the most expensive. Steve grabbed himself a bottle of South African Windhoek Lager, a fine beer, and the only one on the African continent brewed in strict accordance with the German purity laws that made that country's lagers the best in the world. Archie himself was mixing vodka with bottles of beer, and knocking the stuff down his throat with such ferocity that Steve started to suspect he had a drinking problem.

He didn't look pissed, but then alcoholics never do. They learn how to hide it.

'Does the MoD know anything about this?' asked Steve, standing next to Bruce.

DEF was nicknamed Death Inc. in the trade because of the extreme danger of the missions it took on. But although Bruce had started out on the wilder fringes of the industry, as the Private Military Corporations had grown in power and influence, so he had also moved closer to the Ministry of Defence. His company took plenty of contracts from the government, and although it was privately owned, Bruce was careful never to take on any mission that might offend either Whitehall or the Pentagon.

'This one really is off the books,' answered Bruce with a terse shake of the head. 'Nobody knows anything about it except for the men in this room . . . and I hope to God no one ever finds out.'

'But—'

'Put it this way,' continued Bruce, taking a sip of his cognac, 'everyone is fed up with Kapembwa making speeches denouncing British imperialism and blaming us for his problems when anyone can see it's his government's fault that people are starving and the country is falling apart. There used to be a lot of British business done with Batota and there could be again . . . once the bastard is dead.'

Archie had cranked the music up louder, drowning out any attempt at conversation. 'Knockin' on Heaven's Door' was blasting out on speakers so carefully built into the walls you couldn't even see them. It was the Guns 'n' Roses version, not the Dylan original.

As Axl Rose screeched the words of the dying deputy over the swirling, slashing guitar riff, Archie suddenly addressed them all.

'That's what we'll call it!' he exclaimed, his face reddening. '"Operation Heaven's Door."'

'I'll bloody drink to that,' said Ollie. He raised a shot of vodka, slapped Maksie on the back, and downed it in one gulp.

After another hour of heavy drinking, most of the guys were starting to stagger towards their bedrooms. Steve's head still felt clear enough. He walked along the clifftop towards his room, changed into his trunks and headed back towards the pool. Another swim might clear his mind before bed.

The water felt warm and soft as he dived in. The pool nestled next to the cliffs, with a patio looking out over the ocean, and with few clouds, it was bathed in the soft glow of the moon. Steve did a couple of quick lengths to freshen himself up. It was past midnight, but he already guessed it would be a while before he could get to sleep. Too much on his mind.

He spun around when he heard a splash.

He could see a body moving underwater, and for a moment figured that a boozed-up Ollie and Maksie had tossed Nick into the water. On a second glance, he spotted the long hair twisting under the water. Samantha Sharratt broke through the surface and took a gulp of air. The water was glistening across her slim body, and her hair was clinging to her elegantly sculpted face.

'Too much blood on your hands to sleep, Mr West?' she asked.

'Nothing I've ever done has stopped me from getting a good night's kip,' Steve replied.

She swam to the side of the pool, sprang out and poured two glasses of champagne from a bottle sitting open on the table there. 'You're a soldier?' she asked, kneeling and handing one of the glasses to Steve.

'I was. These days, I freelance.'

'Killed many men?'

'Not as many as you've broken the hearts of.'

She smiled. 'Doesn't it trouble you?'

Steve handed back his empty glass then swam away from her on his back, but still looking straight towards her. 'I never hurt an innocent man.'

'And I never broke the heart of an innocent man either,' said Samantha, jumping in and swimming after him.

'I find that hard to believe, Mrs Sharratt.'

No sooner was the sentence completed than she broke into a peal of laughter. '*Mrs* Sharratt?'

Steve had already reached the other side of the pool. He grabbed hold of the ledge, and looked back towards her.

'You mean you're not married to Archie?'

Sam was trying to stop herself from giggling. 'That dweeb? Christ, no. He's my brother, you idiot.'

He looked straight into her eyes. 'Then . . .'

She paused, her blue eyes looking straight into his. 'Maybe "available" is the word you're looking for.'

'Actually, "lucky day" was the phrase I was searching for,' said Steve with a wry smile. 'But given that it's the middle of the night, I'll settle for "available".'

His hand reached across to touch her wet face. He ran his fingers through her hair, then pulled her gently towards him. For a fraction of a second he could feel her resist, then she yielded. Her arms wrapped around his neck, and her lips parted as he pressed his mouth into hers. Her kiss was liked being punched by a rose: it stung Steve with an intensity that was unexpected. Within seconds, he was gripping her tight to his body, feeling her hands roaming across his back and down into his trunks.

'How about you show me your room, Mr West?' she breathed into his ear.

An hour later, still awake, she was lying entwined in his arms in the bed back in his lodge. Steve could feel her hair lying across his chest, and her soft breath blowing across his face. It was past two in the morning and he was shattered: he'd been pushing himself to the limit for the last thirty-six hours, and Sam had turned out to be a tiger in bed, a woman with a sexual energy, imagination and experience that had left Steve aching with exhaustion.

But still he didn't want the night to end.

Not if that meant she might leave his side.

'The worst part was when they found our parents,' she said.

Steve remained silent, but held her closer to his chest.

'There was an old guy called Lincoln. He'd fought with Dad, and lost a leg, and after that he came to live on the farm and worked as an odd-job man and caretaker. We used to play with him in the garden when we were kids. He was devoted to the family.' She paused, catching her breath. 'The war vets left him alone because he'd fought in the war, but he saw our parents being hacked to pieces, and as soon as he could, he ran for the village and phoned us in London. We'd both moved there by then, and we'd begged Mum and Dad to get out as well, but they wouldn't hear of it. The Sharratts had been in the country for three generations – it was the only life our parents knew. "They can call it Batota or whatever the hell they like," Dad used to say, "but it's my land and I'm staying on it".'

'It must have been hard for you.'

Sam snuggled in even closer to Steve's chest, and he could feel the warmth and suppleness of her body sinking into him. There was a scent to her, a salty mixture of sea and wild flowers that he already sensed could quickly become addictive.

'Everyone's parents die,' she said. 'But you don't expect them to die like that. Yes, it can be hard to live with.'

Her eyes rolled up towards Steve.

'That's why Kapembwa has to be punished,' she said, her voice suddenly alive with steely determination. 'The man has raped the country.'

'The bastard will get what he deserves,' Steve said quietly.

Sam was already kissing his chest. Her tongue was flicking across his skin, stabbing at it in delicate, darting motions, and there was a playful smile on her face as she started to run her lips down towards his crotch.

'There's one thing a girl learns, growing up in Africa,' she murmured.

'What's that?' asked Steve breathlessly.

'How to fuck like an animal.'

He grinned. 'There's hope for the continent yet then.'

Eight

GREAT MOUNDS OF FOOD WERE laid out on a buffet table for breakfast. Steve piled some sausages, bacon and eggs onto his plate, then helped himself to a couple of croissants and a bowl of fruit salad. He felt ravenous, and was tipping as much food as possible down his throat to try and recharge himself. Sitting down at one of the tables looking over the sea, he took a long hit of coffee. The rest of the unit was already up, tucking into their own grub. By the looks of them, Maksie and Ollie were the worse for a hard night's drinking. Only Bruce looked fighting fit.

'You'll make your decisions shortly, and I don't want to pressurise you, but if you have any doubts then I want you to know that you'll be taking out one of the nastiest, most corrupt rulers in the world,' said Archie.

Like Bruce, he looked fresh and well-turned out: unlike Bruce, he must have had two dozen or more drinks last night. A man who can hold his booze, noted Steve. Anyone who could do that usually had an iron constitution.

Sharratt had switched on a flat-screen TV showing documentary footage from Batota.

'This used to be the bread-basket of Africa,' continued Archie. 'It has some of the most fertile land in the whole world and, on the highlands at least, one of the most temperate climates. It also has some of the best infrastructure, huge deposits of raw materials, and some of the hardest-working people on the planet. And look at it now. People are starving because they don't have enough to eat. The opposition is beaten into submission by Kapembwa's thugs. The jails are filled with decent, law-abiding men who were just trying to support their families. This mission – it will be a movement of liberation.'

As the guys chatted among themselves over their breakfast, Steve could tell that they didn't need any more persuading. Their minds were already made up.

Ollie was still trying to put together enough cash to buy Katie the house he'd promised her down in Dorset.

Ian had spent too much of his life in a jail in Ulster and couldn't find a way of settling back into civilian life.

Nick wanted another adventure, and was too young to grasp that every mission took you a step closer to death.

Newton didn't have much choice. Archie had paid a lot of money to break the guy out of jail; he wasn't about to say no to him. And it didn't look like his career prospects were in great shape for any other line of work.

And Maksim? Well, the Russian had allowed himself to be tricked into betraying the unit during their last job together in Afghanistan and, although they had forgiven him for that, he'd been left with a desperate desire to prove himself as good a man as any of them.

Steve speared a sausage, and glanced out at the ocean. And what about me, he wondered.

'If I may quote someone I know,' said Ollie, sitting down next to Steve with a second plateful of bacon, sausages and eggs, ' "you'll be making a few quid, and giving a right mean bastard a malleting. And a man can't ask for much more from a day's work than that".'

Steve grinned. He knew that Ollie was quoting the words he'd used himself in Afghanistan right back at him. Across the terrace, Sam had just emerged. She'd tied her hair back in a ponytail, and was wearing a tight pair of black jeans and a red T-shirt. A string of beads was slung around her neck. Taking a plate of fruit salad, she winked at Steve, a lustful expression playing on her lips, then sat down next to Archie.

'I might just be in,' said Steve, looking back at Ollie.

'What changed your mind?' Ollie paused, then glanced at Sam. A knowing expression crossed his face. 'OK, I get it.'

'It's not—' started Steve. But then he paused.

The truth was, Sam *was* the reason he was taking the job.

'Looks like we're fighting for the same thing,' said Ollie.

'I'm not about to get married.'

'We need the money.'

'Jesus, mate, if that girl really cared about you, she wouldn't be pressurising you to buy a house you can't afford – and if *you* loved *her*, you wouldn't be risking your neck like this.'

'Leave it,' Ollie said coldly. 'We've got an evil bastard to assassinate.'

Steve pushed his breakfast aside. Sam had already left, and Archie and Bruce were calling the men together.

'The time for talking is over,' said Bruce. 'Any man who wants to can leave now, and we'll pay for his flight home.'

He looked around at the faces in front of him.

Nobody spoke.

'Then let's get started,' he said. 'If we're going to get this done, then we need to crack on.'

Archie led them through the hallway to a conference room. It was at the back of the house – a long, thin room dominated by an oak boardroom table, and surrounded by thickly upholstered leather armchairs. There were TVs on the wall tuned to Bloomberg, CNBC and BBC News 24 via satellite connections, and a bank of computer screens. At the head of the table, a man was seated. He looked about fifty to Steve, and you could tell at once he was a soldier. You could see it in his build: for a man of his age, there was still a steeliness to his muscles and a tone to his skin that told you immediately that he was in fearsome shape. And you could see it in his eyes as well: they were grey, like granite, and stared straight into each man as they shuffled into position.

'My name is Ken Tokley,' he said, glancing around at them as they sat down at the table. 'I was once a Colonel in the South African Defence Force, and after that I worked for the Bureau of State Security, or BOSS as it used to be known, in intelligence. These days, I'm just a farmer – officially, anyway.'

He grinned. 'I'm told you boys are planning a job.'

'Ken knows more about the Batotean military than any man alive,' said Archie. 'He'll tell you what you're up against.'

Tokley stood up. He was a big man, with greying hair and skin that had been burned dry in the sun. 'Ben Kapembwa hasn't managed to stay in power for a quarter of a century without having some serious protection around him,' he began. 'There have been plenty of assassination attempts on the man over the years, but he is as slippery as a snake. He's damned difficult to catch, and when you get close to him, he's damned difficult to kill.'

He paused, taking a sip of the cup of coffee that had just been placed in front of him.

'The main Batotean Army is a shambles – you don't have to worry about them,' he went on. 'The men don't get paid, they don't get fed, and they haven't got any kit. On any given day, at least half of them will have buggered off back to their villages. If any shooting starts, the other half will piss off as well. But within the Army, there is a hardcore of well-paid, well-trained men, and they're the boys that keep Kapembwa in power. There is the Central Intelligence Organisation, the secret police. You have to remember that Kapembwa started his career as a Marxist guerrilla; he learned how to run a police force from the East German Stasi – and they were the business. So these men know their jobs and they are brutally efficient. The CIO has spies everywhere. That means however you choose to get in or out of the country, you're going to have to reckon on the CIO keeping tabs on you. The same is true of any locals you might get to help you.'

Tokley chuckled to himself. 'The way the CIO operates, I wouldn't be surprised if they had a man in this room.'

Nobody else laughed, but Ian was already glancing towards Maksim with a suspicious look on his face.

'Next, you have to worry about the Sixth Brigade. It consists of 3,500 men, and they are the elite of the elite. They are trained by the North Koreans, and they usually have a dozen of their officers stationed with them. The Sixth are tough and nasty. The discipline is brutal. But they have all the food and kit they need, their families are all well taken care of, and they are all devoted to Kapembwa.

'Inside the President's entourage, there are two other men who really count. The first is a guy called Esram Matola. He's the senior military commander, and he's worked alongside Kapembwa since the guerrilla wars. He's a fanatical disciplinarian. Step out of line, and he'll have you flogged to death – and that's if you're lucky. He works with a Korean called Sungoo Park who, according to insiders, mainly exists to make Matola look good. Park's in charge of training, weapons – and punishment. He's good at all three of them, bloody good, but mainly the third.'

Tokley attempted a smile. 'With any luck, you won't meet either of them. And if you do, God help you.'

On the screen behind him, he flashed up a picture. It showed a bearded Englishman dressed in green combat fatigues. Steve recognised him at once Guy Wallace. Among mercenaries, the man was notorious. An Old Etonian, he'd been a Colonel in the SAS, then started working for himself in Africa. He was a soldier of the old school, harking back to the days before mercenaries transformed themselves into the smoother, more respectable private military corporations. He'd been mixed up in a series of coups in Africa, and found himself thrown into various jails, but he usually managed to talk his way out of them and get himself another job. He was written up constantly in the British papers, and at least two books had been published about him, including one ghost-written autobiography. Total wanker, thought Steve to himself. Back in the Regiment, Wallace was regarded as a fraud and a phony, a man who spent more time courting publicity than doing any proper fighting. The way most of the guys Steve knew saw it, real mercenaries fought their wars quietly and efficiently behind the scenes. They didn't bring a photographer from the *Daily Mail* along with them.

'This is Guy Wallace,' said Tokley. 'Some of you might have heard of him. He's been knocking around Africa for years, involved in different coup attempts and working for different dictators. For the last two years, he's been a senior military adviser to Kapembwa. The way I heard it, he was in a jail in the Congo, and Kapembwa cut some deal to get him out. He's the guy who brings in the foreign fighters they need to keep the regime in place. If you want to take out Kapembwa, then you're going to have to figure on getting past Wallace as well.'

'So how exactly are we going to get through to the President?' asked Steve. As he glanced around the table, he could see that everyone was thinking the same thing.

Some jobs are impossible.

Even for Death Inc.

Except Bruce, noted Steve. Dudley was looking as inscrutable as ever, but there was a hint of a smile in his eyes, enough to tell you that a scheme had already been cooked up.

'We've thought of something,' said Archie. 'I'm not a military man, so I'm not qualified to say whether it will work, and it's your lives that are on the line, but the plan is there if you want it.'

Tokley pointed. On the screen, he'd now flashed up a map of Batota. With his finger, he gestured at the north of the country. 'This is Talabeleland,' he said. 'And the people there have never liked

Kapembwa, right from the start. There's a renegade military commander up there called August Tshaka who's raised his own army and effectively declared UDI against the government in Ibera. He's tough and he's resourceful, and the official Army is in such a bad state they can't do anything about him. He's been holding out in a guerrilla war for more than a year now, and his prestige and his forces are growing by the day. Kapembwa is starting to get worried about the man.'

Dudley stood up, standing next to Tokley. 'The President has vowed to execute Tshaka, and to do it before the elections, which are scheduled for a few weeks' time. Elections are a sham in Batota, as we all know – but there is still an issue of prestige. Kapembwa has pledged he'll capture Tshaka and kill him with his own hands, and if he doesn't make good on that pledge he'll lose respect. In African politics, once that happens you're already dead.'

'Wallace is out recruiting,' said Tokley. 'He's looking for a bunch of hardened mercenaries who can get up to the north of the country and capture Tshaka.'

'So here's the plan,' said Dudley. 'You boys get yourself recruited by Wallace. You take the job to go and capture this Tshaka bloke, then once you've got him, you deliver him precisely where the President wants him. That gets you into the country, and it gets you armed, and no one over there will suspect anything. When Kapembwa comes down for the execution, you turn the tables on him, put a bullet through the bastard's head, then you make your escape over into Tuka or Botswana.'

He looked around the table, his eyes settling briefly on each man in turn. 'Job done.'

'It's crazy,' snapped Steve. 'We shoot the President and the whole sodding Army will descend on us.'

'We need a decent chance at getting away,' said Ollie. 'This mob might be known as Death Inc., but we're not laying down our lives that cheaply.'

'It's a suicide job,' said Ian sourly.

Archie had already walked around the side of the table. He rested his hand on Newton's shoulder.

'Why don't you tell them your story,' he said quietly.

Nine

NEWTON TOOK A SIP OF coffee before starting to speak. He still looked skeleton thin, and his eyes were hollowed out but some colour was returning to his face. 'I was born in Southern Batota, in a town called Khalaki – part of the Nshani tribe – the same as President Kapembwa,' he stated. 'Our father worked on a tobacco farm, but both my twin brother and I wanted to be soldiers. When we turned eighteen, we joined up with the Batotean Army, and we told the Recruiting Sergeant we wanted to be posted with the Corto Scouts.'

'What the hell are they?' asked Nick curiously.

'The Batotean SAS was closely modelled on the British Special Forces, but it was called the Corto Scouts,' Archie explained. 'The name was taken from the explorer Courtney Macdonald Pantlin. Within the Scouts there was one black unit, which was used mainly for ambushes and for missions behind the lines.'

'Sounds like they were on the wrong side,' said Nick.

'There's always guys like that,' said Ian. 'In Ulster, there were good Catholics who didn't mind fighting for the British.'

'Who says it's the wrong side anyway?' shrugged Archie. 'They were fighting for a country called Batota and that was a damned better place to live in than what's there now, and that was true for the black man as well as the white.'

'That's not the issue,' said Ian fiercely. 'It's about self-determination. And it's about self-respect.'

'There's not much point in self-respect when you're hungry,' said Ollie.

'Shall we skip the political discussion?' interrupted Steve. He looked back towards Newton. 'Go on.'

'Like I said, we were brothers, we were fit and young and strong, and we didn't have any trouble getting accepted into the Scouts,' continued Newton. 'We did our basic training with the Eighth Commando Division. That unit was the closest thing to the Foreign Legion ever put together. There were Germans, Irish, Japs – all sorts. You could sign up for the Eighth and no questions were asked, none answered. They were rough men, on the run many of them, but good soldiers, and as fierce as the sun is hot. After a year, we were assigned to the Scouts . . .'

He paused, taking another hit on the coffee.

'We got transferred up to Nafa Nafa, a collection of grass huts up near Lake Hasta where the selection for the Scouts took place. For eighteen days, we had no rations; we had to live off the land, learning how to drink water from the belly of a wild animal, and cook snakes and maggots so that you drained the poison out of them. Both of us passed with ease. We were waiting for our first assignment when one of the Generals came to see us. He sat down with us and asked us about our village and our family. Then he pointed out that we were both Nshani, the same tribe as Kapembwa, the man leading the rebellion.

'They needed someone on the inside, he told us. So he asked my brother if he'd go back to the village, where he'd be given some papers to show that he'd been at college in Angola for a year. He'd join up with the rebels, become a loyal soldier fighting for Kapembwa, but in reality he'd be a sleeper, the eyes and ears of the Scouts within the enemy camp, just waiting for the right moment – and when that moment arrived, they'd call on him. Meanwhile, I'd join up with the

Scouts, but I'd also be the point man, the guy who had to make contact with my brother when he was needed. The General said it was a brave decision, and if we didn't want to do it he'd understand, but for my brother there was no question. If you join an outfit like the Scouts, you put yourself in the hands of your commanders, and you don't start asking questions.

'I stayed with the Scouts while my brother joined Kapembwa's Army. That was 1978. I didn't make any contact with my brother, and I didn't expect to for a few more years yet. The idea was to let him rise within the ranks and then use him as a spy. Then in 1980, Batota surrendered, and a few months later Kapembwa was the President. I guess that's the way it goes in warfare, certainly in Africa. One day you're the rebel, the next you're the President. The Scouts didn't want to hang around to see what the new regime was like. We'd been the fiercest defenders of the old country – and the new government hated the black unit more than the rest of the Scouts. They saw us as traitors, and we'd have been executed as soon as they had the chance. So the night the old flag came down, we slipped quietly across to South Africa. Some of us joined up with the Recces, as the South African Special Forces were known. Others amongst us became mercenaries. Quite a few just melted into the townships and got jobs doing anything that was available. And me? I stayed as a soldier. I fought with the Recces for a couple of years, then I found work as a mercenary, fighting in Mozambique, Angola, anywhere they needed men who knew how to fire a gun, and where you got paid a decent wage-packet at the end of the week. Eventually, I got mixed up with the wrong job, and ended up in Broken Ridge . . . and the rest you know. I haven't seen my brother since the day he left the Scouts to go and join Kapembwa's rebels.'

'But let me guess,' said Ian. 'His name was Esram.'

Newton nodded. 'That's right,' he replied. 'He changed his surname to Matola when he switched sides, so that he could never be traced back to me.'

Ian tapped his fingers on the table. 'And let me guess something else,' he said. 'The General? His name was Ritchie Sharratt.'

Archie smiled. 'The very same,' he said. 'I heard about the story of the twin brothers and the sleeper in the enemy camp from my dad. I knew he'd never been used because the war was over much faster than anyone expected. But I also knew that Esram was still there, and that he'd risen to be the man in charge of the President's security. That's why I paid you boys to break Newton out of jail . . . because he's the key.'

'So here's how it will work,' said Bruce. 'You take out the rebel, then when the President comes down to execute him, you take the bastard down. Newton will remind Esram of his old loyalties, and he'll hold the Army back because he's the guy that controls it. Afterwards, you boys can make a clean break out of the country.'

Steve hadn't often seen Bruce look pleased with himself. He was a tough, sombre Scotsman, who only ever made jokes at the expense of other men.

But he looked pleased with himself right now. Like a fox who had just found a dead rabbit.

And why not? thought Steve. The plan had been thought through with ruthless precision.

'How can we know that Esram will co-operate?' demanded Ian.

'He's my brother,' said Newton.

'Brothers have been known to betray each other,' said Ian. 'It's been a quarter of a century.'

'He owes me,' said Newton. 'Anyway, if we reveal he was a sleeper for the Scouts then he'll be executed on the spot. He won't have any choice.'

'Then why can't he just let us into the Presidential Palace, allow us to finish the bastard, and then get a flight home?' asked Steve.

'The President is obsessive about his security,' said Tokley. 'He sleeps in different houses every night, and switches his guards every few days. Esram might be in charge, but he can't just let a bunch of assassins walk straight in. The only way to hit him is to get him out of the capital, and away from his own guards, then Esram can let you boys do the business.'

'Trust me, this is the only way to get to him,' said Newton.

Bruce looked around the room. He pulled out a clutch of BA tickets. 'Any of you boys want a seat on the eight-fifteen flight to London tonight?' he said.

Each man shook his head in turn.

'Just checking,' he said. 'Right – there's a coffin with President Kapembwa's name on it, just waiting to be filled.'

Ten

THE FARM WAS HIGH ABOVE sea-level, off a rugged dirt track. Steve steered the Land Rover Discovery through the rolling fields, ignoring the clouds of dust kicked up by its wheels. They'd hired the car at the airport after borrowing Archie's private jet and flying up from Cape Town to Pretoria, and Steve was thankful they'd insisted on a four-wheel drive. 'Christ, how can a man live up here?' he grumbled. 'It would drive me crazy.'

By South African standards, Chris's farm on the Mpumalanga Highveld in the north-east of the country up close to the border with Mozambique wasn't particularly remote. The nearest town was thirty miles away, and there was a hospital only sixty miles distant. But it was still the only building that could be seen on the flat plain that stretched as far as the eye could see. There were 2,000 acres to the farm, all of them planted with grains that grew well in the mild, wet climate, but with just a few guys and three big tractors to keep it all in order.

'Think he's home?' said Ollie.

Steve shrugged. 'With this place to look after, I don't reckon he's going anywhere.'

As soon as they'd accepted the job from Archie, both Steve and Ollie had known that Chris was the first man they wanted to put on the team. He'd been with them in Afghanistan, and they knew the quiet, burly South African was vital to the mission. He'd spent a career in the Recces, the feared South African Special Forces, fighting in the bush wars, then he'd bought himself this farm and tried to make a new life for himself on the land. When they'd found him in London, he was up to his ears in debt, the farm had been repossessed by the bank, and he'd been scratching around for work as a mercenary. But with the money he'd made from the Afghan job he'd paid off the debts, got the deeds back from the bank, and bought in enough seed to make the farm productive again.

'Well, I'll be buggered! Steve bloody West and Ollie sodding Hall,' said Chris, bounding up to meet them.

The whitewashed bungalow consisted of three rooms, with a couple of pick-up trucks parked outside, and a small vegetable garden off to one side. It looked out over field after field of corn and maize. Chris was dressed in jeans and sweatshirt, his skin tanned from working the fields. But he looked well, like a man who was at home: not the fish on dry land he'd been in London.

'Great place,' said Ollie, stepping out of the Land Rover and onto the small porch of the bungalow.

'It's bloody fantastic, man,' said Chris. 'This is the life, I'm telling you.'

It was just after four in the afternoon, the end of the working day for a grain farmer. Ollie had mapped out the team they'd be needing for the job, and they'd decided to get Chris on board as fast as possible. They'd get to see him tonight, then fly the unit back to London tomorrow to start bringing the rest of the guys on board. There was no time to lose. A presidential election was looming in Batota, and they only had a couple of weeks to get Kapembwa's name off the ballot paper. Permanently.

Steve took the beer Chris had just offered him and sat down on the porch. In most of South Africa, grain was planted around January, and at this time of year, the fields had just been cleared and the earth turned. You could smell the soil on the dry, dusty breeze, its aroma rich and fertile and earthy. As he looked around the farm, it reminded him of the garage he'd bought from his uncle: a place where a man could put down some roots and find himself some honest, peaceful work. For when the fighting was over.

'Working out OK up here?' he asked Chris.

The other man nodded, taking a hit of his own beer. 'Better than I could have hoped,' he said. 'Grain prices have been soaring, and we've started planting some of the crops used for biofuels, so we're beginning to make some decent money. It's going to be OK this time around, I can tell.'

He rested his beer bottle in his hand and looked straight at Steve. 'There's a job, isn't there?'

Steve nodded. He glanced around. A pair of workmen were putting a tractor away but they were out of earshot. 'President Kapembwa,' he answered. 'There's some guys who want him finished off . . . and we've taken the gig.'

'The man's a bloody bastard,' spat Chris. 'He deserves it.'

'You're our Steven Gerrard – the first name we want to put on the team sheet,' said Ollie. 'You know this territory and how to fight your way through it better than any other man we know.'

Chris paused. He was a big man, with dark hair and strong bull-like features, and murky blue eyes that hid what he was thinking. There were a couple of tattoos on his thick forearms, and he was swatting a fly away from one of them.

'I'd like to go, boys.'

And yet in the tone of his voice you could hear a *but*, noticed Steve.

The door to the kitchen opened, and a women stepped out, carrying a tray with some sandwiches and some crisps on it as well as three more bottles of beer. Thanking her, Ollie grabbed one of the sandwiches hungrily, eating it in a couple of bites.

'This is my wife, Cissy,' said Chris proudly.

Steve looked at the woman. It took a moment for him to adjust. She wasn't what he'd expected. The Recces were fine soldiers, and there was no man he'd rather have alongside him in a foxhole than Chris, but they weren't known for their commitment to multi-culturalism. The girl must have had something special to get Chris to try and make a mixed marriage work.

From the kitchen, a baby started to cry. Cissy disappeared inside, and within seconds reemerged. A three-month-old boy was suckling at her breast. 'This is Mike,' said Chris.

Again, you could hear the pride in his voice.

Cissy excused herself, slipping back into the kitchen to change the baby's nappy.

'You've got a good set-up here,' said Steve.

Chris nodded, took a sandwich and chewed on it in the slow thoughtful way an ox chews on a bale of hay. 'So when do we start?'

Steve met Ollie's eye. There was no need to discuss it; they both knew what they were thinking.

'This job is too dangerous for a man who's just had a kid,' said Steve flatly.

Chris looked straight at him, the surprise evident in his eyes. 'Of course it's bloody dangerous! You think I don't know that?'

'Mike needs you, Cissy needs you,' said Ollie.

Chris took a swig of his beer. 'Mike needs a dad who goes out into the world and fights for what he believes in,' he said firmly. 'And I believe Kapembwa is a right evil bastard, and if there's a bullet heading his way I want to be on the team that's holding the gun.'

'We've got a plan, and we think it's a good one,' said Steve. 'But that kid needs a dad.'

'I'll be all right.'

Steve shook his head. Out in Afghanistan, they'd lost Jeff, and he'd been one of Steve's best mates. He'd had to go and talk to his mum and explain to her what had happened to her son, and it had been one of the worst days of Steve's life.

'I'm not going to be the guy who has to tell Cissy she's bringing up that boy by herself,' said Steve. He stood up and started to walk towards the car.

Chris grabbed the sleeve of his shirt.

'I told you, I'll be all right,' he growled. 'I know how to fight in the bloody bush better than any man alive or dead.'

'You're not coming,' said Steve, pulling himself free. 'And that's final.'

Eleven

THE PARTY LOOKED TO BE in full swing by the time Steve and Ollie returned to the mansion. It had taken them a couple of hours to get back to the airport, an hour while the jet cleared for take-off, then a forty-minute flight to Cape Town. It was past ten at night. The rest of the unit looked to have eaten well, and were getting down to some serious drinking. Nick had moved on from the Stella to vodka shots, and was reminding Maksie that the Welsh knew even more about hard boozing than the Russians. Ian was sampling a glass of vintage Bushmills and Bruce was working his way through the South African reds. There were five girls with them, two blondes and three brunettes, each of them in their early twenties, wearing short denim skirts, knocking back cocktails, and dancing around to the music.

Archie was slapping one of the girls on the bottom and punching the air as Queen's 'We Will Rock You' blasted out of the speaker system.

Steve looked around for Sam. But there was no sign of her. And although he tried to fight it, he couldn't help feeling deflated.

'Where's Chris?' asked Ian. 'I thought you'd gone to get him.'

Steve shook his head. 'He's shacked up with a local girl, and had a kid.'

'Jesus!' shouted Ian, struggling to make himself heard above the racket of the music. 'I'll be getting hitched to Ian Paisley's daughter at this rate.'

'We told him we couldn't take him,' said Steve. 'This is no job for a man with a new baby.'

'We could have used his expertise,' said Ian.

'We'll be fine.'

Archie was handing out more drinks, and organising a couple of the girls into a wet T-shirt competition. They were out on the terrace next to the pool. Maksim had grabbed a hose and was spraying water over a pair of the girls, their bodies glistening in the soft moonlight. Steve couldn't be certain, but he suspected Archie had paid them to be there tonight. There was no other plausible explanation for how Melanie, the girl hanging onto Ian's arm, and cheering Maksie on as he sprayed more water across her friend Lana, would choose to hang out with a bloke as ugly as the Irishman.

I've nothing against the guys enjoying themselves, Steve decided. They've a tough mission ahead. Probably the toughest they've ever been on.

But Archie seemed to be softening them up: it was as if he was trying too hard to get them on his side. We're mercenaries, Steve reminded himself. We fight for money. You don't have to lay on some local slappers to get us onto the battlefield.

'This reminds me of my mum's club,' said Nick, taking the hose from Maksie and spraying down the brunette. Her T-shirt was clinging to her breasts and her wet hair was swaying in time to the music.

'Club?' said Ollie, standing next to him. 'What club?'

But Nick had clammed up again.

Ian and Steve were now standing right next to him.

'Come on – what club?' Steve wanted to know.

'Nothing,' snapped Nick.

'There's only one type of club that looks anything like this,' said Ian.

'Leave it,' growled Nick.

'A lapdancing club,' Ian went on cruelly.

Steve laughed. 'You're kidding us, right?'

Nick went bright red.

'Wow – a lapdancer,' said Ollie, grinning. 'I thought you said she worked in B&Q.'

'Yeah, well, if your mum was a lapdancer, I don't suppose you'd be bragging about it either,' said Nick, a drunken anger evident in his tone of voice. 'She works at the Sensations Club in Cardiff. How else is she supposed to make ends meet? That's why I wanted to take a PMC job in the first place, to make enough money to get my mum out of the club.'

'Christ, I hope she's better-looking than you are,' said Steve.

Ollie was still chuckling. 'Isn't she a bit old?'

'She's only thirty-two.'

Ian was looking straight at Ollie, then back at Nick. 'Thirty-two? How's that possible? I thought you were twenty, Nick. She couldn't have had a kid when she was twelve, could she? I mean, even in Swansea that's a bit young.'

'She was fourteen,' Nick mumbled.

'So let me see – that makes you eighteen,' said Ian. 'Not twenty after all.'

'Jesus,' said Ollie. 'If I known how old you were, I'd never have agreed to take you to Afghanistan.'

'Well, I'm bloody eighteen now, aren't I?'

'Old enough to get into your mum's club,' said Ollie.

'I'll organise your stag night there, mate,' said Steve. 'We can have a right good piss-up and get Nick's mum to lay on a few dances for us.' He looked at the boy. 'What did you say it was called again?'

'Fucking leave it,' the young man snapped, walking away.

'Sensations, Cardiff,' said Ollie, laughing. 'I want the VIP table.'

Nick had already drifted away, and was dancing with one of the girls. Steve stood by himself, watching the fun, but not in the mood to take any part in it.

'I can get some extra girls in if you want,' said Archie, standing next to him.

'That's OK. I think I'll get an early night,' Steve told him.

'You don't like to party?'

Steve looked at Archie sharply. 'Not all of these guys will necessarily make it back from this job alive,' he said. 'For me, that takes the edge off the celebrations.'

Steve strolled back to his lodge, collected his trunks and walked down towards the beach. There was a slight breeze but the night air was still warm. He splashed into the waves and swam out fifty feet. There was a heavy swell in the water, and he could feel the currents whipping across him. As he turned around and swam back to the shore, the waves were breaking over him in strong, powerful gusts, and it was only when he stood up and cleared the water from his eyes that he saw the woman standing in front of him.

She was wearing a white bikini which, in the pale moonlight, only highlighted the soft golden tan of her skin.

'Where were you?' said Steve, taking her in his arms.

'I didn't want to come to the party,' she said. There was a smile playing on her lips.

'Shy?'

Sam shook her head, letting her long pale hair catch the breeze blowing in from the sea. 'I fuck better when I'm sober,' she said.

Christ, thought Steve to himself. You could spend a lifetime looking for perfection in a woman, and not get any closer than this.

He pressed her lips close to his mouth and could feel her tongue flicking up to meet his. Her grip was strong, and her lips salty as she led him away to a small cove on the side of the beach where a circle of black rocks formed a discreet, natural curtain. Sam was tugging Steve down into the ground, kissing his chest and running her hands down the length of his back.

'Take me,' she muttered huskily. 'Take me right now . . .'

Their lovemaking was quick and urgent. With the waves snaking around their feet, Steve pushed her down into the sand, pressing close to her body until he could hear her start to moan in pleasure. Within minutes, they were lying in each other's arms, exhausted yet satisfied.

'There's something about you,' Sam said, nestling in his arms. 'My father would have liked you. He admired soldiers.'

'I'm nervous,' said Steve, looking into her huge eyes.

'Of the mission?'

'Not that,' he answered, with a curt shake of the head. 'I'm worried I might not see you again.'

'I'll be in London,' she said. 'I spend most of my time there anyway, working with the World Species Fund. We fight for the protection of endangered animals.'

'Come and see me,' said Steve.

Her tongue lashed upwards towards his. 'I'd love to,' she said, pulling him towards her wet and naked body.

Archie shook each man warmly by the hand as they gathered in the departure lounge of Cape Town Airport. It was time for them to take a short break before the mission – to go home and get organised.

'I'm bloody grateful to you boys,' he said. 'And if there's anything you need, just ask.'

His eyes were clear and bright, noted Steve. Archie had been plastered on vodka, cognac and beer last night, a combination which in Steve's experience took a savage revenge on you in the morning, but he looked as fresh as a newly-born butterfly. Nick and Maksim, by contrast, looked like a pair of gutter hounds. Ollie was the only man among them who could really hold his drink, but you needed to keep him as far from the bottle as possible: the man was a liability to both himself and his mates once he had a few drops of the hard stuff in his bloodstream.

'One question,' said Ian. 'You bought some papers recently that belonged to the explorer Charles Simkins. Anything interesting in them?'

'Who the hell was he?' interrupted Ollie.

'Charles Simkins was one of the colleagues of Oswald Fitzpatrick, the founder of Batota,' said Archie. 'He negotiated a document that came to be known as the Simkins Concession – that was the deal under which the British South Africa Company bought the mineral rights to the country from King Hstalongula, the African ruler of what is now Batota. Over the years, the concession formed the legal basis for the later white takeover of the country.'

'And his personal papers came up for auction at Sotheby's earlier this year,' said Ian. 'I looked it up on the web. Archie here paid over half a million pounds for them.'

'I'm interested in the history of my country.'

'It's a lot of money for a souvenir.'

'That depends on how much money you have,' said Archie. 'To me, it's loose change. I'm hoping to build a Museum of Batota one day, a place historians can study the joint black and white heritage of the country. Simkins's papers will be core to that. He was the real founder of the nation.'

He looked closely at Ian. 'But that's just history,' he said. 'What you boys are creating is the future.'

'Where I come from they're the same thing,' said Ian. 'History has a funny way of coming back and biting you in the bollocks.'

Up on the screen in front of them, their flight for London was being called. Bruce nodded the men towards the gate.

Suddenly, Steve heard a shout.

Chris Reynolds was bounding towards them. Dressed in black jeans and a blue sweatshirt, there was a small canvas bag slung over his back. 'You're not going without me,' he said.

'Christ, man, we already told you,' Steve said irritably. 'This is no job for a bloke with a new kid to look after.'

'And *I* said I'm coming.'

Bruce handed him a boarding card. It was clear to Steve that the two men had already spoken. How else would Chris know which plane they were on, and have a seat already booked for him?

'I thought—'

'You need someone who knows how to fight in Africa, Steve,' said Bruce sharply. 'Every continent has its own style of warfare. Chris knows what the rules are in this part of the world.'

'It's too dangerous.'

Chris looked straight at Steve. He was a big slow man, with a ponderous manner, but like an ageing ox he had a steady determination to him. 'It's personal,' he said. 'I have my own reasons why I want Kapembwa dead.'

'Such as?'

'I just told you, it's personal,' repeated Chris.

'Fantastic,' said Ollie, clapping him on the back. 'Pleased to have you back on the bus, mate.'

Steve glanced back once at the airport before stepping through the departure gate.

Next time we're on this continent, he thought, we'll be kicking off a small war.

And once you start one of those, there's no way of knowing how it will finish.

Twelve

T HE FARMHOUSE WAS DOWN AT the end of a long, twisting lane, surrounded by fields that at this time of year were damp and lifeless. As he looked out, Steve couldn't help but be reminded of the place Chris had built for himself out in Africa, bathed in brilliant blue sunshine and surrounded by wide open spaces that a man could feel still needed to be conquered.

It wasn't hard to understand why blokes had gone out to places like South Africa or Batota. There was a freedom, a sense of adventure out there, which could never be found at home.

'Let me do the talking,' said Ollie. 'He's my kind.'

'What kind is that then?'

'A public-school tosser.'

Steve grinned. 'OK, you're doing the talking,' he chuckled. 'You boys should get on like a house on fire.'

They'd touched down at Heathrow early this morning after an overnight flight from South Africa. There wasn't any time to lose. Over the next two days, they'd need to put together the rest of the team they needed for the job. That meant tracking down the other men who'd been with them in Afghanistan: the Gurkha warrior Ganju Rai, an expert in stealth fighting, the organisational and logistics maestro David Mallet, and Dan Coleman, the Australian Special Forces trooper who knew more about weapons than any man Steve had ever met.

But before they did any of that, they had to get themselves hired by Wallace. Until they had done that, they hadn't even touched first base.

Guy Wallace lived in a big old stone farmhouse set deep into the Dorset countryside. Bruce had called him from South Africa – the two men knew each other from the old days – and said he had some guys who might be up for a job in Batota if he was still recruiting. Wallace had told him to send them straight down. He needed some fighters and he needed them fast.

On the drive down from London, Steve and Ollie had run through their lines. They wouldn't mention that they were working for Bruce. They'd just say he'd made the introductions. And they certainly wouldn't mention Archie Sharratt. You had to be pretty desperate to sign on for Kapembwa: only men who were millimetres away from the gutter itself were likely to take that shilling. The way they'd tell it, they were both strapped for cash, and were up for anything.

'Mr West and Mr Hall,' said Wallace, stepping out from behind a tractor. 'I've heard plenty about both of you. Most of it bad . . .' He laughed to himself.

The courtyard of the farmhouse was covered in hay and mud. There was a pair of horses in a stable, both of them neighing. Wallace led them inside. The house was built of stone, with low beamed ceilings, and Steve had to stoop to get through to the kitchen. From the musty smell, it was clear that Wallace lived here alone on his occasional trips back from Africa. No woman would allow it to get into this state.

Wallace put a pot of freshly brewed coffee on the table. He was a tall man – thin, with strong muscles, and a greying beard that made him look all of his fifty years. In his runny, blotchy eyes you could see the effects of half a century of drinking and fighting; at different stages in his career, Wallace had spent around a decade in African jails, and the brutal conditions had taken their toll. Yet he moved with a catlike agility, and there was rough intelligence to his face. Steve knew of cars that were just the same – and he usually bought them for the dealership if he got the chance. In another decade, they'd be scrap metal, but for now there was plenty of punch left in their engine.

'So you boys are interested in a trip to Batota?'

Steve nodded. He and Ollie were gazing around the walls, on which dozens of newspaper clippings were pinned, all of them about Wallace. *The Madman of Chad*, ran a headline from the *Daily Mail*. *Etonian Mercenary Held in Mozambique Jail*, said a piece from *The Times*. There were countless others in a similar vein, many of them starting to yellow with age.

'Then I'm your man,' Wallace said, sitting down and pouring out the coffee. His voice was loud and smug: the man was already grating on Steve's nerves.

'Benjamin Kapembwa and I go back a fair few years, and I daresay he trusts me more than he would his own brother. He listens to me, and there aren't many men in the world who can say that. Probably none, and certainly none with a white skin. People reckon the country is broke, and of course they've got their problems, but Batota is still rich in minerals, and the mines are still working, so there's plenty of money sloshing around the place. You just have to get your hands on it, that's all.'

'We heard you were looking for some men.' Ollie spoke for the first time.

Wallace rapped his knuckles on the wooden kitchen table. 'There's a nasty fight going on around the Talabeleland border,' he said. 'A man called August Tshaka is leading an insurgency. He's a brutal thug even by African standards and he's a right pain in the President's backside.'

'Can't the Army deal with him?'

Wallace shook his head. 'It's a rabble,' he said. 'Only the Sixth Brigade is worth anything, but we need to keep those boys in Ibera in case the locals start getting restive. The rest of the Army couldn't shoot itself in the foot without help. The President has promised he'll capture Tshaka and blow the bastard's brains out. And that's exactly what we're going to do.'

He looked straight at Steve and Ollie. From a box on the table, he took out a thick cigar, caressed it for a second, then lit it from the flame of a greasy, oil-fired lighter. 'We need a small unit of men to get up to Talabeleland for us and capture the sod.'

'We've got ten guys,' said Ollie. 'And we know what we're doing.'

'Backgrounds?'

'SAS, Blues, SASR, Spetsnaz, Recces, Gurkhas, Provos . . .'

Wallace grinned.

It was hard not to be impressed by the collective fighting experience of the team. So long as you didn't mention the Welsh teenager, Steve reminded himself.

'So how come you want this job?'

'We need the money, simple as that,' said Ollie. 'We're not fighting for anything other than the pay cheque.'

'There's Iraq, Afghanistan . . .'

'All the good work is gone. It's just convoys and bodyguarding. We need some proper fighting and some proper pay.'

Wallace rapped the table-top again, blowing a thick cloud of smoke upwards.

'We'll pay each man three thousand dollars a week,' he said. 'And for each man, there will be a fifty-thousand-dollar bonus – once the bullet goes into Tshaka's head.'

'Two conditions,' said Ollie. 'We choose our own guys and our own kit. And we don't take any orders from anyone apart from ourselves.'

'Done.'

'When shall we start?' asked Ollie.

'How about yesterday?' said Wallace. 'There's a nasty old scrap going on up there, and we need to get it sorted as fast as possible.'

'We'll be there in three days,' said Ollie.

Wallace stood up and shook both men by their hands. 'I guess they don't call your mob Death Inc. for nothing,' he said. 'It's been a bloody hard vacancy to fill and we're glad to have you on board.'

Thirteen

THE HOUSE WAS SET ONE road back from the seafront, along one of the trim suburban streets on the outskirts of Eastbourne. Last time Steve and Ollie had been here, Ganju Rai had been living with his grandfather, another ex-Gurkha who'd fought with the British in the Second World War. Now, he was by himself. The old man had died two months ago.

'Sorry to hear about the old guy,' said Steve as Ganju let them in.

There was a hint of sadness around Ganju's tough, dark eyes, but he hid it well. He'd lost his brother fighting with the British Army in Bosnia and was left with the responsibility of supporting his sister-in-law and her children. If the Army paid decent pensions to the widows of its men, the little family would have been all right: life was cheap back in Nepal. But it didn't – a point that rankled with Ganju, as it did with all the men the Gurkhas fought alongside – so he'd been forced to quit the Army and make a living as a mercenary to keep the family afloat.

'A Gurkha never dies,' Ganju said now. 'He just moves on and comes back as something else.'

'Your grandfather will probably come back as a tank,' said Ollie.

Ganju smiled at this, then said: 'There's a job, isn't there?'

It took Steve ten minutes to run through the mission. As he spoke, Ganju listened thoughtfully, sipping on the cup of jasmine tea he'd poured himself. At the end, there was only one question. 'Can we be certain that Newton's brother will still co-operate after all these years?'

Steve paused. The same question had been worrying him.

'It's war,' he said flatly. 'Nothing's certain. But the odds are good enough for me.'

'Then I'm in,' said Ganju. 'Anything's better than sitting around in this empty house wondering where my grandfather has got to.'

'Good man,' said Ollie.

Next, Steve and Ollie took the rental car up towards Worpledon, a small village close to Woking. It was past nine by the time they arrived at David Mallet's house, but he seemed happy enough with the interruption. His wife Sandy was busy getting the twins to bed: in those circumstances, any excuse to get out of the house was a good one, he remarked as he got in a round of drinks in the local pub. It was getting on for a year now since they had seen David, not since they'd brought him back from Afghanistan just about in one piece.

'Christ, mate, I think you looked better out on the front line,' Ollie commented.

David took a sip of his pint. 'I think I'd got more sleep as well,' he said. 'I mean, have you ever heard twins screaming their lungs out?'

'Something like a Challenger at full blast?' said Steve.

David nodded. 'But noisier.'

Steve grinned. 'There's a job – but I can't exactly promise you peace and quiet.'

David listened intently. He already had two kids from his first marriage, two teenage boys, both at public school, with the fees going up by 10 per cent a year. His ex, Laura, was always hassling him for more money, and now he had the twins to take care of as well. Even the half million they'd taken away from the Afghanistan mission hadn't put the guy in the black. 'The thing is, boys, I'm broke,' said David.

He started to explain.

Of the half million he'd brought back from the last job, £350,000 had gone straight to Laura: he still owed her that from the divorce settlement. The school fees had eaten their way through another fifty grand, and that was just for one year. He'd spent fifty or sixty in the last year just looking after Sandy and the twins, and the taxman had run away with the rest. 'I tell you, I don't know how a man's meant to support a family, the amount of money everything costs these days.'

'There's a job,' said Steve.

David drained his pint. 'I don't care how risky it is,' he said. 'Just get me on the plane. I need the money.'

Steve glanced down at the number plate attached to the sky-blue Jaguar E-type. G-SPOT, it read. 'Christ!' he exclaimed. 'Who the hell put that there? It's the tackiest thing I've ever seen.'

'Customer's orders,' said his Uncle Ken, who'd been minding the garage whilst Steve was away for a few days. 'A football agent from up in Cheshire, and you know what that mob are like. They don't really do sophistication, especially when it comes to women.'

'Bloody waste of a good Jag . . .'

'The bloke is paying full whack for the motor, Steve, and that means he can paint it yellow with purple stripes if he wants to. It's just business.'

'At least it's not an Aston Martin,' sighed Steve. 'I'm not exactly a religious man, but there are some limits to the amount of sacrilege I'm prepared to tolerate. And putting tack like that on a DB5 would be a step too far.'

Grabbing himself a coffee, he stepped into the back office. Ever since he'd been a boy, it had always been Steve's plan to buy out his Uncle Ken's share in West & Hallam, a dealership in vintage British cars based in Leicestershire. Messing around in the garage with old Jaguars, Aston Martins and Austin Healeys was his passion: one reason why he'd left the Regiment was to make enough money to buy his share in the business, and he was only ever going to do that as a mercenary. With the money from Afghanistan, he'd bought a stake in the garage, as well as buying himself a small cottage on the outskirts of the town to live in. But the stock – three E-types, two of the Jag Mark II, three DB5s and a pair of Austin Healey 3000s – wasn't shifting.

'Cash flow,' shrugged Ken. 'That's what the business is about. Without cash flow, it's just messing about with old cars.'

'I know,' said Steve. He glanced down at the books. But accounts weren't his thing. Never had been. That was why he had joined the Army instead of going into the City like his brother – the Golden Boy Mum and Dad were always going on about.

After dropping Ollie in London, Steve had driven up to the cottage last night, kipped down, then come straight into the office of Hallam & West. He and the rest of the team had forty-eight hours before they were leaving for Batota. By then, they had to put all of their lives in order, and get hold of as much kit as they could source in London. With Ganju and David on board, they were short just one man. Steve had already called Dan Coleman, the Australian SASR man who'd been with them in Afghanistan, but so far they hadn't had any reply. All they had was a mobile number and that kept going straight through to answerphone.

Surely Dan would be up for it, thought Steve. There wasn't any kind of scrap the Aussie didn't want to get into the thick of.

Steve spent the day in the garage, getting his head around the books and checking that the two cars that had found buyers were in good enough condition to be shipped out. But the place wasn't making any money, that much was clear. It doesn't matter how much you try to deny it, Steve told himself. I need that cash I'll be making in Batota to keep this place afloat.

'I could use a favour,' he said to Ken, as they walked together back to the cottage.

It was an old farmer's lodge, with a couple of bedrooms, a sitting room and a small kitchen. Steve hadn't done much to the place since he'd bought it: he'd shipped in his clothes, got himself a satellite dish, a Sky Sports subscription, and a home cinema system, but that was about it. One of these days he reckoned he'd get around to painting the walls. Maybe when he got back from Batota, and had some serious cash in his pocket again.

'Where are you going this time?'

Ken was in his sixties now. Steve's father's brother, he'd spent ten years in the Royal Engineers before setting up the garage. He'd never had any kids of his own – he'd been married once but his wife had run off with another bloke while he was in the Army – and he'd latched onto Steve as a surrogate son. They were men cast from the same rough gun metal, Steve would sometimes reflect. He certainly had a lot more in common with Ken than he did with his own family: he'd fallen out badly with his own dad over joining the Army, and he was fed up with hearing about how well his brother was doing at the bank.

'Batota.'

'Bloody hell, Steve, what for?'

'It's a job,' said Steve tersely. 'I need you to look after the garage for a couple of weeks.'

'Who are you fighting?'

Steve pushed open the gate that led through to the small front garden. 'It's a set-up,' he said. 'We're going in for the Government . . . but we're being paid to turn on them.'

Ken shook his head. 'Africa's a graveyard for men in your trade,' he said. 'You make sure you look after yourself.'

'Everywhere's a graveyard for a PMC,' said Steve. 'Otherwise they wouldn't be hiring us.'

'But Africa . . .' Ken paused. It was a grey, overcast evening, with heavy clouds looming in the distance, and it was already pitch black even though it wasn't yet six o'clock. 'There were plenty of guys I knew who went out to fight in Africa in the mercenary wars of the 1970s. You could make good money in those days in Angola,

Mozambique, the Congo – even in Batota. But a lot more went out than ever came back.'

'Like I said, we'll look after ourselves.'

'But there's blood in that soil, Steve,' said Ken. 'And it's thirsty for more.'

Steve had pushed open the door. A light was already on.

'Steve . . .'

His mother. Lois West was sixty, but was still a fine-looking woman. She had shoulder-length black hair, and a trim, pert figure without an ounce of extra weight on it. She remained, in Steve's view, flawless: the only mystery was how she'd put up with living in Bromley with his dad for so many years.

Steve glanced towards Ken. He must have told her Steve was back for a couple of days. How else would she know that she could find him here today? And who else would have given her a key to let herself in?

'Steve, I just had to see you,' said Lois, planting a kiss on his cheek. 'Your sister's arranged a Christening for the new baby for the week before Christmas and I wanted to make sure you were going to be there. And then you might as well stay down for Christmas. Your brother will be over on the day, and—'

'You could have sent an invite,' said Steve. 'Or just texted me.'

Lois sighed. 'And the chances of a reply were what, exactly? One per cent, two per cent.' She turned around and started walking through the house, picking up a couple of old motoring magazines as she went and chucking them in the bin. 'It's a lovely cottage, Steve, but it needs brightening up. You know, it's about time you settled down.'

'Maybe he will soon,' said Samantha, stepping into the room.

Samantha.

Steve took a deep breath. How the hell did *she* get here? Last time he had seen her, she was in South Africa.

'She seemed such a lovely girl I thought I'd let her in,' said Lois.

'And you did ask me to come and see you when we both got back to England,' said Sam, kissing Steve on the cheek. 'So here I am.'

Steve grinned. The truth was, she was probably the person he most wanted to see right now. And dressed in tight blue jeans with a bright red sweater, she looked fantastic, her tanned skin and golden-blond hair the perfect antidote to the cold winter's day outside.

'Now you boys get some drinks, and us girls will rustle up something to eat,' said Lois, disappearing with Sam into the kitchen.

'A half-open tin of beans and a microwave burger,' said Steve, thinking about the contents of his fridge. 'That should be a slap-up meal. Maybe we should go to the pub?'

Sam flashed him a smile. 'Don't worry,' she said sweetly. 'We've already bought some proper food.'

Fourteen

'GET A BLOODY MOVE ON, mate, we haven't got time to waste,' shouted Ollie from the driveway.

Steve paused for a second. Sam was still holding him in her arms. Her skin felt soft and warm, and her hands were gripping him with a tightness that went beyond the merely physical. Last night, Lois and Sam had cooked up a delicious meal, and then shared a couple of bottles of wine with Ken. After he had left, Lois had gone up to bed, leaving Steve and Sam alone together. The two women had got on brilliantly. Steve had had plenty of girlfriends over the years, but none of them had been serious. They certainly hadn't been the kind of girls who'd spend half the evening chatting to his mum. In fact, most of them you'd be too embarrassed to introduce to your parents at all.

'You'll be back soon, won't you?' she said.

'I promise.'

'You'd better be,' she said, trying to stifle a choke in her voice. 'I promised your mum I'd get you to that Christening. She showed me a picture of the baby. He's *so* sweet.'

Christ, thought Steve. *A bird ganging up with my mum . . . that's the last thing I need.*

He climbed into the rental car. Ollie was picking him up and driving him down to London because they now had just one day left to make their final preparations. They were taking the unit up to

Aberdeen tonight for a final briefing from Bruce, then getting a flight for Madrid in the morning. From there, they'd connect onto a flight for Johannesburg.

They had kit to source.

And they were still a man short.

'You getting serious with that girl?' said Ollie. There was a sly grin on his face.

'Maybe.'

'Well, I hope she's a better bet than the last bird you took up with.'

Steve knew perfectly well what he was getting at. In Afghanistan he'd hooked up with a Russian girl, Orlena, who'd placed her brother Maksim in the unit and then turned out to be betraying them. 'I did a full body search,' he replied. 'And I couldn't find any tracking devices.'

'I bloody hope so,' said Ollie. 'It's going to be dangerous enough out in Batota without our own team trying to kill us as well.'

It was a two-hour drive down to the flat on the Battersea side of the Thames that Bruce allowed his men to use as a base when they were in London. Along the way they discussed the men and kit they still needed. Nick, Ian, Chris, Maksim and Newton had all kipped down there for the night and the place was already smelling like a barrack room. There were the remains of a take-away curry on the table next to the TV when Steve and Ollie joined them. Chris had been out scouring the shops for kit they might need. He had stocked them up with boots and rucksacks and medicines, but didn't want to get any kit that looked military. South Africa had a strict ban on its own citizens working as mercenaries, and it was even tougher with foreigners. The last thing they needed was trouble from immigration: and that was precisely what they'd get if they landed at the airport looking like the Foreign Legion.

'We'll pick up the kit we need in Jo'berg,' Chris said. 'There's not much in the way of military gear you can't buy there, so long as you know the right people.'

Steve nodded. 'We just need one more man, then.'

There was still no answer from Dan, and with less than twelve hours to go, they couldn't rely on the Aussie any more. If he'd gone AWOL, then he was going to have to miss this one.

Steve had rung around a few guys he knew from the 'circuit', as the network of former soldiers who hopped from one war zone to the next was known. So far, he hadn't found anyone. Operations in Iraq and Afghanistan meant there was plenty of demand for well-trained soldiers. The oil price was still high enough for the exploration companies to keep pouring money into small, volatile countries – and they needed guys to protect their kit. There was plenty of easy money to be made in the security industry right now, without flying into Batota and kicking off a revolution. Nor did anybody want to fight for Guy Wallace. They were too many stories of men being tortured to death in African jails after failed coup attempts. 'No bloody way,' said Darren Millar, an ex-Regiment guy Steve had once fought alongside, when he got him on the phone. 'Suicide jobs – that's Wallace's speciality, and this one sounds like the craziest of the lot. You can keep me on the subs bench, thanks very much.'

'How about you?' Chris asked, glancing across at Ollie. 'Found anyone?'

Ollie shook his head. 'There's only one choice,' he answered. 'Roddy.'

'Christ, no,' snapped Steve. 'Not that bloody clown.'

Roddy Smarden was a schoolfriend of Ollie's who'd served alongside him in the Household Cavalry, specialising in communications and signalling. A Fulham Road public schoolboy, he ran a travel business called The Big Ski Adventure Company that took City boys off on escorted tours to some of the world's most dangerous black runs. But after a Merrill Lynch trader suffered brain damage on a trip to Norway, business had dried up. He'd been on the bus for the Afghanistan trip but jumped off at the last moment. Steve reckoned he was the worst kind of public-school tosser: arrogant, smug, and with no backbone.

'Woddy the Wanker?' frowned Ian.

'He's all right,' said Ollie. 'Back in the Blues, there was no finer soldier.'

'He's an idiot,' Steve said flatly.

'Maybe we're all idiots for taking this job,' Ollie responded. 'But we're a man short, and right now he's the only bloke we've found who's willing to come.'

On the departures screen, the BA flight for Aberdeen was open for boarding. All nine men were ready, each of them casually dressed in jeans and a sweatshirt, their kit bags slung over their shoulders. We look like a bunch of oil workers heading back up to the rigs for a two-week shift, decided Steve. But if you looked closely, you could see the edginess in each man's eyes. Every time he set off for a mission, Steve could feel the adrenaline running faster through his veins, knowing that he was putting himself on the front line of experience, taking risks and challenges that most people could never contemplate. Maybe that's what makes me do it, he wondered to himself. Or maybe I'm just too stupid to understand the chances I'm taking.

'Where's Roddy then?' he questioned Ollie.

The other man was glancing around the crowded terminal. It was just after five in the afternoon and Heathrow was thronging with travellers.

But there was no sign of Roddy.

Ollie had already switched on his mobile, was stabbing at the dial button and cupping the phone to his ear. By the time he looked back towards Steve he was bright red. 'Roddy's at Gatwick,' he said. 'Apparently he thought we were flying from there.'

Steve chuckled. 'Then he's missed the sodding bus, hasn't he?'

'And I nearly missed it as well,' said a voice.

Steve spun around. Dan Coleman was standing right behind him. The Australian was a big man, at least six two, with shoulders like steel girders and a jaw so thick and square it looked like breeze block.

His hair was dirty blond, and his grin was rough and rugged. There weren't many guys Steve would avoid getting into a fight with, but Dan was one of them. He'd trained with the Special Air Services Regiment, as the Australian special forces were known, but he'd spent a year in a military jail after a UN report had blamed him for the deaths of two children in a fire-fight in the border country between Pakistan and Afghanistan. Steve had no doubts the judges had got it wrong. The Aussie was among the straightest men he'd ever met: with the enemy, he was about as subtle as a cruise missile, but off the battlefield he was the kindest, gentlest man ever born.

'Bloody hell, boys, I hear there's a big scrap on,' said Dan, slamming his massive fists into Steve's back and leaving him temporarily winded. 'Beer, sunshine, and all the AK-47 ammo you can stuff into your belt? You can't kick off the fun without the Aussies on board.'

'Where the hell have you been?' said Steve.

'Sorry, mate, I lost my mobile in a bar in Barcelona. Legless doesn't even begin to describe it. I only just managed to get Vodafone to give me a new one and let me access my messages.'

'Christ, we're flying out to take on one of the most brutal regimes in the world, and one bloke can't find the airport and another can't find his phone,' said Steve. 'We're going to need some arse and elbow lessons before we get started.'

He shook his head, but secretly he was pleased. In a fire-fight, there was no one he'd rather have standing next to him than Dan.

'So you're coming?' said Ollie.

'Batota? During the cricket season? Of course I'm sodding well coming!'

'Then let's go,' said Ollie. But as he started to lead the unit towards the departure gate, he suddenly froze in his tracks. The word 'Ollie!' was being shouted from somewhere behind him.

'It's Katie,' he muttered to Steve. 'For God's sake, tell her something about where we're going. Just don't mention Batota.'

'You didn't tell her?'

'Of course not,' Ollie said, exasperated. 'She'd be worried sick. We're supposed to be getting married in less than four weeks.'

Katie was hurrying towards them. She was wearing a black dress with suede boots and an overcoat wrapped around her shoulders, her auburn hair reaching down over the back of her neck. Steve didn't like her much: she was too sharp and bitter for his tastes. But there was no denying that she was a beautiful woman. Her olive skin was as rich and subtle as a summer's sunset and her blue eyes could pierce you like a sword. Men's hearts would melt as she walked by: why she'd stuck by a loser like Ollie when she could have chosen any of the millionaire hedge fund managers in the City remained a mystery to Steve.

'We're off, babes,' said Ollie, giving her a hug.

'Where are you going?' she demanded. She was looking mainly at Steve, as if she didn't expect a straight answer from her fiancé.

'Morocco,' he answered blandly. 'We're doing some oil-rig work for a couple of weeks. Nothing more dangerous than a bit of passive smoking from the Arab oil workers.'

'He needs to be back a week before the wedding,' she said bossily. 'There's still tons to do.'

'You can trust us,' said Steve. 'We're mercenaries.'

Even Katie laughed at the joke. But then. 'I want him back, Steve, and I'm putting you in charge of making it happen.'

'Like a best man,' said Steve cheerfully. 'I think I can handle that.' Then, turning to the group, 'Now for Christ's sake, let's move, boys. It's time to get this show on the road. We haven't even left the airport and already it's chaos.'

As he glanced back, he could see Ollie kissing Katie goodbye. If he can't even tell her where he's going, he wondered to himself, then why the hell is he marrying her?

Fifteen

THE LAND STRETCHED OUT INTO the distance across rolling, damp hills, and you could just make out the rugged shores of Loch Kinord. The manor house was fifty miles due east from Aberdeen, in the wild interior of Scotland, dominated by sprawling moors interrupted by forests of birch. Heavy rain was falling and it was already dark, obscuring the view, but the landscape still had a brooding, powerful beauty to it, and Steve could see at once why Bruce was drawn to this place. He'd bought the estate with the money he'd made from DEF, and although land was cheap in the north of Scotland compared to the rest of the country, it must still have cost a small fortune to buy and another to maintain. The old stone house had ten bedrooms, a small farm, and 1,000 acres of woodland, as well as its own shooting and fishing.

This is what he fights for, decided Steve, taking a sip of the single malt whisky from the nearby Glendronach Distillery. Just like I fight for my cars, and Ollie fights for Katie. Every man needs something he can make a home out of, even if some of us struggle to spend much time there.

'Africa's not like fighting anywhere else, boys,' said Bruce, looking around the assembled unit. 'And so I've asked Hugo MacAskill here to tell you what he knows.'

The man standing in front of them was at least sixty, with orange hair and white pasty skin, but he had a strong jaw and serious, dark green eyes. He'd been in the SAS during the 1960s, according to Bruce, then joined in some of the mercenary wars that raged through Africa in the 1980s. He'd fought with the Batoteans, with the Portuguese in Mozambique, and for the mining companies up in the Congo. He spent a decade fighting in Africa when it was a battlefield in the Cold War, with Russian- Chinese- and American-backed armies vying for control of the region. He'd taken on Stasi fighters advising the guerrillas in the Congo, and a renegade brigade of hardened Vietcong veterans who'd been sent to stiffen the rebel forces in Namibia. And although he'd made it back with nothing worse than a couple of bullet wounds to his thighs, he'd known plenty of men whose corpses would have rotted beneath unmarked African graves many years ago.

'Since Bruce has asked me here to tell you what I know, I've three messages for you,' MacAskill began. He looked around the oak-panelled library, where the men were sitting on club armchairs surrounded by shooting magazines and prints of dogs and horses. 'First, never underestimate the African fighting man. He may not have the discipline that some of you guys are used to. He may not have the kit or the back-up, and his officers may not have any training to speak of. But he's brave, and he's not afraid to die – and that makes him a formidable enemy. Get into a fire-fight with an African platoon, and you'd better make sure you've got enough ammo, because the bastards are going to keep coming at you until there is no one left alive. A lot of them will be high on dagga – what they call the weed in Southern Africa – and the local stuff is so strong it does things to a man's mind. Makes him think the bullets will just bounce off him . . . and a lot of those men are so strong that sometimes it will seem as if they really do.'

He paused, draining a glass of neat Glendronach. 'Next, make friends with the weather. Contrary to what a lot of people imagine, Batota isn't that hot. The climate in Ibera isn't even as hot as London. But it's the rainy season and that's going to make it hard for you.

You've never seen rain like you get in Africa. It will come down in great sheets. You won't just be wet through, you'll feel as if you're drowning. Your clothes will destroyed; none of your guns will work. And you know what? There won't be a damned thing you can do about it.

'Lastly, get used to the brutality. Africa is a cruel continent. Don't ask me why, but it just is. I'll tell you one story. I was part of a small unit of foreigners making raids in Mozambique in the late 1970s for the Batoteans. We were hitting some of the guerrilla bases used by Kapembwa's men. They didn't want to use their own guys because they weren't meant to be in Mozambique. We came into this one village, and the guerrillas decided that the people there must have been helping us. They rounded up the twenty-seven workers in the village, most of whom were migrants anyway, then hacked the men to death one by one, making their wives and children watch. Why did they do it? We never had any idea. They were just making a point. But you have to remember, people in Africa are going to be afraid. No one will help you, no one will want to talk to you. And whatever else happens, don't get taken alive. You might think that "a fate worse than death" is just a phrase. In Africa, it's the literal truth.'

For the next hour, MacAskill was happy to be cross-examined, telling the men everything he knew about the terrain they'd be fighting across, and the kind of kit they should take with them. When he'd finally wrapped up the session and gone up to bed, Steve said to Chris, 'What happened to you?'

Chris remained silent.

Steve persisted. 'You said this job was personal – so what was it?'

Chris took a sip of his whisky. He didn't speak often, and when he did the words were slow and measured, but once he got going he was like a car with no brakes: he didn't stop until he crashed into a wall.

'There was a mate of mine, a guy called Joe,' he started. He took a deep hit on the drink, his eyes runny and sad. 'Great bloke. We were at school together, ran around the place as teenagers, then joined the

Recces together. Man, I loved that guy. Funniest bastard you ever met and one of the bravest as well. We were in the same unit, went on patrols together. One time, our patrol moved into Mozambique to try and flush out a troop of Kapembwa's guerrillas. Joe set off out by himself one night to try and get a lead on where they were operating. He never came back. The rest of us went out in the morning to try and find out what had happened to him. It took all day in burning hot sun, but we finally found him.'

Chris looked up at Steve.

'The bastards had captured him. They spreadeagled the bloke on the ground and crucified him by sticking bayonets through his hands and legs and then left him out in the midday sun. He was still alive by the time we got there, but only just: it can take a man hours to die like that, days sometimes. He was drifting in and out of consciousness. We ripped the bayonets straight out. But the shock of it killed him. He'd lost too much blood, and too much strength. Just before his eyes closed I told him that if I ever got a chance to take revenge on Kapembwa I'd grab it. Joe nodded, tried to smile, then closed his eyes. There aren't many things I'm certain of in this world, but this is one, if you make a promise to a mate on his deathbed, then you bloody well keep it – and you don't let anything stand in your way.'

Bruce was letting the hunting dogs out of their pound when Steve caught up with him. It was just after seven in the morning, and dawn had hardly broken. 'Thanks for getting Ollie out for me,' said Bruce, watching as the dogs raced off into the damp grass, then out into the woodland.

'The man's a liability,' grunted Steve.

'He proved himself a good enough soldier out in Afghanistan.'

'But he should never have taken that job,' said Steve. There was a thread of bitterness in his voice. 'He put all our lives at risk.'

'He can't settle, Steve,' said Bruce. 'It can take a man years to do that, to figure out what home is, and how he can put down roots there. So you shouldn't be too hard on him.'

Steve shook his head. 'As for the rest of the team . . .' he muttered.

'You're not happy with them?'

'Chris shouldn't be on the unit – he's got a kid to look after. Nick's just a boy. And Maksim turned sodding traitor on us, last time we went into action together.'

Bruce put an arm across Steve's shoulder as they walked out over the wet grass towards the dogs. 'Chris wants to avenge his mate, and Nick wants to grow up – and those are both mighty powerful forces within a man. As for Maksim, he's looking to atone for what happened the last time around, to prove himself as good a man as any of you. Men fight for many different reasons, Steve, but trust me, when you've been around military forces as long as I have, you'll understand that those are three of the best reasons there are for taking up arms. The unit will be just fine.'

A thin, wet mist was covering the hillside. It was just after eight in the morning now, and a car had been booked for nine to take them to the airport. They had already eaten some breakfast, but before leaving, Bruce had insisted on taking them all down to the wood at the bottom of the extensive gardens. It covered about fifty acres in total – rough heather broken up with rows of thick, tall mountain ash and silver birch running right down to the banks of the loch below.

But the tree Bruce was standing next to was an oak.

And it was freshly planted.

It was a cold, blustery morning, and the men could hear the branches creaking above them, as they gathered around the sapling. Bruce looked at the assembled unit of men, his expression solemn. From his green Barbour jacket, he pulled out a small silver plaque; with a hammer, he staked it into the ground. As Steve looked down, he could see that the plaque had only a name on it and a pair of dates:

Jeff Campbell 1978-2008

Jeff, thought Steve. My mate, now buried somewhere in Afghanistan.

'Every time a man goes down, working for DEF, then I plant an oak tree right here in this forest and his name is next to it,' said Bruce. 'And I'm not planning on planting any more. So you boys had better come back with blood still running in your veins.'

Sixteen

THE WAREHOUSE WAS LOCATED IN Aerton, a drab industrial suburb of Johannesburg to the south of the city, not far from Soweto. The road twisted through a series of factories and depots before Chris pulled the jeep up outside Ben Bull & Sons.

'We'll get what we need in here,' he said. 'And if we don't find it, we'll find out where we *can* get it.'

The unit had touched down in the city this morning. They'd flown from Aberdeen to Madrid, then caught a flight to South Africa from there. They had passed through immigration without any trouble. British citizens didn't need a visa. If they'd been asked, they'd have said they were here on holiday, but all of them were waved in, no questions asked. They'd checked into the City Lodge, a three-star place with a pool a couple of miles down the highway from OR Tambo International. Newton and Ganju had stayed behind in the room, as Newton was still building his strength back up and Ganju was keeping an eye on him. Nick and David had gone out to buy a pair of second-hand jeeps by scouring the used parking lots. Chris, meanwhile, had phoned around his old Recce mates to find out which of them had the best black-market arms-dealing operation in the country.

And that, as it turned out, was Ben Bull.

The factory made garage doors. At least on the ground floor, that is. It occupied a fifty foot by thirty concrete shed, and most of the day there were twenty guys in there sweating over their machinery. But night had fallen now, and that meant the place was empty. Except for the owner.

Ben gave Chris a tight bear hug. He was a huge man, six feet five and weighing in at three hundred pounds. He had a thick beard, half-black, half-grey, and there was a film of sweat covering his face. Maybe back in the Recces, he'd been a decent physical specimen, decided Steve. He'd have had to be: in their prime, the Recces were the finest special forces unit the world had ever seen. But in the years since then, he'd turned into a ruin very fast.

After the introductions were made, Ben took them inside and offered them all some beers, but for Chris and Dan buying weapons was a serious business: for Dan, it was the only thing worth turning down a beer for.

The workshop covered the entire ground floor; there was a smell of lathes and oil in the air. Ben led them through a small doorway then down a flight of stairs, then through another door which, Steve noted, was double-locked with what looked like a hardened steel mortice deadlock. Laughably, Chris had explained to them on the way over, South Africa had strict gun control laws. Everyone was meant to get a police licence to own a weapon. In effect, all it meant was that the police could waste time hassling law-abiding citizens, whilst the criminals – and there were plenty of those – could get hold of all the weapons they wanted. Most of the white farmers went to guys like Ben to stock up on the munitions they needed. Even suburban families had more heavy-duty firepower tucked away in a safe room than the average police station in a normal country. Shotguns, automatic rifles – even hand grenades: they were all standard kit along the leafy avenues of middle-class Johannesburg.

Downstairs was a long thin basement, thirty feet deep and twenty across, with three rows of metal shelving. The room was immaculately clean, its temperature controlled at a constant seventeen degrees. 'Good stuff,' whistled Dan, as he cast his eyes around the room.

South Africa was not only one of the most heavily armed societies in the world, it was also one of the leading arms manufacturers: international sanctions in the last years of apartheid, coupled with vicious border wars, meant the country had no choice but to develop its own arms industry, and the kit had to be good enough to match Soviet-bloc-supplied guerrilla weapon for weapon. Among professional soldiers, weapons from three countries were most prized for their technology and durability: Israel, South Africa and Russia. Of the three, the Israeli kit was the most technically slick, but the South African one packed the most punch. Just by working with the local manufacturers, and getting hold of shipments made after-hours in the factories, a dealer such as Ben could operate an armoury as sophisticated as any in the world.

'Where you going?' asked Ben.

'North,' answered Chris.

Ben just nodded, the fat around his triple chin wobbling as he did so. He was both a Recce and an arms dealer, and the code of both professions meant you didn't ask any unnecessary questions. But north could only mean one thing. Batota.

'You'll need plenty of kit then,' he said. 'It gets rough up there. Worse every year, from what I hear.'

They had already put together a checklist of what they would need. Assault rifles were an essential: they'd take AK-47s if they could find some good ones because they were sturdy, reliable, easy to look after, and there were so many of them in Africa that they could always steal some extra ammo if it became necessary. They'd need some decent machine pistols, plus some rocket-propelled grenades (RPGs), hand grenades, some quality plastic explosives – and enough ammunition to keep them supplied even if they came up against a small army.

On the racks of assault rifles was a selection of guns made by

Vector Arms, a company now based in the US that specialised in making replica AK-47s mostly from Hungarian, Polish and Bulgarian parts. Chris was familiar with their stuff: it was reliable, well put together, and brand new. He took down an AKSW, its version of the AK-47, made with a black polymer hand-grip and a light-blond wood stock, tested its weight and feel, and handed it to Dan. Dan took a minute to assess the weapon, then nodded. They'd take a dozen, at $600 each: one for each man, and a couple of spares. The Vector AK came with a 30-round mag: they'd take twenty-four, allowing each man a spare for his webbing, and twenty boxes of ammo. Ben had a full range of AK-47 accessories – different grips, flashlights and laser sights – but none of them interested Dan very much. The AK was never any use as a precision weapon; it didn't have the range or the accuracy. But there were a stock of AK bayonets. Of the three Ben had on the shelves, Dan picked out the Chinese-made Norinco 84S-1, a simple bayonet with a black, stubby stock that slotted neatly on the underside of the weapon, and a short, polished steel blade that could be simply stabbed into your enemy and should kill him with one twist. Like most Chinese weapons, it was designed to kill quickly and effectively. They took twelve.

'And this,' said Ben. He was pointing to an old Vector line. The RPD had two additions to a basic AK-47: a hundred-round drumfeed that could be slotted underneath the weapon, and a simple bi-pod that could be used to rest it on. Together they turned the weapon into a very simple machine gun, the bullets feeding out of the drum, whilst the bi-pod held it in position. In a tight corner, it would give you the firepower of five or six men, allowing a couple of blokes to provide as much cover as a whole platoon.

'Two of those as well,' nodded Dan.

Next they needed pistols. After looking at the range of thirty handguns that Ben kept in stock they eventually decided on a set of replica Uzi machine pistols. Machine pistols take their name from the German word *Maschinenpistole*, meaning sub-machine gun, and they'd been widely used in the German Army from the First World War onwards. A machine pistol had an automatic cartridge, making it the natural weapon for sustained blasts of close-quarters fire. The Uzi had been designed by Uziel Gal, a German Jew who was born in the Weimer Republic, and had moved first to England and then to Palestine to escape the Nazis. His brutally simple weapons combined the best of the German and later the Israeli armament industries. The Uzi had been adopted by the Israeli special forces, and there were few better adverts for a weapon than that. Over the next two decades, the Uzi had been put into service by the German Army as well as by the US Secret Service. After President Reagan was shot, it was Uzi machine pistols the Secret Service pulled out to provide covering fire whilst the President was evacuated.

'If it's good enough for Reagan, it will do for us,' said Ian.

They took a dozen, plus ammo.

For the next half-hour, they picked out knives, webbing, boots, socks, compasses and helmets. They took three RPGs plus a box of twenty-four missiles, and a box of C-4, the British-made plastic explosive that was standard issue for armies around the world.

'We used to nick this stuff from your boys all the time,' said Ian. 'And a bloody good bang it makes as well.'

Next, they looked at the hunting rifles. As Chris pointed out, the chances were they were going to be finding themselves out in some wild country. 'And that means wild animals as well,' he said. 'We might be able to stop a patrol, but an angry rhino is something else, man.'

The Holland & Holland – the British-made .375 Magnum hunting rifle – was a classic big-game weapon. Designed in 1912, it had been imitated plenty of times over the next century, but had never been bettered. Its massive bullets weighed up to seventeen grams, with enough punch to bring down a elephant. It was the classic African safari shotgun, tested over the generations by big-game hunters.

'We'll take two,' said Chris, aware of the size of the bill they were running up. 'If we meet anything with a skin thicker than Ian's, then these will be the guys we want on our side. I know they're expensive, but when you are going one on one with a rhino you don't want to be counting the pennies.'

Neither of the H&H's Ben Bull had in stock were new. One was ten years old, sold at auction by one of the safari parks; the other had been in a farming family for a couple of generations. That was fine with Steve. After ten years, an H&H was just starting to get oiled in. Like a Bentley, these were machines that were built to last. A new one would just need a lot of breaking in before you could be certain it was shooting true.

Chris had one more item on his shopping list.

A KPV.

Ben smiled. He took them through to a back room, then pulled off the dust-sheet. The Russian-built KPV was one of the big beasts of any battlefield. A heavy machine gun, it had first been developed in the late 1940s but had been radically modified since then. In truth, it didn't need much updating. Its job was to spit out big bullets at a terrifying rate and it already did that effectively enough. The *Krupnokaliberniy Pulemyot Vladimorova*, to give it its full military name, had two substantial wheels, armour-plating to protect its operator, and a big 1.3 metre barrel that on automatic could spray bullets from its ammo belt up to 500 metres at a rate of 550 rounds a minute. The Russians had originally designed it as an infantry weapon – like many Russian weapons it was named after its designer, Semjon Vladimirow – to be used as the Red Army advanced on Western Europe, but it was terrorists who'd learned its real strengths. Hamas, for instance, had turned it into a brutally effective anti-helicopter weapon. Its .57 calibre bullets were among the most powerful in the world. Even the Israeli pilots were nervous of it and, as Ian pointed out, not much frightened that country's armed forces. Out in Iraq, the insurgents had used it for roadside ambushes: even the American armour wasn't strong enough to shield their vehicles from its murderous fire.

'I didn't realise you had many of these in Africa,' said Ian.

Ben chuckled. 'There isn't a weapon in the world you don't get out here,' he answered. 'The Russians gave them to the Cubans, and the Cubans shipped them over to help out their guerrilla friends.'

'And then they wind up here?'

'These people always need money . . . and this is valuable kit.'

'How much?' asked Steve.

It was Archie Sharratt's wallet they were dipping into, and that seemed deep enough. But Steve hated the way that arms dealers took advantage of Private Military Corporations, always assuming you were on some huge, unlimited expenses contract. Sometimes it was true. But if there was spare cash to be made, it should be the guys putting themselves in the line of fire that were making it. Not the blokes in the grubby backrooms putting huge mark-ups on the kit they'd have to take with them.

Ben might be a mate of Chris's from the Recces, but Steve wasn't sure he liked him.

'Twelve thousand dollars.'

'Ten.'

Ben shook his head. 'Twelve,' he said flatly. 'I can get good money for one of those. Maybe even ship it to Iraq.'

'With twenty thousand rounds included?'

'Ten thousand.'

'Done.'

By the time they completed the transaction, Dan was already in the corner of the warehouse, inspecting some of the latest kit. It was always the same with Dan, Steve reminded himself. It was like taking a petrol-head to a car showroom. He just couldn't help himself from trying out all the toys.

Dan glanced back at Ben with a glimmer in his eyes.

'Is that an STW?' he asked.

Ben waddled towards him. His weight slowed him down, but like any tradesman he could move quickly enough when a customer was eyeing up the most expensive item in the store.

'You familiar with those?' he asked.

Dan was holding the box in his hand. 'STW stands for see-through-wall, right?' he said crisply. 'The technology was developed by the Israelis, like most of the best kit. Basically, it's a radarscope which you can fit onto any gun with a strong armour-piercing bullet. It has an impulse radar that emits very short blasts of high-frequency electronic pulses, then it uses a complex piece of software to literally reconstruct an image of what is happening on the other side of the wall.'

Ben nodded. 'You can look straight through the wall and shoot the bastard on the other side of it.'

Ian was already holding the box in his hands. 'For real?'

'For real,' said Dan. 'It's experimental, but the American police have been using them in hostage rescues. And the Israeli special forces, of course – it's just that you don't get to hear about that.'

'And I reckon if you're planning to assassinate a man,' Steve said without thinking, 'that's the kind of kit you need.'

'Assassinate a man?' repeated Ben.

Steve was already cursing himself for having spoken. If you were heading north from South Africa, there was only one man a gang of international mercenaries would be going to assassinate. And his name started with a K.

'Who is it you're about to assassinate exactly?' pressed Ben. His dark beady eyes were looking straight at Steve. It seemed that the code that said arms dealers didn't ask questions was about to be broken.

'Our business is our business and it stays that way,' Steve said steadily.

Dan was glancing from man to man.

'We'll take it,' he said, holding out the STW box.

'I've got something else,' said Ben.

He started to show them another complex piece of electronics, so new that it too was still packaged in a steel crate. 'It's called a high-power electromagnetic system or HPEMS for short, and it's made by the American company EIA Aerospace. They're selling them to the police . . . but to special forces as well.'

'What does it do?' asked Ian.

'It puts out a high-strength microwave signal over a radius of up to fifty metres, and that disables any vehicle it comes into contact with,' answered Ben. 'It literally turns the machine right off. The idea is to put them on police choppers. They can fly above a car making a getaway and stop the bastard by flicking a switch. But they are obviously handy for the military as well.'

He paused to wipe a bead of sweat from his face. 'Particularly an assassination squad. One that was going after a President, for example.'

'We'll take it,' said Ian.

Chris arranged for the consignment to be ready by midnight, whilst Steve added up the damage and settled the bill. It came to $32,000 in total, paid for with a fresh roll of $100 bills that Bruce had given them before they left Scotland. He'd given each man six gold Krugerrands as well, since once they got into the wilds of Batota, gold would be the only currency worth having. The jeeps should be secured by the end of the day, then the unit would bring them round here, collect the weapons and start the drive north. It would be safer to move at night. If the South African police came across a group of foreign mercenaries with enough munitions on them to take out a small army, they'd sling them straight in jail. And probably beat us to death as well while they are about it, Steve thought grimly.

Ben turned his bloodshot eyes to look at them. 'Good luck,' he said. 'The bastard deserves it.'

Steve remained silent. The arms dealer could think what he liked.

There was no way he was confirming or denying what they were here for. He could draw his own conclusions.

They'd be heading north later tonight, and the last thing they needed was any word leaking out about what they were really planning. If Wallace suspected they were there to hit the President, they'd be executed on the spot.

Seventeen

D AWN WAS BREAKING AS THE Talek Bridge loomed into view. Steve glanced at Newton, sitting next to him in the front of the Nissan Navara pick-up truck driven by Ganju. The man was leaning forwards in his seat, staring up at the massive steel structure.

'You're home,' said Steve.

'What's left of it,' Newton answered quietly.

They had been driving steadily through the night. David and Nick had brought them two vehicles: the Nissan was for carrying the heavy kit, including the KPV, a massive lump of metal that weighed almost fifty kilos; the Toyota Land Cruiser was for taking the rest of the guys. The kit was in the back of the Nissan, covered with plastic sheeting and thick strips of plasterboard. If anyone asked them, they'd say they were just delivering some building supplies up to their farm. Chris was driving the Toyota, a big SUV with a 4.7 litre engine and enough space to accommodate the other guys. They'd stopped once so far to buy themselves ten jerry cans, filling them with thirty gallons of diesel. Once they got across the border, and from there on into Batota, fuel might be in short supply, warned Chris. The last thing they needed was to run out.

'Slow up,' said Steve to Ganju.

The Gurkha brought the Nissan to a stop by the side of the road and Steve stepped out onto the rough tarmac, looking up at the bridge ahead. It had been named after Alfred Talek, the founder of the Talek mining conglomerate and one of the business associates of Oswald Fitzpatrick. Just to look at it, decided Steve, was a reminder that this border had always been about business and trade. And even now, it probably still was.

There were people everywhere. The Limpopo was a big, muddy river that started up in Botswana and snaked its way through Zimbabwe, Batota and South Africa. The bridge was heavily armed, but that didn't stop a constant flow of refugees risking their lives to make the crossing. Famine and political beatings were now common across Zimbabwe: up to a million people had already fled the country and many more were joining them every day. The situation was the same in Batota: most of the refugees came to South Africa. There wasn't much food or work for them there either. But at least they weren't going to get driven into camps and beaten to death by Kapembwa's thugs.

'We can drive straight across?' asked Steve, looking towards Chris in the Toyota.

Chris nodded. 'Everyone's coming in the other direction,' he said. 'The only people trying to get into Batota these days are soldiers and journalists – and the journalists aren't trying very hard.'

About fifty yards to Steve's left there was a mobile film unit, with a satellite dish beaming back reports from the border about the upcoming Batotean presidential elections. No one expected Kapembwa to lose. He never did. But there was still plenty of interest in how he was going to fix the result. At this time of the morning, all the journalists were asleep. The refugees were still moving, however – a relentless flow of bedraggled humanity, trudging wearily towards an unknown destiny. The bridge itself was heavily guarded by the South African Defence Force. The sentries were checking the papers of everyone who came through. Plenty were being turned back: South Africa had enough problems of its own. That didn't mean that no one could get through. Handing fifty dollars to the border guards was enough to get a man across the bridge. For the girls, it was cheaper, so long as they were attractive. They were taken into the sentry huts: if they didn't mind having sex with a couple of the guards, they'd be let through as well. Anyone who didn't have the money or a body to sell had to take a more direct route.

The river, which measured thirty feet across, was swollen at this time of year by the rains further upstream; great torrents of muddy water were flowing through it. On the South African side was a six-foot-high barbed-wire fence. But there weren't nearly enough soldiers to protect it, and as Steve knew from fighting in Bosnia, a fence without any soldiers next to it was just an obstacle to cut your way through. Strung along the river were small rafts, no more than a few logs tied to air-filled jerry cans, floating across on the current, each with two or three people on board. When they hit the banks, they'd scramble up into South Africa, crawling underneath the fence through holes that had already been dug in the mud. Sometimes they'd have streaks of blood across their faces and chests as they stumbled into their new country. But nobody was trying to stop them; they simply ignored the soldiers and started walking down the side of the road. Where they would end up it was impossible to tell, judged Steve. They probably didn't even know themselves.

'Just drive straight through,' said Chris. 'The Sixth Brigade is waiting for us on the other side. And nobody messes with them, not even the South African Army.'

The air was heavy with repressed violence as they approached the bridge. You could smell it everywhere, noted Steve. And you could see it in the sad and weary eyes of the mothers carrying their hungry babies on their backs.

Ganju had pushed the Nissan up into second gear. There were plenty of people in front of them, but they edged away as the vehicle moved towards them. A soldier stepped out, looking at them suspiciously. He was carrying an R5 assault rifle. The soldier looked well-trained to Steve; he'd think twice before getting into a fight with this man. They had given Wallace their planned time of arrival and he'd messaged back that the Sixth Brigade would be waiting for them. The soldiers must have got the message across the bridge, since the South African troops didn't even ask for their passports or papers, or show any interest in searching the back of the pick-up truck. Just as well, thought Steve. We've got a whole armoury back there.

'Here we go then,' he said.

'And may God be with us,' the Gurkha replied quietly.

'We'll need more than that,' Newton put in from the back seat.

Steve nodded. The guy was right. Plenty of men had tried to assassinate Kapembwa over the years, but somehow they'd ended up in their graves while he remained in the Presidential Palace.

A soldier was flagging them down on the other side of the bridge.

'We're meeting Colonel Samuel Yohane,' said Ganju, winding down the window.

The expression on the face of the soldier suddenly changed. He stood bolt upright, kept his rifle gripped tight to his chest, and pointed them to the side of the road. Ganju pulled the Nissan into a lay-by, checking that the Toyota was right behind them. Steve climbed out of the vehicle. Behind them, a woman with a screaming toddler at her side was arguing with a border guard. Steve tried to block out the noise. He hated the sound of women and children crying. Chris had already climbed out of the Toyota, with Ollie right behind him.

A man was striding towards them. Tall and strong, he had a thick, muscular face, perfect white teeth, and a wide grin belied only by the hardness of his dark brown eyes. He was dressed in an olive-green battlefield uniform and one of the distinctive purple and gold berets that marked out the Sixth Brigade from the rest of the Batotean Army. At his side, he was wearing a QSZ-92 pistol, manufactured by the Chinese weapons supplier Norinco since the late 1990s. Among the most advanced handguns in the world, it was still only available in limited quantities within China's People's Liberation Army. Whatever the Sixth Brigade might lack, decided Steve, it wasn't munitions. Or guts either, he reckoned.

'You are Mr Wallace's men?' the Colonel demanded, looking first at Steve, and then at Ollie.

'Ready for work,' said Steve crisply. 'We were told you'd escort us into Batota.'

Yohane stretched out a fist and shook hands with each man in turn. He nodded towards two Chinese-made military jeeps fifty yards down the road that would escort them into Batota. Both had six men inside, the second one a 50-cal machine gun strapped to its back.

'We'll move out in a convoy,' said Yohane. 'One of our jeeps will go in front, the other behind your two vehicles. If there's any trouble, let us handle it.'

'Happy to, mate,' said Steve, trying to remain cheerful. 'We'll stick to the fighting we're paid for.'

If Yohane got the joke you couldn't see it on his face. His expression remained solemn and implacable. He might be an African, decided Steve, but the North Korean training had left its mark on him. He handled himself with the icy cruelty you only found in Asian armies.

'Excuse me,' he said, his tone clipped.

He walked towards the sentry post, brushing aside the soldiers dealing with the angry mother. With one swift movement, he yanked her hair backwards with his left hand. With his right, he drew the QSZ-92 from its holster, pressed it into the side of the woman's head, and without a moment's hesitation put a single shot into her brain. For a fraction of a second she remained lifeless in his hands, then dropped to the ground, blood starting to seep from the neat wound that had been cut into her skull. Yohane knelt down to wipe away a speck of blood that had splashed onto his polished black leather boots, tossing the crimson-stained handkerchief next to the woman's corpse.

'Take the child away,' he ordered the soldier. 'And put this body in the river.'

He walked back towards Steve and Chris, a thin smile playing on his lips. 'That's how the Sixth Brigade deals with traitors trying to leave our motherland,' he said. 'I thought it might be interesting for you to have an idea of what Batotean discipline consists of.'

It took every ounce of willpower for Steve not to kill the man on the spot.

He could feel the hatred of the man and everything he represented flooding into his veins. Brutality towards women and children was, the way Steve reckoned it, a step across the line. That wasn't soldiering, it was just thuggery. They had enough munitions in the Nissan to take out the whole border post. The Colonel would be the first to die. But no, he told himself. There's no point in taking out one soldier: there will be another thug, just as brutal, ready to step into his bloodstained boots. We're here to mallet the man who created this hellish situation. Nothing should distract us from that.

'Fine,' he said, his voice tense. 'Let's crack on.'

Steve glanced back once towards the child. A boy of about three, dressed in ragged clothes, he was shaking with shock and fear. One of the soldiers was already jabbing him with the barrel of his gun.

'Let's move,' he said, gesturing for everyone to get back into the stationary vehicles.

Ganju steered the Nissan back onto the road. Low, dark cloud hung over the flat, scrubby landscape, making the tin shacks of the border town look even more dismal. People were everywhere – refugees mostly, but also shopkeepers selling fruit and drinks, money-changers swapping bundles of local currency for South African rand, and people-smugglers offering to take refugees across the border. Girls were selling their bodies right along the main highway, some of them shouting that they were virgins so there was no chance of catching AIDS. 'Even Nick might be able to score in this town,' said Ollie in the back of the Toyota, but somehow the joke fell flat. No one was in the mood for ribbing one another. They were just looking out of the windows, slowly taking in the sheer scale of the devastation that had swept through the country.

To Ibera, it was a drive of more than three hundred miles, and the road wasn't in great shape. For years now, it had been thronging with refugees. It might have been a decent enough highway once, decided Steve, but now it was covered with potholes. The refugees had left years of debris. There were broken-down vehicles everywhere, abandoned by their owners when they ran out of the petrol that was in short supply right across this area. Most had just been shunted off-road and left to rust. There were mounds of rotting food, with flies swarming around it. And, as you got further up the highway, you could see people dying by the side of the road: elderly men and women who had simply given up the struggle and laid down to die in the forest that was creeping closer and closer to the highway every year.

Nothing stopped the Sixth Brigade, however.

Yohane was leading the convoy in the first of the two jeeps. He was sitting right in front of the open-topped machine, his purple and gold beret glinting in the morning sun. A pair of aviator shades had been pulled down over his eyes. Although the highway was crowded with people, the driver didn't even have to honk. The crowds just parted as they saw the vehicles approach, people scrambling to the sides of the road, and cars and trucks steering wildly into the muddy ditches that ran along the edge of the highway. It was a lesson in how much this organisation was feared, noted Steve. People would happily risk their lives rather than hold them up for a single second.

That's because they knew what they'd get.

A bullet straight between the eyes.

Even so, the journey was a long and hard one. It had been eight in the morning when they crossed the bridge, and Steve reckoned it would be late in the evening before they made it to Ibera. Along the way, he was watching, observing, drawing in as much information about the country as he could. It was a lesson he'd learned when he was still training with the Regiment. The more you knew about the territory you were fighting in, the better your chances of survival. Sometimes it was just knowing the routes out, at other times the type of kit you could pick up along the way. Whatever it was, you never knew when it was going to give you that millimetre of an edge against your opponent.

But what can I learn about Batota? he wondered. Except that a cyclone of chaos has already swept through this country.

He thought briefly about Sam. As he saw the miserable poverty to which the country had been reduced – one dirt-poor village after another rolling past, abandoned farms and disused factories everywhere – he began to get a sense of the anger that burned within her. To see your parents murdered was bad enough. To see the country you were raised in sent back to the Stone Age was more than anyone could bear.

Without lusting after vengeance.

It was after ten at night by the time the convoy entered the dusty villages that surrounded Ibera. The road came in from the south of the city, running close to Lake Abayo, a manmade waterway created by the damming of the Nanyama River in the 1960s. After that, the roads twisted through the big leafy suburbs, built for the white elite during the 1970s. Looking out on the buildings was like being transported to an old American TV show, Steve thought. Big comfortable houses with space for a couple of cars on the driveway and a barbecue and a swing for the kids out the back. It looked a bit like the more prosperous parts of Bromley, the place where he'd grown up. Except here you didn't get the sense of suffocating safety so familiar from a middle-class London suburb. Far from it. You could feel the tension bristling through the night air.

Many of the houses were abandoned now, with weeds crawling across their driveways and verandas, their gardens turned into jungle.

Others had been taken over by Kapembwa's war veterans, his state-licensed thugs who roamed the streets terrorising the local population. Groups of boys, some of them no more than twelve or thirteen, could be seen sitting around on the lawns toting their assault rifles and smoking dope. A few of the old white families had stayed on, and some of the houses had been bought by middle-class black families, but even driving past you could see that the city was fast turning back into a ghetto.

Give me Bromley any day, thought Steve. It never gets this dangerous – not even on a Saturday night outside Wetherspoon's, when they've got a three-for-two offer on the alcopops.

The convoy drove steadily forwards. You could feel the lurking menace all around you, but nobody was going to attack the Sixth Brigade. Nobody was that crazy.

Yohane's jeep steered through the outer parts of the city, then headed towards the centre. It skirted around Churchill Avenue, the site of the President's Residence. Barriers came down at six o'clock every evening to seal off the road surrounding the building. The restriction was taken seriously: anyone straying into that part of town after the curfew was likely to be shot on sight. Even when the Presidential motorcade came out of the compound, drivers were required by law to pull over and stop. Maybe that was why Kapembwa had survived assassination so long, Steve thought.

The barracks were situated three miles to the north of the city centre. Steve had seen plenty of military camps over the years, both living within them, and attacking them. But he hadn't yet seen anything with the same air of ugly violence as the headquarters of the Sixth Brigade. The building was on its own piece of derelict land, off a main highway, with only an abandoned factory close by. There was an eight-foot wall all around it, topped with barbed wire and broken glass. Searchlights from the two twenty-foot-high turrets next to the main gate swept the surrounding city in long, aggressive arcs. At the front were two big steel gates, with sentry posts on either side, both of them manned by four soldiers.

Yohane swept forwards, barking orders at the sentries, his jeeps only slowing fractionally as the soldiers scurried to get the gates open. As Ganju steered the Nissan inside and brought it gently to a stop on the tarmac, Steve glanced around. Another six sentries were standing right inside the gates. Straight ahead of him were six blocks where he guessed the ordinary soldiers slept, followed by an officer's mess, a canteen, then an arsenal, and finally a parade ground and shooting range. Next to the latter one piece of equipment that Steve reckoned wasn't part of the typical furniture of a military camp.

A gallows.

Steve stepped out of the jeep.

We're here, he thought grimly. In the pay of the beast.

As the men piled out of the vehicles, Wallace was already walking stiffly towards them, the embers of a cigar still smouldering in his mouth. He shook Ollie by the hand – the only man present he rated as his equal, noted Steve – then took a step back.

'I hope you had a good journey, boys,' he said, taking the stub of the cigar from his mouth but leaving a trail of smoke around his face. 'And you have my thanks for getting out here so quickly. There's work to be done, plenty of it, but we'll crack on with that in the morning. The Colonel here will show you to your barracks. Get a good night's sleep and I'll see you in the morning.'

The barracks contained thirty beds, in two rows of fifteen; it had a wooden floor and a coal-fired burner at one end. It was the kind of hut you'd see in Second World War movies: built purely for survival, with no regard for the comfort of the men. But they'd only be here for a couple of nights at most. Steve had slept in much worse places. It would do fine.

'Make yourselves at home,' said Yohane. 'There's food on the table. Help yourselves.'

As he left, Maksim and Nick had already checked out the grub. It was piled up on a wooden table. There were six loaves of bread, a big bowl of lukewarm beans, two different types of salad, and plates of cold chicken and ham slices. On the side was a bowl of tinned fruit. All the men started to heap their plates with food. None of them had had anything proper to eat since they left Johannesburg almost twenty-four hours ago and they were ravenous. Steve squeezed some chicken between two thick slices of bread, stuffed some tomato and lettuce on top and took a huge bite. He was feeling better already.

'So far, so good,' he mumbled.

'We haven't started yet,' said Ollie, taking a spoonful of beans.

'And we haven't got anything to drink,' growled Maksim.

Steve tossed the Russian a carton of apple juice.

'I said drink . . .'

Nick brought out a bottle of vodka, pouring a shot of the liquid into each man's cup, then emptying the rest into the fruit bowl. Steve didn't usually drink much whilst he was on a mission, although he knew plenty of men who did. He liked to have a clear head going into battle. But he could feel the alcohol unwinding him, and he was thankful for that. The tension has been eating away at him. He didn't mind risking his life when he had to, but he had never attempted this kind of deception before. Relax, he told himself. You'll feel better once the action kicks off.

'One drink, guys, then we get some kip,' said Ollie sternly. 'We don't know what tomorrow has in store for us yet, but we can be bloody sure it's going to be a long hard day, so the more rest we can get the better.'

The men finished their food, then unpacked the kitbags. The barracks room was clean and there were fresh sheets on the beds. In the corner, David had lit up the brazier, creating a gentle warmth that radiated through the room.

'So what the hell have you been up to since last year?' Steve asked Dan.

The Australian shrugged. 'Getting into trouble, I guess.'

Steve looked at the man closely, and he could see Ollie doing the same. Dan had spent a year in a military jail on charges of letting a couple of Afghan kids die in a fire-fight when he was with the SASR. When he said he'd been in trouble, it usually meant something serious.

Dan took a hit of his drink. 'I came back from Afghanistan and I had half a million quid sitting in an offshore bank account,' he said. 'More money than I could ever have dreamed about.'

'Less than we were promised,' interrupted Ian.

'But still more than we'd imagined,' said Dan. 'I spent a hundred of it paying off my parents' mortgage. My dad's been truck-driving in one of the iron ore mines for the last twenty years and that's a hell of a hard life for a bloke. Even so, that still left me with four big ones. There's only so much money a man can spend on beer and women . . .'

'Don't count on it,' Maksim put in.

'Maybe for an ugly bastard like you,' said Dan, grinning. 'Anyway, I went travelling for a bit, then found myself in Majorca, and I reckoned it wasn't such a bad place. Bit like Oz, really. One day, I met this bloke Dudley who was selling his pub out there and it gave me an idea. Majorca doesn't have an Australian bar. Unbelievable, I know, but there you go. I ended up paying the bloke three big ones for the place. My plan is to do it up, rename it "Dan's Beer Bar" . . .'

'Good title,' said Steve. 'Original.'

Dan nodded. ' "Dan's Beer Bar" it says over the top. Then underneath it says: "Ice Cold Beer. Red Hot Girls. You Lucky Bastards".'

'Maybe you could get Nick's mum to work there,' said Ollie.

'Leave it,' snapped Nick. 'My mum's getting a proper job.'

'So what went wrong?' asked David.

'Like I said, I paid three big ones for the place,' said Dan. 'But it was a ruin. The inside needed gutting, it needed a garden you could drink in, a new kitchen, the works. I'd met this Polish girl, Irenka.

Blond hair, blue eyes, a real knockout. She was working as a waitress at one of the bars in Palma, which was how I met her. So Irenka starts helping me with the bar, and it turns out her brother back in Krakow is a builder, so I paid for him and three of his mates to come over and do the work on the place. Irenka and I went away for a couple of weeks, while the work got done.'

Dan took a hit on his drink. 'By the time we got back, the brother had pissed off with all the money I left for him. When I went back to find out from Irenka what had happened, she'd pissed off as well. Un-bloody-believable. All I had for her was a mobile number. And that turned out to be dead.' He shook his head from side to side. 'So I'm stuck with a ruin of a bar with no money to do it up. It's costing me a fortune just to keep up with the taxes on the place.'

'Poles,' Maksim spat. 'You can't trust the bastards.'

'Women either,' said Ian.

'Polish women,' muttered Maksim, opening up a fresh bottle of vodka he'd hidden in his rucksack and topping up everyone's mug. 'I'd rather sleep with Nick than one of those bitches.'

'Let's skip past the geo-political rivalries, shall we?' said Ian.

'We'll get you the money, mate,' said Steve. 'With the haul from this job, you'll make it the best Aussie beer bar in the whole of Spain.'

'The whole of the Med,' agreed Ian.

'And if that isn't something to drink to,' said Ollie, raising his glass, 'then I'd like to know what is.'

Eighteen

UY WALLACE POINTED AT A map on the wall. It showed the northern half of Batota, the border dominated by the massive Lake Hasta. A section measuring 100 square miles was marked out in red. 'This is where the bastard is holed up,' he said. 'And this is where you're going to get him.'

The unit was sitting in the planning room of the officer's mess. They had been woken just after dawn by a bugle call, and as they brewed up some coffee and ate some breakfast they could see the Sixth Brigade being put through its early-morning drill on the parade ground. There was no doubt they were a formidable fighting force. There were 300 soldiers in the barracks, and each one of them looked immaculately turned out, drilled and equipped.

If it comes to a fight, we'll just have to hope they are not on the other side of it, Steve reflected. Three hundred of them against ten of us? We wouldn't have a chance.

Wallace had collected them from the barracks at eight sharp and led them through to the operations room. It was sparsely furnished, with a single wooden table, one window overlooking the parade ground, and a series of maps and charts that detailed every inch of the country. It was from here, guessed Steve, that the President kept his real grip on the country. It wasn't politics or tribal history that kept him in office, whatever you might read in the papers. It was the rifles of the Sixth Brigade.

Wallace was describing Tshaka's forces. At his side was his main North Korean military adviser, Sungoo Park. The Korean was a small man, no more than five foot six, with cropped black hair and close-set dark brown eyes. As he walked into the room, there was a punchy smell of cheap aftershave. His expression was tense, and he spoke in a clipped, hurried English, but you could see the military intelligence in everything he said, Steve thought. Park might be a cruel man – ruthless, as well – but there was nothing inept about him.

In total, Tshaka had taken control of an area of 100 square miles, declaring effective Independence. Government troops couldn't go into the area. Nor could the police or the tax collectors. The rebel leader was building his strength for an assault on the capital. 'We can't be sure when it's coming, or what his strategy will be when he decides to strike, but strike he will, we can be certain of that,' Wallace said heavily.

'We need to destroy him – and destroy him now,' said Park.

There was emphasis on the word *destroy*, noted Steve. The North Koreans fought with a brutal savagery that flattened all opposition. Park wasn't the man who was going to change that tradition.

'There's a Presidential election coming up in three weeks,' said Wallace. 'I don't suppose our man is in any danger of losing, he never is . . .' Chuckling to himself, he took a cigar from the breast pocket of his olive-green battlefield uniform and rolled it between his fingers but left it unlit.

'But there's an issue of prestige on the line, and we need Tshaka dealt with right away,' he continued, his eyes glancing at each man in turn. 'There aren't going to be any medals for this one, boys, but there's a meaty cheque at the end of it, and that's worth fighting for.'

'So where is he most of the time?' asked David.

'Right here,' said Park, tapping the map with his short, stubby finger. 'A place called Elephant's Point on the shores of the lake. The closest town is called Binga, about fifty miles down from Avalanche Falls. He plans all his operations from there, and lives inside the fort most of the time. The bulk of his troops are out on the front line, protecting his territory from our soldiers. Our intelligence is that there are fifty crack troops stationed at Elephant's Foot at all times, tasked with protecting Tshaka.'

'That's the place to strike,' said Wallace. 'Get into the fort, and bring the bastard out.'

'It would be easier to get him when he's on the front line,' said Ian.

Wallace was looking at him suspiciously. 'Why?'

'He won't have so much protection around him,' the Irishman said. 'The fort is where he's most heavily guarded. Get him in a jeep, in the middle of some hard fighting, and he'll be easier to snatch.'

'We don't have the intelligence,' said Wallace. 'We'd need a man on the inside to tell us where he was and when we could take him.'

Steve glanced between both men. Wallace was right. If they were going to capture Tshaka out on the battlefield, they'd need to know where he was. And that did mean a man on the inside.

'He knows we want to kill him, and he's not stupid,' said Park. 'There are three jeeps he uses to go out in, and two choppers. On any day, he might be in any of them.'

'How about meetings?' said Ian. 'In the Provos, we'd get a politician's schedule, then plan a hit . . .'

'This is Batota, not Westminster,' said Wallace. His tone was acidic. 'Tshaka is a guerrilla leader. He doesn't go to committee meetings.'

'The fort it is then,' said Ollie. He glanced towards Ian, noted that he'd fallen silent, and added: 'We know where he is, we just have to figure out a way of getting him.'

Wallace was grinding his fists together, and chewing on the unlit cigar. 'You men are all professionals, and it's your lives on the line,' he said. 'So I'll let you choose your own way in.'

'Maybe some kind of nerve gas,' said Maksim. 'In the Spetsnaz, we'd get chemicals into a building, put everyone to sleep.'

'And most of them died, the way I heard it,' said Steve.

Maksim shrugged. 'In the Spetsnaz, we don't worry about casualties.'

'Tshaka must be taken alive,' said Park.

'Then no chemicals, it's too dangerous,' said Dan. 'There isn't anything that's reliable enough to disable the men inside the camp without killing someone.'

There was a brief silence among the men as they calculated the odds. Ten against fifty? Maybe that's why they had to bring in outsiders, reckoned Steve. It wasn't just that the Sixth Brigade couldn't spare the men. They didn't fancy the odds.

'There's a reason why the first thing any military commander has done for about five thousand years is build himself a fort,' said Ollie. 'Because they are bloody difficult to capture.'

'That's why I'm saying we grab him on the outside,' said Ian.

'We already told you, we don't have the intelligence,' snapped Wallace.

'We could lie up in wait,' said Ollie. 'Find a spot on the road, then stage an ambush as soon as he drives past.'

'He's got three cars,' said Dan. 'If we get the wrong one, he knows where we are and he comes to get us.'

'We could tunnel in,' suggested Nick.

'Thanks,' said Steve, turning around to grin at the young Welshman. 'I think you suggested that last time. Keep watching the Second World War DVDs.'

Nick went red in the face.

'How about we just blast the bastards,' said Dan. 'Go straight in the front door, RPGs and cannon turned on full whack.'

'The famous stealth tactics of the SASR,' said Ian sourly. 'And we have to get this guy out alive, remember?'

'You got a better idea?' Dan said nastily.

Steve took a swig from a bottle of water. It wasn't even nine o'clock on the first morning of the mission and already tempers were starting to fray. This was going to be harder than it looked. And it *looked* sodding hard.

'Maybe Newton could smuggle his way in?' said Ganju. 'If we had a man on the inside, that might help.'

Wallace shook his head. He was looking closely at Newton, assessing the man. 'It won't work, not in the time available,' he stated. 'Tshaka only has his handpicked troops inside the fort. They are his version of the Sixth Brigade. He won't let anyone inside until he's known them for years.'

'A siege,' said Ollie. 'Like I said, commanders have been building forts for five thousand years. So we'll do what their enemies have been doing for centuries to defeat them. Surround the fort, and put barrage after barrage of munitions into the bastards. If nothing else, we can starve them out.'

'Thanks for the Sandhurst tutorial,' Steve sighed. 'He's got a whole army less than a hundred miles away. A siege only works when you've got total control of the territory, *and* overwhelming numbers.'

'So what's the bloody SAS suggesting then?' growled Ollie. 'The usual? Run in with guns blazing and hope it's the other bloke who gets his balls shot off?'

Another silence.

It didn't matter how you looked at it. A fort was bloody hard to capture.

'There is a way,' said Chris slowly.

Steve looked towards him. The South African didn't speak very often. His opinions were rarely ventured, but when they were, there was a determination to his voice that commanded respect. Chris had spent more time on battlefields than any of them: he knew what made the difference between victory and defeat. 'I know some guys who fought in the Batotean bush wars,' he said. 'They had something called a Fireforce unit, based on that Rhodesian units of the same name . . .'

'What the hell's that?' asked Nick.

'Batota is a high country – the greater part of it is over two thousand feet above sea level – and it's hot as well, so most of it is unsuitable for conventional military helicopters,' Chris explained. 'But in the mid-sixties, a French company called Société Turboméca started developing small gas-chamber engines that would work in a chopper. You could use them even at these altitudes and temperatures. Once the Batotean Army got hold of some Alouette choppers fitted with the new type of engines, they were in business. The Fireforce units consisted of four or five men. They'd be on stand-by waiting for a guerrilla attack, or any intelligence on the location of the rebels, then they'd scramble into action, come blasting in with the chopper, and inflict some heavy casualties on the enemy. The Fireforce boys scored more kills than any other unit of the Batotean Army.'

Steve was looking at him closely. 'You're saying we come in by chopper?'

Chris took a sharp intake of breath. 'We kit out the right kind of machine, so there's room for the men and at least one machine gun. But there's no point in trying to parachute down into the fort – they'll just shoot us to pieces. Instead, we take advantage of the fact that, at these altitudes, a chopper can drop very fast out of the sky. We come in high, then drop down suddenly to about thirty feet over the parade ground. We roll out ropes, and scale right down into the centre of the fort, our guns blazing on automatic . . .'

'Chopper and boat,' Ollie interrupted. He stood up and walked towards the map, tapping it with his finger. 'Chris is right about the Fireforce units. Nobody knew better how to fight in this kind of territory than they did, and we should use the same tactics.'

He pointed to the lake. 'The fort's other vulnerability is its proximity to the water. We've already bought ourselves a KPV and that's one of the most lethal machine guns ever built. We strap it to the front of a boat, and come in close from behind, with the engines switched off so we can't be heard. We stay in constant radio communication with the chopper . . .'

He paused, looking around the room, the plan forming in his mind as he spoke.

'Five men in the air, and five in the boat. The boat opens up first, laying down a barrage of fire into their arses. While the boys in the fort are running around trying to find out what the hell is happening, the chopper drops out of the sky, four guys jump out and let them have it hard, straight into their backs.'

Ollie punched his fists together. 'They'll be dead before they know what's hit them.'

Steve nodded, listening to every word. Maximum speed, maximum aggression, the motto of the Regiment. It was the way he'd always fought, the way he liked to fight. 'It might just work,' he muttered.

And even as he spoke, he knew he was reflecting the views of every man in the room.

None of them minded risking their lives so long as they had a plan they believed in and which gave them a chance of getting out alive.

'What about Tshaka?' demanded Wallace. 'How will you get him out alive? It's going to be like a slaughterhouse in there.'

'He's the commander,' said Ollie. 'He'll stay inside the officer's mess, and once we've dealt with his men, we can bring him out and get away in the chopper.'

'You can't be certain. He might be killed—'

'It's a battlefield,' said Ollie with a shrug. 'Nothing's ever certain. There's no way of capturing this man without a risk of him being killed.'

Wallace lit his cigar with a greasy lighter that smelled of fuel. 'To the Fire Force then,' he said, blowing a plume of smoke up into the air. 'And may God be on your side. Because you're bloody well going to need all the help you can get.'

Nineteen

S TEVE CAST HIS EYES OVER the machine. The Alouette III was a stubby little helicopter with a thick, bulbous nose and a short tail – a design that made it perfect for high-altitude flying. It was fitted with an Astazou XIV engine, designed to perform even in intense heat, and although it was built to run on jet fuel, if you ran out of that, it would run on petrol as well. In an emergency, you could even get it into the air using diesel. Like the men inside it, it could live off the land. Which was what made it right for the job.

At Steve's side, Chris was running his hands along the exterior of the chopper. He'd never piloted one himself, but he'd spent plenty of time in the back of an Alouette: the South African Air Force had bought dozens of them. Steve was used to the machine as well. The Pakistani Air Force used them to patrol the al-Queda-controlled wild, mountainous borderlands between their own country and Afghanistan, and back in the Regiment he'd been on joint missions with them. It wasn't the most modern chopper in the world – the first Alouette had been designed in 1959, and the III first came into service in 1970 – but it had been used in countless combat zones and to Steve that meant it was reliable, tested and rugged.

'How's she running?' asked Chris.

They were standing on a small, military airstrip ten miles north of the barracks. Steve, Chris and David had been driven straight out here after the meeting broke up. David was the most experienced pilot in the unit. Steve could fly a chopper if he had to – it was part of standard Regiment training – and so could Dan, but David was the man with the most flying hours on his CV so it would be he who took the controls. Wallace had introduced them to Josiah Katana, the chief engineer of the air base, who had taken them out to check the Alouette.

'Perfectly,' answered Katana immediately. 'We don't have a huge Air Force here in Batota. If we have a machine like this, then we look after it.'

Gazing around the airstrip, Steve could see that that much was true. There was a pair of MIG fighters and an elderly Antonov troop carrier and a Pakistani-built Nanchang trainer aircraft, but otherwise Ibera seemed largely undefended from the air. A modern, well-equipped Army could take this place in a couple of days, he reflected. If they wanted to.

'How about armour?' he said aloud. 'We could be taking some heavy incoming fire as we approach the fort.'

'It's got steel plating right along the underside,' explained Katana. 'The Alouette can absorb a huge amount of incoming fire, that's one of its main strengths. You can take any number of bullet-holes to the skin, and so long as the pilot is alive, you'll be OK. Punch a hole in the rotorblade and she'll stay up. Even if the tail rotor fails you can still get clear of the battlefield and bring her down safely.'

'So what are her vulnerabilities, would you say?' asked David.

Katana thought for a minute before replying. 'A direct hit to the engine or to the main rotor gearbox is going to finish you off. Those are the two parts of the machine you need to protect.'

Steve looked across at David. He was the man who was going to be flying the machine. Ultimately, it was his call. He spent a couple more minutes poking around inside the engine, then checking the blades. 'We'll take it,' said David finally.

Together with Wallace, the three men climbed inside the compact cabin. The Alouette held six men plus the pilot at standard capacity, but this one had had two of the passenger seats removed to create more space for loading kit on board or for evacuating wounded soldiers. At the side, there was an FN 7.62mm MAG machine gun, again a leftover from the old Batotean Army, which had bought most of its armaments from the Belgian manufacturer Fabrique Nationale. David pulled back on the throttle, letting the powerful rotor swing into action, and in the next moment Steve could feel the machine start to jerk into the air. It wasn't built for comfort, he could remember that much from the time he'd flown in an Alouette in Pakistan. It stuttered on its climb, the engines filling the cramped cabin with a deafening roar. But it took off cleanly and quickly, accelerated fast, and could drop out of the sky with terrifying speed. For the job in hand, it would do just fine.

The Alouette had a top speed of 124 miles an hour. David swung it out over the fields that lay to the north of Ibera, opened up the throttle to take it up to full speed, then brought it back towards the Sixth Brigade barracks, landing it neatly on the parade ground. As he climbed out of the cockpit, he looked pleased enough.

'She flies fine,' he said tersely. 'She'll get us in, and hopefully out again, in one piece. And that's all that counts.'

By the time they got back to the Operations Room, Ollie had already started drawing up more detailed plans of the way they wanted the raid to unfold. It was a second-by-second plan: a raid like this was going to depend on precise timing. David would fly the chopper and Steve, Ian, Maksim and Dan would drop down from the air. Ian would create some homemade stun grenades to lob as they came in for the assault: the more disorientated the troops were, the less resistance they'd offer, and the easier it would be to take them out.

They'd fly out tomorrow to a small town called Gull's Wing, about 100 miles up the lake from Elephant's Foot, and the closest piece of territory controlled by the Government. The fort there would give them shelter for the night and a chance to ready themselves for the attack. There was a twenty-five-foot, armour-plated cruiser they could use for the assault from Lake Hasta. The KPV could be fitted onto its front. Ollie, Newton, Nick, Ganju and Chris would lead that charge, blasting the side of Tshaka's stronghold with rockets and machine-gun fire.

'There are probably about a hundred things that can go wrong,' said Ollie, when he'd finished drawing up the first draft of the battle plan. 'But with any luck, only about fifty of them actually will. And in that case, we should get out of there alive.'

'How long do you need?' asked Wallace.

'We've a day to train,' said Ollie, 'but we'll get down to Gull's Wing tomorrow. The closer we are to the target, the better.'

'Then tonight we'll eat . . . and toast the success of your mission.'

By six, dinner was served. Wallace and Park had set out a table on the veranda of the officer's mess. It was a grey, dark evening, with the threat of thunder in the air. The long wooden table was piled high with food: bread, salad, fruit and rice. On a long, wood-fired barbecue, sausages, chicken breasts, pork strips, steak and fish were being grilled, creating a delicious aroma that reminded Steve how hungry he was. There were ten crates of lager and ten bottles of a locally-made rum. There might be a shortage of food across Batota, but the Sixth Brigade wasn't going hungry, noted Steve. Or running dry. It was the first rule of any dictatorship. *Keep your crack troops well-fed.* Kapembwa was following it to the letter.

'We've lined up a performance for you,' said Wallace, pulling out a chair and sitting down. He offered each man a cigar, but only Maksim accepted. 'This country used to be one of the largest tobacco exporters in the world,' Wallace said. 'Most of the farms have collapsed, of course, but they still make a damned fine cigar if you know where to buy them. You should try one.'

'We've got a war to fight,' said Ollie. 'We need to stay fit.'

Wallace laughed. 'I've been smoking all my life and it's never done me any harm.'

Ollie was about to say something but he could already see Steve glancing at him and decided to stay silent. The men had all loaded their plates with food and helped themselves to a bottle of the lager. It was nothing special but it was ice cold and it was alcoholic so it would do.

'You don't get mercenaries in Africa like the old days, so it's good to see you boys out here,' said Wallace. He drank half a bottle of beer in one gulp and knocked back a rum chaser. 'Back in the sixties and seventies, this was where soldiers of fortune could really make their mark. There was Angola, Rhodesia, the Congo, Mozambique. The Batotean Army was like the bloody Foreign Legion, there were so many different nationalities in it. Put a gun in a man's hand and a green and gold shirt on his chest, and suddenly he was a warrior.'

'There's still work for soldiers,' said Ollie.

Wallace nodded. 'Iraq, Afghanistan – it's all PMCs now,' he agreed. He poured himself another generous shot of rum and knocked it back in a single gulp. 'The business has been taken over by bloody management consultants. They've got flipcharts and PowerPoint presentations and contracts from the UN. It's all a load of bollocks.'

He grabbed the bottle of rum, poured more into his glass then slammed it down onto the table.

'There are endless bloody rules and regulations and so-called peacekeepers. But Africa . . .' He pushed his uneaten food away and torched up his cigar, a smile spreading across his lips as the alcohol and tobacco started to calm him. 'In Africa, they still fight like soldiers. Here, strength and determination are all that count. It's kill or be killed – the way a man should live.'

'And how far has it got them?' said Ian.

Steve glanced across at the Irishman. He had been thinking exactly the same thing himself. He didn't like Wallace or his methods. But they were here as hardened mercenaries, apparently interested in nothing apart from making themselves a few quid as quickly as possible. Let that mask slip for a single second, he reminded himself, and they were as good as dead.

'I'll show you how far it's got them,' growled Wallace. He clapped his hands together. 'I promised you a performance. Well, you're going to get one.'

Park had already stepped up from the table. The clouds were growing darker, and off in the distance Steve could see the first cracks of lightning starting to split open the night sky. The Korean was barking something at the Sergeant, who disappeared inside the barracks. Within moments, 100 men had formed a steady line on the parade ground, facing the officer's mess. The bayonets on their rifles were gleaming. In front of them, the Sergeant was dragging a man in uniform, his hands manacled behind his back. The prisoner was no more than twenty-one or twenty-two, judged Steve. There was a look of fear in his big brown eyes. Behind him, two more soldiers were carrying a wooden rack, eight foot high and four wide, shaped like a crucifix. They placed it down on the parade ground, halfway between the men and the mess, so that it was thirty feet in front of where the unit were sitting. The Sergeant roared at his men, then the soldier was strapped to the wooden frame, his arms and legs bound into place with rough leather belts.

'This guy missed parade this morning,' said Wallace, relighting his cigar. 'We'll show you what kind of punishment commands respect in Africa.'

A zigzag of lightning was followed by a peal of thunder so loud and savage it was like a bomb exploding. A man was walking out into the parade ground, carrying a bamboo stick. Steve recognised him at once. Yohane.

Yohane glanced over at Wallace, nodded curtly, then took a couple of paces forward. He was standing five feet away from the soldier. Even at this distance, Steve could see the man was sobbing with fear. Like every member of the Sixth Brigade, he was an immaculate physical specimen, tall and strong and fit. But he clearly knew the kind of punishment he was about to get. And also knew that he might not live through it.

Yohane drew the bamboo cane backwards, approaching the target the way a confident footballer approaches a penalty: with a short, precise run that puts maximum power into the shot without sacrificing accuracy. He lashed the cane into the man's back, cutting through the cotton of his tunic and slicing into the open flesh beneath it. There was a split-second delay as the man attempted to bury the agony somewhere within him, but he could no more control it than he could control the thunderstorm rolling through the night sky. A howl of pain ripped through the air, as brutal and piercing as any Steve had ever heard. Reaching forwards, he poured himself a shot of the rum and knocked the liquid into the back of his throat with one swift movement of his hand. It looks like a long night, he decided grimly. I'll need some hard liquor running through my veins to get through it.

The rain had already started to fall, bringing howling gusts of wind with it. Yohane delivered second blow, then another. Each time the soldier cried out in pain. On the third stroke, the blood started to flow freely. The cane had cut deeply into the skin, slicing open the veins. The rain was beating into the man, soaking into his skin, washing the blood out onto the parade ground, until it was stained crimson. And still the blows kept coming, each one delivered with the same savage force.

'Christ, man, he's going to die,' snapped Ian.

Wallace turned to look at him, a sneer of contempt twisted onto his lips. 'So? He's just a nigger.'

Nick stood up. He'd had a couple of beers, but from the look in his eyes he was stone cold sober.

'He's a human being, you bastard,' he said, a steely edge to his voice. 'He's taken his punishment, now tell that cunt to stop.'

Wallace blew out a puff of cigar smoke. 'Don't give me lessons on discipline, Taffy. I tell you, he's a nigger. This is the only language they understand.'

'In the Spetsnaz, it's just the same,' shrugged Maksim, taking another swig of the rough spirits. 'Men get beaten to death all the time.'

'Nobody believes a word you say,' scoffed Nick. 'Last time out, you sodding betrayed us.'

Maksim started to stand up, swaying violently towards Nick. 'I was tricked!' he roared. 'I betrayed no one!'

Nick pointed to the parade ground. 'Then bloody stop this.'

Maksim lunged towards him, but in the same instant Dan and Chris had leaped to their feet, grabbing hold of the Russian and pushing him back into his seat.

'Leave it, Nick,' Steve said, his tone quiet but determined.

For a moment, he wondered if Nick was about to thump him, and he wouldn't have blamed the boy if he had. What they were witnessing was barbaric, a ritual that had no place in any army. But they couldn't let Wallace know that: and Nick should be mature enough to realise that for himself.

On the parade ground, Yohane had finally stopped, throwing the cane to the sodden ground.

The Sergeant stepped forwards, took a second to check the man's pulse, then judged him dead. With a knife, he sliced open the man's wrist, then held a water flask to the open wound, catching the blood as it emptied into the metal container. When it was full, he walked over to the first man in the line of soldiers, waited whilst the man raised the flask to his lips, took a sip of the fresh blood, then passed the flask down the line.

'In Africa, the men still believe that if you drink the blood of another man, then his courage will be your courage,' said Wallace.

'Maybe they'll let us have a drop,' said Steve.

'You might need it,' granted Wallace. 'You're going into battle tomorrow, and so long as you come out ahead you'll be bloody well paid. But if any of you cross me . . .' he gestured at the parade ground, '. . . then you know what kind of vengeance I'll take.'

'Jesus,' muttered Steve softly to himself.

The sooner we are out of this madhouse the better.

Twenty

T HE SKIES WERE CLEAR AND blue as the Cessna Skymaster flew
due north over the wide open countryside. Steve had been
looking down as the farmland and forest outside Ibera faded
into the wilder bush country, then at the great blue expanse of Lake
Hasta. All the time, he was judging his bearings, mapping the
geography or the territory so that it was stamped on his brain. From
tomorrow, they'd be fighting their way through this country. The
more they knew about it, the better.

'The lake!' shouted Wallace, straining to make himself heard over
the roar of the engine and the rush of the wind outside.

The single-engine aircraft had space for five passengers. Wallace
was at the controls, with Steve, Dan, Ian, Nick and Ganju riding
alongside, while David flew Ollie and the rest of the unit up-country
in the Alouette. They had driven up to the airfield at first light, all of
them anxious to get up north and crack on with the mission. From
what they'd seen last night, they'd agreed the sooner they stopped
working for Wallace, and got the man who paid his wages safely into
his coffin, the better. They were mercenaries, and they didn't mind
killing men if they had to, so long as the rules were clear and they
deserved the malleting. But Wallace . . . he'd strayed into psycho
territory.

We're all feeling the worse for wear, decided Steve. And it's not the
local rum making us feel that way.

It's the job.

Wallace pulled on the throttle and the Cessna shook violently as it started to drop a couple of thousand feet through the sky. Steve gripped the side of the plane as it shuddered, the bolts holding it together groaning under the pressure. But Wallace knew what he was doing. He let the engine rip again, steadying the plane on a new cruising altitude of 8,000 feet. They were low enough to get a close look at the ground, but high enough to be out of reach of small-arms fire. This was, after all, enemy territory. And at this altitude, only a SAM missile could take them down.

They were tracking the contours of the lake. It arced in a quarter circle, irrigating the land all around it, so it was rich with green trees. The country was lush and beautiful, but Steve could already guess it was very different once you got down on the ground. The animals would be wild and the trees and the grasses would hold you up, making it virtually impossible to escape. Luckily they'd have the chopper to get out in. There'd be no way out marching across country this rough.

'Elephant's Foot!' shouted Wallace, pointing straight ahead. 'We'll make one fly-past so you boys can take a look. Any more than that, and Tshaka will start getting suspicious.'

He chuckled to himself. 'And we don't want the bastard to know you're coming for him.'

Steve found himself listening closely to the laugh. There was something he didn't like about it, as if it was a warning. Could Wallace be sending them into a trap? Maybe the assault on the fort was just a decoy action whilst the real attack was launched elsewhere. Or maybe it was just a probing attack, designed to soften up the fort for a full-scale assault by the Sixth Brigade. I certainly wouldn't put it past Wallace to be using us as pawns in a much larger game, he thought.

He strained to get a view of the fort. Even at 8,000 feet you could get a sense of the strength of the place. Its position on the lake looked out onto clear water so there was not much chance of taking cover behind the bend if you approached by boat. Ollie would have to come in hard and fast for his assault. On the other three sides of the fort, the forest and scrubland had been cleared at least 100 yards in each direction. Again, there was no cover, making it impossible to stage a surprise attack. A single mud track led up to the fort, twisting its way through the forest. Trees had been felled for twenty yards on either side, the path regularly cleared to stop it growing back. Again, the Commander was making certain there was no possibility of an ambush. Nobody could get anywhere near the road without exposing themselves to fire.

'We've learned something already,' Dan said to Steve.

'Yes – that the man's a professional,' said Steve.

Dan nodded. 'Which means we're going to have a fight on our hands.'

Steve knew he was right. Inside, even from this distance, the fort looked both well-defended and well-maintained. There was nothing sloppy or amateurish about it. Tshaka was expecting to be attacked, and had made plans to defend himself. The man was disciplined and organised, and knew his stuff – and that was going to make him a formidable opponent.

'Look,' said Ganju quickly.

Steve followed the man's finger. The Gurkha was the most acutely observant man he'd ever fought alongside, a solider who could spot a weakness in even the best dug-in defences. It was part of his tradition. The Gurkhas were famous for their formidable bravery, but it was mixed with cunning, and planning. They hit their enemies hard, and without fear, but they always made sure they were aiming for the weakest spot.

'Water pipes,' continued Ganju. He was already scribbling on a pad of paper he'd opened on his lap. 'There's a set of two, coming in and out of the lake. I reckon one is taking out the sewage, the other is bringing in water for washing, maybe for drinking as well.'

'And?' prompted Steve.

'And the pipes are coming in overground and through the wall of the fort,' said Ganju. 'That's lazy. They should have put them in a deep trench. The wall is going to be weaker where they've fed the pipes through. So that's where we put in the main RPG rounds. Our chances of bringing down the wall will be far higher then.'

Steve just nodded. As so often, Ganju was completely right.

Wallace had already started to bank the Skymaster into a turning circle, pushing it out over the lake. They'd spent as much time as they could risk flying over the fort today. Tshaka had no Air Force and had to tolerate surveillance from the Central Government's planes, but more than one reconnaissance flight a day would be noted and put him on the alert. They headed back out over the lake, making for Gull's Wing.

It was just after eleven by the time they landed. The airstrip was just a dusty stretch of baked and hardened mud to the west of the fort. In wet weather, there would be no way you could bring a plane down here. Even in the dry, Wallace circled the Skymaster twice to get the measure of the strip before attempting to land the plane. Its wheels bumped viciously along the rough ground, the plane rocking violently as Wallace slammed hard on the brakes.

As he hopped down from the cockpit, Steve could feel the humidity in the air. It was much wetter than down in Ibera. You could feel the moisture everywhere, making your lungs sticky and bringing the sweat straight out onto the surface of your skin. In the distance, you could hear the squeals of birds in the forest, creating a nervous edge to the air. I've only been here about five seconds, thought Steve. And I don't like the place already.

They stepped smartly towards the fort. The Alouette had already landed, and Ollie and the rest of the men were inside. Looking around, Steve could see at once why Wallace wasn't using any of his own men to try and take out Tshaka. This fort was left over from the old Batotean regime, and was nothing more than a remote border post. The walls were seven feet high, made from breeze blocks, creating a well-defended square of about 100 square yards. But it was nothing like Tshaka's fortress. At the back, the forest was creeping up: weeds, grasses and trees were growing all over the rear wall, and there was enough cover there for a whole platoon of troops to launch a surprise assault. The walls had been whitewashed once, but the paintwork had long since faded away, leaving the concrete exposed to the humidity, which over time would weaken it: a couple of well-placed RPG rounds would blow a hole right through it. At the entrance, a pair of guards at least stood to attention when Wallace started leading the men through. But their uniforms were dirty and frayed, and one of them was wearing trainers rather than boots. Their rifles didn't look that clean either.

A rabble, decided Steve. This lot weren't going to be able to fight anyone.

Ollie and David were already standing next to the chopper unloading the kit, as Steve strode across to meet them. In total, he reckoned there were 150 soldiers based here, but none of them looked fighting fit. The barrack house was dilapidated, and the officer's mess didn't look any better. There was a terrible smell coming from the crap-house, suggesting it hadn't been cleaned for weeks. Outside of the barracks, a group of men were playing cards and smoking dope. To the left of the parade ground, another group of guys had got a game of football going.

'Shame we can't fight these blokes,' said Ollie, shaking Steve by the hand. 'I reckon they'd collapse in no time.'

'We might be, soon enough,' answered Steve quietly. He glanced back towards Wallace, but he'd already slipped away to talk to the camp's commander.

'What's Tshaka's fort like?' asked Ollie.

'A lot better than this dump,' said Steve. 'I can see why the President is worried about Tshaka . . . he looks a lot more on the ball than his own Army.'

'Defended?'

Steve nodded curtly. 'It's a professional outfit. We'll have a fair old scrap when we go in.'

'Then we'd better crack on,' said Ollie.

Ollie and David had already drawn up a plan for the day's activities, making the best use of each man's skills.

Ollie would sort out the boat, fixing the KPV machine gun to its turret and loading up the RPG rockets. He'd take it out on the lake to make sure each man knew his drill. David would take the Alouette up for a spin with the men on board. They needed at least one practice run, maybe two. For most of them, it was a while since they'd last attempted an airborne assault. There were few more difficult military manoeuvres. It required a precise combination of raw courage and perfect choreography. Like ballet dancing under heavy fire – that was the way Steve remembered his instructor at Hereford describing it. Once false move, and you were already a corpse.

'Ready?' said David, as he gunned the engine on the chopper.

Steve was sitting in the back along with Ian, Maksim and Dan. 'Ready,' he rapped in reply.

The Alouette's heavy blade swiped through the air, and with a sudden jerky movement it was rising up into the sky. It rose quickly, even in the hot, thin air, swaying up to 1,000 feet. David pushed it out over the lake. He'd already flown it up from Ibera this morning and was getting used to the controls. The machine ran smoothly enough. Like a vintage car, it wasn't cluttered with a lot of modern electronics. It was about as simple as a lawnmower and the better for it. Electronics were fine when you had an American aircraft carrier with a full team of mechanics to keep them working for you, thought Steve. Out here, the less you had to worry about the better.

David twisted over the lake, and pointed back towards their fort. 'Get ready, boys.' he yelled over the roar of the engine.

The Alouette suddenly plummeted: David was bringing it right down to 200 feet, and for the drop itself, it would come down to fifty.

They had coiled four lightweight but sturdy nylon ropes onto winches on the side of the chopper. The winch would regulate the speed of your drop as you threw yourself from the side of the machine, allowing you to land at roughly the same speed as on a parachute jump. Each man was gripping onto his rope with his hand, since as soon as you hit the ground, you had to form a tight square and start shooting. There was no time to unhook a harness. It was hands or nothing.

Steve could feel his stomach rising into his chest as the chopper dropped down. It was always the same, and there was no point in fighting it. They'd be coming in low for the attack, and when you did that, even a man with a constitution like old boots started vomiting. The Alouette was hurtling towards the fort, skimming over the surface of the lake, inching down all the time as David co-ordinated the flight so that it would hit fifty feet just as it hovered over the centre of the parade ground.

A hundred yards, judged Steve.

Fifty . . .

Thank Christ this is just a practice, he told himself grimly. I need a run at this before I do it with blokes shooting straight into my balls.

'Go, go!' screamed David.

Steve took only a fraction of a second to glance from the side of the chopper. He'd been through this drill dozens of times with the Regiment. He'd done his basic parachute training by jumping again and again from a tall wooden platform on the end of a rope and he'd seen a few blokes break ankles and legs. He'd done fifty parachute jumps, ten of them in combat zones, and two of them under hostile fire. But it didn't matter how many times you did it. You could still feel the fear creeping through your veins as you chucked yourself into the void. Your blood froze and your heart pumped furiously. 'Go,' Steve repeated to himself. *'Just sodding go.'*

He held on tight to the rope as he fell, releasing just enough grip from his fingers and knees to keep himself moving down. The updraught from the chopper's blade was creating a vicious blast of air that shot straight upwards, dragging a cloud of dust and dirt swirling into them. As you dropped down through it, you were completely blinded. Steve held tight to the rope, taking less than three seconds to shimmy down its entire length. He hit the ground with a thud, letting his knees bend to absorb the pressure. In that same instant, he whipped his AK-47 from his chest webbing, knelt down and started firing the mag full of blanks he'd loaded into the gun. Above him, David was jerking the Alouette hard into the sky, and slowly the dust cloud was starting to clear, making it possible to see the fort.

Ganju was standing right next to him.

With his AK-47 pointing into Steve's chest.

Steve stood up, wiping the dirt out of his eyes and glancing around at Dan, Ian and Maksie. If they'd been doing this for real, it looked as if Ian would have died.

And me as well.

'OK,' Steve sighed. 'Let's keep doing this until we get it right.'

David had taken the chopper up for a clean getaway, and was circling around before bringing it back in to land. Steve checked his watch. It was just after noon. They could do another couple of practice runs, then they had to start assembling their kit and getting some rest.

They weren't going to perfect the manoeuvre in the time available. But there was no point in worrying about that now. They just had to crack on – and reckon they'd get it right when their lives were on the line. After all, he reminded himself, there was nothing like facing a real live enemy with real live bullets in his guns to get you focused.

Down by the lake, Ollie and Chris were fixing up the boat.

It was a military patrol vessel, at least twenty years old, and manufactured locally. Its steel hull was painted a dark green. There was a small cabin down below with room for three men, and plenty of space for another six men on the deck. Modern patrol boats were made from aluminium for greater speed, but Chris reckoned this one would do just fine. It had two 400-kilowatt diesel engines, which could get it up to a top speed of forty knots if you pushed it hard enough. There were 300 litres of fuel in its tank, fully loaded, enough to get it down to Elephant's Foot and back twice over, and a generous allowance in a country where diesel was in short supply.

Chris had already fired up the engine and taken her for a spin around the lake. 'She runs fine,' he said gruffly. 'We'll get there in one piece.' He pointed towards a scaly pair of eyes staring at them from the far side of the lake. 'So long as the crocs don't get us, of course.'

Over the course of the afternoon, Ollie and Chris fixed the weapons they'd need. The heavy KPV machine gun was bolted onto the front of the boat, and space cleared for its cartridges. Ollie loosened off a few rounds, wounding one of the crocodiles in the process, as he tested the set-up. The boat swayed viciously in the water from the KPV's massive kickback, but the hull was deep enough to hold it steady. On the back of the boat was a pair of MAGs, machine guns made by Fabrique Nationale of Belgium. The MAG – it stood for *Mitrailleuse d'Appui Général* or General Purpose Machine Gun – was one of the most widely available firearms in the world, and all the men were familiar with how it worked. The boat was fitted with the 60-40 model, designed for fighting vehicles, and they were fitted on a swivel platform, giving a single gunner a 360-degree arc of fire.

As they inspected the boat, Ollie and Chris were satisfied that it was well defended. Next, they started to load the RPGs. They had two launchers they'd brought up from Ibera with them, plus twenty rockets. A man on either side of the boat, sitting just back from the KPV, should be able to get a clear shot at the fort. As they came in, they'd be laying down heavy fire from the KPV plus the two RPGs, and they'd have the two MAGs to protect their flanks. For such a small vessel, it was an awesome line-up of firepower.

'All set?' asked Ollie.

Chris shook his head. 'We need a searchlight,' he answered. 'We're coming in just as dawn breaks, and there could well be some mist on the lake. We might not be able to see anything.'

While Chris retrieved a searchlight from the fort, Ollie checked and double-checked the engine, making sure that everything was working smoothly. When they were finished, they returned to the base. It was already after four in the afternoon, and the air was heavy with moisture.

Ian had spent the day making a series of six stun grenades that would be dropped on the fort just as the chopper came down. Similar to the grenades he'd used in the jail break-out, he'd based them on the American M84 grenade, a variant of the basic SAS device known as a 'flash'n'crash' because it generated both a blinding flash of light and a vicious swirl of noise that could totally disorientate an enemy for up to a minute. The M84 used a mix of magnesium and ammonium, both of which Ian had bought in Johannesburg. They were mixed into a compact tube, with a short fuse wire that should give them a detonation time of precisely five seconds. The men would tip them down into the fort as the chopper swooped in for the attack. Within five feet of detonation, the grenade would produce 170 decibels of sound, which is about 30 per cent louder than standing right underneath a 747 at take-off. The flash would be bright enough to temporarily blind anyone not wearing protective glasses. All four men coming down on the ropes would be wearing protective glasses and ear mufflers – enough, they hoped, to give them a crucial edge over the soldiers they'd be fighting on the ground.

Nick had been zeroing all the weapons: every new gun had to be tested, particularly if you were about to take it into battle. He was the best shot among them, and he took each rifle and pistol, set himself a target, then fired and fired until he could be certain that its sights and aim were true. Every time he fired, he muttered, 'Kill,' silently under his breath. It was hard, patient work, requiring hour after hour of concentration. But one faulty weapon could make the difference between success or failure. Nick worked methodically, getting each weapon just right before he marked it down as ready for use. By the end of the afternoon, two of the AK-47s and one of the Uzis had been discarded. The rest were OK.

Ganju had been fixing up a two-way radio. Dawn would break at just after six in the morning, according to the weather forecasts they'd seen back in Ibera. They wanted to come in for the attack just as the light was hazy, so that their enemy would still be sleeping, but also so that there would be some light to shoot into. The boat would take around three hours to get to the fort, the chopper about half an hour. They had to co-ordinate the attack perfectly so that they went in at precisely the same time – and that meant they needed radio contact. Ganju set up a short-wave system using electronic transmitters that would keep the two sides in constant communication but shouldn't be on any of the frequencies monitored inside the fort. If they were overheard, that would spell disaster: the attack could only work if they had total surprise on their side.

'Let's eat,' announced Steve. 'And then we rest.'

Dan and Newton had cooked up a basic meal of grilled pork, beans, salad and rice. All the men were hungry from the day's labours. Nick had brought an iPod with him, loaded up with Bruce Springsteen, Coldplay and Snow Patrol. 'Stick to Bruce,' said Steve, as Nick attached the MP3 player to a speaker system in the officer's mess. 'None of us blokes likes any of that modern rubbish.'

Steve chewed on his food as a rousing chorus of 'The Rising' boomed out of the speakers. He thought briefly about Jeff. He'd loved The Boss, carrying his complete works around with him on his iPod, along with Stevie Wonder and Prince. He looked towards the sky, swallowing hard on his grub, and washing it down with a glass of water. Another hell-hole, listening to Bruce, with all of us getting wound up because we're nervous about going into battle, he reflected to himself. At moments like this, it's hard to understand why we do it. For the excitement – or because none of us know how to live a normal life any more?

Dan was talking about his bar in Majorca, and Maksim was saying that he'd definitely bring some Russian builders down for the summer to finish the place off. But the conversation was desultory. Steve could feel the anxiety in the air. Men were always nervous before a battle, it was part of soldiering, but this was different. None of them minded a fight, so long as it was a fair one and there was a chance of coming out alive. But the assault on the fort looked close to impossible. Fifty men against ten. Those weren't odds anyone could face calmly.

We should never have taken this job, he thought. It was Ollie's fault. If that useless tosser didn't drink and gamble so much, none of us would be here.

'I want to be on the chopper,' said Nick, sitting down next to Steve.

Ollie was sitting a few yards away from him, with Dan and Newton at his side. Dusk was starting to fall, and out in the forest you could hear the wails of an animal on the prowl. At the front entrance, half a dozen wounded men were being dumped off in a truck and hurriedly carried inside the fort. It was clear that up on the front line, about five miles from here, the Government forces were taking a terrible beating. A couple of the men being carried through on stretchers looked like they'd had half their faces blown off, whilst another pair had taken heavy shrapnel wounds to their legs. The medical facilities were rudimentary: one tent, staffed by a single nurse, and a doctor who'd long since run out of most of the medicines you needed in a field hospital.

'You want to do *what*?'

'The chopper,' said Nick firmly. 'I want to come with the guys in the chopper.'

'Then you're sodding crazy,' snapped Steve. But he could tell from Nick's face that he desperately wanted to go. He was reddening, not with embarrassment the way he usually did, but with anger.

'You left me behind the last time,' said Nick. 'This time I want to be right in the thick of the action.'

'And you know how to jump out of a chopper?'

'I did it in the Territorials. I'll be all right.'

'This is under fire, mate, when your life depends on it. You need experience.'

'Like Ian? He's just a Provo.'

Steve thought for a moment. 'That's different. We need Ian to bomb the bastards.'

'I can drop the stun bombs,' said Nick.

Steve shook his head from side to side. He admired the boy's guts. Nick was probably the only man among them whose insides weren't churning at the thought of the drop tomorrow. Coming in by parachute was bad enough. Dropping off a rope into enemy fire was among the most terrifying experiences soldiering had to offer. If Nick knew what it was like, he wouldn't be volunteering. But he was young, he had no sense of danger, and although everyone was like that once, once you'd had some battles under your belt, you knew that sending a man without experience into a fire storm like that was just throwing away a life.

'You can have my place,' shouted Maksim, grabbing hold of his crotch. 'There's too many girls haven't had a taste of these yet to get them shot off in the morning.'

'Deal,' Nick said immediately.

But Maksim had stopped joking. 'Sorry, no way,' he muttered.

Ollie had already stood up and was walking across to join them. He put his arm around Nick's shoulder and steered him towards the medical tent. One of the wounded soldiers had been slung across the rickety operating table. The nurse was lying down on his chest, trying to keep him still while the doctor hacked off his left leg just above the knee. The man was swaying, blood foaming from his mouth. They'd pumped him full of morphine, but had no proper anaesthetics to knock him out before they started the operation. If the wound didn't kill him the trauma might well do the job, realised Ollie grimly. He had seen it happen before – men so psychologically damaged by being operated on in the field they lost the will to live.

Nick started to heave, throwing his food up onto his boots. He spluttered, wiping the vomit from his mouth with the back of his hand, spitting onto the ground when he'd finished.

'That's real soldiering, Nick,' said Ollie. 'You drop out of a chopper in a real contact and it only takes one bloke with an automatic rifle to get a good aim and he's going to rip your legs to shreds. If you're lucky you'll die before you hit the ground. And if you're unlucky, we'll have to bring you back here to get your leg sawn off by this butcher. So you listen to me. I've got a berth for you on the back of my boat, holding a MAG, because you're the best bloody shot I ever saw, and if some bastard starts creeping up behind me then you're the guy I want shooting him.'

Ollie paused, then took Nick back to where the rest of the men were eating.

'That all right with you?'

Nick nodded but remained silent.

'Right,' said Ollie, as he rejoined the rest of the men. 'Some of us are going to be heading out of here long before dawn, and by the time we see the sun rising again we'll have the scrap of our lives to deal with. So I think we all need a drink.'

Steve stepped forwards. 'I think we've had enough to drink,' he said.

Ollie looked at him sharply. 'I haven't,' he said. Picking up one of the beer bottles, he removed the lid and downed it in a single draught. 'Maybe some cards as well,' he said. 'Some of you boys are going to be worth a few quid in a couple of days and I want to lighten your wallets a little.'

'Christ, man,' Steve said irritably, 'haven't the bottle and the card-table got you in enough trouble already? You need to be on that boat by one-thirty and it's already eight . . . get some sleep, for God's sake.'

'I need a drink.'

'And *I* need to be fighting alongside blokes who aren't so pissed and so tired they can't shoot straight.'

Ollie took a step forward, so that he was standing two feet away from Steve. He wiped the grime and sweat from his face with the back of his hand. 'If anyone wants a drink, I say they can have one.'

'Well, I say they can't,' said Steve. 'And that's an—' He paused.

'What? An order?' There was a sneer in Ollie voice. 'I thought this unit was Regiment rules. Each man's voice is equal.'

From the corner of his eye, Steve could see Wallace walking across to join them, two bottles of rum in his hand.

'Ollie's in charge,' growled Wallace.

Steve looked at him furiously

'He's the officer, and in my book that makes him the bloke who runs the show. Doesn't matter whether it's regular Army or a bunch of money-grubbing chancers like you boys, the man who went to the right sort of school knows how to command. That's the way it's always been and that's the way it stays.'

He stared at them all, but especially at Steve. 'And if he says you boys can have a drink, then it's all right with me.'

Wallace removed the top from a bottle of locally brewed rum and slammed it down on the table.

'This job is dangerous enough without any bloody piss-heads around,' Steve objected angrily.

'Proper soldiers get their courage from a flag or an idea,' said Wallace. He laughed, and lit his cigar. 'But mercenaries? Ours comes from a chequebook or a bottle – and quite often both.'

'This is my unit now, mate,' Ollie told Steve. 'Now *you* get some bloody sleep.'

'Oliver's sodding Army, is it?' growled Steve. 'Well, good luck to you, you bastard. I hope you get shot to pieces.' And he stalked off towards the barracks room.

Without watching him leave, Ollie took a hit of the rum and started to deal out some cards. 'I'll deal you in, mate,' he said, glancing towards Dan. 'Maybe I can win that bar in Majorca off you.' He let the rum wash through him. 'Ice Cold Beer, Red Hot Girls,' he said, laughing to himself. 'Best advertising slogan I ever heard.'

Twenty-One

OLLIE CHECKED THAT EACH MAN was in place, before giving a signal to Ganju at the wheel. The patrol boat slipped smoothly out into the quiet waters of Lake Hasta, and started to push forwards. It was just after one-thirty in the morning, and although the sky was covered with dark clouds, so far there was no sign of rain. For that at least they could be grateful, decided Ollie. This job was going to be hard enough without fighting the weather as well.

Newton was in charge of navigating. He was the man who knew the lake, although in reality it was a simple enough task: just hug the shoreline and they'd get there soon enough. Tshaka didn't exactly have a Navy but he had a couple of patrol boats that kept order on the lake. Even though it was the dead of night, they had to be constantly on their guard. They were close to enemy territory now, and once they crossed that line, there was no going back.

Each man knew his role for the assault. Chris would man the KPV, because he was the strongest among them, and the heavy machine gun had such a brutal kick-back on it, it took the strength of an ox to keep it under control and on target. Ollie and Newton would take the two RPGs and put shell after shell into the wall of the fort. They already knew the position of the water pipes and would aim the shells straight at them: with any luck, the wall would be weak enough at that point for the explosives to bring it down. Ganju would stay at the wheel of the boat, and Nick would handle the MAG at the stern to shoot up anything coming at them from behind. If any of Tshaka's troops started to rush them, it would be his job to mow them down with the machine gun before they got anywhere close to the vessel.

Ollie was looking straight ahead, as the vessel ploughed steadily on. The diesel engines were rumbling and he was in no doubt that they could be heard from the banks. There was no way of moving without being detected. But they were keeping 100 yards from the shore, and with the thick clouds filling the sky, they should remain invisible if not inaudible.

Let's hope so anyway, he thought grimly. If we have to fight our way through to Elephant's Foot we're as good as done for.

His head was starting to clear. Last night, he had stayed up until eleven drinking the best part of a bottle of rum with Maksim and playing cards with Nick and Dan. The game had drifted into a stalemate, and by the end of it, they'd all been too drunk to remember what they'd been betting anyway. He got his head down for a couple of hours' kip, then woke up at one, had a final shave, packed his kit and his webbing with everything he'd need for the battle, and led the men down to the boat. Maybe Wallace was right, he thought with a thin smile. Maybe you did need to be made of the right stuff to lead the unit – and although Steve might be one of the bravest, most resourceful soldiers he'd ever met, when the crunch came he didn't have it. In the end, he wasn't an officer. And that made a difference.

Newton caught Ollie's eye. His finger was pointing to the map. 'We've passed into Tshaka's territory,' he said quietly.

Ollie nodded, his face determined. 'Then it's begun.'

Steve threw the remains of the coffee down the back of his throat. It tasted like filth, but he wasn't going to let that bother him now. Another forty-eight hours at most, he decided, looking into the dark clouds swirling overhead, then I'll be sitting back in a five-star suite in a Johannesburg hotel getting Samantha to wash bubbles over my back, sipping champagne, and watching Batota choose a new President on CNN. She'd be plenty grateful for seeing Kapembwa dead, thought Steve. And offhand, he could think of a dozen different ways she could demonstrate it.

We just need to get through the next couple of hours, he told himself. And keep our wits about us.

It was three-thirty in the morning, and he was sitting on the porch of the officer's mess. Ollie had led out his guys a couple of hours ago. The men going in on the chopper could get a bit more kip. The attack was scheduled for six, and the flight should only take half an hour, which meant nobody needed to get up before five. The better rested they were, the better they'd fight, but Steve could never sleep before a battle. He preferred to sit on the porch feeling the night breeze on his skin than lie around tossing and turning in bed.

Across in the field hospital, a man was groaning. The bloke who'd had his leg amputated had died in the night, his body put down to the side of the medical tent for burial in the morning. From the sound of the other guy, it didn't look as if he'd make it to the morning either. Kapembwa is losing this war, decided Steve. You could see it in the beating his troops were taking. It wasn't hard to understand why he wanted Tshaka dead. If the rebel commander lived, pretty soon he'd be strong enough to march on the capital.

For the next half an hour, Steve stripped down his AK-47, wiping each part clean, and reassembling it. Taking care of your weapon was basic drill and he never forgot it. He made sure the mag was full, and so was the spare. Once that was done, he carefully ran through the kit he'd be carrying with him. Every man had his own selection, and sometimes it had to be varied for the local conditions, but Steve had carried the same tools since his first live contact back in the Regiment. He always put his Kevlar body armour on first, and his webbing over that: if he needed something, he wanted to be able to get to it quickly without taking off the armour.

Inside, there were two pouches for maps, in case they got lost. There were two grenade pouches, both filled, and four long thin pouches for rifle magazines. The South-African-made AKs had thirty-round mags, which meant he had 150 rounds on him, including the rounds in his clip. But the first rule of any assault was also the simplest: you could never have too much ammo on you. Next to those were the field dressings: if you went down, you weren't going to be in any fit state to fix yourself, so you put those on the outside so one of your mates could rip them off and patch you up. Steve always carried at least two. One bandage would hold in about a pint of blood, but if you took a nasty hit, you were going to need two, minimum. He stuffed in enough food and water to last twenty-four hours: if you couldn't eat or drink, you were no use to anyone. Finally, he packed in a knife and a compass, whilst around his neck he clipped into place an old Army dog tag, plus a vial of morphine. At his side, he had a hard hat: it wouldn't stop a high-velocity bullet, but it would deal with shrapnel, and any glancing rounds. He checked and double-checked that everything was in place, not because he was likely to find anything missing, but because it stopped him from dwelling on the battle ahead.

'Christ, this coffee tastes like crap,' said David, joining Steve on the porch.

Inside, Ian, Maksim and Dan were hauling themselves out of the simple metal beds inside the barracks and washing themselves down.

'I can see why it's the Kenyan coffee that's world famous and not this rubbish,' continued David. 'I mean, you never see Batotean coffee in Tesco, do you? Not even in Aldi. Now we know why.' He drained the last of the tin mug, and took a slice of dry bread and some fruit to eat.

'What do you reckon on those clouds?' said Steve, pointing upwards.

David stared into the sky, a worried frown on his forehead. It was dark in the fort. There was no mains electricity, the power coming from a diesel generator that was switched off for most of the night to conserve the fort's meagre supply of fuel. The clouds were blocking out the moon and the stars, and only the oil torch Steve had lit earlier was providing any light on the porch. Yet even through the darkness, you could see the dampness in the clouds.

'Any chance of a weather forecast?' David asked.

Steve laughed. 'Out here? This mob haven't even got any anaesthetics in the medical tent.'

Both men were silent for a moment. They knew it was madness to attempt a chopper attack in the rain. In any kind of proper military action, the soldiers would have access to detailed weather information. Without it, they were flying into the unknown. And that was the one place you never wanted to go.

'If it starts to rain heavily, that's going to make things tricky,' said David. 'We need speed – it's the only advantage we have – and the rain will slow down the approach. If there are gusts of wind as well, it's going to be hard to hold the chopper steady.'

'Meaning?'

'You ever been dangled on the end of a rope like a puppet?'

Steve shook his head.

'You might be about to find out what it's like.'

'My stun bombs will still work,' said Ian. He helped himself to a cup of coffee, and joined them on the porch.

'Doesn't matter what the weather is like,' he continued. 'We'll still get the flash and the bang – and that should throw them off balance.'

'I'll tell you another thing,' said Maksim. 'If the weather's bad, the last thing they'll expect is a bunch of madmen dropping out of the sky.'

'I know it doesn't make any difference to the Spetsnaz, mate, but surprise means bugger all if we're all already dead.'

'You reckon we should abort?' said Ian.

'The way I heard it, Ollie's in charge now,' said Steve. 'We'll let him decide.' He stood up and started pulling his webbing into place.

'Don't listen to any of that public-school-man crap,' David advised. 'I've been on that treadmill and all it got me was a temporary job on the Algerian oil rigs. And that's about as far down the career ladder as you can get. Me and a few Somalis who couldn't even make it to Britain as asylum seekers. So just ignore Wallace's bullshit. It's where a man's going that counts, not where he came from.'

'Well, I reckon we're going straight on then, and getting the sodding job done,' said Steve. 'We'll radio through to Ollie and make a decision closer to the target.'

Ollie looked up into the sky.

He wasn't sure he'd ever seen such total darkness. The clouds were a thick, low blanket lying across the lake, smothering any light from the moon or stars. Ganju was steering the patrol boat steadily forwards but he was using the charts and the compass and its onboard radar. There was no point in trying to look at anything. If you held up your hand, you could barely even make out your own fingers.

Africa, thought Ollie to himself. It had the most brilliant, orange sunshine during the day, the warmest, most embracing light you had ever felt on your skin, but then when the sun went down, the nights were cold and dark and hostile, as if you were about to be sucked into an abyss. 'How far?' he hissed.

'We've covered about fifty miles,' Newton whispered. He was using a tiny flashlight to read the map. 'We're already into Tshaka's territory. We see anyone now, we should assume they're an enemy.'

I'm already assuming that, thought Ollie. I've been assuming it for days.

'We're on track,' murmured Ganju. 'It's three-thirty in the morning, so we should be getting close to the fort by around five. We'll slow right down for the final approach. We don't want to let the enemy know we're coming.'

That's for sure, thought Ollie.

He could feel a smattering of rain on his cheeks.

'Christ,' he muttered quietly. There were just specks of rain. But they were damp and cold, and blown sideways in the wind: the kind of raindrops that warned of stormy weather ahead.

The Alouette lifted jerkily into the sky.

David was crouched over the controls, pulling on the throttle to coax more power out of the engine. The clouds were thick, and the wind was starting to howl up from the lake, buffeting the chopper as it groaned and heaved itself upwards.

Steve was sitting right behind him, with Dan at his side. Opposite them, Maksim and Ian were hanging onto the metal handlebars. Ian had lined up his six stun grenades in a neat row, ready to be tossed onto the ground. The Alouette had open doors for ease of access, but that meant it was a far from pleasant ride. The chopper was rocking from side to side as it climbed, and Steve's insides were starting to feel as if they'd been put through a washing machine. Clutching the handlebars, he closed his eyes for a second. Just punch your way through this, he told himself, gritting his teeth.

At 5,000 feet the standard cruising altitude for the Alouette, the chopper started to level out. They had pulled through the low-lying clouds, and were suddenly bathed in the light of the moon. To the east, the sun was starting to rise. It was a brilliant orange, sending shafts of light bouncing across the clouds beneath them. For a moment, Steve just stared into it, breathless at the beauty of the scene. It was strange how the world often looked at its most stunning in the moment before you went into battle. A reminder, he reflected, of what you might be about to leave behind.

David had already charted their course across to Elephant's Foot. They were flying due east, straight into the sunrise, and tracking the contours of the lake. Then they'd tack south, before turning around and attacking the fort. They'd drop down low for the last three miles, skimming the surface of the ground, flying at between seventy-five and a hundred feet. They had no intelligence on whether the fort was equipped with radar, but they had to assume that it was: at that height, they'd be flying low enough to stay safely below any radar screens.

Ian was looking down into the clouds below them. The rising gale was swirling through the sky, slowing the chopper down as it struggled to press through the headwinds. 'It looks like a storm to me,' he shouted above the roar of the three-blade rotor.

'When we're ten miles out, we contact Ollie on the radio,' yelled Steve. 'We'll make a decision on the weather when we've spoken to him.'

He didn't want to abort. None of them did. Once you'd psyched yourself up to go into battle, there was nothing worse than having to stand down.

But a helicopter drop in a full-blown storm?
That was madness.

The rain was starting to lash into Ollie's face.

The sun was rising in the east, creating a soft, hazy glow across the lake. Ganju had turned the engine right down, so it was running at little more than a murmur. He'd steered the boat out to a couple of hundred yards from the shore, but the rain was making so much noise as it hit the lake it was unlikely they'd be heard even up close.

Ahead, Ollie could see a crack of lightning opening up the sky. He took a deep breath, counting the time before he heard the clap of thunder to try and get a measure of how far away the storm was. It could be centred twenty miles ahead of them, and they were still ten miles from the fort, which meant they wouldn't be fighting right in the thick of it. But we'll be close, decided Ollie. Maybe too damned close.

'Get Steve on the radio,' he said Ganju. 'We need to see if he can get a fix on the weather from the air.'

Newton had taken the wheel whilst Ganju was fiddling with the radio. It was a simple two-way transceiver of the type used by armies right around the world for close-combat communications. There were up to 1,840 different channels, and Ganju had added a simple scrambler as well. Unless the fort was equipped with high-level detection equipment, and so long as they restricted communications to no more than four- or five-second bursts, there was very little chance of the conversation being detected. 'Come in, come in,' hissed Ganju into the receiver.

Ollie was staring straight ahead. As the sun rose, there was a thin layer of mist on the water. The rain was coming down harder all the time, lashing into his face, seeping into his clothes and boots. It was impossible to see more than a dozen yards ahead, but from the charts, he could see they were approaching the final bend that would take them in close to the fort.

He checked his watch. Ten minutes to six . . .

Not much time left.

'Come in, come in,' Ganju said urgently, louder this time.

'Chopper receiving, chopper receiving,' came the reply. Even through the haze and crackle, Steve's voice was clearly recognisable.

'What's the weather like?' Ganju asked. As he spoke, another crack of lightning was followed by a rattle of thunder.

Ollie was looking towards Ganju, waiting for the reply. At his side, Newton was steering the patrol boat relentlessly forward. The bend was looming ever closer. A point, judged Ollie, of no return.

Get round that bend, and they'd be visible from the fort.

We'll have to stand and fight. No matter what odds we may be facing.

'What's the weather like?' repeated Ganju.

There was a burst of static. Then silence.

'Repeat, chopper, weather update,' said Ganju. 'Attack today question. Decide now . . .'

Ollie was glancing between Ganju and the radio. But there was nothing.

Just another piercing stab of lightning, a rolling blast of thunder and rain lashing hard into his face.

'Christ,' he muttered out loud. 'We can't attack in this.'

Steve slammed his fists together in frustration. He pushed the headphones away. Sweat was forming on his face.

'We've only sodding lost radio contact,' he snarled.

'It's the storm,' shouted David. 'The lightning . . . it's fucked the shortwave radio.'

Steve stared down at the clouds swirling beneath them. There was a flash of purple – evidence of lightning. It was almost certainly raining heavily down there. The weather was about to get rough . . . brutally rough.

'We're five miles from the target,' David bellowed. 'Either we abort or we drop down through the clouds now.'

Steve glanced into the faces of the men around him. They were tense, frowning – hanging onto the handlebars for dear life.

'We bloody do this!' shouted Maksim above the wind. 'The Spetsnaz had a simple rule. When you throw a punch, you never pull it.'

'We can't contact Ollie.' Ian spoke next. 'Even if we're pulling back, there's no way of warning them, and we can't leave them to go in by themselves. They'll be slaughtered.'

'He might have decided to pull back,' Steve said.

'Nah. He's too obstinate,' said Ian.

Next, Steve looked at Dan. They could only do this if each man agreed. He wasn't going to force anyone to drop down into a firefight like this.

Each bloke had to make his own decision.

The Australian nodded curtly, without a moment's hesitation.

Steve clamped a hand on David's shoulder. 'We're on, mate,' he said, with a tense grin. 'Drop this bastard out of the sky.'

*

'Tell them to pull back!' shouted Ollie.

The patrol boat was nearing the bend. A vicious wind was spinning across the lake, kicking up waves that were hurling spray across the bow. The vessel was swaying in the stormy waters. It was impossible to see more than a few feet in front of them.

Ollie addressed himself to Chris and Ganju.

'It's bloody madness,' he roared. 'They can't bring that chopper down in this storm, and we can't hold this damned ship steady enough to fire into the fort.'

Both men nodded their agreement.

Ganju was working the radio furiously. He was twisting the knobs, trying to get a signal, but it was useless. 'It's the storm!' he shouted. 'We're not going to get through.'

'With any luck, Steve will pull back,' said Chris.

'I wouldn't count on it,' Ollie told him. 'We've all seen that bastard in a scrap. The man doesn't know when he's beaten.'

Newton was steering the patrol boat around the bend. Suddenly, through the mist and the rain, the fort at Elephant's Foot was clearly visible.

Up above them, there was a roll of thunder, so loud and close it sounded as if the earth around them was opening up. Then there was another sound.

The rotorblades of a chopper.

Ollie spun around. Half a mile behind them, the Alouette was skimming across the lake. Within a minute, it would be over the fort.

'We're going in!' he bawled.

And God help us.

Twenty-Two

THE CHOPPER WAS KNOCKED SIDEWAYS as it plunged suddenly into the low cloud. It bounced for a second, then started its descent. David was struggling to hold the machine steady, while Steve was clinging desperately to the handlebar, and repeating the same words over and over again.

'*Our Father, Who art in heaven, hallowed be Thy name . . .*'

Then: 'Sod it,' he muttered out loud, as the Alouette jerked and swayed, and the first blast of rain lashed in from the open doorways. 'It's too late to start praying now.'

At his side, Maksim was spewing up the rum he'd drunk last night. Dan coughed – once, then twice – then heaved his guts onto the floor. He was far too experienced a soldier to try and hold it in: when you were flying a helicopter below the radar, the ride was so rough even a dead man would start throwing up. The sooner you got it over with, the better. But Steve was still fighting it, holding his stomach tight as the Alouette jolted and rocked through the air.

The pit of the machine was like a sick bowl, the vomit mixing with the rain and swilling around their boots, creating a vile, foamy stench. Steve couldn't even look at it, but the smell was enough. He heaved, throwing up into the mixture, then wiped his mouth with the back of his hand, spitting as he did so.

The chopper was descending rapidly towards the lake. David

steadied it at seventy-five feet from the surface. The rain was intense, with great sheets of water falling in front of them, and Steve knew at once they had made a mistake. You should never even contemplate a chopper attack in this kind of weather.

Too late to turn back now.

Up ahead, he could see the patrol boat steaming up close to the port. The men were lined up on its prow, trying to hold themselves steady as the vessel dipped and rose in the waves.

'We'll be there in ten,' shouted Steve. 'Get ready.'

The land was passing beneath them, then they were skimming over the walls of the fort. They'd planned for Ollie to start bombing the walls before the chopper dropped out of the sky but that part of the assault had already gone pear-shaped. David was cursing as he battled with the controls of the Alouette, shouting at the engines as he tried desperately to coax enough power from the machine to stabilise it.

Ian was knocking the stun grenades down onto the ground.

'Ear-mufflers, glasses!' he yelled.

Next, there was a huge explosion – a sound so brutal and cruel it cracked open the air. Steve had only just pulled on his mufflers and his glasses as the noise erupted from the ground, making every bolt and join in the Alouette shudder and shake. It was followed by a flash of pure white light, as blinding and intense as the hottest sun, and for a moment even the storm itself appeared quelled into submission by the force of the explosions.

'*Go, go, go!*' screamed Steve.

He could see a moment's hesitation in the faces of the men around him. They were the bravest soldiers he'd ever met, but even the stoutest heart wasn't built for a task of this magnitude.

'*Just bloody go!*' he yelled, almost shredding his lungs with the volume of the command.

Unhooking his rope, he flung himself from the open chopper, and immediately could feel himself dropping through the air.

And as he glanced down, it looked as if he was falling through the gates of hell.

Ollie flinched as the noise of the stun grenades rocked out over the lake. Then he permitted himself a brief smile.

'Bloody madmen,' he said to Chris.

But there was no time for a reply. Through the spray and wind, the fort was looming up at them. At 100 yards' distance, you could see the strength of its walls. The thick slabs of concrete rose up out of the ground, presenting a formidable obstacle. Rainwater was pouring off its sides, creating hundreds of tiny streams down to the lake, and the few yards between the shore and the wall were already a churned, muddy mess.

Ganju had slowed the engine to a crawl, steering carefully, his eyes rooted to the radar as they completed the last few yards of their approach. The lake might well have been mined, he judged, with only a narrow, clear channel left for Tshaka's own men to get in and out. Touch one of those and the patrol boat would be blown into the sky.

'Steady!' yelled Ollie, wiping the spray from his face.

Smoke was rising from inside the fort, he noted. The stun grenades had ignited one after another, creating a pyrotechnic display of awesome power. The flashes lit up the dark morning sky with brilliant light, whilst the echo of the explosions filled the lake with a ghostly noise.

'Ready your firing positions,' Ollie commanded.

Chris was at the KPV and Nick had manned one of the two MAGs at the back of the boat, whilst Ganju was holding the wheel steady. Ollie and Newton had picked up the two RPGs, positioning the heavy steel tubes on their shoulders. Ollie was scanning the ground, following the water pipes up to the wall. He held himself as still as he could.

'*Fire!*' he bellowed.

As he spoke, a wave kicked into the prow, jerking the boat

upwards. Ollie loosened off his rocket, the device fizzing through the air. It missed the wall entirely, exploding inside the fort. Ganju's rocket fared only slightly better, striking the wall two feet below the parapet, knocking loose some dust and concrete, but not doing any real damage.

We have to strike the foundations, Ollie told himself. That's the only way we're going to blast through the wall.

'Steady the boat, steady the boat,' he shouted towards Newton.

Yet even as he spoke, another strong wave rocked into the side of the vessel.

'Bloody hell,' he spat angrily.

This is a sodding disaster.

Steve hung onto the rope for dear life.

He was hurtling down into the fort. The stun grenades were still fizzing and popping all around him, the echoes of the blast fading only slowly. The afterglow of the flashes created a hazy, yellow light, like stepping right inside a light bulb. The chopper was jerking in the sky, due to the brutal weather, and the wind was starting to pick up force as the impact of the explosions, which had briefly sucked most of the air out of the fort, started to subside. Steve began to sway from side to side.

He looked down. Even though he was at the end of the rope, he was still fifteen feet from the ground. Suddenly, the Alouette twitched upwards: Steve was twenty feet from the ground now. Broken ankle territory, he told himself grimly.

'Drop – fucking drop now!' he yelled to the other men. But they all had ear mufflers on to protect them from the stun grenades, so there was no way they could hear anything.

Steve let go of the rope.

Tucking his legs up into a foetal position, he took the impact of the landing on his side. He rolled to absorb the blow, and felt a horrible punch in his ribs as he did so. In the same movement, he whipped the AK-47 from his chest and rolled once more before turning himself upwards into a crouching position. The parade ground where they'd come down was still filled with smoke, making it impossible to see more than a few feet ahead, but Steve knew the enemy would have been aware of the assault for at least a minute now, and that was more than enough time to prepare a response.

Everything depended on hitting the enemy with such total force and shock that they were destroyed before they could organise themselves. If they got into a fair fight, then the unit was done for.

He slammed his finger hard on the trigger. A lethal burst of fire blasted out of the weapon.

Behind him, Maksim had taken up the same position, his AK locked onto automatic, spewing out bullets. Dan had crashed to the ground, swearing violently as he rolled with the impact and struggled to get his gun into position. Ian had attempted to throw himself into the fort but the rope had snagged on his foot, and had suddenly jerked him upwards, turning him upside down. The Alouette was starting to lift itself back up into the air, pulling Ian upwards by the foot. The man was screaming in agony.

'Cut him down, cut him down!' yelled Steve.

Through the clearing smoke, he saw a figure starting to run towards him. Lifting his AK-47 to his face, he pulled the trigger and slotted two bullets cleanly into the man's chest.

Christ, please let David see what's happening, Steve told himself as he turned around to see Ian lifted upwards.

Dan was running towards Ian with his knife, while up above, David was trying to lower the Alouette.

Dan leaped up, grabbing hold of Ian's legs and slashing at the rope with his knife. The nylon was strong but eventually gave way, and both men came crashing down to the ground, swearing and shouting as they did so. The chopper was lifting back into the sky, but 100 feet away, a machine gun had started to splutter into life. Fire and metal was pouring from its short stubby barrel, directed upwards into the innards of the chopper.

The Alouette was twisting into the sky, but there was thick black smoke billowing from its gearbox, and even from the ground you could hear the engine spluttering.

'Where the fuck is Ollie?' screamed Steve. 'We're about to take a beating here.'

Ollie looked into the smoke and debris, but could see that so far they hadn't put much more than a scratch on the surface of the wall. Chris had opened up an intense blast of fire, but even the heavy-calibre bullets of the KPV weren't doing anything more than chipping away at its surface.

A unit of three men was advancing towards them on the shore, a patrol sent to find out what the hell was happening. When they saw the boat, they opened fire with their automatic rifles, the bullets smattering its skin. Nick immediately swivelled around the MAG, cutting down all three men with lethal efficiency.

'Cover me!' he yelled, and jumped into the water. The patrol boat was still ten yards into the lake, swaying in the choppy waters. Nick started to wade ashore. Behind him, Newton had grabbed his AK-47 and was peppering a line of bullets over Nick's head to prevent anyone stepping out to confront him. As Nick emerged onto the shore, he ran for the short jetty, grabbed a rope and tossed it towards the boat. The rain was beating hard into him but he held himself steady as Ganju caught the rope and twisted it around the boat's prow. Putting all his strength into it, Nick started to haul on the rope, tugging it into the jetty, steadying the vessel as he did so.

'OK – hold it right there,' shouted Ollie. 'Just bloody hold it.'

In an instant, he had raised the RPG and slammed a missile straight into the wall. This time, with the boat steadied, it exploded just where the pipes went in. At his side, Ganju had done the same.

Another direct hit. The pipes broke open, sending water flying everywhere, and the wall above was starting to splinter. Ollie reloaded, fired, then reloaded again. The KPV was filling the wall with a constant barrage of lead, spitting and chewing at the concrete.

Then, a crash.

The defences were broken.

A cloud of dust kicked upwards, as a section of wall five yards wide collapsed onto itself. The debris was instantly soaked by the rain, creating a sodden mess of rubble. As the dust started to subside, beaten down by the rain, there was a flurry of activity behind the wall, as a group of soldiers rushed into position.

Chris lined up the KPV. 'Get your head down!' he bawled towards Nick.

Nick threw himself to the ground as Chris opened up with the huge machine gun. He could feel a solid wall of hot lead fly over his head. The bullets sprayed into the wall, cutting down the men who had fallen into the breach. The rattle of the gunfire mixed with the screams of the dying men, the pitiful sound echoing out across the stormy lake.

'Another RPG round,' shouted Ollie.

He put a missile into the breached wall, then another. Mounds of brick spat into the air as the explosions blew chunks of the defences apart. More screams howled upwards, as the detonations and then the shrapnel sliced chunks out of the men desperately trying to defend the fort.

'Charge the bastards,' Ollie ordered. Then, without a moment's hesitation, and without waiting for any replies, he gripped hold of his AK-47 and started to run towards the wall.

David sensed immediately what the trouble was. A bullet had smashed the gearbox to pieces. A lucky shot? he wondered grimly. Probably not. The soldiers down there knew what aircraft the Government forces had, and they knew their weaknesses. The unit should have thought of that, and used a machine they weren't familiar with, he realised now. Too late.

The Alouette was finished.

There was still enough power in the engine to climb up to 800 feet. The cabin was starting to fill with grimy black smoke. The carbon monoxide was swirling everywhere but, with the doors open, there was little chance of suffocating. David felt strangely calm. He knew precisely what he was going to do. Now all he had to do was finish it.

He kicked as much power as he could into the rear rotor and steered the chopper out towards the lake. The main blade was still turning but spluttering badly. The rear rotor was doing its job, but as the main blade lost power, there soon wouldn't be enough power to steer by. He could see the fort, a mix of smoke and fire, beneath him. He could also see the patrol boat, tethered to the jetty now, and Ollie leading his men into the breach in the wall. And then he could see the rough waves of the lake, its surface whipped up by the wind.

The main blade was weakening all the time, turning slower and slower. You could hear the shot-up gearbox grinding, sparks flying as metal scratched against metal. It wasn't generating enough power to maintain its altitude any more.

Any second now, the Alouette would literally drop out of the sky.

Taking one long, hard breath, and then, without even looking down, David Mallet tossed himself from the side of the Alouette and started to fall towards the lake.

Steve watched the chopper tumble out of the sky and into the lake, spitting smoke and flame as it started to break up. 'There goes our exit, boys,' he said sternly. 'We stay and fight here, and we'll die if we have to, because our bus home just crashed.'

He took a brief, anxious second to assess their situation. Totally fucked? No, not yet. Not while they were still standing, anyway.

The fort at least was in total disarray. They had landed towards the back of the parade ground, close to the main entrance. Ten yards to their left, there was a shooting range that would provide some cover. At the back, the dust and noise kicked up by the RPG rounds suggested Ollie had breached the wall. A dozen men had come out to rush them as the chopper landed, but the stun grenades had done their work with lethal efficiency. The troops on the ground had been so overwhelmed by the sudden power of the attack, their first response had been feeble and confused, and the few men who had tried to counter-attack had been easily cut down by the guns of the men bailing out of the chopper. Their corpses were lying all around them, wounds cut open in their faces and chests, the sodden ground already red with their blood. A couple were still alive, moaning pitifully, but there was no way anyone could help them now.

The real test, Steve knew, was about to begin.

A column of ten men was preparing to break out of the main barracks.

'Take cover,' he shouted, pointing towards the shooting range.

He held himself steady, laying down constant fire from his AK-47, moving backwards as he did so. The four men retreated in a steady line, putting round after round of ammunition into their opponents. It was only ten yards but it felt like fifty, as the bullets started to spit into the ground around them. The rain was still falling hard, soaking through their clothes and turning the ground to mud. But, as the smoke cleared, the visibility was improving.

We can see the enemy now, Steve told himself.

And they can see us.

He threw himself behind the wooden fence that was used for target practice. Three feet across and five feet high, it was sturdily built and there was a steel plate down its centre. On an assault in Bosnia, back in the Regiment, Steve had learned that a firing range was the perfect place to take cover: it was built to withstand bullet after bullet. He checked that Ian, Maksim and Dan were safely in place then peered out around the wall.

A kid was running towards them, a hand grenade clutched in his fist.

The lad was no more than ten, judged Steve. Short and stocky, he had a goofy smile on his face, and was wearing a fake Manchester United shirt. He pulled the pin from the grenade and kept on running, heading straight for the wall. Christ, thought Steve. A child soldier. You get them all over Africa. *And they're using him to kill us.*

He lined up the child in the sights of his AK-47, but his finger jammed in the trigger. In his mind, he could see the kid's brains getting blown apart by the bullet, his crooked smile disappearing for ever, and he couldn't do it.

Then the child fell. A bullet had smacked into his face, blowing it half away, whilst his body tumbled on top of the grenade. He was blown apart, his intestines flying out across the fort.

'You bloody bottled it,' snarled Maksim, smoke still rising from the barrel of his AK-47.

'He was a child,' Steve said.

Maksim shrugged. 'He was going to kill us.'

Steve knew he was right.

'That's a weakness,' the Russian said. 'And a soldier shouldn't allow himself any of those.'

There was no time for Steve to reply. Ten men were advancing steadily towards them, laying down round after round from their assault rifles. The bullets were cutting into the wall, chewing up clumps of wood. Steve took aim, planning to bring at least one man down, but the fire was too intense. He couldn't line up any kind of a shot without getting his face blown off. At his side, Ian had ripped free a grenade, tossing it over the parapet, but before it could explode, one of the men had kicked it away, so it exploded harmlessly twenty yards away.

We're pinned down, realised Steve. We can't move out of here, and we can't strike back.

And where the hell has Ollie got to?

Twenty-Three

OLLIE WAS LEADING THE CHARGE through the breach that had been blasted in the fort's wall. There were mounds of rubble strewn across the ground and, amidst the debris, the corpses of a dozen men who had died trying to hold the defences.

Ollie heard a groan to his left. He looked around and saw a man's hand reaching out towards him. He was horribly mutilated, his torso ripped to shreds, and one leg blown clean off, but he was still hanging onto life. Ollie grabbed his Uzi and put two clean pistol shots through the man's face, killing him instantly. We're not giving these bastards any chance to regroup themselves and start fighting back, he told himself fiercely.

'Take the barracks!' he shouted.

Looking through the fort, Ollie reckoned at least half the soldiers inside had died in the initial assault. There were twelve men down at the wall, and another eight corpses were spread out close to where the chopper had come down. They must have died when Steve and his boys had put down their first rounds of fire.

Fifteen yards to his left, the officer's mess was quiet. Ollie reckoned Tshaka would be holed up in there while his men repelled the attack. Twenty yards to his right, the main barracks building was still held by a group of men with a machine gun. And across the parade ground, ten men were steadily advancing towards where Steve had taken cover behind the shooting range.

Ollie took a second to assess his options. They had to help out Steve and his guys. But they had to take out the machine gun inside the barracks as well. If they didn't, they'd get mown down as they tried to cross the parade ground.

'Newton,' he snapped. 'The gun.'

'It's . . .'

Ollie knew at once what the man was about to say.

It's suicide.

But Newton was the only one among them who'd never proved himself in combat. If there was a nasty scrap to be fought, that meant he was the man holding the short straw. Even though they needed him to talk to his brother, they couldn't let him duck a scrap. He knew it himself: it sounded as if he'd been about to say something, but he'd caught the words before they escaped his lips.

'I'll go,' was all he said.

There were almost certainly men stationed at every point round the barracks. The only way to take out a machine gun was to come around the back. But Tshaka's guys looked professional enough to have stationed a guard to protect their flanks. If anyone came close, they'd get gunned down.

'I'll go with him,' said Nick quickly.

The two men veered right. The back of the fort was empty now, and Nick and Newton had the advantage that no one could see them as they approached the barracks block from behind. There was a long back wall to the block, made of wood, with a doorway at the side. The only windows were at the front.

'I'm going in,' said Newton.

'Don't be fucking stupid,' Nick objected.

But Newton had already clamped the Uzi into his fist.

'They're not sending me back to Broken Ridge, or any other jail,' he said. 'I've had my first taste of freedom in ten years, and if I have to pay for that with my life, then I won't be complaining.' Kicking back with his heels, he then threw himself at the door.

It crashed open easily enough. Newton was a big man, and even though his weight had whittled away during the years in prison, there was enough of him to bring down most obstacles. He rolled onto the floor, his shoulder already badly bruised, and screaming with pain. Two guards were standing by the door, and another three men were manning the machine gun. Raising the Uzi, Newton slammed his finger on the trigger and the bullets spat from the barrel of the gun in a hot, angry barrage. The Uzi was capable of firing 1,000 rounds a minute: its rapid bursts of fire were what made it so deadly in close-quarters combat, but also incredibly difficult to control.

The first guard took six rounds to his chin. By the time Newton adjusted his aim, the man's jaw had been splintered into a dozen different fragments, and most of his face had been shot clean away. He was staggering around, blinded and dying. The second guard took a dozen bullets to his chest, collapsing to the ground in a heap of blood. Without even releasing his finger from the trigger, Newton turned the Uzi towards the machine gunners. One of the three men had managed to draw his own handgun and put one bullet straight into Newton, but it was caught by his Kevlar body armour and, apart from a tear to his shirt, and another nasty bruise to his chest, he was unhurt.

The Uzi's 9mm bullets ripped into the men in an unstoppable assault of flying metal. None of them were wearing body armour and it wouldn't have made any difference anyway. More than fifty rounds flew into them in the space of a couple of seconds, and although the Uzi wasn't capable of much accuracy, the bullets were puncturing lungs, hearts and brains. In a fraction of a second, all three men had died. Newton released his finger from the trigger. The magazine was empty. The pain in his shoulder was intense and his chest was injured from the bullet to his body armour.

'Drop it, drop it, drop it!' shouted a soldier. He was standing at the back of the barracks block, twenty feet away, pointing his AK-47 straight at Newton. 'One move and you're a fucking dead man.'

There was no time for Newton to reload. He'd be dead before he even reached for the mag.

In the doorway, Nick raised his own AK-47 to his shoulder. He took only a fraction of a second to compose the shot. The soldier was cleanly lined up in his sights, but Nick already knew he'd only get one crack at this. If the man wasn't killed instantly he'd put enough shots into Newton to finish him in less than a second. Adjusting the aim by a micro-millimetre to make sure the bullet would blast into the man's skull right in the centre of the forehead, he muttered softly, '*Kill*,' and squeezed the trigger.

'Thanks, mate,' said Newton with a crooked half-smile as the man crumpled meekly to the ground, his brains already shot out.

Nick grabbed him by the hand, and pulled Newton to his feet. He ran towards the machine-gun post, and looked out into the parade ground. The ten men were still advancing steadily on the shooting range, laying down a murderous rate of fire straight into the position held by Steve and his unit.

'Go, go, go!' shouted Nick, looking back to where Ollie, Ganju and Chris were stationed. 'The gun is down . . .'

Steve was starting to lose count of how many bullets had shaved past him. A dozen, two dozen – it didn't make any difference, did it?

The ground all around them was churned into a hot muddy soup of dirt and lead. The rain was lashing into their position and a fierce wind was whipping through the fort. All four men were hunkered behind the wall, their guns at the ready. In front of them, the wall was steadily being chipped away, its edges splintering as the bullets pummelled into it. Maksim had already lobbed another two grenades over the top, but both, like the one Ian had thrown, had been kicked away by the soldiers.

'We need a stun grenade,' said Steve, glancing towards Ian. 'Something to distract these blokes long enough to put some ammo into the bastards.'

'None left,' Ian said tersely.

'Christ, man, couldn't you have brought some more?'

'Well, why didn't you bloody bring them?' growled Ian. 'This operation was meant to be wrapped up in the first three minutes.'

'Well, it sodding isn't – and we need something to break out of here.'

'A volunteer,' said Dan. His voice was strained and there was rainwater running down his sturdy face.

Steve remained silent. He knew exactly what Dan was getting at, and it wasn't a comfortable thought.

'One bloke gets out there and puts some fire into those men, distracts them – then the rest of us let them have it from the other direction.'

'Suicide,' granted Ian. 'The bloke won't stand a chance.'

'I know,' said Dan. He fell quiet for a second. 'But it's better that one bloke dies than all of us. It's the only way.'

'We draw straws,' said Maksim.

'No straws,' said Steve firmly. 'We'll give Ollie another five seconds to bring up the cavalry. After that, *I'll* go . . .'

His lungs were already bursting as he opened his eyes. He'd tried to hit the water with his legs and arms together, to minimise the impact of the fall, but the waves and the wind had knocked him off-course and it had turned into a belly flop that even his kids would be embarrassed by. A wave crashed over his head, and although he struggled to stay focused, David could feel himself briefly losing consciousness. Fatal, he told himself, as his brain became woozy. Lose it underwater and you'll drown within a couple of minutes.

He kicked back with his legs. He reckoned he'd dropped twenty-five feet into the water, but the lake was far deeper than that. It was pitch black, and he was only too aware that there were crocodiles all around him. He wouldn't see them coming, but they could see and smell him, he could be certain of that. Kicking harder, he struggled for the surface, and when he finally broke through, took a huge lungful of air, coughing violently as the oxygen mixed with the water in his lungs. Then he looked around, trying to get a measure of how far he was from the shore. Despite the rain pummelling the water, he could see it was only thirty yards. Taking another deep breath, he started to swim.

A minute later, David pulled himself up onto the shore, panting and bruised.

He looked up at the fort ahead of him. His ears were still clogged from the water, but as soon as they started to clear he could hear explosions and gunfire. 'Jesus wept,' he muttered aloud. 'This was meant to be over by now.'

His AK-47 was gone, but his Uzi machine pistol was still strapped firm to his chest webbing, protected by a waterproof pouch. He pulled the gun free, fired one shot to make sure it hadn't been damaged by the soaking, then started to hurry towards the fort.

A boy was running away. No more than twelve, reckoned David.

He fired two warning shots into the child's path. 'Hold it right there, you little bugger,' he growled.

'Straight into their backs, boys,' hissed Ollie, his voice hoarse and angry.

He, Chris and Ganju had slipped around to the back of the parade ground. The barracks block was to one side of them, its machine gun now silenced. The officer's mess was to their other side. Straight ahead of them, they could see the line of men advancing on Steve's position.

Chris had ripped the drum from his ammo belt that would turn his AK-47 into a crude machine gun. Slamming the drum into the weapon, he held it tight to his chest. There was no time to set it up on a tripod: he was going to fire straight from the shoulder.

'Let rip,' ordered Ollie.

Simultaneously, Ollie and Ganju started firing with their own AK-

47s. Ollie had taken careful aim at one of the men, slotting a bullet neatly into the back of his head, sending the man tumbling to the ground. He felt a brief pang of guilt: there was no military task he hated more than shooting an enemy in the back. But it was Chris who was doing the real damage. The bullets were spitting out of the automated AK at a terrifying rate, punching holes in the line of men. The gun was virtually impossible to control held in your hands, its kickback potentially lethal even for a man of Chris's strength and experience. He held it steady for three seconds, putting twenty rounds into the line and bringing down five of the men before it flew from his hand, smashing into the muddy ground, a couple of live rounds still spitting angrily from its barrel.

Seven of the ten men had been taken down in the first assault, five of them killed instantly, two more wounded, their blood seeping out of them, and washed into the streams of water running across the parade ground. Two men had started to run towards Steve's position. A third had turned, slamming his finger on the trigger of his rifle, but only managing to get off one poorly aimed shot before Ganju calmly put the man's chest in the sights of his AK-47 and punched a bullet clean through his heart.

'Break-out,' snapped Steve. 'The reinforcements are here at last.'

He stepped out from behind the wall, his gun tucked into his chest. Two men were running straight towards them, their faces contorted into expressions of pure hatred: they were charging with the fury of soldiers who knew they'd already lost the battle. With Maksim and Dan, Steve formed a small unit, crouching down and unleashing a volley of fire that ripped straight through the two troopers, stopping them as if they'd been hit by a truck. For a brief moment, they were motionless, before tumbling towards the ground.

Steve raised a hand.

There was no point in using up any more ammo.

The soldiers defending the fort were all dead.

Twenty-Four

S TEVE CHECKED HIS WATCH. IT was only eight minutes since they'd dropped out of the chopper, but it seemed like hours had gone by. The fort had been smashed to pieces. There were bodies lying everywhere, their blood spilled out over the parade ground, but already the fierce rain was washing it clean. The stench of gunpowder and charred metal lay heavy in the air, and yet the howling wind was blowing that away as well.

Ollie walked across to where Steve was standing.

'Christ, man, I was trying to get you on the radio to tell you to abort,' he said. 'There was no way we should have tried this in such bad weather.'

'And I tried to get you . . .' Steve laughed, the relief at finding himself alive and his enemy vanquished suddenly flooding through him. 'And I decided you're such an awkward bastard you'd press on anyway, so I'd better help you out.'

Ollie grinned. 'I'd do the same for you.'

'Don't count on it, mate. Next time, I'm pissing off.'

Within a minute, all the men had assembled on the parade ground. Newton had dislocated his shoulder, and Ian had a sprain to his ankle that would leave him hobbling for a couple of days. There were cuts and bruises on all of them, but it was nothing that wouldn't heal up. For the risk they had run in attempting the assault in this weather, they were in far better shape than they had any right to be,

Steve told himself. Even without the chopper, it had better be a smooth run home.

Because we've already used up our full quota of luck on this job.

Ganju quickly sorted out Newton's shoulder. He ripped a vial of morphine from his webbing, and injected it into the man. Then Chris held him down, while Ganju skilfully wrenched his shoulder back into position. It hurt like hell, even with the morphine, but Newton had the strength to take the punishment. Nick had already told everyone how the man had risked his life to take out the machine gun, and Newton was starting to be accepted as part of the unit. It was only when you were plunged into the ferocious heat of combat that you found out who your mates were, decided Steve – and Newton had proved himself as much as any man. Maybe more so.

'What happened to David?' asked Steve, looking around the parade ground.

Already, he was fearing the worst. He'd seen the chopper catch fire out over the lake, but he hadn't seen David bail out. Maybe he had been trapped inside? Or maybe he'd drowned after hitting the water. It was very easy to lose consciousness bailing out – and if that happened, you were dead.

'I'm right here,' said David, walking across the parade ground to join them.

He was wet through, but then they all were. His clothes were torn, and his eyes looked bloodshot. But he was alive, that was the main thing. He was holding a boy by the torn collar of his shirt. The lad was aged about twelve, with huge frightened eyes.

'This little sod was trying to scarper out of here,' said David.

'He'll raise the alarm,' said Dan anxiously. 'There could easily be reinforcements stationed nearby. The kid goes to get them – we're done for.'

Maksim stepped forwards, his Uzi machine pistol in his hand. 'Then we finish him right here,' he growled.

'No,' said Steve.

'We haven't got time for prisoners.'

'He's just a kid.'

Maksim stepped forwards, raising the Uzi level with the boy's head. The child looked bewildered, too confused even to be afraid.

Ollie grabbed Maksim's shoulder. 'No,' he said. 'Leave it. If the kid makes a run for it, you can shoot him, but until then we leave him right here.'

'I'm not risking it,' stated Maksim angrily.

'You shoot him, we shoot you,' said David.

Reluctantly, Maksim lowered the gun. Steve was already looking towards the officer's mess. They'd taken the fort, but they hadn't taken the man they'd come to look for yet. It was a simple bungalow, fifty feet by twenty, with maybe three rooms inside, constructed from concrete breeze blocks with some white paint on them that had long since faded. The roof was made of corrugated iron, the rainwater splashing off its surface and onto the ground.

'I saw four men rush in there when the smoke cleared from the stun grenades,' he said. 'I reckon Tshaka's in there, and those blokes are protecting him.'

Ollie nodded. The building was thirty yards across the parade ground, with no windows. Nobody could shoot into or out of it. 'Then let's get the bastard out.'

There was one wounded man on the ground, moaning in pain, but Maksim finished him off with a quick pair of bullets to the head. The victim was too badly wounded to be treated, and anyway, they couldn't waste time on casualties. Ollie and Steve marched down towards the officer's block, their guns kept cocked all the time. There might be more men hidden somewhere, they knew, and a bullet could come flying at them any time.

'We know you're in there,' shouted Steve towards the doorway. 'We have control of the fort. If you come out now, you'll be taken prisoner but you won't be harmed. If you don't . . .'

He paused for dramatic impact.

'We blow the place to pieces.'

There was a silence. Steve could hear nothing except for the beating of the rain against the ground, and the rumble of distant thunder.

'We're giving you five seconds!' he roared.

Again, nothing.

Then: 'Get the hell off my territory, Englishman,' shouted a voice from inside the building.

'Three seconds . . .'

'Your bombs don't frighten me.'

'One more second . . .'

'I'm already a dead man – so kill me now.'

Steve counted down the last second.

'Christ,' he muttered out loud.

'He's not falling for it,' said Chris.

'Then we blow the fucker,' said Maksim. He looked towards Ian. 'The Bomber here will have the explosives.'

Steve shook his head. 'We're being paid to bring him out alive. Put a bomb into the place and he'll be killed.'

'Then we storm it,' said Dan.

Steve had already inspected the block. There was only one door and, close to the roof, some air vents that were no more than slits in the wall. It had been built as a bunker as much as a place for the officers to kip down. That wasn't uncommon for guerrilla forts: they'd build in a safe room, the same way you might in a private house, so you could hunker down if you came under attack, and wait for reinforcements to arrive. It looked like Tshaka had been expecting an assault on his fort, and had made his plans already. He could hole up in there, make contact with his army via radio, then wait for the soldiers to arrive.

Smart, he decided. The man had planned for every possibility, and had already mapped out his response.

'We could smoke the bastard out,' said Ian. 'Put some incendiary devices through those slits, then wait for him to run out.'

'Too much rain,' said Steve. 'The bastard won't burn.'

'Or put an RPG round into the wall,' said Nick.

'Same problem,' Steve barked. 'If we bring down a wall, we risk killing him.'

'So we use the see-through-wall kit,' said Dan.

He pulled out the STW they'd bought back in Johannesburg. The imaging device could be slotted onto a standard AK-47, then the mag loaded with armour-piercing bullets. Dan had bought a dozen back in South Africa, and clipped them to his ammo belt. The bullets had a core of tungsten carbide, one of the hardest substances known to man, encased in a softer shell, usually made of copper. The soft skin would peel away on impact, allowing the core of the bullet to push through to the target. Armour-piercing bullets could smash through steel plates: relatively old concrete shouldn't be any problem at all. The bullet was 'hollow-point' as well: that meant the energy wrapped up in the ammunition diffused rapidly on impact, creating a far worse, messier wound on its victim than normal ammunition. But it also meant the bullet wouldn't pass right through the target and hit someone else. It was standard Special Forces training to use 'hollow-point' ammo on hostage rescues. The last thing you wanted was for the bullet to take out the person you were rescuing as well as the guards. In this case, they didn't want to accidentally shoot Tshaka. Just the men around him.

Dan slotted the imaging device into place, then glanced across at Nick. 'Reckon you can make the shot?'

Nick took the weapon in his hands. He flipped open the display screen on the STW device, and pointed the gun towards the building. 'It's a bit like a Nintendo DS,' he said with a grin.

'Should be easy for you then,' said Steve. 'We only brought you along because you got to the end of *Medal of Honor*.'

Nick started to circle the building. The images flashing across the screen were distinct enough: grey shapes against a pale blue background, but clearly distinguishable.

'There are four men inside in total,' he told the others.

Both Steve and Dan were looking at the screen as well. The men were clearly delineated – but which one was Tshaka?

'Take out this one,' said Dan, pointing at the man closest to the door.

'Why him?' asked Steve.

Dan jabbed at the figures on the screen. 'Two blokes by the door, both clearly with their guns cocked. They must be the guards. There are two men further back in the room, so I reckon one is Tshaka and the other is probably the Camp Commander. Take out one of the blokes at the door . . . then see who they rush to protect.'

Steve nodded. It made sense to him.

'Do it,' he said tersely, looking towards Nick as he spoke.

Nick steadied the rifle into his shoulder. The man on his screen was hardly moving, and the distance was only ten yards. In normal circumstances, the shot would be simple; he wouldn't even think about it. But the rain was pouring across his screen, and he'd never used this piece of technology before. He took a moment to compose himself. Just a normal shot, he repeated, again and again. Nothing special.

'*Kill*,' he muttered, squeezing the trigger.

The bullet drilled through the wall. The standard velocity for an AK-47 round is 715 yards per second and Nick's rifle was in perfect condition, cleaned and oiled to ensure accurate and reliable fire. It took only a micro-second for the hardened bullet to shed its copper skin, leaving it embedded in the neat hole it had drilled in the concrete, whilst the tungsten core smashed into the soldier's brain just above his left ear. Any bullet delivered to that spot will be fatal: a tungsten bullet chews up the brain the way a hungry dog chews up a bone.

The man collapsed to the ground, already dead.

'We're giving you five seconds to come out with your hands up,' shouted Ollie, standing close to the wall. 'You are completely surrounded. We can kill you through these walls. If you come out, we promise you won't be harmed.'

In the sky, the thunder was still crashing through the clouds. But from inside the building, there was only silence.

'Good work, mate,' said Steve, patting Nick on the shoulder.

A tense smile was stretched across the Welsh teenager's face.

'Now line up the next shot . . .'

'One,' shouted Ollie.

Nick raised the AK-47 to his shoulder a second time. He'd monitored the movement of the remaining men as the first soldier went down and he noticed they moved to protect the smallest of the three remaining figures. *Tshaka*, he decided. *That's him.*

'Two,' shouted Ollie.

He paused, wiping the rainwater out of his face.

'Three . . . I won't give you another warning.'

'You got the target?' Steve asked Nick.

'Four,' shouted Ollie.

Nick nodded. The soldier was still standing close to the door. They clearly had no idea how they'd been hit or how they should protect themselves. Maybe they thought the sniper had just got lucky, even though firing into a whole building was a million to one shot.

This next one should convince them, he told himself. Nobody gets that lucky.

'Five,' Ollie cried. He looked toward Nick and nodded briefly.

'*Kill*,' muttered Nick, and squeezed the trigger.

Once again, the bullet drilled straight through the wall. Once again, it dropped the target instantly.

'Bloody fantastic kit,' said Dan, watching the man fall on the tiny screen.

'We can keep doing this until you're all bloody dead,' shouted Ollie.

He waited for a second. On Nick's screen, he could see the two remaining men moving cautiously towards the exit.

'We're coming out,' shouted a voice.

The door opened slowly, and two men emerged into the rain, both of them wearing uniforms. The larger of the two must be the Camp Commander, judged Steve. The smaller, he recognised from the picture Wallace had shown them.

Tshaka.

He was only small in comparison to his troops, all of them big men. He looked around five ten, reckoned Steve, was about thirty-five years old, and had the natural authority of a born military leader. According to the dossier Steve had seen, Tshaka had been one of the fastest-rising young officers within the Government forces, a full Colonel before he was thirty, but then had broken away and started fighting for his own region. You could see at once why his men had come with him. Even as a prisoner, he had a bearing and dignity that betrayed not a single trace of either fear or defeat.

Chris stepped up to both men and frisked them for weapons. They were clean. He ordered them to put their hands behind their backs, then snapped Plasti-Cuffs, the cheap plastic handcuffs that were standard issue in armies around the world, to their wrists.

'Who sent you, white man?' growled Tshaka.

'No questions,' snapped Chris.

'Who is your leader?'

Ollie looked straight at the man. 'You can talk to me.'

Tshaka started to walk towards Ollie, his eyes looking straight into the man. 'I saw your helicopter come down,' he said. 'My men control this territory for a hundred miles in every direction. It doesn't matter how you try and break out . . . you'll never make it.'

Twenty-Five

THE BOAT WASN'T BUILT TO take eleven men. Chris pushed Tshaka into the back of the vessel, then clipped an extra pair of Plasti-Cuffs into place to make sure he was securely fastened to the deck. The Camp Commander had been shot through the head, and left next to the jetty. They'd left the boy next to his body, with a warning that if he tried to get help, they'd hunt him down and shoot him. From the expression of fear on his face, it looked as if he believed them.

'OK, let's get the hell out of here,' said Steve when they had got everyone on board.

Ganju had fired up the engine on the patrol boat, and Dan had unhooked its mooring from the jetty. As they looked back at the fort, it was a scene of devastation. A hole had been punched in its main walls and there were corpses lying everywhere. Once the rain cleared, the vultures would start to descend, picking the flesh from the dead, and after that, the forest would start to move back in, reclaiming the fort for the wild.

Steve looked out into the lake. It was turning seven in the morning, and in another hour or two he reckoned the storm would start to abate. Ganju was already steering the boat out into the choppy waters. With the helicopter destroyed, they had no choice but to get back to their base via the lake.

As they started to head upstream, the visibility was improving.

The rain was easing off, and the low-lying mist was beginning to clear. Ganju had been trying to contact Wallace on the radio, but its short-wave transmitter wasn't going to get through to the base from this low-level. There was nothing for it, decided Steve. They'd just have to make their way back on this boat, and hope that none of Tshaka's men saw them.

They were all exhausted from the battle – wet through and bruised. Down in the hold, Chris had brewed up some tea. There were only four tin mugs, but by passing them around they made do. Steve gulped on the hot liquid, letting it warm him up. Once the sun came up he knew they'd start to dry out, but for now he could feel the dampness in every part of his body.

With Ganju at the wheel, Chris was manning the heavy KPV at the front of the boat, and Nick and Dan were guarding the pair of MAGs at its stern. Newton was reading the charts, but having done the journey one way in the morning, and in the dark as well, getting back wasn't going to be a problem.

The rebel leader, even though he was strapped to the metal frame of the boat, looked strangely calm, Steve reckoned. None of them had said a word to him about who they were or why they'd captured him, but the man didn't look like a fool and it wasn't hard to figure out. The President relied on foreign mercenaries. If a bunch of them dropped out of the sky to take you prisoner, then they were taking you to see Kapembwa. And when you got there, you were going to be shot.

So why's he so damned cheerful? Steve asked himself, then followed his question with the answer: Because he knows this lake is crawling with his men and it's going to be hard for us to break through.

And he's probably right.

Ganju had steered out to the centre of the lake, but as the stormclouds blew over them and the visibility got steadily better, anyone out on the lake could see them easily. Steve was keeping his eyes peeled on the waters in every direction, but it was not until just after eight that he saw the first signs of life. A fishing vessel, with a two-man crew, it steered well clear of the patrol boat. By nine, Steve was starting to feel more confident. There was still no sign of the enemy. In total, the journey was going to take four to five hours. Ganju was squeezing as much life as he could from the engine, but they were going upstream, there was no current to help them, and the boat was carrying a lot more weight than it should do – all of which meant that progress was a lot slower than it had been on the way down.

Still, we're getting towards halfway, thought Steve. Maybe we're going to get through OK.

Then he saw it.

It was just a ripple on the surface of the lake to start with. Then slowly, you could see it take shape on the horizon. It was probably originally built as a fishing boat, decided Steve. It measured forty feet, made from hulking steel, starting to rust around the edges, and still with the big winch on its deck that would once have been used to haul in the fishing nets. But there was no mistaking the lump of metal on its prow: a Russian-built AK-630 naval cannon, originally designed for the Soviet Navy in the early 1980s and then sold to sympathetic forces around the world. The AK-630 was a six-barrelled Gatling-style weapon, able to fire both conventional shells and incendiary devices up to a range of 4,000 yards. It wasn't particularly accurate but it could lay down so much fire over such a wide range that it effectively protected a relatively small boat from attack by anything other than a submarine. Certainly, nothing from the air or the sea could touch it.

Steve could feel himself tensing. If those blokes knew how to use that bastard, they were as good as dead.

'Those your guys?' he asked, tapping Tshaka on the shoulder.

Tshaka looked towards the boat and nodded slowly. The same peaceful smile was playing on his lips. And in his eyes, there was a glint of determined resistance.

Steve drew his Uzi machine pistol and slammed it into the man's head. 'I want you to get them on the radio and tell them to let us through.'

Tshaka just shook his head.

'Do as you're told,' growled Steve. 'Or you're a dead man.'

'I'm a dead man already,' said Tshaka, his tone calm and even. 'You're taking me to Kapembwa, I used to fight for him, and I know that he plans to kill me. So you see, since you are delivering me to my executioner, your threats don't have much effect.'

'Look, just tell—'

But Steve's sentence was interrupted by the roar of the AK-630. The cannonfire ripped through the still of the morning, its shells cutting across the stretch of water that still separated the two boats. Suddenly, there were explosions all around, the water churned up by the munitions. A huge wave rocked over the patrol boat, then another, and the vessel was listing from side to side. Ganju had already spun the wheel, trying to steer close to the shore, where they wouldn't be so directly in the line of fire, whilst Chris had opened up with the KPV, pumping round after round of munitions across the lake.

'Get them to stop!' roared Steve into Tshaka's ear.

The guerrilla leader shook his head. There was water splashing across his face, and he was struggling to maintain his balance as the boat was thrown around, but he stayed silent.

'You'll bloody die as well,' Steve shouted.

'Once you've decided to kill a man, you'll find you've lost all influence over him,' said Tshaka. 'I'm surprised the British Army doesn't still teach that lesson. Since I'm going to die anyway, I'd rather you and the rest of your unit died with me. Surely you can see that?'

'Sod it,' muttered Steve under his breath. There was no point in talking to this nutter. 'Lay some fire into the bastards,' he yelled.

Grabbing his own AK-47 he began putting round after round into the boat. At his side, Ollie and Dan were doing the same thing. But the distance meant they were having little impact and the bullets, even if they found their target, weren't going to do much damage to plates of solid steel.

'It doesn't turn,' shouted Maksim.

Steve turned to face the Russian.

'I've trained against AK-630s,' said Maksim, struggling to make himself heard against the roar of gunfire all around them. 'It's a lethal gun, but it can't be turned around quickly. We need to get alongside them, then put an RPG round into the bastards.'

Steve nodded. The Russian was right. The attacking vessel could outgun them, but it couldn't outmanoeuvre them. He rushed up to the bridge, grabbing hold of Ganju. 'Get close to the shore, and get as much speed as possible,' he instructed the Gurkha. 'Nick and Maksim, get an RPG ready. Chris, you put as much heavy-duty fire into the bastards as possible. Everyone else hunker down and get ready to swim for it if we have to.'

Ganju had already swung the vessel violently towards the shoreline. He was dragging as much power as possible from the patrol boat, pushing the diesel engine to the maximum. The waters all around them were rough, the waves kicked up by the explosions making the vessel toss and pitch. It took all your strength just to hang on. Water was smashing into them from every direction, making it impossible to see anything that was happening around them. The AK-630 was still laying down round after round of fire and, as the two boats drew closer to one another, it was getting more accurate as well. Steve could smell the shells exploding in the water, and he sensed it wouldn't be long before they were hit. Chris was holding the KPV as steady as he could. At least when they were returning fire it made it too dangerous for any of Tshaka's men to come out on the deck of their boat. And it stopped the crew manning the AK-630 from focusing on their target.

But we can't hold out for long, realised Steve. They're too strong for us.

'Get more power from the engines!' he bellowed above the din of the battle.

They were as close to the edge of the lake as they could risk: twenty feet at most. The enemy was 200 yards away, closer to the centre of the lake. They were starting to draw level: another fifty yards and they'd be right alongside it.

Nick and Maksim were preparing the RPG, struggling desperately to hold it steady enough to get away a shot.

The AK-630 was turning – but slowly, noted Steve. Just the way Maksim said it would. A few more yards, and they could get an RPG round straight into it.

He could hear a crash, then smelled burning. The boat rocked backwards, the sound of metal screeching against metal splitting through the air. Christ, their boat had hit something, realised Steve. Whether they'd struck a rock close to the shore or been hit by a shell, it was impossible to tell. The boat was still moving but it was losing power fast, carried forward mainly by its own momentum. Water was sloshing across the deck.

Suddenly, they were out of range of the AK-630.

'Fire, fire!' yelled Steve.

Maksim slammed his fist down, releasing the first of the RPG rounds. After the assault on the fort, they only had four shells left. They couldn't afford to waste any. The missile spat through the air, a sheath of smoke left in its wake. In an instant, it had crashed into the side of the boat, exploding against the side of the AK-630, sending sparks shooting out across the deck.

'Again, again!' Steve bawled.

Nick had already reloaded and Maksim fired before the sentence had been finished.

This time, the missile skidded across the deck of the vessel. The gun was smashed to pieces, and two men, their uniforms set alight, hurled themselves desperately into the stormy waters.

The third missile slammed into its side, punching a hole in the hull. The boat was starting to list badly, shipping water as it did so. Five or six men were running onto the deck, but they were charging straight into the murderous fire Chris was laying down from the KPV.

'Save the last round,' ordered Steve.

Nick and Maksim put down the RPG. The lake was starting to fall silent, the guns no longer raging.

But the engine was quiet, and the patrol boat was shipping water.

'It's fucked,' spat Dan, climbing up from the hold, his face covered with grime and oil. 'The engine took a hit from one of the shells. There's no way we can fix it.'

'How long have we got?' asked Steve.

'We'll be down within ten minutes,' said Ganju from the bridge.

Steve glanced towards the shore. It was only twenty feet away, but the boat was leaking badly, and before long it would be under.

'Let's get to the shore,' he snapped, 'and bring as much kit with us as we can. We're going to sodding need it.' Loading his own kit on to his back, he turned to face Tshaka. 'You're not dying today, mate,' he said roughly. 'I've got other plans for you.'

He checked that everyone was getting their gear together. There was no way they were going to rescue the KPV – that piece of kit was going down with the boat. Their AK-47s would be held above their head to make sure they didn't get too wet. 'OK, let's go . . .'

Steve jumped into the water. The lake wasn't too cold and anyway, he was already wet through. He only needed two strokes, then his feet touched ground. He turned around, shouting at Maksim to toss Tshaka into the water. The Russian grabbed the man by his still-handcuffed hands, spun him towards the edge of the boat, then shoved hard. Tshaka was a strong man, but there was no point in resisting, and he tumbled face first into the water. Even though his hands were still bound, he instinctively kicked back and brought himself spluttering to the surface, the way Steve guessed he would.

Grabbing the prisoner by the collar, he dragged him up to the banks of the lake.

It was a short, muddy walk, then a push through the tall reeds that lined the shoreline. Steve shoved Tshaka up onto the banks, then helped haul the men ashore one by one. Within less than a minute, they were sitting exhausted, watching as the patrol boat slowly slipped beneath the waves.

Steve looked across at Ollie. 'This is your army, mate,' he said. 'You can decide what we do now. Because I'm buggered if I know.'

Twenty-Six

OLLIE AND NEWTON WERE STUDYING the maps. Tucked into a waterproof pouch inside Newton's webbing, they had survived the drenching. All of the men were wet through and exhausted, but they knew they couldn't stay where they were. The risk was too high. Pretty soon, Tshaka's men would come looking for them. And this time, reckoned Steve, they'd bring enough men and firepower to make sure there was only one outcome.

'We reckon it's about fifty miles back to the camp,' said Ollie. 'We can walk it in maybe two days.'

'We should track the lake,' said Ian. 'That way it will be easy to follow the route and there won't be too much vegetation in the way.'

Newton shook his head. 'There will be patrols all along the waterfront,' he said. 'We have to get at least ten miles into the interior, then head steadily west.'

'What kind of country is it?' asked Dan.

'A mixture of forest and bush,' answered Newton. He glanced up at the sky. 'It's not too difficult, so long as the weather doesn't turn rough.'

'Animals?' Ian queried.

Newton nodded. 'There are plenty of safari parks around here and the animals roam in and out of them. There are rhinos and elephants, and the Nile crocodiles from the lake take a walk onto the shore when they are feeling hungry. We'll be skirting close to the

Donatsuda National Park, and that has the highest concentration of lions of any area in Africa. There are leopards and cheetahs, and they introduced hyenas a couple of decades back to try and keep the herds of wild impala under control.'

Nick had salvaged the H&H from the sinking boat. 'We've got the right kit,' he said. 'We'll be OK.'

Newton just smiled. 'I don't think you've ever faced a herd of rhino in full charge,' he said. 'They could stop a tank division – never mind one skinny teenager with a big gun.'

'We crack on,' said Ollie quickly, noticing that Nick was about to get himself embroiled in a fight with Newton. 'There's no point in wasting any time.'

They took a few minutes to prepare themselves. It had stopped raining, but there were still dark clouds scudding across the wide open sky and you hardly needed a weather forecast to know that another downpour could kick off at any second. Each man had a change of clothes in his kitbag, but they would save those for later. Steve had done wilderness survival as part of his selection for the SAS: a whole week in the Welsh hills without food or shelter and, as he was quick to point out, once you'd done that you knew all you needed to know about surviving in heavy rain. You had to keep your spare clothes for the night, because if you didn't have some dry clothes to sleep in, then you were done for. It wasn't much fun marching in wet kit, but it was better than dying of exposure and exhaustion.

Newton and David had sketched out a rough route. They would tack five miles into the interior, then head south-west for another five miles. After that, they'd walk in as straight a line as possible for the forty-five miles that should take them back to base. At some point they'd have to break through the front line of the conflict between Tshaka and Kapembwa's men. But they'd worry about that when they got there. For now, they just had to move on.

Ian had cut himself a staff. His ankle was badly sprained, but he could still walk. At times, he rested on Dan's shoulder, and other times Chris propped him up. The first few miles were easy enough. They were walking through the flat scrubland that led down to the lake. There were streams and gullies, and birds that circled in the gloomy sky as they darted between their nests and the waters: huge, ungainly-looking Saddle-Billed Storks, Grey and Goliath Heron that would swoop through the sky like fighter jets, as well as buzzards and Black Eagles and a dozen other varieties that Steve didn't even recognise. In the distance, they could see small herds of impala, the compact, delicate antelope that were the dominant species throughout much of the African savannah. The rams had great black and bronze horns, while the ewes had big dark eyes and black and suede tanned ears that stuck out of their small heads.

It was beautiful country, decided Steve, as he marched steadily over the rough ground. Abundant, rich – and largely empty of humans yet teeming with animals so exotic and varied they took your breath away. It was the kind of country a man could spend a lifetime in and never feel the need for an adventure: everything was already here. You could see why men had fought over it through the generations and were fighting over it still. Such a natural and unspoiled prize could never be surrendered easily: nor, once captured, could it even be defended completely against predators.

They stopped briefly for some lunch – soggy biscuits and chocolate bars from their kitbags – then pressed on. Tshaka was walking silently between Dan and Chris, his hands still strapped behind his back, but he wasn't making any trouble and didn't look like he was going to. If he made a break for it, he'd been told he'd get a bullet in the back of his kneecap, and there was no point in crippling himself for life, not while there was still a chance his men might rescue him.

By four, Ollie suggested they stop for the day. They'd walked twenty miles, and most of them had been up since the crack of dawn. It had been a long and hard day, and there was nothing to be gained by exhausting themselves. They found a small wood, consisting mostly of mopane, the high, heavy trees that were found all over this part of Africa: its wood was so strong it was commonly used for railway sleepers and pit props down mines. They cleaned the dried leaves off the ground, then started to build themselves some shelter for the night. The trees would provide some natural cover if the rains came back. But each man also had a single, strong polythene sheet in his kitbag. Using fallen branches, they created a series of triangular structures, then stretched the polythene sheets across them, to make simple dry hammocks to sleep on. That would stop the dampness in the ground seeping up into their bodies, and the worst of the rain would wash straight off them.

Chris and Dan started to collect some mopane worms from the trees. Mopane wood is so hard even termites can't live in it, but the worms – one-inch-long caterpillars – swarm over its branches. Across Southern Africa, the worms were standard fare. Usually, they are dried and sold in the markets: they have a woody flavour, and make a useful snack in countries where food is often scarce. But you can also cook them fresh from the trees, grilling them alive: they taste something like the not-so-nice bits of a chicken. Chris had suggested catching one of the impala – the bush was thronging with them – but Steve told him not to be crazy. SAS survival drill was to eat worms and grubs, and was right to do so, he reminded himself. A man could waste a couple of hours and use up 500 calories tracking down and killing an animal. Then you had to roast it for another couple of hours, and you'd end up throwing most of the meat away because you couldn't carry it. It was a waste of time and energy when you could just collect a handful of grubs and eat those. 'We'll have a slap-up meal in Johannesburg when we're done,' he reminded the unit. 'Until then, the worms will do just fine.'

Within twenty minutes, a small fire had been built from wood collected on the ground, and the food cooked.

'Not bad,' said Nick, tucking into the plateful of worms. 'Not as good as McDonald's, obviously. But a step up from the curry and lager for a fiver Monday Night Special down at JD Wetherspoon in Swansea.'

'Lager, that's what we need,' said Maksim.

'In your dreams, Maksie,' said Steve. 'We're staying off the booze until this job is done.'

The men were sitting around the small fire. It was dark and they knew the embers and smoke were signals that anyone tracking them could pick up on. But they needed the warmth and they needed some hot food inside them. It was already past dusk, and in the distance, they could see the black thunderclouds gathering in the distance. The chances were they'd get another soaking before the night was finished.

Newton put a cupful of the roasted worms in front of Tshaka along with a cupful of water.

'I can't eat them with my hands bound, can I?' said Tshaka.

'Feed him with a spoon,' said Ollie sharply. 'We're not undoing him.'

Newton shovelled some food to his lips. Tshaka ate hungrily, then took a swig of the water he was offered. 'You're a black man,' he said, looking straight at Newton when he'd finished. 'Why are you working with these white mercenary pigs?'

'I'm a Batotean.' It was said in the same quiet tone of determination that Newton always used, noted Steve, listening quietly by the fire.

'That makes it worse,' said Tshaka. His voice was filled with a righteous anger. 'Kapembwa is the tool of the white man, always has been.'

'Really?' asked Newton. 'He fought against them long enough. Some of us were already soldiers when his guerrilla army was driving the colonialists out of this country.'

'He was fighting for the Russians, and they were white men last time I checked,' said Tshaka. 'Kapembwa was a tool of the Cold War, a Marxist trained in Moscow, and used by the West. Imperialists, Communists – it makes no difference. The problem for Africa has been the white man trying to tell us how to run our affairs. It's time we started looking after ourselves.'

'We don't need any political lectures, thank you,' said Ollie.

'Every man needs political lectures,' snarled Tshaka. 'Let me ask you just one question. Do you call yourself a soldier?'

'Of course,' snapped Ollie.

'Then a soldier fights for something he believes in – he fights for his people,' said Tshaka. 'Look at this country, it's a ruin. The land has been pillaged, the people are going hungry. A third of the population has fled, the rest are starving. And you just fly into the country to kill the one man who is fighting against all that . . .'

Tshaka spat on the ground. 'You're just dogs.'

Steve chewed on his worms. They weren't so bad once you got used to them. Better than the grubs he'd eaten on his survival course back in the Regiment. If you didn't look too closely, the meal could be from any kebab shop on Bromley High Street. Tshaka was an impressive man, he thought to himself. And he was making a solid enough point. If they were just here to assassinate him, the way Wallace wanted them to, then they would in truth be nothing more than attack dogs. But we're not, he reminded himself. We're here to eliminate Kapembwa. If Tshaka knew that, then maybe he'd even be working with us.

'And you think you'll make a difference?' sneered Ian.

'Of course.'

'Change doesn't come from the barrel of a gun,' said Ian. 'We learned that the hard way in my country.'

'In Africa, the barrel of a gun is all we have – and if wasn't for dogs like you we'd sort this out ourselves.'

Ollie had already stepped up to the man, and struck him across the face with the back of his hand. 'We'll have no more of your damned lip,' he said coldly. 'We're just earning our wages.'

He started to organise the night-watch. Some drizzle was already falling and strong gusts of wind were blowing through the trees. One man would remain on duty at all times, switching shifts every hour. When Nick volunteered for the first stint, Newton ran through what to watch for. 'Look for the Black Rhinos,' he said. 'They tend to charge first and ask questions later. The problem is, the rhino can't see very well and it's easily frightened, so if it smells or hears anything suspicious then it's likely to start charging it.'

'I've got some mates like that back in Swansea,' said Nick.

Newton chuckled, then continued, 'It gets particularly angry at humans. The skin on a rhino is so thick, and it's so strong, none of the other animals worry it very much, but it knows a man can kill it with a gun, and it doesn't believe in negotiating. So if you hear any kind of rumbling in the distance, anything that sounds like hooves running, then for God's sake wake us all up and we'll have about five seconds to assemble enough firepower to stop them.'

'Black Rhinos?' said Steve. 'Sam is really keen on preserving them. She works for this fund—'

'Then she's out of her mind,' interrupted Newton. 'They're vicious bastards and ugly as well.'

Steve shrugged. 'Slot them right between the eyes – it's fine with me, mate. We'll just keep it between ourselves, that's all. I don't need a bird getting all soppy on me.'

The hammocks were prepared, and the fire had been snuffed out. The rain was starting to spit down, and in the distance a streak of lightning was splitting open the sky once more. Steve changed quickly into his dry clothes, hanging up the old ones at the end of his bed. They'd still be wet through in the morning, and they'd be uncomfortable to put back on in the morning, but it was better than trying to kip down in soaking kit. So long as you got a decent night's sleep, most things would be OK.

'So, Maksie,' he shouted out across the narrow space that

separated the two men. 'When we finally make it down to Nick's mum's lapdancing club, what songs are you going to pick?'

'I bloody heard that,' shouted Nick from his watch-post.

Maksim was already laughing. ' "Sweet Child of Mine" by Guns 'n' Roses. And you know why? Because it's six minutes long . . . and I like to get my money's worth out of a woman.'

' "Dirty" by Christina Aguilera,' said Dan. 'I just love the way she sings those lyrics.'

'Glad to see SASR's subtle sense of style coming to the fore,' said Ian.

'How about you then?'

'As the only man here with a sense of irony, I'd have to go with "Like a Virgin" by Madonna.'

' "Biology" by Girls Aloud,' David said dreamily.

'I didn't realise you were so up-to-date,' said Ollie.

'I've got kids, mate.'

'I'd go for "Fever" by Peggy Lee,' said Chris. 'I like a slow dance.'

'I'll take anything by the Stones,' said Ollie.

'What is this lapdancing anyway?' asked Newton.

'You've been in jail too long,' said Dan. 'Get us out of here alive and we'll show you. That's a promise.'

'How about you, Steve?' Maksim turned to him.

'I'm a classics man,' said Steve. 'So it's a tough choice, but in the end I reckon it would have to be "Purple Rain" by Prince.'

'So you can spray beer over her belly,' roared Maksim. 'Then lick it off.'

'That's the spirit, Maksie,' laughed Steve. 'I'm getting you to that club for sure.'

Suddenly they were interrupted by a raking blast of AK-47 fire. Bullets were flying everywhere, slicing through the leaves of the trees. Steve stood bolt upright only to see Nick standing above them, his face red with fury. 'Just shut the fuck up about my mum's club, all right?' he spluttered.

'Time to button our lips and crash out, boys,' said Steve with a wry smile. 'Sweet dreams, everyone.'

The rain had beaten down on the forest all night, leaving puddles and mud all around the small clearing where they had made camp. Still, at least we didn't get charged by rhinos, yawned Steve, as he rolled out of his hammock and put his foot straight into a pool of cold water. And nobody tried to shoot us. Out in this hell-hole, that counts as a good night.

They ate a few dried biscuits washed down with some rainwater that had been collected in their drinking flasks overnight, then pulled their wet clothes back on, storing their dry kit back in the bags so they could sleep in it again if they needed to. By seven in the morning, the march had resumed. There were forty miles left to the camp. They were all fit, strong men, and they could cover that distance in nine or ten hours, so long as the terrain wasn't too rough. But at some point, they were going to have to break through Tshaka's lines. And that was going to be a lot harder.

They had completed the first twenty miles by just after lunch. They rested for half an hour, then cracked on. At two o'clock, they saw the first sign of life – a farming village lying just to the right of the path they had mapped out. Newton took them on a two-mile detour that would keep them well out of sight: he reckoned Tshaka's men would have stationed a couple of soldiers in every village, and there was no point in getting into a fight.

The detour took them into the wilder bush country, a great flat plane of tall grasses and stubby trees. Chris was the first to spot the two Black Rhino, recognising the stamp of their hooves and the snort of their massive nostrils from his time fighting in the borderlands between South Africa and Namibia. The Recces didn't fear very much, he reminded everyone, but the Black Rhino was on the list. 'Get the H&H ready,' he hissed towards Nick.

Steve spun around. Those words could only mean one thing.

His eyes scanned the horizon. They were marching through a barren stretch of savannah, with nothing but tall, wild grasses for at least five miles in every direction. There were hills directly to their west, and they'd be climbing them soon enough, but until then there was no cover, nowhere they could run to.

'There,' said Chris.

Steve was straining to see – then his eyes latched onto the rough, tarred skin rippling in the grasslands. A typical Black Rhino was five feet high and twelve feet long, and weighed up to 3,000 pounds, or the equivalent of fifteen hefty blokes. Despite the name, they weren't really black, more a greyish-brown. Their skin was so thick it made a tank seem under-protected. On their heads were two massive, twisted horns, which could grow up to five feet in length: they could spear a man as easily as you stuck a kebab on a skewer, reckoned Steve. There were two of them – both moving towards them at full pelt. Their blood was up and they were spoiling for a fight: another thirty or forty seconds and they'd be upon them.

'Go for the skull,' hissed Chris, his hand resting on his Nick's shoulder.

Nick had raised the big hunting gun to his eye, lining up the shot. He was glancing around, his expression apprehensive.

'I said *go for the skull*!' repeated Chris, louder this time.

'I . . . I . . .' Nick was stammering. His face had turned bright red.

'Christ,' muttered Steve. The boy had frozen.

Whipping his AK-47 from his chest, he locked his finger onto the trigger. Whether its 7.62 calibre ammo would make any dent in a rhino skin, Steve had no idea. But it was better than standing around being skewered to death.

At his side, Ganju had taken out his hunting knife. 'If they're upon us, a gun's no use,' he said tersely. 'All you can do is twist a knife into their eye and hope to break through to the brain before they crush you to death.'

Chris had already realised what had happened to Nick. Pushing him to one side, he'd grabbed the gun from him. The rhinos were only fifty yards away now, clearly visible through the grasses, snorting viciously as they accelerated towards their prey. The H&H cracked brutally as Chris fired the first bullet. He staggered backwards, struggling to tame the gun's kickback, then fired again. The first bullet smashed into the advancing animal, splitting open its skull, and sending the beast skidding to the ground.

But the next shot missed.

And the second rhino, now driven into a frenzy of fear and anger, was only thirty yards from them.

'Get back, get back!' yelled Steve, spraying a dozen rounds of bullets into the animal. They bounced off its thick skin but still carried enough force to deflect its path. The rhino was charging to the left, then gradually noticed that it no longer had its prey directly in its sights, and started to slow down. It looked around, its black eyes cold and damp, yet streaked with a raw, animal fury. Steve kept pumping bullets into its face – but they made no difference.

Then Chris fired the H&H.

The rhino was just readying itself for the final charge straight into the target when the bullet slammed into its skull. It paused, as if suspended in ice, then its legs started to buckle. It dropped to the ground, but was still carried forwards by the momentum of the charge, and it came to rest just ten yards in front of where Chris and Steve were standing. It moaned, a low, pitiful sound, as the last remnants of life ebbed out of the massive corpse.

'Jesus, why would your bird want to save those fuckers?' said Chris, looking down at the dead beast, its thick maroon blood still spilling onto the ground.

Steve shook his head. 'No accounting for women.'

Nick was standing to one side of them, his face distraught. He walked slowly across to the rhino, sidestepping the blood. 'I don't know what happened,' he said, with a shake of his head.

'Anyone can freeze, mate,' said Steve. He put an arm across the lad's shoulder, then pushed him playfully away. Nick tried to smile but his heart wasn't in it. We've trusted Nick too much, reflected Steve. He's only a kid and he's never in been in the proper Army. Just because he can shoot better than any man we've ever seen, doesn't mean he always knows what he's doing. He wasn't up for taking down the rhino: and we shouldn't have expected him to be.

Remember that, Steve told himself. *Don't rely on guys who can't deliver.*

'Anyone for rhino burgers?' said Dan, cheerfully standing over the animal. 'I hear they're not so bad with plenty of ketchup on top.'

'How about the horn?' said Maksim, his knife at the ready. 'I've heard you get good money for them in China. I know some guys who could smuggle it through Russia.'

'We're getting paid well enough,' said Ollie. 'We don't need to get arrested at the South African border for smuggling in a banned product.'

Maksim glanced down at the two long, twisted horns, then folded his knife back into his webbing.

But Ganju still had his knife out.

He was holding out his left arm and, with a flicker of hesitation, cut open a one-inch wound. The blood bubbled to the surface of his skin, before he put away his knife and ripped a bandage from his medi-kit to stick over it. Everyone was looking at him as if he was crazy. 'It's an old Gurkha tradition,' he said simply. 'If a Gurkha draws his sword, or his knife, then blood must be spilled before he puts it away again. If necessary, it must be the man's own blood.'

'Remind me not to ask you to carve the turkey at Christmas,' joked Ian.

Ganju smiled. 'We all live by our own traditions.'

'No one would have noticed if you'd just slipped the knife away,' said Dan.

'We are all accountable for our own actions,' said Ganju. 'It doesn't matter if anyone is watching or not.'

'Right – let's crack on,' Steve said briskly. 'We need to get there before nightfall if we can – and before it starts pissing down on us again.'

He led the march forwards. They had another twenty miles to go before they reached the camp. Newton and Ganju were leading the way, with Dan and Maksim taking the rear. Tshaka was in the middle of the convoy, his hands still behind his back, the same peaceful smile still on his face.

I don't like the way that man looks, Steve repeated to himself. He's too calm.

As if he knows something we don't.

Twenty-Seven

BOTH NEWTON AND GANJU LOOKED worried when they returned from the recce. Steve knew at once what they were about to say even before they'd opened their mouths.

'It's too dangerous that way,' said Ganju. 'We'll get blown to pieces.'

They had stopped a mile behind the front line.

Their fort at Gull's Wing was only three miles away, no distance. But between them was a long front line, held by Tshaka's army, fighting the official Government forces. There were trenches, barbed wire, gun emplacements and patrols. In total, there were 10,000 men in Tshaka's forces and another 15,000 Government troops confronting them. The fighting was sporadic – most of the time the soldiers were happy enough just to hold their positions – but there wasn't much chance of breaking through. If you were spotted, 1,000 men could be upon you in seconds, and even if they weren't top quality troops, that didn't mean their bullets weren't going to kill you.

'Maybe we could go this way,' said Newton, pointing to the map. It was just after seven in the evening, and they'd laid up to rest in a remote patch of woodland. The tall, thick trees gave them cover from the storm the skies were threatening, and made them invisible from anything other than a patrol that stumbled straight into them. Dusk was starting to fall and, in the distance, you could hear occasional bursts of gunfire as the two armies probed and tested each other's positions. 'There's a ridge of hills, then a steep valley that runs though them. You can't dig trenches there, and you can't lay down barbed wire because the terrain is too rough. There might be some patrols out, but I don't think the area is going to be heavily defended because you couldn't put any serious armour through it.'

Steve looked towards Tshaka. 'Can we break through there?'

'You expect me to help you deliver me to my executioners?' Tshaka spat on the ground.

Maksim was advancing towards him, a thick log he'd picked up from the ground in his hand. 'You'll tell us where we can break through, or you'll die right here.'

'Then I'll die here, Russian scum.'

Ian was standing next to him. He'd flipped open the knife he carried in his webbing, and even in the pale early-evening light its blade glistened menacingly.

'Leave it,' snapped Ollie.

'We'll carve the information out of him if we need to,' said Ian calmly. 'Most men will talk if you know where to put the knife. It worked in Ulster.'

'I daresay it did,' said Ollie stiffly. 'But even if you break him, there's nothing to stop him leading us straight into a trap. His best chance of getting out alive is to push us straight towards his crack troops.'

Ian paused, then folded away the blade. In the distance, there was a peal of thunder. The rain would be upon them soon, judged Steve. Another rough night. But that might play to their advantage. If he knew anything about soldiers, they'd be hunkering down, trying to keep themselves dry, probably brewing up some hot tea and grabbing a few quiet ciggies. Even if they were sent out on patrol, they'd be making it as short as possible.

'How far?' he said, looking towards Newton and pointing towards the pass he'd marked out on the map.

'About two miles,' answered Newton. 'It's a steep climb up through the hills, then a clean break through the valley.'

'I reckon it's our best shot,' said Steve.

'We could wait until morning,' said David. 'Do a proper recce of the area?'

Steve shook his head. 'We're too close to Tshaka's lines. If they discover us, we're done for. I'd rather take my chances tonight.'

He glanced at each man in turn. Gritty determination was written into the faces of each of them. They knew the risk they were about to take. They were attempting to break through a military line, with no logistical support, no proper planning and zero intelligence. They had no idea what kind of opposition they might face. In any normal circumstance, they'd be told it was madness. They could run into an overwhelming force from either army. And both sides would shoot on sight.

But these weren't normal circumstances.

The risks were appalling whether they stayed or went. And they'd all rather move out now than spend a night waiting to see if a whole army was about to descend on them, intent on slaughter.

'Then let's crack on,' Steve said crisply.

They took a few minutes to eat some of the dried-up worms they'd brought with them, mixed in with some biscuits carried in their kitbags. The food made them feel a bit stronger. Ollie and David broke the unit up into smaller patrols. If any shooting kicked off, there was no point in them all going down. Newton was the lead man, since he knew the ground best. He'd go fifty yards ahead, and signal any trouble. That would give the others a chance to get away if they encountered a serious-looking force. Newton himself would be a goner, but those were the breaks.

Behind Newton, Steve would lead a four-man patrol including David, Maksim and Dan. Another fifty yards back, Ollie would lead Ian, Chris and Nick, with Tshaka walking between them, still bound and also gagged now. Ganju would drop another fifty yards back to alert them to any trouble from the rear.

'All set?' asked Steve.

The men remained silent.

'Then let's go.'

It was a long, hard march. Dusk had faded into night, and there was a stiff, damp breeze. The moon was totally obscured, but it was too dangerous to use a torch. A narrow path led through the woodlands, then up into the hills. By following that, they could keep from getting lost. But it was slow, hazardous progress, each step measured out carefully to prevent yourself falling over the fallen branches that littered the way.

After a mile, the ground started to rise steeply. The track narrowed and twisted out of the woodlands and into the dense scrub that filled the hillside. A ridge of mountains stretched for about five miles to the east, rising to a height of 2,000 feet. Two miles away, Steve reckoned he could see the lights of the front line. Campfires were burning and, occasionally, there was a burst of tracer fire spitting into the sky. If it was a modern, well-equipped army down there, there would be white phosphorus grenades to light up the night sky. But these boys didn't have money to burn on illuminations and fireworks: they fought the old-fashioned way, with each bullet used to kill a man – and Steve couldn't help but admire them for that.

It was close to ten at night by the time they reached the valley. The rain had kicked in, falling in great powerful waves. Steve tried to ignore it as he ploughed forwards. The track was quickly churned into mud, with streams of water gushing through it, and it took all your concentration to stay on your feet. Dan had already slipped once, cursing loudly as he went down.

'For God's sake shut it,' Steve had hissed. 'You'll bring a whole army down on us.'

Up ahead, Newton had raised an arm to tell the others to stop. Steve told the unit to take a break, while he went ahead to recce the lie of the land. As he arrived at the top of the ridge, Newton had already crouched down low behind the stubby remains of a dead tree.

He handed a pair of field glasses to Steve. Brushing the water from his face, Steve put them to his eyes. It was hard to see through the rain and darkness. The contours of the ground were nothing more than a series of pale shadows. But he could see the way the valley dipped between the hills, creating a narrow channel that ran through to the plains on the other side. And he could see a small glowing light right at its centre.

'I reckon it's some guards,' said Newton.

Cursing the rain, Steve wiped the field glasses clean and took a closer look. He could make out a small tent, with a brazier inside to keep the men warm through the night.

'Tshaka's forces? Or the Government's?'

'Tshaka's I think,' said Newton. 'Kapembwa's men wouldn't be this far forward.'

'How many are there?'

Newton shrugged. 'Six at the most,' he said. 'The tent won't hold any more than that.'

Steve nodded. It sounded about right. 'We'll try to sneak past them,' he said. 'The bastards will probably be dozing, and the rain will help disguise any noise we might make. But if it turns into a scrap, we can handle six blokes. We'll slot them, then make a run for the opposing lines.'

Newton nodded.

'OK,' Steve said. 'I'll go and break the good news to the rest of the boys.'

Within five minutes they were ready to move out. The gags on Tshaka had been doubled in strength to stop him from shouting to his men, and Maksim had explained how he was going to rip each fingernail off both hands if he caused any trouble.

They lined up in single file and started to move down through the valley, Newton still leading the way. The track narrowed as it started to descend the hillside. The rain was lashing into them, streaming off the rough, rocky ground, and churning the path into mud. A couple of times Steve could feel his feet slipping. They marched steadily forwards until they were 100 yards from the sentry post. The path would have taken them straight down and through it, but that was far too dangerous. Instead, Newton led them along the side of the valley, seventy feet up from the soldiers. The ground was rougher here, and there was no track for them to follow. Nor was there anything for your boots to get any kind of grip on. Even Newton was struggling to find a way forwards.

'Oh Christ,' growled Chris as he started to slither.

Maksim had already grabbed him by the wrist, using the immense strength in his shoulder muscles to haul the big man back up again.

'Shut the fuck up,' hissed Steve. He glanced nervously at the tent. It was taking a beating in the weather – the wind and rain smashing into the canvas. Must be impossible to sleep in there, he decided grimly. Somebody would be awake.

Maybe we should have waited until morning.

Suddenly: 'Shit!' screeched Chris.

Steve glanced backwards. This time, surely the noise was loud enough to wake the soldiers.

Chris had fallen again, and this time was sliding down through the mud straight into the valley below. Maksim was scrambling down after him, trying to help hoist him back upwards.

In the commotion, Tshaka had made a run for it. Even with his hands bound and his mouth gagged, he was hurling himself down the side of the valley.

'Bloody stop him,' ordered Steve. He was trying to keep his voice low yet still make himself heard.

Tshaka was only fifty yards from the tent now. Reaching out a hand, Chris managed to get a hold of the man's leg, sending him thumping to the ground and, in the next few seconds, the two men were rolling around like a couple of bears in the mud.

Suddenly there was a burst of gunfire. A soldier had appeared outside the tent, and was spraying the hillside with bullets from his AK-47.

'Lay down some covering fire,' shouted Ollie up above.

Steve ducked, and started to crawl forwards. He could hear Chris scream out in pain as he was struck in the chest. Bullets were flying overhead as Ollie organised a barrage of fire down into the enemy position. Steve fought his way through the mud until he grabbed hold of Chris.

'You OK?' he shouted.

Chris nodded. 'The bullet hit the Kevlar,' he grunted. 'Just winded me, that's all.'

Together with Maksim, the three men started to haul Tshaka back up the hillside. Ollie was directing fire into the tent but the soldiers had already abandoned it, retreating to the defensive mud and sandbag wall they'd built just behind it. Even from this distance, you could see they had a couple of armoured vehicles. One of the soldiers had manned a machine gun and was starting to spray bullets. It was wild, poorly directed fire. But the valley was a narrow one. Sooner or later he was going to hit someone.

And it's going to be one of us, decided Steve. 'We need some cover,' he said, 'or we're going to get bloody slaughtered out here.'

Ollie, Chris and Nick were frantically pushing together all the mud and rocks and wood they could find, to create a rough wall. Ganju was digging frantically in the churned-up ground. There was no natural cover on the hillside: no decent trees, no walls, no ridges of land they could sneak behind. All they could do was make their own foxhole. Steve threw himself into the work, scrabbling at the mud with his bare hands. The bullets were still spitting up from the tent, but in the dark and through the rain, it would take a lot of luck for any of them to hit their target. Within minutes, a rough foxhole was constructed: a trench, three feet deep and five long, with a mud and rock wall in front of it. Steve paused for a moment, leaning back to recover his breath. The rain was still coming down hard and without any drainage, their foxhole was already starting to fill with water. It was cold and damp, the water seeping into his skin.

'Bloody hell,' he muttered out loud. 'What now?'

'We hold them, subdue their fire, then break out,' Ollie said tightly.

'And how exactly are we going to do that?' David enquired.

Both Steve and Ollie were straining to look over the roughly constructed wall but the bullets were winging right past them. The troops were dug in inside a pair of armoured vehicles, which controlled the narrow path through the valley, putting down round after round into their enemy.

I'm buggered if I know, thought Steve.

'Sniper fire?' Nick suggested.

Steve shook his head. 'There's no way you can get a shot in there.'

'RPG?' That was Maksim.

'We've only one left,' said Ollie. 'Our chances of a direct hit from this distance and in this weather are minimal. Then we've used up our ammo.'

'OK – we sneak along the back and come at them from behind,' said Maksim.

'You give it a go if you want to, Maksie,' said Steve, 'but it looks bloody dodgy to me. And we need all the blokes we've got to hold this position.'

'Then what?'

'Scarper,' said Steve. 'Put down some fire, then head back into the interior and find another way through.'

'Run away?' snapped Maksim. 'Never.'

'Call it a tactical retreat,' said Ollie with a rough smile. 'I know the Spetsnaz don't do tactics, but—'

'There's nowhere *to* go,' said Newton. 'Now they're onto us, they'll use dogs to track us down. There's no interior to disappear into.'

'Radio,' said Ganju quietly. 'Wallace is only three miles away. Get him on the radio, tell him our position, and he can bring reinforcements in.'

'Do it,' said Ollie.

Ganju had already unhooked the shortwave radio from his kitbag and was twiddling the dials, trying to get onto the right frequency. The weather didn't help. In the storm raging around him, the signals would all get scrambled. 'But it's only three miles,' he muttered to himself. 'We must be able to get through.'

'Anything?' said Ollie, his voice tense.

'Not yet,' Ganju said irritably.

'Keep trying.'

The gunfire was coming closer. Of the two armoured vehicles, one had started to move forward, its big tyres churning through the mud. The machine gunner was raking the hillside with fire, bullets peppering their position. A grenade was lobbed into the air. It landed twenty feet in front of their position, exploding as it crashed into the muddy ground. A huge ball of fire and smoke kicked up into the air, and in the next instant, mud was raining down on their position.

'Wallace, Wallace,' hissed Ganju into the radio.

Sodding well reply, thought Steve. Or else we're all done for. But all he could hear was crackle and static.

A flash of lightning suddenly illuminated the valley. Fifty yards below them, Steve could see the single armoured vehicle, the machine gunner raking the hills. The man who'd lobbed the hand grenade was clearly protected behind the machine gun, preparing the next assault. He's finding his range, realised Steve. Pretty soon, one of those grenades is going to land right on top of us.

Fifty yards further back, two more vehicles were advancing down the track, making a total of four. They looked like regular SUVs, but they had been armour-plated and had machine guns built onto them.

Steve grimaced. He looked towards Ganju.

'I'm doing the best I bloody can,' snapped the Gurkha.

It was the first time Steve had seen the man lose his rag. That was how bad their situation was.

'We've got to drive that vehicle back,' Dan said.

Ollie nodded. 'Wait until it advances closer, then give them the RPG.'

Behind him, Steve could hear a burst of life from the radio – '*Come in, come in . . .*' – and recognised the voice even through the crackle. The same Old Etonian drawl he'd taken a dislike to back in Britain. Wallace.

But right now, he thought, *I'm sodding pleased to hear the smarmy git.*

'We need assistance,' said Ganju. 'Repeat, assistance.'

Newton grabbed the receiver, spitting instructions on their position into the machine. Then, as he waited for the reply, the static returned. 'Did you hear? Repeat, did you hear?'

'It's gone,' said Ganju. 'There's nothing to do now but pray he heard.'

Another grenade exploded in front of them. This time it was only ten feet away. You could feel the ground all around you tremble, and the rain temporarily stopped, blocked out by the heat and smoke, before coming back as a shower of hot mud and stone.

'I'm not staying here to get killed,' shouted Maksim. 'If I'm going to die, it's with my guns on automatic.' He started to run forward, his finger jammed on the trigger of his AK-47, firing wildly.

'Give them the RPG,' yelled Ollie. 'Before that Russian nutter kills himself.'

Dan had placed the launcher onto his shoulder, while Chris loaded the missile. Taking a brief second to steady himself, Dan then fired it straight into the armoured vehicle. It hissed through the air, then exploded on impact. A huge flame leaped into the air, followed by a plume of thick black smoke, but it was soon washed away by the torrential rain. As it cleared, you could see that one man had been killed, and the vehicle had been damaged but not immobilised. Its thick steel plating had absorbed the worst of the explosion.

'They don't realise it's our last missile,' said Dan, watching as the vehicle started to back away.

'But they soon will,' said Chris. 'And then they'll be back – we can be sure of that.'

Minutes ticked away. Steve sat back in the muddy pool of water. How long could it take Wallace to get here? he wondered. Ten minutes, maybe fifteen. They had a few dozen rounds of ammo left per man, and a couple of hand grenades each, but no heavy weaponry.

Maybe they should make a run for it.

It would be better than dying in this muddy ditch.

'*Kill*,' muttered Nick to his left.

Steve glanced upwards. The second of the two armoured vehicles was advancing into the valley. Nick had put a couple of rounds into its skin, but he might as well have been using a peashooter for all the difference it made. It was edging forwards, the driver testing and probing to see if there were any more RPG rounds coming their way. But as it advanced, the driver was growing in confidence. The machine gun opened up, peppering the foxhole with bullets; these were sticking in the mud and stone, but before long the wall would collapse, Steve knew. Even Maksim had retreated, rejoining the rest of the unit.

A grenade was flung towards them, detonating fifteen yards away. Then another. This time it was just ten yards. The acrid smell of sulphur drifted on the fierce wind.

'Right, boys, let's die with our boots on if we have to,' said Ollie. 'We can't wait for Wallace. We'll make a fighting break-out.' He grabbed Tshaka by the scruff of the neck, hauling him up to the air. 'At least this bastard will go down with us,' he growled.

Each man picked up his gun, and slotted its bayonet into place.

There wasn't any point in arguing about it, decided Steve. All they could do now was gamble their lives on breaking through.

They formed themselves into a tight unit. Newton led the way, followed by Steve, Maksim and Dan. Chris, Nick, Ganju and David brought up the rear. Ian was hobbling in the centre of the group, holding on to Tshaka.

'Straight over the top,' shouted Ollie. 'Then down into the valley beyond the last vehicle.'

They started to run, loosening off round after round from their AK-47s as they did so. Steve was pushing himself, his heart thumping in his chest, the way illuminated only by the tracer fire of the machine gun tracking their every step. You could feel the bullets peppering the mud all around you. It must have been something like this when you went over the top into no-man's land in the First World War, he decided in one of those odd seconds of clarity that sometimes came upon him in moments of maximum danger. Running for your life, through heavy fire, knowing that if you went down, you'd be left to die slowly in the mud.

The plan was to charge across the top of the valley, putting down enough fire to keep their opponents at bay, until they could safely drop down on the other side of the armoured vehicles. Then they could move steadily along the valley, fighting running skirmishes if necessary, until they reached the Government lines.

It wasn't much of a plan, Steve acknowledged. And right now, it didn't look as if it was working.

A grenade had exploded ten yards in front of them, and in the smoke and flame it kicked up, there was no choice but to stop. Dan had rolled one of his own grenades down towards the attacker, but it didn't detonate close enough to the soldiers to do any real damage. The valley was fiercely illuminated in the explosions and tracer fire, and the noise of the detonation mixed with the thunder to create a murderous barrage of noise that screamed and swirled around your ears.

Steve dropped to the ground, wiping the mud and grime from his face. 'We're not going to get through!' he shouted.

He glanced backwards. The men from the first armoured vehicle had sent a patrol up the hillside, trying to flush them out. They couldn't retreat now, he realised. There was nowhere to go.

Only straight into the fire.

He looked across at Ollie. The man's face was a mixture of determination and fear. All of them had dropped down into the mud to avoid the bullets spitting across the hillside. Ian had pulled Tshaka down with him, but the man was struggling like a caged bull and it took a pair of vicious blows across the face to calm him down.

They couldn't survive for long like this, Steve knew. They'd be taken to pieces by the grenades and the advancing troops. He pointed towards the first armoured vehicle. It had been damaged when the RPG round struck it, and the machine gunner had abandoned his post. If there were only one or two men on board, they could take it, use it for cover, and launch a fight back.

'Think we can charge it?' he panted.

'If we can't, we'll die trying,' Ollie gasped back.

Each member of the unit knew they had no choice but to risk their lives on one last desperate throw of the dice. If the machine gunner got hold of his weapon, they were all corpses. The chances of dying were far higher than the chances of surviving, and that simple fact was hammering into the hearts of each one of them.

'Bayonets?' said Maksim.

Steve nodded. 'Fix 'em.' He slotted the sharp steel blade onto the underside of his AK-47 and snapped the last of his full mags into place. He waited for five seconds whilst each man did the same, then waved them forwards. With guns outstretched, a small, human wave of steel and gunpowder rose up out of the mud, like corpses rising from a graveyard, and started to advance on the enemy position.

Steve began to run towards the vehicle. It was fifty yards away, all of it downhill, and they could cover the ground in a few seconds. He loosed off a few rounds just to the let the enemy know they were in a scrap, then accelerated hard. To the right, the men in the other armoured vehicle were starting to fire into them. Up on the hills, the soldiers flushing them out were turning their fire downwards. Steve pushed harder, driving himself forward: every second you were exposed to the murderous fire increased your chances of getting hit.

Nick was the fastest of them, and he bounded onto the vehicle first, a roar blasting from his strained lungs as he vaulted into the wall of thickly armoured steel. Dan, Chris and Maksim were on it in a flash, and suddenly the blades of their bayonets were everywhere. It was savage, hand-to-hand combat. In total, there were four men manning the vehicle, but they had been taken by surprise, and were now outnumbered. Nick had sliced open one man's stomach with his blade, whilst Chris slashed his own bayonet across his throat, emptying a pint of blood instantly. Maksim had shot one man straight in the face, sending him reeling backwards. A third was standing straight in front of Steve, reaching for his hand gun, but before he could get a grip on the pistol, Steve had already stabbed him hard in the chest with his bayonet, puncturing a lung and leaving him gasping for oxygen. The gun dropped from his hand. Steve drew out the blade, blood still dripping from its tip, and was about to stab him again, but Ollie had already put a bullet straight into his heart.

Dan and Chris crouched behind the vehicle.

'Take cover, take cover!' shouted Chris.

Steve flung himself behind the vehicle, looking around. He counted the bodies as they took over, checking each man in turn to make sure they were OK.

We've survived.

For now, he reminded himself.

Up ahead, the three remaining armoured vehicles had seen what had happened. And they were turning their fire straight into them.

Twenty-Eight

CHRIS HAD GRABBED HOLD OF the machine gun, spraying bullets towards the soldiers on the hillside. Two of them had been cut down by the gunfire, but the rest had scuttled back to the armoured vehicles.

Steve checked his mag. Three bullets left. Then he was out of ammo.

All ten men were sheltering behind the vehicles, with Tshaka still bound and gagged next to them. They were soaking, covered in blood and mud, and running dangerously low on ammo.

Up ahead, the armoured vehicles were advancing steadily towards them, their machine guns laying down heavy fire. Steve was rifling through the clothes of one of the corpses, ripping a mag from his chest webbing, but there were only another four bullets left in the clip.

'What's the next bright idea?' he said to Ollie.

'Pray.'

'Thanks, mate,' Steve said tersely. 'But there are military graveyards full of men who were doing just that.' The vehicles were only 100 yards ahead now, advancing in a tight formation. Less than a minute, and they'd be upon them.

'Use this bastard as a negotiating tool,' said Ian, grabbing hold of Tshaka.

'That's surrendering,' objected Chris.

'It's better than fecking dying,' shouted Ian. 'It's—' But the sentence was cut off by a huge explosion as one of the armoured vehicles ahead of them ignited. Flames were pouring out of the machine and lethal shards of shrapnel were flying everywhere. Steve ducked to avoid any of it hitting him. The screams of two men being incinerated split through the air, whilst another man jumped to the ground, his back covered in flames. He threw himself into the sodden mud, trying to put out the fire, but it was already too late: the flames had gripped his uniform, and within seconds the heat had melted his lungs.

Then another explosion.

And another.

'Watch out for shrapnel!' shouted Ollie. 'Get your heads down.'

Pulling his hard hat into place Steve hunkered down under the steel coating of the vehicle they were squatting behind. With shrapnel, you had to protect your head and your heart. A wound anywhere else could be fixed. Not in the head or heart, however. That killed you.

He listened as round after round crashed into the opposing vehicles.

He recognised the sound. It was the L118, a British-made artillery weapon, sold around the world and universally referred to as the 'Light Gun'. In service since 1975, the 'Light Gun' was a small artillery piece that could be dropped into the battlefield by helicopter or towed on a Land Rover. Its 105mm cannon could fire six to eight missiles a minute over a range of 17,000 yards, and its night-imaging kit meant it was effective even in the dark. Steve had trained with them plenty of times, as had most soldiers around the world: along with the American-manufactured variant, the M119A1 Howitzer, it was one of the most widely available field guns in modern military armouries.

I'd recognise the meaty thump of its shells anywhere, Steve told himself. And I'm sodding glad it's on our side. He counted five, six, then seven missiles crashing into their target, each one detonating with deadly impact. The heat rolled in waves through the valley, and his lungs were aching as the oxygen was sucked out of the air. But there could be no doubt about what was happening.

'Wallace?' said Steve, glancing towards Ollie.

Ollie wiped some of the grime from his face. 'Just in the nick of bloody time as well.'

The gun fell silent as suddenly as it had started up. The roar of the cannon faded, and the smoke cleared. Steve waited a few more seconds, making sure it wasn't just a lull in the combat, then looked down the valley. The armoured vehicles were smouldering wrecks, broken to pieces by the heavy shells blasting into them. Debris was lying everywhere, much of it still burning. Six corpses were visible on the ground, and there would be the charred remains of more inside the vehicles. One man was staggering forwards, clutching his face, clearly blinded from the way he was walking. Nick had already picked up his rifle and slotted a pair of bullets into his chest to finish him off. In the circumstances, it was the kindest thing to do, reflected Steve. They were decent soldiers, and they'd given a good account of themselves, but they'd lost and there was no point in any of them complaining about their fate now.

'Let's get the hell out of here,' he shouted at the others.

Dan had grabbed hold of Tshaka, and Chris was helping Ian. The unit moved at a swift jog through the valley, hopping over the puddles of burning diesel. Wallace's men were clearly visible a half-mile down the track. He was leading a convoy of four heavily armoured Land Rovers, with a single Light Gun planted in front of them, manned by a crew of three men. Steve picked up his pace, running across the slippery ground. We don't want to hang around here any longer than we have to, he said to himself. Who knew where Tshaka's army might have some reinforcements tucked away?

Wallace was sitting on top of his Land Rover. The still fierce rain was spitting into him, but he'd managed to keep his cigar alight, the thick smoke drifting across his dark face.

'I knew you boys were going to need your nappies changed at some point,' he said. 'I should have hired myself some proper soldiers.'

'They'd be welcome to the job as well,' said Steve calmly. 'We've got your man – but I can see why the President's boys are taking a beating.'

Dan had pushed Tshaka forward, and Wallace's men had already grabbed him by the shoulders and shoved him roughly into one of the waiting Land Rovers. He was still gagged, incapable of speech, but even so you could see the anger and fury in his eyes. He hadn't expected to be taken alive, realised Steve. For the last two days since he'd been captured, he had remained quietly confident that his men would free him. And now that he had been handed across to Wallace, he knew exactly the fate that awaited him.

He didn't mind dying, thought Steve. But at the hand of his sworn enemy? That wasn't a fate he'd settled for.

Ollie led the men into the back of a waiting truck. They climbed in one by one, settling down on the wooden floorboards, their heads lowered and their eyes strained. The truck kicked into first gear, pulling out onto the track and starting the short journey back to the fort at Gull's Wing. We'll talk when we get there, decided Steve. Maybe start to unwind. We are all shattered by the battle we've just been through, and it will take a while to get ourselves back in shape.

And this job's not even over yet.

We've still got a President to kill.

There were no lights in the fort when the truck drew up at the main gate. Six soldiers were stationed at the entry post, and another thirty inside. It was just after eleven at night – less than thirty-six hours since they had moved out of here, Steve reminded himself. But it seemed like a lifetime ago.

Just one more day, he told himself. *And then we're out of this hell-hole.*

Wallace was already out of his Land Rover, leading Tshaka towards a cell block, barking orders at his men. They had to reckon on Tshaka's army getting wind of where their leader was, and what was about to happen to him – and that meant they had to be prepared for a possible counter-strike. No one in the fort was getting any sleep tonight. They would remain on high alert until the job was finished.

Ollie was helping each man down from the truck. They walked wearily across to the barracks room, the same one they had slept in two nights ago. There was a table spread out with food, and some buckets with clean water, soap and towels.

'Christ, I could eat a bloody horse – I'm starving,' said Dan, picking up a couple of sandwiches and some chicken and stuffing them into his mouth.

Steve dipped his hands into a bucket. He could feel the dried blood and grime caked to his skin, and felt a sudden urge to wash himself completely clean. There were no showers, and the water was cold, but it felt good all the same. Ripping off his torn shirt, he splashed water all over himself, picking up the soap and rubbing it into his skin. There were nicks and cuts across his body, and they'd all need washing to make sure he didn't pick up any infections. Some of us eat, some of us wash, he reflected: it's just a way of shaking the smell of death from us.

'Bloody good show, boys,' said Wallace, walking into the room carrying three bottles of rum under his arm. 'We thought you were goners when you didn't call in on the radio.'

He chuckled to himself as he broke open a bottle. 'I was already wondering where the hell I could get some more madmen to take out Tshaka's fort. But you pulled through. It was a job well done – and if that doesn't deserve a bloody stiff drink, then I don't know what does.'

He poured the rum liberally into a series of mugs, and handed one to each man.

'To the President,' he said, raising his mug into the air and knocking back the shot of alcohol in a single gulp.

Steve held his hand rock steady. Dan, Chris, Ollie and, naturally, Maksim, were all drinking and refilling their cups. He'd never criticise a man for having a drink, not after what they'd just been through. But he couldn't toast the President. As he looked into Wallace's grey, soulless eyes, he could feel only contempt for the man. He was nothing but a hired gun, a killer who sold himself to the highest bidder. We're not like that, he reminded himself sharply. We fight when we have to, as the money is good. But only if the cause is morally OK.

'So what's the drill now?' asked Ollie.

'We've already radioed in to the President,' said Wallace. 'He's going to be getting a chopper down here at first light tomorrow. His chief security man Esram Matola is bringing him.'

'And then?'

'We don't want to waste any time with the execution,' said Wallace, taking another hit of the rum. 'As soon as the men get here, we'll strap that Tshaka bastard to a stake and get the big man to put some bullets into him.'

He opened up the second bottle of rum and put it on the table. Maksim immediately grabbed hold of it, pouring a measure into his cup.

'So you boys have a drink, then get your heads down,' Wallace told them. 'You can watch the show tomorrow morning. Then, if you want to, you can take a few days to see the sights, or you can all bugger straight off home.'

As he turned and left the room, Ollie poured himself a stiff drink, waiting until the door was shut before speaking. He checked no one was listening outside, then he glanced across at Steve. 'The job's just beginning.'

Steve nodded. 'We need a plan,' he said. He looked at Newton. 'How should we play it?'

'As soon as Kapembwa lands, he'll have my brother with him,' said Newton. 'I'll walk up to him and shake his hand. After I've whispered in his ear, I'll know that he's agreed to the plan. I'll nod to you twice, like so . . . then we wait for Tshaka to be executed. As soon as the deed is done, we put a bullet through the President. My brother will stop the troops from retaliating. Then we make our escape.'

'I think we should have something ready,' said Ian. 'A back-up plan.'

'There is no need. The plan is a good one,' Newton told him sternly. 'My brother controls the Army totally, and he'll do what I say.'

Ian shrugged. 'All the same, I don't like to hang around after an assassination.'

'We'll get a boat ready,' said David. 'We're only a mile from the lake. Let's secure a boat tonight, then get straight on that when the job's done and get clear into Tuka in less than an hour. We can catch a flight home from there.'

'We'll arrange that tonight,' agreed Ollie. 'And we'll have a jeep ready as well. I don't think any of us want to hang around this shit heap any longer than strictly necessary.'

'That's my country you're talking about,' said Newton sharply.

'We're taking your word for that,' said Ian in a suspicious tone. 'I just hope it's true.'

Twenty-Nine

STEVE TURNED IN HIS SIMPLE metal bed, trying to get some sleep. But the air was hot and sticky and humid. And you could smell murder in it.

He checked his watch, a Luminox Navy Seal diving watch, originally developed for the American special forces; his Uncle Ken had given it to him the day he was accepted into the SAS. It was just after four in the morning. After running through the plan last night, Ian, Steve and Ganju had slipped down to the lake and managed to wake up one of the fishermen sleeping on his vessel: they told the guards on the gate they needed some air. Steve had promised him one of the gold Krugerrands he carried on his belt and left one as a deposit. The one-ounce coin was worth $1,000 – more than enough to persuade the man to be waiting for them tomorrow morning, ready to ferry them across to Tuka.

At least we've got that sorted, Steve thought. With a bit of luck, by tomorrow lunchtime, we'll be sitting in the departure lounge, waiting for a plane back to London.

He thought briefly about Sam, wondering what she was doing and when he might see her again. He couldn't remember a time when a girl had made such an impact on him. A soldier needs something to march for, he reminded himself. Sometimes it was a flag, sometimes an ideal. And sometimes it was a woman – and in this case, the woman was Samantha. She needed a man who could avenge her parents and her country: it was her way of coming to terms with her past. She'd chosen Steve for that task and, so far, he hadn't any complaints about that.

Still thinking about her, he closed his eyes, determined to catch an hour or so of kip before the action kicked off again.

At five-thirty, David and Ollie were waking the unit up. The men were still exhausted by the battle they'd been through, but as soon as Dan brewed up a jug of coffee, the adrenaline and their training started to kick in. There was still fighting to be done. And until the last blow was landed on their enemy, none of them would be able to rest and recuperate properly.

'Foot OK?' Steve asked the Irishman.

Ian nodded. 'Painful, but I'll be all right,' he replied.

There was some bread and fruit left out on the table to make a simple breakfast. Steve washed and checked his webbing. The AK-47 was just about out of ammo, the grenades were gone, and even the Uzi was running dangerously low on supplies. The heavy weaponry had all been left behind. If anything went wrong, they didn't have much to hit back with.

'All set?' he enquired of Newton.

The man nodded, but remained silent.

'Good. We've a busy day ahead,' said Steve tersely.

As they stepped out of the barracks building they saw that the rain had eased up, but it might return at any moment: you could feel it in the stickiness of the air. Wallace had already led his men out onto the parade ground. They were as shabby and disorganised as the first time Steve had seen them. None of them knew how to drill properly, and none of them had any idea how to hold their weapons. There were only two fighting forces in this country, he thought – the Sixth Brigade, and Tshaka's guerrillas. And one of them was about to get beaten.

'A good morning for a hanging,' said Wallace. He lit up his cigar and choked violently as the smoke flooded his lungs.

'If you like that sort of thing,' said Steve flatly. Up above, he could hear the sound of a chopper. It was still above the clouds, but quickly dropped down, and within seconds the Chinese-built Z-11 military helicopter had landed on the parade ground. Based on the French AS 350B, the Z-11 weighed two tons and had room for six seats. A huge cloud of dust was kicked into the air as it came into land, and a few of the soldiers scuttled out of the way. The pilot killed the engine, allowing a minute for the dust to settle before pulling out the steps that allowed Kapembwa to step out into the fort.

'Ever met a President before?' hissed Ollie at Steve's side.

'Not one I'm about to assassinate,' he answered with a half-smile.

Kapembwa was in late middle age, but was still a strong, commanding figure as he stepped confidently from the helicopter and down onto the ground. Of medium height and build, his hair had greyed but was still thick, and had been combed carefully into place. He was wearing a dark charcoal suit with a white open-necked shirt and a baseball cap. As his eyes swept through the fort, you could feel the man's presence immediately: imperious and cruel, his was the look of a man who came to command and conquer. And, if necessary, destroy.

Matola was walking steadily at his side. Over six foot, he was dressed in full military uniform, with a handgun prominently displayed on his belt. You could see the resemblance to Newton right away. It was there in the cut of his face and the shape of his eyes. Twin brothers, thought Steve. They may have separated a couple of lifetimes ago, but you could see the bond instantly.

'Tshaka is here?' said Kapembwa, looking straight at Wallace.

'Yes, sir,' Wallace replied respectfully.

'And who are the men I need to thank?' Kapembwa went on.

'These chaps,' said Wallace, nodding towards Steve and the rest of the unit.

Kapembwa took a step forward, offering Steve his hand. He shook it. But the man's handshake was limp and cold, as if the blood had been drained out of his veins.

'Who is your leader?' Kapembwa asked.

'We don't have one,' Steve told him.

A slow smile – the smile of a crocodile – started to crease the older man's lips. 'Every order of men must have a leader.'

'Not us. We work for each other.'

'Trust me, I know more about politics than you do, and I know that you have a leader,' said Kapembwa. 'Even if he hasn't revealed himself yet.'

We'll see about that, mate, thought Steve. But he remained silent.

'You have captured a dangerous criminal,' continued Kapembwa. 'For that, Mr Wallace will make sure you are well paid. But you should know as well that you have earned the gratitude of the Batotean people.'

Not like we will in the next few minutes, thought Steve. *When we put a round of bullets into you.*

'Bring out the prisoner, Mr Wallace,' commanded Kapembwa.

Wallace barked an order to one of his men. A minute later, Tshaka was led out of the cell block, and marched across the parade ground. The barrel of an AK-47 was jabbing into his back. He carried himself with dignity, noted Steve. He was striding purposefully towards his fate, even though he must know there was little chance of escape. A blindfold was strapped around his face, his hands were tied behind his back, and his uniform was torn and dirty. There was a smell of blood and dirt clinging to his skin. But he showed not so much as a flicker of fear as he was led towards a stake that had been hammered into the centre of the parade ground.

'I've waited a long time for this moment,' said Kapembwa, a thin smile on his lips.

Newton had taken five steps forward and was shaking Matola by the hand. The two men were remaining calm, betraying no emotion. But as Newton turned around, there was a tight smile drawn on his lips. He whispered a word into Matola's ear, then looked back to Ollie and nodded twice.

The message was clear enough.

We're on.

'He looks tense,' muttered Ian, standing at Steve's side.

'You'd be sodding tense if you were about to kill your President.'

Ian was edging back.

Behind them, a Land Rover was parked close to the fort's main gates. It was idle, but the key were still in the ignition. The soldiers in the camp had all been lined up on the other side of the parade ground to watch the execution. One man had been given a camcorder to hold, and another was taking snaps with an ordinary digital camera.

I'll watch the show from here, decided Ian.

Just in case.

'Bring me a gun,' barked Kapembwa.

'Which weapon, sir?' asked Wallace.

The man thought for a moment, the same way a wine connoisseur might hesitate while deciding which vintage to choose.

'A Heckler and Koch USP,' said Kapembwa.

Good choice, thought Steve. With 9×19mm parabellum ammunition, the Heckler was a modern German weapon, good enough to be chosen as the standard firearm for the German Army or *Bundeswehr*. Say what you like about the Krauts, reflected Steve, they knew a bit about weaponry. The *Bundeswehr* didn't put in an order for a couple of hundred thousand handguns without knowing they were buying quality.

From the corner of his eye, he could see Ian edging closer to the Land Rover. Instinctively, Steve did the same, with Nick following along at his side.

In the sky, some rain was starting to spit out of the heavy clouds. It'll be sheeting down in a minute, thought Steve. But the poor bastard on the stake won't be around to feel it.

And neither will the President.

Kapembwa held the Heckler & Koch in his right hand; he was just twenty feet away from his target. His hand was rock steady, noted Steve. You could still see that he had been a guerrilla leader long before he became a politician. 'You're ready?' he asked the prisoner.

'Remove my blindfold,' said Tshaka.

'Shut up,' snarled Wallace.

'No,' said the President. 'Remove it.'

Wallace nodded towards one of the soldiers. The man stepped forward, cutting free the cloth covering Tshaka's eyes, allowing it to drop to the ground.

Kapembwa squeezed the trigger.

The bullet slotted neatly into the side of Tshaka's head. His body jerked, as if a bolt of electricity had shot through him, then slumped. Blood was starting to seep out of his forehead.

Kapembwa squeezed again on the trigger.

A double tap, thought Steve. Right out of the Regiment textbook.

The second bullet caught Tshaka on the cheek, slicing open the skin, then drilling into the bone of the skull. But the man didn't so much as twitch. The first bullet had already killed him.

Tshaka was slumped forward, only the ropes binding him to the stake holding him upright.

'That's the end of your rebellion, my friend,' said Kapembwa softly.

Steve glanced towards Newton.

Now, he thought to himself. Pull your Uzi, and let the bastard have a taste of his own medicine.

Thirty

EWTON HAD PULLED THE UZI from his webbing. His finger was resting on the trigger. A bead of sweat was running down the side of his face, but otherwise he was calm and composed.

With a flick of his wrist, he pointed the gun straight towards Dan, Ollie and the rest of the men. In the same moment, Kapembwa turned around with his own gun. So did Wallace and the thirty soldiers standing right behind him.

'Don't even think about moving,' growled Wallace.

Steve could see at once what was happening.

They had been betrayed.

Behind him, Ian had already jumped into the Land Rover and fired the engine into life. Steve hurled himself into the back of the vehicle, Nick at his side. The wheels were skidding against the dusty surface of the parade ground as Steve thrust out a hand, grabbing Nick by the wrist and dragging him up. As Steve looked back, Wallace's men were jabbing their rifles into the rest of the unit, forcing them to throw their weapons to the ground.

'Move out!' he shouted at Ian.

The command was unnecessary. The Irishman had already slammed his foot on the accelerator, and was climbing up through thirty then forty miles an hour.

They were heading straight towards the exit.

Wallace had seen what was happening and started barking orders to his men. He pulled his own gun and fired one, then two rounds into them, but they flashed harmlessly past. The Land Rover was swaying as it hit the exit. With a sickening thud, it smashed into the guard at the gates, and you could feel it shake as the big tyres crushed the man's lungs. Ian just slammed his foot harder to the floor, swerving the Land Rover out onto the dirt track then down towards the lake.

'What about the others?' shouted Nick.

'There's no time.'

'We can't—'

'We're going to the lake!' yelled Steve, making sure Ian had heard him.

He looked back towards the fort. He'd seen the look of anguish on the faces of each of the men as the guns jabbed into their backs. There's nothing we can do, he told himself grimly. There are thirty soldiers in there, they are holding our mates hostage, and we're short on ammo. If we go back in, it will be a bloodbath.

And it will be our blood.

But we will be back, he vowed.

Soon.

The Land Rover was jerking wildly as it bounced over the holes and bumps in the track. Ian was driving at a breakneck speed, struggling to control the machine as it climbed up to sixty. It was a suicidal speed, but there was no choice. As soon as Wallace had his prisoners under control, he'd be scrambling his men into action.

'If you see something, shoot it,' Steve muttered towards Nick. He had already pulled the Uzi free from his own webbing, but through the dust kicked up in their wake, it was impossible to see anything apart from the occasional flash of forest and grassland.

Ian brought the Land Rover skidding to a shuddering halt at the edge of the jetty. Steve was flung forwards as the car braked, and it took all his control to stop himself from loosening off a few rounds from the automatic pistol. Maybe I'm going to die here, he thought to himself. But it's going to be in a battle, not an accident.

'Move!' screamed Ian.

The three men started to run towards the waiting fishing boat.

Ollie could feel the cold steel tip of an AK-47 jabbing into his back. 'Stand totally still,' barked the soldier. 'Or you die right here, right now.'

Up ahead, he could see the Land Rover, with Ian at the wheel, spin through the gates. He'd seen Steve and Nick climb on board, and he was cursing himself for not having had the wits to stand closer to the vehicle.

But it's too late now, he told himself. And we won't get a second chance.

'Drop your weapon,' the soldier ordered.

Ollie stood still. At his side, he could see Dan, Chris, Ganju, David and Maksim, all standing immobile. Newton was whispering something into his brother's ear and the President was folding away the gun Wallace had given him. Some light rain was starting to spit across the parade ground. Maybe I've had worse mornings, thought Ollie bitterly. But right now I can't think of any.

'Drop it.' The AK-47 was digging into his skin, the metal growing warm and sticky from the sweat running off Ollie's back.

'Do what he says,' snapped Wallace, looking across at Ollie. 'We don't give a damn about shooting you right now.'

Ollie fished inside his webbing and drew out the Uzi. He could feel a stab of regret in his chest as it landed on the ground, but he knew there was no choice. He didn't rate their chances of survival very highly right now, and he wouldn't have minded going out in a blaze of gunfire. But he knew he'd be dead before a single shot was fired. If I'm going to throw my life away, he told himself, I'll make sure I take some of these bastards down with me.

A soldier stooped to pick up the weapons each of the men had thrown on the ground.

'Bind them,' commanded Wallace.

Ollie thrust his hands behind his back. He could feel the Plasti-Cuffs snapping into place. The plastic was tight, cutting uncomfortably into his skin. Across the parade ground, Kapembwa was walking with Newton and Matola back towards the waiting chopper, pulling the steps up behind them as they climbed inside.

'The men who escaped,' Wallace shouted to one of the soldiers standing closest to him. 'I want them caught and shot. Show them no mercy.'

Steve heard the roar of a vehicle crashing down the dirt track, followed by the rattle of an AK-47, its bullets cutting through the damp morning air. Leaping from the side of the Land Rover, he started to run towards the jetty.

'I can hold them,' shouted Nick.

'Just sodding run,' yelled Steve.

Ahead, Ian was hurrying towards one of the three boats tied up to the mooring. It was a simple fishing vessel, thirty feet long, with a Honda outboard engine. The fisherman was standing right next to it. By now, Ian was already standing on the open deck, shouting at them furiously to get on board.

Steve glanced around. Nick was racing past him, jumping onto the boat. Behind him a Land Rover was hurtling down the dirt track towards them; there was no way of knowing how many men were on board, but bullets were flying in every direction.

He looked towards the two fishermen standing by their boats. Both men were young, twenty or twenty-one, with strong, lean bodies, their muscles strengthened by long days hauling nets from the lake. Drawing his Uzi, he jabbed it towards them. 'Disable your boats,' he shouted.

Both men remained still.

'There's no time,' yelled Ian.

There has to be time, thought Steve. If those soldiers get hold of a boat, then we're done for. They'll chase us across the lake.

Behind him, the Land Rover was screeching up towards the jetty. Steve took aim.

Squeezing hard on the trigger, he pumped the few remaining rounds of ammo into the engine of one of the boats. It took six shots before the engine caught fire, sending a sudden shaft of flame shooting upwards, and a cloud of black smoke into the air.

'You fucking bastard,' shouted the fisherman, lunging towards Steve.

Steve put one bullet into the jetty next to the man's feet. It was enough to stop him dead in his tracks. Suddenly, he heard a burst of gunfire behind him. The Land Rover had screeched to a halt. Two soldiers were leaning out of its side, putting down round after round of fire from their AK-47s.

With no time to waste, he ripped the one remaining grenade from his chest, pulled the pin and dropped it into the second vessel. No sooner had he released it from his hand than Steve lunged into the boat. Ian had already gripped the motor, and kicked off into the water. The sound of gunfire echoed all around them.

Behind them the grenade detonated. Splinters of wood shrieked across the lake. A ball of fire ripped into the air, and whether either of the fishermen had survived, it was impossible to tell. Through a wall of flame, the soldiers were setting up a volley of fire but could see nothing clearly through the clouds of smoke.

Ducking down to the bottom of the boat, Steve let the spray wash over him. Ian had put the engine on full throttle, squeezing every last ounce of power out of its four-horsepower engine. The boat was picking up speed as it steered through the choppy waters and towards the Tukan border.

Less than a mile, Steve thought to himself. And then at least we'll be out of this sodding country. And we can start plotting our strike back.

'Move it towards the damned truck,' Wallace bellowed.

Ollie remained motionless, still dazed by the suddenness and violence of the attack. He'd already figured that Newton must have been betraying them from the start. But Archie Sharratt as well? It hardly seemed possible.

'I said *move!*'

The soldier jabbed the butt of the AK-47 hard into his back. It was like having a baseball bat smashed into your spine. Reluctantly, Ollie started to walk forwards. A Hyundai Cargo Truck had pulled up at the exit to the fort. One by one the men were being pushed inside. The surface was made from flat boards, and there was building debris clinging to its surface.

'What's happening?' asked Ollie, turning around to look back at Wallace.

'We're going to put you on trial for plotting to assassinate our President,' said Wallace.

He laughed to himself, and relit the stub of the cigar in his mouth.

'And then we're going to bloody execute you.'

Thirty-One

THE JETTY LOOMED UP OUT of the pouring rain.

Steve stood on the prow of the small boat, waiting until he was close enough to reach out and grab the wooden pier. It had been a tough journey. The wind was blowing hard across the lake, and the rain had kicked in when they were just a few hundred yards away from the Batotean shore. At times, it was so heavy, you could only see a few feet ahead of you. Nick and Ian were bailing water out of the boat, whilst the fisherman, Kingston, steered, and Steve used his compass to keep them heading due north towards the Tukan shoreline.

At least the rain means we're invisible, Steve had consoled himself as he felt the storm lashing into his clothes. Even if they had a boat, Wallace's men would never find them in weather this rough.

'Where are we?' said Ian, climbing onto the jetty.

'Place called Siavonga,' answered Kingston, using a rope to secure the boat.

Steve glanced down the main street. It was a dusty little place, with fifty or so houses, and three or four shops. There were some fishing boats, and a pair of pleasure cruisers that took tourists out on runs into the lake, but this was the rainy season and even the Germans and the Dutch didn't go on safari then. Only a couple of fishermen were on the dock, repairing their rods and lines, and one taxi driver was standing next to a battered old Toyota waiting for any trade that might be passing.

'How much do we owe you?' asked Steve, looking back towards Kingston.

'Three thousand dollars.'

'I thought—' Steve started to protest, but Kingston was ready with his reply. 'I've risked my life for you, man,' he said. 'I can't go back to Batota now. I'll have the army on my back, and if they find me, they'll kill me. I don't care about that. The whole country is going to hell anyway. The fish in the lake are the only things that are worth anything, and that's not much. But if I'm going to start again, it will take money. And you owe me.'

'He's right – we owe him, Steve,' said Ian sharply.

Steve backed away. The pair of fishermen at the dockside were looking at them warily, and they were both big, hulking guys with muscles toned from years of hauling nets. If it came to a ruck, there was no doubt whose side they were going to be on, he decided.

'This isn't his war,' Ian continued. 'He didn't ask to get mixed up in this.'

True enough, acknowledged Steve. Each of them were carrying three gold Krugerrands, worth about $1,000 apiece. Steve took three from his belt and handed them across to Kingston with a pat on the back. 'Good luck,' he said – and meant it.

The three men started to walk towards the single taxi. The driver had already opened the door for them, a thick smile on his lips. He'd seen the three gold coins. The strange men on the jetty might look rough, but they had money, and that made them a rarity in Siavonga.

'You're paying for the rest of the trip,' Steve said, glancing across at Ian.

'In that case, we're travelling economy,' Ian replied with a rough smile.

They asked the taxi driver to take them to the only money-changer in town – an Egyptian called Hazem, who offered to swap one Krugerrand for the local currency, the Tukan kwacha. The official rate was three point two kwacha to the dollar, which made the gold coins worth $3,200. Hazem offered them $2,500 and allowed himself to be haggled up to $3,000. They were still getting ripped off, Steve knew, but they had more important things to worry about right now.

'Take us to the best hotel in town,' said Ian, climbing back into the taxi.

'I hope they've got some grub,' said Nick. 'I'm bloody starving.'

Ollie reckoned he had a bruise for every pothole the truck had crashed through. By the time it finally pulled up, his bones were aching and he was wet through from the rain that had poured down on them as they travelled towards Ibera. They had spent the last fifteen hours strapped in the back of the truck whilst it made its way south, twisting through the traffic, with a two-vehicle military escort. Even with the soldiers clearing the way, it was still a painfully slow journey, with constant obstacles on the road.

But that hardly mattered Ollie thought. It wasn't as if things were going to get any better when they arrived.

'Move yourselves,' barked Wallace.

Ollie stood up and started to lower himself out of the truck. It was night now, with heavy clouds covering the city, and there were only a few lights illuminating the parade ground where the truck had pulled up.

But Ollie didn't need any light to recognise it.

The Headquarters of the Sixth Brigade.

The very last place in Batota they wanted to be right now.

A reception party of ten soldiers had lined up to greet them, each of them armed with an AK-47. The six men climbed out one by one until they were all standing on the ground. One of the soldiers slammed the butt of his rifle into Ganju's ribs, then gestured towards a nearby building. One by one they started to walk. They were taken into a barracks block, then down a flight of concrete stairs that led into a damp basement. One light bulb provided all the illumination, but it was enough to see the four cells. In the first, two men were chained up, but the light was so bad, it was impossible to see anything apart from two pairs of beaten, starving eyes.

One cell door was open.

The soldier threw Ganju inside, then motioned to the rest of the men to follow. As the door slammed behind them and the key was turned in the lock, Wallace relit his cigar, the flame from his lighter briefly revealing the blood and excrement that covered the walls and the floor.

'Just in case you boys were wondering what the drill is,' he said with a cruel grin, 'we're going to try you, then we're going to execute you. So if I were you, I'd pray for a quick death. It's the best you can hope for now.'

The receptionist at Eagle Wing Lodge wasn't impressed, decided Steve. And frankly, who could blame her? Three blokes, wet to their skins, their faces muddy and bruised, and with what looked like full military kit attached to their chests. I wouldn't want us checking into the hotel either, he thought.

Putting 1,000 kwacha down on the table, he said, 'We need a room badly.'

'*Three* rooms,' said Ian. 'I'm not sharing with this bloke.' He flashed the receptionist a rough grin. 'I mean, just smell him.'

The Eagle Wing was the closest to an upscale hotel you could find anywhere in the area. Located five miles from the town, it had a fine position on a ridge of high ground looking down onto the valley and then the lake below. With thirty individual wooden huts, it was built for the safari tours, but this was way out of season, and the place was empty, kept open with a skeleton staff until the rains were through. The reception fronted a bar and restaurant, and was decorated with pictures of big game. The woman at the desk was eyeing the notes on the table. Steve put another 200 down. 'That's for you,' he said.

Taking the money, she folded it into her tunic then pushed three room keys across the desk. 'Welcome to the Eagle Wing,' she said, with a forced 'have-a-nice-day' smile. 'And enjoy your stay.'

Steve took his key and started to walk towards lodge number twelve. The rain was still falling heavily as they stepped through gardens lushly planted with flowers and trees. From their vantage point, they could see clearly out across the lake and, at this height, straight into Batota.

'We're going right back,' Steve told the others.

'I know,' said Ian. 'But first we rest . . . and plan.'

'We can't leave Ollie and the rest of the boys there,' said Nick. You could hear the anger in his voice.

'It's three men against a whole country,' said Ian wearily.

Steve nodded, still looking out across the lake. 'I know,' he replied, his voice threaded with quiet determination. 'But it's the right three men . . . and the wrong country.'

Thirty-Two

STEVE HELPED HIMSELF TO A bowl of cereal, a jug of coffee and a carton of orange juice from the breakfast bar. The clouds had cleared, and the lake was a dazzling, deep blue. Birds were skating across its surface, and over in the distance, you could see the wide open spaces of the safari parks.

A beautiful country, he thought to himself. If only there weren't so many madmen screwing the place up.

Ian had persuaded him they should get some sleep and get their strength back, and although he'd disagreed with him at the time, now that it was morning Steve could see he'd been right. He'd put his head down, and crashed for twelve hours straight. By the time he woke up, the impact of what had turned into forty-eight hours of non-stop fighting was starting to fade. The bruises and the cuts were still there, but the spirit and determination were back. And that was what counted.

We'll get our mates out, he told himself, pouring milk on top of his cereal. But we have to plan our way in and out again. Otherwise we're just throwing our lives away.

'We've got work to do,' said Ian, sitting next to him, with Nick at his side.

From a single glance, it was obvious that both of them had been up for a couple of hours. They were washed and shaved, and wearing some fresh clothes that they must have bought at the lobby desk.

They looked like a pair of out-of-season tourists: it was only if you got up close that you became aware of the fury in their eyes.

'There's something you should see.'

Steve stood up and followed Ian into the hotel bar. There was a TV in the corner, tuned to CNN. The weather forecast was playing right now – more heavy storms were forecast for South and Central Africa – but the headlines were coming up next.

'Watch,' muttered Ian.

Steve looked straight at the screen.

'Our top story this hour,' said the newscaster. 'President Kapembwa of Batota foils an assassination plot. CNN reporters are not allowed into the country, but our Southern Africa correspondent Kenneth Mialich reports from Johannesburg. Ken . . .'

Steve's eyes tracked the screen as a man in a white open-necked shirt appeared.

'A dramatic day in Ibera,' started the reporter. 'Veteran leader Benjamin Kapembwa claims to have foiled an assassination plot sponsored by Britain and other Western governments.'

Footage of Kapembwa speaking to an angry-looking crowd flashed up on the screen.

'He has accused the British Government of conspiring with a group of white mercenaries to assassinate him and to bring back colonial rule,' continued Mialich. 'He said they'd been working alongside the rebel leader August Tshaka – who has now been executed – and were planning to assassinate him too, as a prelude to a full-scale coup.'

The report cut to Kapembwa booming into a microphone. 'The British want to bring the white man back to rule in Batota.' he said. 'They want the white men to take over the farms once again, to run the factories, and to own the Government. But we have defeated them before – and we will defeat them again.'

Back on screen, Mialich continued the story. 'The arrested mercenaries have been named. Ollie Hall, formerly of the British

Army's prestigious Household Cavalry, is reported as being the leader of the group. He is joined by five other men, named as David Mallet, another Englishman, Chris Reynolds, a South African, Dan Coleman, an Australian, Ganju Rai, a former Gurkha, and Maksim Perova, a Russian citizen. A spokesman for the British Foreign Office said in London this morning that they had no knowledge of the plot, but refused to say whether the Government would be asking for their release. The statement went on to say that the UK can't condone mercenaries, nor can it help British citizens who may have broken the laws of a country they are visiting.'

'And what's the view on what's likely to happen to these men, Ken?' asked the newscaster.

'A trial is being organised for the next couple of days in Ibera,' answered Mialich, looking straight to the camera. 'We'll have to wait for that for the next stage in this drama.'

'And do people think there really was a coup attempt?'

'It's certainly very convenient for the President,' answered Mialich. 'There's a Presidential election in a few days, and with the Batotean economy in ruins, the threat of foreign military intervention is about the only thing that could rally support back to his cause. Against that, these are all men with military backgrounds, August Tshaka has been killed, and they were arrested in Batota – so something may have been going on. At this stage we just don't know the full story.'

'Thanks, Ken,' said the newscaster. 'And now to other news. It was another turbulent day for global stock markets . . .'

Ian stood up and switched off the television.

'Bastards,' muttered Steve, grinding his fists together. He took another hit of his coffee. 'Sharratt must have planned this from the start,' he continued. 'But what the hell is the man playing at?'

'I think I can tell you,' said Ian.

Both Steve and Nick were looking straight up at him.

'There's a computer with a web connection in the lobby, and I've been doing some research,' Ian continued. 'After I saw that our men had been arrested and accused of plotting to murder the President, I checked out the prices of Sharratt's hedge fund. It jumped in the City yesterday, up by almost thirty per cent. The reason? Well, one of the companies it controls just announced a major new deal. It's discovered some serious platinum deposits in Eastern Batota. Tons of the stuff, apparently, and platinum trades at two thousand dollars an ounce, making it more than twice as expensive as gold. The mining company Sharratt controls has just been granted a twenty-five-year licence by President Kapembwa to exploit the mine.'

'What an arsehole,' muttered Nick.

'Exactly,' said Ian. 'I reckon Sharratt was playing us for suckers right from the start. He wanted the mining licence, so he offered Kapembwa a deal. He'd find some boys to take out his enemy for him, then he'd set them up with an assassination plot. It was all designed to whip up public sympathy for him ahead of the elections. If there's one thing that plays well in Africa, it's the threat of the old white colonialists coming back and seizing power again. He just needed a gang of mercenaries to be the fall guys.'

'And Sharratt chose us,' said Steve, his tone hard and bitter.

'Precisely,' said Ian.

'OK – we were going to kill the bastard for money, now we'll do it for revenge,' said Steve. 'And once we've done that, we'll hunt down Sharratt and finish him as well.'

'The question is how?' said Ian.

Steve was thinking. He was looking out of the window, out at the lake, and out into Batota. There has to be a way, he told himself. It's just a question of finding it.

At that moment, the receptionist walked into the bar. 'Mr West?'

Steve looked around. 'Yes?'

'There's someone to see you.'

Steve paused. Me? *How the hell could anyone know I'm here?*

'Who is it?'

'They want you to come and meet them in the lobby.'

'Tell them I'll be there in a moment,' said Steve curtly. He glanced across at Ian as soon as the woman left the room. 'Maybe one of Wallace's men?' he said.

Ian nodded, his expression tense. 'Or one of Sharratt's guys,' he said. 'I reckon he figured we'd all be executed by his mate Kapembwa and he wouldn't have to worry about us any more. The last thing he wants is to have us out in the open. Even if we can't get Ollie and the boys out, he knows we'll track him down, and when we find him we'll empty every last pint of blood out of his lying, treacherous body.'

Steve nodded, permitting himself a smile. There was no mistaking Ian's anger. No one pursued a vendetta like an Ulsterman, that much was certain. Get into a grudge fight with one of those guys, and it could last for centuries.

'But how would he find us here?' interrupted Nick.

'The taxi driver, maybe?'

Ian nodded his agreement. 'Word gets around a place like this pretty fast. We're not safe here.'

'I'm going to see who it is,' said Steve. He'd already unhooked his Uzi from his belt. Taking three bullets from Nick, he slotted them into the mag. 'Make sure I'm covered,' he told the other two.

Steve stepped out towards the lobby, his gun concealed inside his loose-fitting shirt. As he did so, he checked behind him, noting that both Ian and Nick were ready to spring into action.

If it was one of Wallace's or Sharratt's men, they'd gun him down on the spot.

But the lobby was empty.

'She's waiting for you in the garden,' said the receptionist.

'*She?*' The surprise was evident in his tone.

The receptionist was looking at him suspiciously. She hadn't liked the look of the three men much when they checked in yesterday, and it was clear from her expression that she was regretting having taken their money.

'That way,' she said sharply. Her tone suggested she couldn't wait to be rid of them.

Steve stepped out into the garden. He looked around, glancing through the flowers and the shrubs that filled the lawn running towards the lake. There was an eerie silence, with just a light breeze rustling through the flowers, and that made him uncomfortable. He sensed he might be drawn into a killing ground.

Drawing the Uzi from his belt, he placed his finger on the trigger, ready to unleash a blast of automatic fire.

Then he saw her.

She was standing with her back to him, looking out into the lake, but he'd recognise her flowing blond hair and the subtle curve of her hips anywhere.

Samantha.

Hearing him approach, she turned. Her eyes looked towards the gun, then up into Steve's face.

'You can put that away,' she said. 'You don't have to shoot me. I'm not the enemy.'

Thirty-Three

THE AIR INSIDE THE CELL was warm and sticky, like being stuck inside windowless toilet that hadn't been cleaned for years. Ollie turned on his side. When he glanced at his watch, he saw that it was only just after five in the morning. He'd slept fitfully through the night, never for more than a few minutes at a time, and he could feel the exhaustion in every bone in his body. 'Bastards,' he muttered under his breath for the thousandth time in a row. *Whatever the plot was, how could we possibly have fallen for it?*

There were six of them, all locked in a cell that measured just twelve foot by eight. The basement was plunged into near total darkness, and there was a film of sweaty, dirty damp on the walls. Across the floor were strewn a few old rags, but no straw, and nothing you could use as a bed. There was a bucket in the corner to use as a lavatory, but it was already full, and the smell from it mixed with the sweat and the stench of the men to create a punching, ugly aroma that ripped up your lungs with every breath. On the wall, Ollie noted a single word had been scratched into the old stone. *Hell.*

'Why the understatement?' quipped Dan when he read it.

True enough, thought Ollie to himself as he looked at it again. Hell itself must surely be better than this place. They had been led down here last night, and offered neither food nor water. Nor had anyone said how long they'd be kept locked up. They had been given nothing to drink during the long drive down to Ibera, and most of them were starting to get dehydrated even then. They were in an even worse state now.

Ollie tried to close his eyes. They were lying three abreast on the hard stone, and even though most of them had learned early during their military careers to kip down anywhere, it wasn't easy. Even Maksim was finding it hard, and they had never heard the Russian complain about the conditions before. In the end, Ollie just lay still in the darkness, gnawing away at the only issue that now mattered.

How are we going to get out of here?

A torchlight flashed suddenly through the dark space. All of the men sat up, rubbing some of the sweat and grime out of their eyes. A guard was approaching them, an elderly man, with hair turning white, a slight stoop to his back, and two buckets in his hand. Stopping by the first cell, he unlocked the door, pushed one of the buckets through an opening in its bars, then moved silently towards the next cell. He flashed the torchlight on the men, and for a brief second Ollie's eyes recoiled from the glare. The man then pushed the bucket into their cell, along with a single tin cup.

'Food,' he said, his tone harsh and rasping. 'There will be nothing else until that's finished.'

Ollie watched as the man turned away, and climbed back up the stairs. They're trying to break us, he decided. But why?

They've already said they're planning to execute us. What more can they want?

'Grub's up, boys,' said Dan cheerfully, reaching across to the bucket.

'Let me guess,' said David. 'Some lightly smoked salmon with scrambled eggs and a plate of hot buttered toast.'

'No – I think it's caviar on black bread, with a vodka shot to chase it down,' said Maksim, grinning.

'Or maybe some croissants, cooked to perfection, with some fresh marmalade, and a bowl of fruit salad,' put in Ganju.

'Or a bowl of hot porridge, with a shot of brandy in it to get you awake,' said Chris.

'You're all wrong. It's a Full English,' said Ollie. 'Sausages, bacon, eggs, mushrooms and fried bread, with a big mug of tea and the sports section of the *Telegraph* to read.'

'With your boys winning at the football,' said Dan.

'Now it really is a fantasy,' said Chris.

'Sorry to disappoint you, lads,' said Dan, glancing into the bucket 'but the menu isn't quite living up to our expectations.'

The cell fell silent. If Dan didn't rate the grub, that really was a bad sign, decided Ollie. The Aussie would eat anything.

'Give us the good news,' said Chris finally.

Dan's face had turned a sickly colour. 'It's mostly water, but I suspect they've mixed some sewage into it. There's a dead rat floating on the top. Not sure if we're meant to eat that or not. There's quite a few old potato peelings, some bits of carrot . . .'

'It could be puke,' said Chris.

'Thanks, mate,' said Dan. 'I was trying to look on the bright side.'

'I think I'm losing my appetite,' said David.

Ollie took the cup and plunged it into the bucket. Whatever Wallace was planning for them, he didn't reckon it included poisoning them in their prison cells. If he wanted them dead, he'd have let them have a bullet in the head back in the fort. Throwing the water down his throat, he struggled to hold it there.

'We have to drink, and we need to eat something,' he said, once he'd got the swill down into his stomach, and managed to suppress the violent urge to vomit. 'I'm not planning on dying here, so let's get some food inside us until we can figure a way out of here.'

Chris took a swig from the cup Ollie had just handed him. 'Could use a little salt,' he said, wiping some of the grime away from his mouth.

'And maybe some pepper – freshly ground of course,' said Dan, picking away what looked unpleasantly like some rat hair that had lodged itself in the half-inch of stubble that had grown on his chin since the mission had begun.

'Gallows humour,' snarled Wallace. 'I'm glad to see you boys have got the measure of the situation. Because the only way you're getting out of this fix is on the end of a rope.'

He had just walked down the stairs and was leering into the cell, his rough face illuminated only by the dull amber glow of his cigar stub. Standing directly behind him was a man in his fifties, dressed in a dark blue suit and with an attaché case in his hand. His face was solemn, and he remained two paces behind Wallace, but looking straight into the eyes of the men locked up in front of him.

Dan turned around and, from the end of his tongue, flicked a slither of potato peel straight into Wallace's face. 'Do you mind keeping the noise down, mate,' he said belligerently, 'we're trying to have some breakfast here.'

Wallace removed the peel from his cheek. 'You'll regret that,' he said.

'Yeah, it was a waste of some good grub.'

Wallace turned around, and gestured to the man in the blue suit. He edged up to the front of the cage, his face wrinkling up as he did so. It's the smell, decided Ollie. The bloke hasn't got the stomach for it.

'My name is Clement Mobani,' he said. His eyes swivelled from man to man, the disdain evident in his expression. 'I am a prosecutor for the Batotean Government,' he continued. 'You are being charged with conspiracy to murder in connection with a plot to assassinate our President. I need hardly tell you that these are grave charges, and the penalty under Batotean law is death.'

'OK, OK, now tell us the good news,' said Ollie with a rough grin.

'I'm afraid there isn't any good news, Mr Hall. If there was, you wouldn't be here.' He drew a spotless white handkerchief from his pocket, and wiped his forehead. 'A trial is being scheduled. But it would be better for everyone if you agree to sign a full confession before then.'

'What about a defence lawyer?' said Ganju.

Mobani's smile was both gentle and mocking at the same time. 'I'm afraid for a crime of this severity, that won't be possible,' he replied.

'Nice system,' said David.

'You'll find that Batotean justice is far superior to the British system,' said Mobani. 'And we certainly intend to take no lessons from colonial dogs like you.' He opened the attaché case. 'I have six confessions already prepared. I just need your signatures.'

'Piss off,' spat Dan.

Wallace leered closer into the bars of the cage, flicking some ash down on the men inside. 'Learn some bloody manners.'

'Learn to stick to a bloody contract,' snapped Dan.

Wallace backed away.

'You hired us to do a job and we've risked our lives doing it well,' snarled David. 'And this is how you repay us.'

'You boys took your chances – that's the business you're in,' said Wallace. 'There's no use in complaining about it now. So sign.'

'Or what?' said Ollie. 'You've already said we'll swing.'

Mobani raised a hand. 'Trust me, a confession would be better,' he said with quiet determination. 'There are better and worse ways of dying.'

Maksim suddenly lunged forward, grabbing hold of the bars. His face was red with anger, and he was spitting straight at the lawyer. The bars were vibrating as he put all his brute-like strength into rattling them, but they were buried deep into the foundations of the building and nothing short of a bulldozer was going to break them.

'Just let me at him!' he roared.

'You getting the message?' said Ollie, looking straight at Wallace.

'You'll sign soon enough,' Wallace replied angrily. 'Or you'll suffer the consequences.'

Thirty-Four

STEVE COULD FEEL THE MUSCLES in his right index finger stiffening on the trigger of the Uzi. For a brief but vivid second, he realised he might have been about to squeeze it. He'd already pictured the bullet he was going to put through Archie's head, savoured its smell in his imagination, and the same went for his sister as well. It had been a trap right from the start, and she was the honey at its centre. He could see that clearly now.

But then his fingers relaxed.

Maybe some men could shoot a woman they loved. He'd met guys who wouldn't give it a second thought. But not me, he told himself. There might be a bullet with her name on it somewhere, but it's not in the barrel of my gun.

She took two steps towards him, her face tired, and her eyes smudged with tears.

'Put the gun down, Steve,' she said.

Steve folded the Uzi back into his webbing.

She ran towards him, throwing herself against his chest. For a moment, Steve could feel a surge of anger, then repulsion, yet as her breasts heaved against his chest, the fury subsided and he realised how pleased he was to see her again.

'What happened?' he asked.

She looked into his eyes, then collapsed into tears. It was like one of the thunderstorms they'd just been marching through: a sudden violent wave, unstoppable in its force. Her whole body was shaking as the tears rolled down her cheeks. Steve held her tight. 'It's OK,' he said.

'I'm so sorry,' she said, her voice still choking, even though she had finally managed to bring the sobbing under control. 'I had no idea what Archie was planning, I really didn't. He's a bastard – he has been, ever since he was a kid. I thought he was trying to do something about what happened to Mum and Dad, but he was only out to make some money for himself. That's all he's ever been interested in – that's why he got on so badly with Dad.'

'Very convenient that you've only found that out now,' Ian said malevolently. He was standing behind them in the garden, with Nick at his side.

Samantha looked up, her eyes bloodshot. 'I knew nothing about it, that's the honest truth,' she said, her tone hurt. 'I saw the news this morning about you guys being arrested and I guessed at once what must have happened. As soon as I heard about Archie's fund having an investment in the platinum mine as well, I could see he must have planned it from the start. Behind the scenes, Archie's being dabbling in African politics for years. That's the only reason his fund has done so well.'

'Then how did you find us so quickly?' said Nick.

Nick wasn't usually a man to press difficult questions; he took most things on trust. But it was a fair question.

'I could see that six men had been arrested, plus Newton must have been a traitor from the start,' Samantha told him. 'That left three men. I figured you must have escaped to this side of the lake.' She shrugged, wiping the tears out of the smudged mascara on her face. 'Three white guys, paying for a room in cash? You weren't so hard to find.'

'If she can find us, so can Wallace,' said Steve.

Ian nodded.

'What are you going to do?' asked Samantha.

'We can't stay here,' said Steve. 'Not if we're that easy to find.'

'We should go to Ibera,' she said.

Steve grimaced. 'There's only one place I'm planning to go with a member of the Sharratt family, and that's a funeral,' he said. 'And it's not going to be mine.'

He could see the wounded look on her face as he finished the sentence, as if she'd just taken a punch, and he regretted saying it. Maybe she was on the level. Maybe she really had known nothing about what her brother was doing. And, if so, there was no point in taking it out on her.

But there's nothing I can do about it now, he told himself impatiently. Maybe I can look her up one day.

Right now I've got six mates to save from the gallows.

'Let's get our kit, guys,' he said, turning around to Nick and Ian, 'and then let's get the hell out of here.'

Samantha took a step forward, so that she was standing between the three men. 'Where are you going?'

'You think we're going to tell *you?*' Ian laughed harshly. 'Just so you can tell your brother?'

Samantha ignored him, looking straight at Steve. 'I can get you into Ibera so you can break your men out.'

'So you can deliver us into the same jail, you mean,' sneered Ian.

'Leave it,' Steve said. 'If she's got a plan, we should listen to it.'

'*Listen* to her?' the Irishman growled. 'You must be crazy.'

'I think she's on the level.'

Ian took a couple of steps forward. He was standing right in front of Steve, so close he was practically headbutting the man. 'Steve West and his piece of skirt, eh? We're not falling for that one again. Now let's get the hell out of here.'

'Have you got a plan for getting us into Batota?'

'I can come up with a better fecking plan than being led straight into a firing squad by a woman who's working for the enemy!'

'Then let's hear it.'

Ian turned away, his expression furious. 'I can't seriously believe I'm listening to this. You're thinking with your trousers again, mate. Try using your head for once.'

For a minute, all three men were silent.

'If she's got a plan, then I think we should at least listen to it,' Nick said finally.

Thirty-Five

OLLIE GLANCED ANXIOUSLY AT MAKSIM. The Russian was prowling the perimeter of the cell like a caged tiger, his eyes wild with anger. He was breathing heavily, occasionally gripping the bars and shaking them violently, until dust and dirt was loosened from the bricks holding them in place.

'Christ,' Ollie muttered to David. 'We can't keep that bloke banged up in here too long. He's going to do someone an injury soon.'

'What happens if we sign?' David asked.

'They'll kill us,' said Ollie. 'We sign, they'll take us out and have us shot. We're just being used as pawns in a political game.'

'But we could still sign . . .'

'I'm not signing anything,' Ollie said immediately.

'I don't know about you,' said David, 'but sometimes you just reckon your number's up, and the best thing is to crack on with it.'

'We'll be all right,' Ollie told him.

David looked around despairingly. The cell was dark and crowded, they'd long since finished the foul food and stinking water, and the usual stomach-ripping smell was drifting from the bucket in the corner. 'Sure looks that way,' he said bitterly.

'Steve, Ian and Nick got away,' said Ollie. 'They'll do something.'

'Three men against a whole country? I'm as optimistic as the next bloke, but I've got more chance of being invited to take a Jacuzzi with

285

the entire crew of Girls Aloud than they have of getting us out of here.'

But Ollie was looking straight ahead. Two soldiers had just walked into the cell block, both of them carrying AK-47s held tight into their chests, and carrying sturdy wooden truncheons. They walked up to the door.

'We want Oliver Hall and David Mallet to come with us,' barked the first soldier.

Ollie could feel his heart thumping in his chest. He'd already reckoned there'd be some roughing up to get them to sign the confessions. But he hadn't expected it to start this quickly.

'That's me,' he said, stepping forwards. David was standing right behind him.

The soldier stuck a key into the door, unlocking it with a single, swift movement. He swung it open, grabbing hold of Ollie by the forearm. In the same moment, Maksim roared and lunged at the man. He sank his teeth straight into his arm, drawing blood that dripped across his face, making the man scream in pain. But the second soldier was quick, bringing his truncheon down hard onto the back of Maksim's neck. The Russian was momentarily paralysed by the blow, the nerves in his spine seizing up, then he started to stagger away as wave after wave of pain rolled through him. The first soldier pulled himself upwards, then punched Maksim hard in the chest, throwing him to the ground. Then he dragged Ollie roughly from the cell.

'Move!' he snarled.

Ollie stepped out into the corridor. He felt bad for not helping Maksim, but the Russian had lost it. Even if they had managed to overpower the soldiers, they'd be stopped on the way out. There were 500 elite Sixth Brigade troops in this barracks. If they were going to escape they needed something more sophisticated than a ruck.

'Up the stairs,' ordered the soldier, shoving Ollie in the back.

With David at his side, he started to walk.

'Ever done torture training?' hissed David.

Ollie nodded.

'Just stay inside the box,' David advised.

The box, thought Ollie grimly. He'd been through the torture drill as part of his basic training, the same way most officers did, but of all the different skills he'd acquired during his time in the Blues, that was the one he most hoped he'd never have to use. The technique was first developed by the Americans during the Vietnam War, for soldiers captured by the Vietcong. It had been widely taught in Western armies ever since. You created a mental box inside your head, a place with sturdy psychological walls, filled with all the things you most valued in life, and you retreated into that space, and tried to ignore whatever indignities were being inflicted upon your body.

Easy to teach, decided Ollie. Not so easy in practice.

'That bad, you reckon?' he said aloud.

David nodded. 'They're not bringing us out for a nice cup of tea, that much is for bloody certain.'

They broke into bright sunshine. It was just after eleven in the morning, and another five soldiers were waiting to escort them across the dusty parade ground. They stepped up into a small square building made from rough concrete breeze blocks.

'This way,' snarled the soldier, jabbing Ollie once again with the butt of his AK-47.

He stumbled inside, struggling to keep his balance as the force of the blow rattled down his spine.

It was just a single room. There was a light bulb hanging from the ceiling, and a stale smell of blood and sweat reeking out from the slabs of slate on the floor. The walls were lined with bricks, and there were no windows, making it hot inside. Small, compact and, most importantly of all, soundproofed, noted Ollie. Just the way you'd design a torture chamber.

He looked up. The North Korean Sungoo Park was standing

straight in front of him. He was dressed in a plain khaki uniform, with heavy black boots, and an electric cattle prod in his right hand. Directly behind him, a noose was strung up to a metal bar attached to the ceiling, and next to it a single wooden chair.

'Christ,' muttered Ollie under his breath. A hanging.

'Stand to attention!' snapped Park.

Ollie stood up straight. What's in my box? he wondered to himself. Katie? Not really. If she wasn't determined to live like a City banker's wife, whilst married to an Army officer, then he might not be in this mess in the first place. His dad? Not likely. He'd never forgiven Ollie for going into the Household Cavalry in the first place, then he'd never forgiven him all over again for not being able to hold down the job in the City he'd wangled for him when he quit the Army. No comfort there. Nor from his mother either. She'd died in a car accident when Ollie was just three and he could scarcely remember her. Maybe Lena, the Italian nanny who had looked after him from the age of three to eight, before he'd been packed off to boarding school and a succession of aunts, holiday camps, and au pairs who looked after him during the holidays. Yes, Lena, he reflected. He used to climb into her bed sometimes when he was scared in the night, and there was nowhere else for him to go. With her long black hair, deep brown eyes, a permanent, infectious giggle, and a scent of boiled sweets, she was the person he'd crawl up next to in his own personal box. But Jesus, he thought to himself. A nanny you haven't spoken to for twenty-three years. It's not much for a man to cling onto in what might well be his final few minutes on this earth.

'I've summoned both of you up here because you are the only two officers amongst the men we captured,' Park announced. He was a short man, with intense, wiry muscles. But there was a hardness within him that suggested he was made out of pressed steel.

'This isn't the army,' said Ollie stiffly. 'No officers . . . just men.'

Park attempted a thin smile but it soon vanished. 'Oliver Hall.

Once of the Household Cavalry – your Queen's own bodyguards. There is no more prestigious regiment in the British Army.' His eyes flashed across to David. 'And David Mallet. Formerly a Major in the Irish Guards – the Regiment that draws upon the cream of Britain's Catholic public schools.'

'I'm glad to see you're such an expert on the British Army,' Ollie said sarcastically.

'We like to know our enemy.'

'And so do we.'

Park paused for a moment. He was playing with the cattle prod like a relay baton. At a rough glance, Ollie reckoned it had about 4,000 volts in it. Enough to give even the tough hide of a bullock a nasty jolt. On a man – well, it wouldn't be lethal, but it would still hurt like hell. Cattle prods, as the name suggested, had been developed by farmers to control their herds, but the Chinese People's Liberation Army had deployed them as a crowd control and torture device; Park must have picked up the technique from them. Delivering sharp, intense bursts of pain, they wouldn't kill you, nor would they leave the incriminating body burns and cuts that most other tortures did. Yet they could still break a man.

'Whether you use army ranks or not is no concern of mine,' said Park eventually, weighing each word carefully. 'You are still the only officers, and I suspect the men look to you for guidance. It is the same in any military organisation. So, it is to you that I shall address my remarks. We would like you to sign a full confession—'

'Saying what?' interrupted Ollie.

'Saying you came to Batota to assassinate President Kapembwa, and you were in the pay of big business and its British colonial masters.'

'It's bollocks,' Ollie said immediately. 'We were set up to provide a show trial for your President. And you know it.'

'It would be better for you to sign.'

'So you keep saying.'

Park took a step closer, peering straight into Ollie's eyes. 'As an officer you have a duty towards your men,' he hissed. 'And in this case, the duty says you should minimise their suffering. You know you'll sign eventually so let's just get it done.'

Ollie remained totally silent. Lock yourself up in your box, he reminded himself. Don't let them frighten you.

'Very well, we'll play this your way,' continued Park coldly. He nodded towards the noose.

'I'm going to hang one of you as an example to the others,' he said. 'Once they see your corpse dangling from the rope they'll sign quickly enough. So I'd like one of you to volunteer to be the man who puts his head into the rope whilst the other goes down to explain to the others how we deal with prisoners who don't obey orders around here.'

The statement was delivered crisply, without a trace of emotion.

Christ, thought Ollie. He really means it.

'Come on, come on,' the short man said impatiently. 'Which of you is it to be? We don't have all day.'

Ollie took a step forward.

'Bugger it, Ollie, you don't—' started David.

'You've got four kids, mate,' said Ollie, struggling to keep his voice level.

'We'll draw straws,' said David.

'We'll do no such thing,' retorted Ollie. 'I got us into this mess.'

'But—'

Park pointed his cattle prod straight at David. 'It's been decided.' He turned to Ollie and smiled. 'I'm glad to see that a sense of honour still survives among British soldiers. I would hate to think even that had died.'

He gestured towards the chair. 'Stand on that please.'

Ollie walked uneasily towards the chair. His legs were surprisingly steady, but his stomach was churning. There were plenty of times he'd thought about dying. There had been a few close shaves, enough for him to feel at least on nodding terms with the Grim Reaper. But he'd always imagined his number would get called, if called it was, on a battlefield with a gun in his hands.

Not with a rope around his neck.

He took a single step up onto the chair.

One of the soldiers placed a stepladder next to it, then placed the noose carefully over Ollie's neck. He could feel the rope against his skin, its rough knots edging into his throat. The man then tightened the noose so that it gripped his windpipe, but still left him room to breathe.

Ollie could feel a bead of sweat run down his chest. Lena, he thought again, retreating into his box. He'd been too young to think about it at the time, but she was quite a minx. He wouldn't mind climbing into her bed again, he decided. Except she'd probably be at least fifty by now, and have a Sicilian husband who was even more scary than the Korean bastard standing right in front of him.

She might have a daughter though, Ollie decided. Almost certainly did. He permitted himself a brief, tight smile, one that took his captors by surprise. Lena's daughter, he repeated to himself. That might be someone for a man to live for.

'All I want you to do is sign the confession,' said Park, looking up at Ollie.

'Piss off,' snapped Ollie.

'Hanging is a slow, painful death . . .'

'I heard it was quick.'

'Not the way we tie the noose. The rope doesn't break your neck, so you'll just slowly suffocate.'

'Just get on with it.'

'A signature, that's all.'

'You're wasting your time.'

If Park was annoyed, his expression, cold and unyielding, didn't betray it.

He drew back his leg, preparing to kick away the chair on which Ollie was standing.

Moses Atouba was a tall strong man, with friendly eyes and a broad smile. He was wearing pale khaki shorts and a grey sweatshirt. As Samantha led them towards him, Steve was glancing around suspiciously, still unsure whether she was leading them into a trap. Any sign of trouble, and they'd move out by themselves.

The African was standing next to a Hyundai Santa Fe SUV, with a decent-sized 2.4 litre engine. The vehicle had been extensively modified, with outsized wheels and tyres fitted to take it across rough terrain. The back had been remodelled to create seven seats, and there were tanks fitted to its rear to carry the extra petrol and water you might need on a long journey.

'You can get us into Batota?' said Steve.

The man nodded.

'Moses is with the World Species Fund – the same outfit I do work for in London,' said Samantha crisply. She stepped up to the vehicle, removing a small folder of papers out of the glove compartment, with the air of a woman who liked to take charge. 'We have signed papers from the Minister of the Interior giving us access to the country.'

'Until they spot the three white mercenaries sitting in the back,' said Ian.

Moses opened up the Hyundai. He rolled back the seats, then pointed towards the floor. It was made of thin plywood and, when he pulled it back, it revealed a hidden compartment. It measured about eight feet by five: a tight squeeze for three blokes.

'We'll put you in here,' he said, looking back towards Steve. 'It won't be comfortable, and I can't promise to drive that fast, but it should be safe.'

'If they search the car they'll find us,' said Steve.

'They won't,' said Sam. 'We'll bribe the guards, and we'll show them the papers. When you have connections with Kapembwa's henchmen – and these papers prove that we do – they won't want to hassle us.'

Ian was shaking his head. 'We'll be sitting targets,' he said. 'We should take our chances by ourselves.'

'How exactly? By swimming across the lake?'

'We'll get a boat, then we tab our way down to Ibera.'

'It could take days,' argued Steve. 'Our mates could be dead before we get halfway there.'

Ian looked towards the Hyundai. Then he glanced at both Sam and Moses. It was clear from his face he didn't like the plan much.

Then he shrugged, and pulled open the door. 'If I could think of any other way of getting there, I'd take it,' he said. 'But as I can't, it's Ibera next stop . . .'

Park swung his leg hard into the chair, sending it skidding across the floor.

For a second, it seemed to Ollie as if he was suspended in air. With his hands still strapped behind his back by the Plasti-Cuffs, there was nothing he could do to stop himself from falling. He muttered a silent prayer, and closed his eyes. If you're going to go, he reminded himself, then at least do it with your head held high.

He dropped straight towards the floor. For a brief second, he could feel the noose tightening around his neck, strangling the oxygen out of his throat. He was gasping for air.

The rope snapped. Ollie opened his eyes and found that he'd already fallen to the ground, crashing hard into the stone floor. Unable to shield his fall with his arms he'd taken a nasty bruise to the chest. Sweat was pouring off him, and he was shaking with fear.

Compose yourself, man, he told himself. Don't let the bastard know he scared you.

Ollie glanced up towards the ceiling. The noose, he realised, had been attached to the ceiling by some flimsy, twisted thread: it would obviously break as soon as it had to take the weight of a man. He'd heard of the fake hanging being part of the bullying of new recruits back in the Army. It happened in the Paras, although never in the Blues, so far as he knew.

And there was a good reason for that. Even for new squaddies, it was a brutal trick.

Park pulled Ollie up off the floor. 'You don't break easily, Mr Hall,' he said smoothly. 'But you'll break all the same . . . they always do.'

Thirty-Six

THE BORDER CROSSING WAS JUST a single wooden shack. Six soldiers were standing inside it, all of them armed with AK-47s, checking the papers of the passing traffic. Six cars and trucks were parked ahead of him as Moses pulled the Hyundai up into the line. Most of them were Batotean vehicles returning home. Few tourists came here any more; even the safari business had largely died. There wasn't even much trade. Not many people in Batota had any money, and the Tukans had largely given up doing business with them. The bills didn't get paid.

'Got your papers ready?' Moses asked.

Sam nodded. They had crossed over the Hasta Dam, following the road that linked the two countries and would eventually take them down to Ibera. On one side, the lake stretched out into the distance, its surface shining in the bright afternoon sunshine. On the other, the Zambezi River, from which the lake was fed, continued the long journey that started in Angola and finally ended spilling out into the Mozambique Channel that separated that country from Madagascar.

It was at moments like this, as she looked out onto its breathtaking scenery, that Sam realised she'd been born an African, and would remain an African. It was in her blood, and if that blood had to be spilled, then that was just the price that the continent demanded.

She glanced ahead. One truck driver had been led away for

interrogation, and she could feel her pulse racing in fear. The border guards rarely got paid any more: bribes and extortion were the only way they could make a living. She'd heard stories of women being gang raped while male drivers and passengers were beaten and robbed.

'Papers,' said a soldier, leaning into the side of the Hyundai. He was a tall, strong man, and he smelled of tobacco.

Moses handed across his own Tukan passport, then Sam's. She had both British and Batotean documents, and used the African one this time. The soldier looked at the picture, then up at her. There were whites left in Batota, but not that many, and they were more often going out than coming back in again. Moses produced three ten-dollar bills he'd stashed in his breastpocket and handed them across. 'For you,' he said quietly.

The soldier took the money. There was more, but Moses knew it was a mistake to pay a bribe that was too generous. If they thought you had a lot of money on you, they'd just rob you, then kill you and tip the bodies in the lake to make sure the theft wasn't reported.

'Your business?' the man said.

'We work with the World Species Fund,' said Moses. 'We have permission to track down and monitor some of the last wild herds of Black Rhinos.'

'What's in the vehicle?'

'Just food, water, photographic equipment and medicines.'

The soldier was gesturing to one of his mates. A second soldier walked towards the car, and from his manner, Sam judged he was the more senior of the two men. They were surveying the car, and you could see the greed in their eyes. Sam was starting to feel nervous. She'd called ahead to Archie, who was already in Ibera, and explained that she was on her way to the city, and to make sure there wouldn't be any problems at the border. But there was no way of knowing if the border soldiers even listened to the government any more.

'We need to search the car,' said the second soldier.

Sam leaned across. She had a letter personally signed by the Minister of the Interior guaranteeing safe passage through the country for any senior staffer of the World Species Fund. Handing it across, she flashed half a smile. The soldier took the letter, stopping for a brief chat with his mate.

There was a flicker of indecision on his face, Sam noted.

Then he handed the letter back. 'On your way,' he said tersely.

Moses kicked the Hyundai up into second, then third gear and pushed on down the track. From the sentry post, they heard a scream as one of the truck drivers was given a beating. From here to Ibera was a drive of 365 kilometres along the R14 Highway. There was relatively little traffic. Fuel was in such short supply that few people were taking their cars or trucks out. There were plenty of robbers on the road, and any decent-looking vehicle was always at risk of a hold-up, but they managed to drive a couple of hours and cover 100 kilometers without incident.

At five in the afternoon, Sam asked Moses to pull off the main road. He drove 500 metres down a dirt track, then pulled into a small, shaded copse of woodland. Sam climbed from the Hyundai, opened up the back, and lifted the fake floor.

'Jesus,' muttered Steve, climbing out first. 'Remind me never to be buried alive with a Welshie and a Mick. The bloody smell in there would make a skunk faint.'

He took the bottle of water Sam had just handed him, and took a long, hard swig on the lukewarm liquid before passing it across to Ian and Nick. Both men drank as much as they could. They had spent the last three hours lying squeezed up side by side in a temperature that was getting above 40 degrees, and with the carbon monoxide from the exhaust pipe swirling up around them, and with every bump and pit in the worn-out road shattering straight through their spines. A thin film of grime and sweat covered every inch of their bodies, and it took a couple of minutes to readjust their eyes to the glare of the late-afternoon sunshine.

'I still reckon we should have taken the scenic route,' said Nick cheerfully.

Sam handed around bananas and some biscuits, and the men chewed their way through them, keen to get as much liquid and food down their throats as possible to prepare for the rest of the journey.

'Any chance of sitting up front for a while?' Ian asked Moses.

The African shook his head. 'There could be police or Army checks anywhere along this highway, and certainly on the roads in Ibera,' he said.

'I don't know how much longer we can hold out in there,' said Steve.

'We'll be there by nightfall,' Moses told him. 'No later than eleven.'

Steve took another slug of water, stretched his muscles and climbed back into the Hyundai. 'Then let's crack on.'

Ollie was still shaking, recovering from the shock of the hanging. He was sitting in a corner of the cell, slowly piecing his thoughts back together as David explained to the rest of the men what had happened.

'We did that all the time in the Spetsnaz,' chortled Maksim. 'I remember one guy – Vladimir, I think he was called – he was so fucked up by the whole experience, he hung himself for real a couple of days later.'

'Very comforting, mate,' said Ollie sourly.

'The point is, they are determined to break us,' said David. 'And we have to ask ourselves how long we can hold out.'

'I'm not signing any bloody confession,' said Dan.

'No matter what they do to us?'

All the men in the cell fell silent for a moment.

'Do you reckon Steve and the boys can do anything?' asked Chris.

'I'm sure they'll try,' said David. 'But it's a hell of a big ask.'

'We don't sign yet,' said Ganju, his voice threaded with quiet determination. 'We play for time, because that's the only thing we have going for us. Make them wait for us to agree to sign, then delay again when we've said we will. That way, there's more chance for Steve to get us out of here.'

As he spoke, a group of six soldiers appeared, walking straight towards their cell. Wallace was standing in front of them, looking around menacingly. 'I've got another treat for you boys,' he said harshly. 'I hope you're ready for it.'

Reluctantly, the six men stood up and followed Wallace through the dark cell block and up onto the parade ground. It was just after six in the evening and all of them were dog tired. Their muscles and limbs were aching, and they had been given nothing more to eat or drink since the bucket of swill that had been handed to them in the morning. The soldiers were jabbing them with the barrels of their assault rifles as they shunted them across the dusty ground.

'Form a line, you miserable bastards,' Wallace ordered.

He was standing right in front of them, with Park at his side. There were another two dozen soldiers standing directly behind them, their purple and gold berets gleaming in the sun. Wallace started to walk up and down the line, looking into the faces of the men.

He's scrutinising us for weakness, decided Ollie. Trying to figure out which of us is most likely to crack. And that will be the man he chooses as his next victim. It's standard bully boy tactics, he reflected. He probably learned them at Eton.

'Him,' he snapped, nodding towards Chris.

Two of the Sixth Brigade soldiers stepped forward from their line and yanked Chris hard out of the group.

He's got the wrong bloke, thought Ollie. Chris isn't the weakest man here. Not even close.

'Christopher Reynolds,' Wallace said, looking him up and down contemptuously. 'A bloody Recce were you, man?'

Chris remained silent, his face defiant.

'I reckon your boys inflicted some nasty injuries on Sixth Brigade soldiers, back in the old days,' continued Wallace. 'What was it you used to call the black soldiers? "Kaffirs"? "Niggers"? "Bushcats"?'

The two soldiers dragged Chris back twenty yards. Wallace was walking behind them, leaning down into the man. 'Well, I reckon they'd like a bit of payback.'

He turned towards the other five prisoners. 'You blokes ever seen a crucifixion, African-style?' he enquired.

They all remained silent, rooted to the spot.

'He's bloody kidding,' hissed Ollie. 'It'll be the same as the hanging. He's just trying to frighten us.'

'Four bayonets,' Wallace rapped out.

Four of the Sixth Brigade men stepped smartly forwards, the bayonets on their rifles glinting menacingly in the late evening sunshine – each one twelve inches of hardened steel, sharpened to lethal precision. One of them grabbed Chris then thrust him hard onto the ground. There was sweat pouring off the man's face, and a wild, burning anger lighting up his eyes. This was the same way his mate had died. Another soldier thrust his knee hard into Chris's chest, pinning his back into the dirt, whilst the third held onto his right arm, splaying his hand onto the ground. Drawing back his rifle, he then, with a sudden movement, thrust the bayonet downwards, piercing the flesh in Chris's right hand. The scream that blasted through the evening air was filled with terror and hatred. The soldier was leaning heavily on the bayonet, pushing the spear deep into the ground so that there was no chance of the man it was pinning down breaking free. His comrade was grabbing hold of Chris's left arm, splaying it down and pressing the palm close to the dust whilst another soldier speared his bayonet into the bone and muscle.

Another scream.

'Jesus, man!' objected Ollie. His face was red with anger as he looked across at Wallace.

Maksim was struggling violently, and so was Dan, both men trying desperately to free themselves from their captors so they could rush to Chris's aide. Maksim briefly broke free, but he only ran three yards before three huge, beefy soldiers brought him crashing to the ground, pummelling him with their fists. Slowly, he was dragged back to the line, whilst only a few yards away, they could hear Chris choking back the pain from the freshly opened wounds.

'He's a professional soldier, just like you,' growled Ollie, still looking at Wallace. 'This is no way to treat a man.'

'He's Afrikaans scum,' spat Wallace. He turned back towards the soldiers standing over Chris. 'Now the legs,' he shouted.

Chris was kicking violently, but he didn't have the strength to match the two soldiers who grabbed hold of his right leg, and pinned it hard to the ground. Again, a third lifted his gun, twisted it slightly so the bayonet was perfectly angled, then thrust it down. It struck Chris just above the ankle, splintering the bones with a sickening crunch, then slicing through the flesh and digging into the ground below. With a swiftness that suggested the Sixth Brigade men were well practised in administering this punishment, they did the same to the left leg. Chris's cries of pain were getting fainter each time, and yet, as the volume and strength of his lungs started to weaken, there was also more despair in them.

Wallace stepped up to inspect the body. Chris was splayed out on the ground like a starfish, all four limbs bayoneted into the ground. His back arched up in agony, yet as he did so, his flesh stretched into the blade cutting into him, making him scream in pain, and emptying fresh trickles of blood onto the parade ground.

With a curt nod of his head, Wallace thanked the soldiers and dismissed them.

He walked the ten paces back to where Ollie and the rest of the men were standing. 'Apparently some of the revisionist historians say that crucifixion wasn't so bad,' he said, pulling out a fresh cigar from his breast-pocket and wafting it under his nose to enjoy its smoky aroma. 'But it looks bloody painful to me.'

Ollie remained silent.

'We'll leave the bastard out for a few hours, and let the flies and the cockroaches have a bit of a chew at him,' Wallace said conversationally. 'And we'll bring you boys out later tonight to take a look at him. Then I'll give you a simple choice. You can start making those confessions I want from you. Or else you can draw lots for which one of you fuckers is going to be next.'

He nodded towards the soldiers.

The prisoners were marched back towards their cell, Chris's howls of pain still fresh in their ears.

The heads of the men were down, noted Ollie.

We're about to find out how much punishment we can take, he told himself grimly.

Thirty-Seven

NOT MANY PEOPLE WENT OUT in Ibera at night, not any more. Most of the bars and restaurants had closed down, and those that were still open were short on customers. Police and Army patrols roamed the streets at night and shot people on sight for any minor infringement of the law. Those that weren't shot got shaken down for bribes Most evenings, a deathly silence fell over the place by ten. With few lights left working, it was a city shrouded in darkness and fear.

When Steve climbed out of the back of the Hyundai, his limbs were stiff, and his back ached in a dozen different places. Ian and Nick followed, looking exhausted. They'd pulled into a suburban side street on the northern edge of the city, full of solid detached 1950s and 1960s houses that had been built by people trying to recreate the Home Countries.

Except no one was trying to kill you in the Home Counties. At least, not with AK-47s. Not yet anyway.

'Where the hell can we go now?' Ian asked.

'I know a place,' said Sam. 'There's a backpacker's hostel close to the centre of the city where three scruffy-looking white guys aren't going to attract too much attention to themselves.'

Steve glanced at his watch. It was just after ten at night.

'Then let's go,' he said tersely. 'We haven't much time.'

*

Ollie could smell the alcohol on the breath of the soldiers who pushed them roughly up the stairs and out onto the parade ground: a mixture of beer and rum – a combination that could make men wild with fury. *Wallace is giving them the booze for a reason*, he calculated. *He's expecting something nasty to happen. And soon.*

A drunk soldier is a brutal soldier. Every commander knows that simple rule.

Ollie exchanged a worried look with David. It was clear he'd had the same thought.

This is about to turn even rougher.

They stumbled out onto the parade ground. Dusk had fallen now, and although the night was cloudy, there were flashlights beaming down into the enclosed space. The soldiers marched them straight across to where Chris had been crucified. Ollie could see Wallace and Park already standing there, and he felt a sickening thud inside his chest. He prided himself on having a strong stomach. He'd done a few days in A&E as part of a medical option on his basic training, and a bit of blood and gore didn't faze him. But a man staked to the ground and left to die? One of your mates? It was going to take a constitution of iron to look at that without throwing up or breaking down.

'Looks like your man's bought it,' said Wallace.

Ollie glanced down.

Chris's face was twisted into an expression of indescribable agony, his once strong, solid features recast into an ugly mixture of pain and despair. His wrists and feet were shredded where he'd tried to buck himself free. And the ground all around him was stained crimson.

'Blood loss is what gets the bastards,' said Wallace, his tone matter of fact. 'You can survive the wounds from the bayonets OK on an African crucifixion. They'll heal, but you have to keep yourself still. Every time you wriggle around, you open up the wounds again, and lose more blood. I reckon your mate knew that. He was trying to hold himself steady, but it's just so bloody uncomfortable . . .'

He shook his head sorrowfully from side to side. 'I'll say this for the bugger, he might have been a damned Recce, but he had some guts in his belly.'

'Give us some spades, and we'll dig him a grave,' said Ollie stiffly.

Wallace lit up his cigar, then glanced across at Park. 'You hear that, Sungoo? This joker thinks his man's getting a funeral.'

'He's a soldier,' snapped Ollie. 'He deserves to be buried with dignity – just like we all do.'

'Maybe some nice cucumber sandwiches for the wake,' said the Korean, a thin smile creasing up his face.

'Just a spade will be fine,' said Ollie. 'That's all I'm asking for.'

Ignoring him, Wallace gestured to one of the soldiers. The man stepped up to the body and pulled the four bayonets roughly from the ground one by one, flicking away the blood, bone and skin from the edge of the sharp blades. Then two more men picked up Chris's body and started to walk towards the barracks room with it.

'We'll show you what we do with the corpses of our enemies around here,' Wallace said coldly.

The soldiers had already whacked each of the five men with the butts of their guns, guiding them forwards. Ollie could see at once where they were going. The interrogation room. The same place they'd tried to hang him.

Already he could feel his heart sinking.

'Through the door,' shouted the soldier at his back, pushing Ollie forward.

He stumbled into the room. It was brightly lit, with a row of three flashlights up against one wall. There was a camcorder set up on a tripod in front of it.

'Stand right there,' growled the soldier.

Ollie stood with his back to the wall. Dan, Maksim, David and

Ganju were all standing next to him. The soldier brought in Chris's body and dumped it down on the ground. Christ, thought Ollie. They're going to film something.

One of the soldiers knelt down and stabbed a knife roughly into Chris's throat, then twisted it. As the blood started to gush from the opened-up vein, he put a cheap plastic container underneath to catch it. When he'd finished, another soldier took his place. He was holding a hacksaw in his hand. As he knelt down, he started to saw into Chris's neck, the blade chewing into the bone and skin until it was completely severed. Picking the head up by the hair, he then placed it in a big bucket of water.

'Your friend was a brave man, we'll give him that,' said Wallace, looking up at the five men in front of him. 'And in this country, the men believe that bravery is like a vitamin – you can acquire it by eating it. So they're going to mix that blood with their rum, and that head is going to soak in that bucket of water, and in the morning the men are going to drink the liquid, and that way the courage will be transferred.'

'It's barbaric' Ollie spat.

'Now, now, Mr Hall,' said Wallace. 'Respect for other people's cultures. Surely they're teaching that at Sandhurst these days?'

'It's you that's the savage, man!'

'Indeed – as you're about to discover.'

He clapped his hands together and Park stepped forward holding a white card with a series of words stencilled onto it in thick black ink. *We are agents of British-American imperialism*, it read. *We have been sent here by our governments, and by the mining and oil conglomerates, to assassinate President Kapembwa and to bring Batota back under the heel of colonial rule.*

'We want you to stand in front of the camera and read out this statement,' Park said.

Ollie could feel his chest tightening. He was afraid, he didn't mind admitting that, at least to himself. Wallace was a killer, insane – of that there could be no question – and he'd stop at nothing to get what he wanted.

But I'm not bloody reading that, he told himself with grim determination. It doesn't matter what they threaten us with.

Wallace suddenly jumped forward. He'd grabbed hold of David, wrestling the man to the ground. Two soldiers immediately stepped in, pinning him to the floor by pressing down on his chest, leaving David gasping for breath.

'If you haven't read that statement in ten minutes, then this man is next,' threatened Wallace.

The backpackers' hostel occupied an old colonial building in one of the smartest districts of Ibera, in the north-east of the city. The streets had once been home to the grand mining and farming families, as well as the diplomats posted to the capital, and the houses were big, with ten or eleven bedrooms, pools, and gardens that would have been lush if anyone had had the time and money to look after them. Three of the old buildings had been turned into cheap hostels for travellers, the rooms converted to dorms where you could get a bed and meal for the equivalent of a couple of quid a night, and along the street outside was a string of internet cafés and shops selling phone cards and walking boots.

It'll do, decided Steve, as they pulled up in the Hyundai. Just so long as we can stay safe until we break our boys out.

Sam slipped inside to secure them a room. A minute later, the owner stepped out to great them. With straggly black hair tied in a ponytail, and a multi-coloured T-shirt, he looked like a bass player from Aerosmith on a bad day.

'You boys can kip down in room seven,' he said, handing across a key. 'There's some space for Sam in the women's dorm. Grab yourself a beer on the terrace, and I'll get the cook to heat you up some stew.'

The beer felt cold and refreshing as Steve opened up the bottle and started to pour it down his throat. There were five other people still up, even though it was just after eleven. Only gap year students and intrepid travellers were still trying to come to Batota, and that meant the backpackers' hostels were one of the few bits of the economy still making any money. At one table, a pair of German students were drinking beer and sending texts on their mobiles. On another, a tough-looking Scottish woman in her sixties was reading a Joseph Conrad novel. Then there was a pair of Canadian blokes in their forties, serious wildlife buffs, with thick beards, sturdy walking boots and a small pile of books on all the different animals in Batota.

Steve smiled and nodded to each of them in turn, said good evening, but then walked out into the garden followed by Nick and Ian. He didn't want to be overheard, not by anyone.

'How long do you reckon we have?' said Ian.

Steve shook his head. 'The bastard won't hang around.'

He looked at the TV hooked up in one corner of the bar. It was tuned to the Government-controlled Batotean Broadcasting Corporation, and the nightly news was just starting. The newsreader was announcing that the executions of the foreign mercenaries were scheduled for ten o'clock tomorrow morning.

As he listened to the words, Steve took a sharp intake of breath. 'Christ,' he muttered to himself.

Then a picture of Ollie flashed up on the screen. He looked terrible, noted Steve. His face was covered with stubble, sweat and grime, and his eyes were haggard and bloodshot. In a slow, mechanical voice, he started to speak. 'We are agents of British-American imperialism. We have been sent here by our governments, and by the mining and oil conglomerates, to assassinate President Kapembwa and to bring Batota back under the heel of colonial rule.'

One by one, the rest of the men appeared on the screen, each one of them reciting the same statement. David, followed by Dan, by Maksim, and then by Ganju. You could see the anger in each man's eyes, but also sense the despair.

They've done something to them, realised Steve. Something bloody awful to get them to read that crap.

'The execution of the foreign mercenaries and the agents of imperialism will take place in the morning at the Juberra Jail in Ibera,' the newsreader repeated. 'But first they will be taken through the city, and paraded at the election rally that our glorious President is holding in the National Stadium so that the Batotean people may demonstrate that they will never again be brought under colonial rule.'

On the screen, a shot of Kapembwa suddenly flashed up. He was wearing a bright red top and a black baseball cap, and there was a hint of venom in his eyes.

'The Batotean people will never again fall under the tyranny of the British, the Americans or the mining companies,' he said, looking straight into the camera. 'They can send their mercenaries, their dogs of war, but we will never be defeated. And tomorrow, these men will pay the ultimate price for the treachery to which they have confessed.'

'Notice something?' said Ian, standing next to Steve.

A cool night breeze was blowing through the garden, and the scent of the jacaranda trees that lined the streets in this part of town wafted through the air.

'What – that he's a sodding nutter?' said Steve.

'Well, that's true enough, but something else . . .'

Steve shook his head.

'There was no sign of Chris,' said Ian, his tone tense.

Steve already knew what he was saying. He'd noticed it himself as the men were paraded past. He just didn't want to think about what it meant. Not right now anyway.

'That's right,' said Nick, putting his beer down. 'Where the hell was Chris in the line-up?'

Steve looked across at Ian. Someone would have to explain it.

'They must have done something bad to get Ollie and the boys to

309

read that rubbish,' said Ian. 'And Chris will have been the guy they did it to. He's a Recce, after all.'

'Dead, you reckon?' said Steve.

'Yeah, I reckon,' Ian replied heavily. 'Or as near as makes no fecking difference.'

Thirty-Eight

WALLACE SLAMMED THE DOOR SHUT on the cell. Some food had been put down on the floor. Nothing much. Two loaves of stale bread, some black and squishy bananas and a bucket of water. Ollie sat down on the hard ground next to it. It didn't make any difference what the food looked like. He didn't feel like eating.

'You boys get some beauty sleep,' Wallace said mockingly.

Nobody replied. Then: 'What's it to be?' asked David. 'The bullet or the rope?'

'We'll make it a surprise for you,' said Wallace. 'I wouldn't want to stop you from getting a good night's sleep.' He chuckled to himself as he walked back up the stairs to the parade ground, leaving the men alone in their cell.

'Thanks for saving my skin,' David said to Ollie and Dan.

Ollie shrugged. 'There wasn't any choice,' he said flatly. 'They'd have crucified you the same way they crucified Chris. They were going to murder us all, so we did the right thing. Gave them their confessions and bought ourselves a bit more time.'

'If we're going to die, it should be the bullet,' said Maksim, mashing up some banana into a lump of hard bread and chewing on the sandwich. 'A soldier's death – that's the least we deserve. In the Russian Army, a soldier always gets a bullet.' He laughed. 'Actually, so do the criminals and the politicians. No rope factories, you see.'

'Or the sword,' said Ganju, his tone reflective. 'A man should have the right to die by his own sword. That way, it is easier for his soul to be transmitted from one body to the next one.'

'You really believe that?' Maksim asked.

'It is the tradition of *samsara*,' said Ganju quietly. 'All your actions in this world are added up, and they determine your destiny once your soul is reborn. Our bodies are like a coat. When it's worn out, we put it aside and put on a new one – but the soul carries on.'

'What are you coming back as, Maksie?' said Dan.

'A mad bull, I reckon,' growled Ian.

'A barman in a brothel,' Maksie replied. 'An expensive one.'

'And I'll own the bloody place,' said Dan. 'The man with the tab that never runs out.'

'I think I'll be the barman at a lapdancing club – something a bit more upmarket,' said Ollie.

'Maybe Nick's mum's gaff,' grinned Dan.

'Doesn't sound that classy to me,' said Ollie. 'I mean, given the state of Nick, what the hell can his mum look like?'

'We've got less than twelve hours,' said Steve, glancing at his watch.

They were looking at a street map of Ibera.

'The Sixth Brigade barracks is here,' said Ian, pointing to a spot on the map towards the north of the city, and only a couple of miles from where they were spending the night. 'If we reckon they are keeping them penned up there because it's the safest place, then they will have to come down these roads here to get to the National Stadium out in the south-west of the city.' He was tracing a finger down a row of streets. 'In order to be paraded at the rally at ten in the morning, then they need to come down this one.' He jabbed at the Akwa Road, a wide avenue that cut through the west of the city. 'And that's where we strike.'

Steve was studying the map, running the calculations in his head, trying to get a fix on the odds. Whichever way you looked at it, they weren't great. Not great at all.

'You certain?' he asked.

'Got any better ideas?' said Ian tersely.

Steve shook his head. They couldn't break into the Sixth Brigade headquarters. There were hundreds of soldiers there, all of them skilled operators, and there were only three of them. Once they were in the National Stadium, there could be fifty or sixty thousand people inside. The journey through the city was the only possible point of weakness. *They had to strike there.*

'We can stop the vehicles,' said Nick.

'With what – our bare hands?' said Ian.

'No, with the kit that Dan bought,' said Nick. From his kitbag, he pulled out the HPES, or High-Power Electromagnetic System, they had bought from the arms dealer back in Johannesburg. 'It stops vehicles, right?' Nick went on. 'So they'll be bringing our boys on a truck. We use this to stop it dead in its tracks.'

'You certain it'll work?' said Steve.

Nick shrugged. 'I've got no idea – we haven't tried it yet. But I reckon this will be the morning to give it a go.'

Steve and Ian exchanged glances. 'If anyone can make it work, Nick can,' Steve shrugged.

Ian nodded. 'OK, Nick, you rig up your toy, and then your job is to stop the truck.' His eyes flashed up towards Steve. 'I'm going to put together some homemade bombs. Nothing too lethal – I don't want to turn the place into Hiroshima. But there will be a convoy of troops coming down with the main vehicle carrying our boys, we can be certain of that. I'll create enough smoke and noise that they think there's a fire-fight breaking out, and that will draw enough troops from the convoy to give us a chance of rescuing them.'

'You take care of that,' agreed Steve, 'and I'll rush the main vehicle. I'll slot the driver, then take control of it and drive the hell out of there. You boys will have to jump on the back, or else melt into the crowds and chaos and make your own way home as best you can.'

Ian nodded his head, his face tight with concentration. 'The men need to be prepared,' he said. 'If they know what's going down, then they can help overwhelm the guards.'

'I can do that,' said Sam.

Steve looked towards her. He'd hardly noticed her leaning over the map, listening to every word of the discussion. Her hair was tied behind her, and her face looked pale and drawn, but there was determination in her eyes.

'Like how?'

'I've been texting my brother.'

'He knows we're here!' exclaimed Ian.

Sam shook her head. 'Just me,' she said quietly. 'But I can go and visit the men in the cell first thing in the morning if that would help.'

Again, Steve exchanged glances with Ian. Both of them needed no more than a look to confirm they were in agreement. The mission they were about to take on was so high-risk already, it didn't make much difference how many chances they took.

'Could you get to see them alone?' said Steve.

Sam nodded. 'My parents sent me to a convent school for a couple of years. I'll tell Archie they might want a brief religious ceremony if they're going to be hanged in the morning. He'll let me see them.'

'He trusts you?' said Ian.

'I'm his *sister*.'

'OK, you're on,' Steve decided. 'Get them alone, and tell them there's going to be a break-out as they approach the stadium. I'm going to find you some pocket-knives. If you can, try to find a way of slipping them through to them.'

He looked towards Nick. 'You practise with that kit, laddie. Make sure you know it inside out. We can't afford any screw-ups.'

'And by the way, it's *not* a rhino – got that?' Ian put in.

'That wasn't my bloody fault,' said Nick, his ears turning bright red.

'Drop it,' snapped Steve. Ian was good enough at his job, but his tongue had a cruel lash to it. This was no time to be knocking Nick's confidence. They were three men against impossible odds, and they were going to need all the self-belief they could dig out of themselves to have any chance of pulling this off.

'Ian, we'll start sourcing your kit,' he went on. 'What do you need?'

'I want some oil drums, a metal hacksaw, about twenty gallons of diesel, a packet of triple-A batteries, and two old-fashioned phones,' the Irishman said. 'The Bakelite ones, with the dials on the front.'

Steve just grinned. Ian regularly came up with a list of bizarre odds and sods. But he could turn them into one hell of a nasty bang when he needed to.

'Neil can get those for us,' said Sam, referring to her friend who ran the hostel. 'He knows every black-market dealer in Ibera. It's only the diesel that's going to be expensive. There's a terrible shortage of fuel in this city.'

'Won't he be suspicious?'

'Yes, he will,' said Sam. 'But we're old friends. We used to smoke dope in the same gang as teenagers. He owes me some favours.'

'I thought you just said you went to convent school?'

Sam flashed a smile. 'Convent girls are always the worst. I'm sure you know that.'

Steve looked straight into her clear blue eyes. 'Thanks.'

Sam shrugged. 'It's OK. I owe you.'

'That's one thing you got right,' said Ian sourly.

Thirty-Nine

DAN CHEWED ON THE BREAKFAST that had just been pushed through the door. There were two loaves of hard bread, some more of the mouldy bananas, and a few scraps of chicken that were already starting to reek of decay. The smell from the crap bucket was, as usual, filling the cell, and the walls were running with moisture.

'Still, look on the bright side, mate,' Dan said to Ollie. 'At least you're off the hook for the wedding.'

Ollie chuckled. 'Katie's going to be bloody furious,' he said. 'The flowers are all booked, everything. That Kapembwa bloke's got no idea of the bollocking he's going to get.'

'Maybe your mother-in-law will save us,' said David.

'Or yours. You've got two of them.'

'I know.' David shook his head. 'I should have taken the hanging while I had the chance.'

Ignoring the banter, Ollie checked his watch. It was just after eight in the morning. No time had been scheduled for the execution, but Wallace had used the word 'morning' – and that meant it would be sooner rather than later.

'Not long to go,' he said, his tone serious. 'If Steve's going to try something, he hasn't got much time.'

'I reckon he'll be working on it right now,' said David. But there wasn't a lot of hope in his voice.

'No chance. He's just buggered off home,' said Dan. 'That's what I'd do.'

'Thanks, mate,' said David. 'I'll remember that, next time you need rescuing from a tight spot.'

'I didn't mean that,' Dan said, 'but it's bloody useless, isn't it? There's sod all that can be done for us now. The others might as well save their own skins.'

'There's always a way,' said Ganju, his voice fierce with determination.

'Oh yeah? Like what?'

'Just take it easy, boys,' said Ollie sharply. The tension was getting to them, he could tell. And when they were facing an imminent execution, who could blame them? Like most professional soldiers, they'd learned to come to terms with their own mortality. But this was different.

Being murdered wasn't something any of them had counted on.

'Nick will do something,' growled Maksim. 'I don't know about the Irishman. Too clever for his own good, I reckon. And Steve?' He shrugged. 'Steve's a realist. He takes risks when they've a chance of paying off. When they haven't, he walks away. But Nick's a good man, probably the best of us. He'll try something.'

The sentence had hardly been finished before a shaft of light broke through into the cell as the upper door was opened. Ollie could hear footsteps on the stairway. His heart froze. Maybe that was Wallace, coming to lead them towards the firing squad, or whatever miserable way of ending their lives he had chosen. For the first time, he sensed himself becoming afraid. Like many condemned men, he dealt with the terror by ignoring it, pretending it wasn't happening, focusing on the present and forgetting about the future. But once the executioner arrived . . .?

He wanted to carry himself with dignity to the end. But he was no longer sure he'd be able to.

Think about Lena, he urged himself. *It worked last time.*

More footsteps, he realised, glancing up. There were two people there at least. Then, out of the shadows, emerged the last man he had expected to see.

Archie Sharratt.

With his sister at his side.

'I just wanted to thank you boys for all your hard work,' said Archie, standing a few feet back from the cage. 'Just a shame you're not going to get paid.' He chuckled to himself.

Maksim had already thrown himself against the bars, his face twisted with anger, spitting violently. 'You bastard!' he roared.

Archie backed away uneasily. 'Easy soldier,' he said. 'Getting mad won't get you anywhere.'

'How about getting even, then?' suggested Ollie.

'It's a bit late for that, my old sausage,' said Archie.

'There's always time,' Ollie told him.

'Not for you boys. But that's business for you. Stock prices can go down as well as up, as it says on the investment ads. And this morning, the market is shorting mercenaries.'

Ollie walked closer to the bars, aware that his dark, stubbled face, caked in scabs of blood, presented a horrifying picture. 'Except that it's you who will be shorted.'

For a brief moment, there was a flash of fear across Archie's face, but he quickly composed himself. 'I'll see you at the hanging,' he snapped. Then he turned to look at Sam. 'Let's go.'

'I want to speak to them,' she said.

'What the hell about?' Archie asked irritably. 'They're dead men.'

'They might have some messages for their loved ones.'

'These scum?' Archie sneered. 'Even their mothers couldn't love them.'

Sam looked at him sharply. 'I was at convent school, so I know how to give these men the last rites. Please, Archie – I only need five minutes.'

'Bollocks.'

'I really want to do this, Archie.'

'Have it your own way.' He turned around and marched briskly up the stairs. Sam remained silent until she was certain he'd slammed the door behind him.

'We've no messages for *you*, you double-crossing bitch,' started Dan.

Sam ignored him, stepping closer to the cell, blinking at the foul smell that seeped up out of the enclosed space like an open sewer.

'Steve's going to break you out,' she hissed.

Ollie paused. It took a moment for the information to sink in. Could she really be working with Steve, and not her brother? he asked himself.

'Christ,' he muttered under his breath. Maybe there was hope for them, after all.

'There will be an ambush on the way to the stadium,' she murmured. 'When the truck stops, you must overpower your guards.' Reaching inside her top, she pulled out a small canvas bag and pushed it through the bars. 'There's some pocket-knives to help you.'

'Why the hell should we trust you?' Dan wouldn't let it drop. 'It was your brother who landed us in this mess.'

'Don't believe me, believe the knives,' Sam told him. She had already turned around, and was heading for the stairs. 'I can't stay any longer,' she said. She crossed herself. 'May God be on your side.' And then she was gone. The door clanged shut.

Ollie dipped his hand into the bag. Inside was a set of five small knives, with two-inch blades, inconspicuous enough to fit inside a man's sleeve, but still with enough punch in them to rip out a guard's throat.

It doesn't matter whether she's on the level or not, he told himself. The knives give us a chance of escaping.

And right now, that's all that counts.

*

Steve looked down at the map. It was eight in the morning, and none of them had slept all night, but a shower, a jug of orange juice and a pot of hot coffee had refreshed them all. Steve could feel the tension within him as he traced the route of the Akwa Road for the hundredth time. He'd been in a lot of fights in his life, both for his country and for his wallet. More, probably, than any sane man should get into. But he knew one thing for certain: he'd never gone into a battle where he cared as much about the outcome as he did today. They were a rough bunch of boys, ugly and violent, with the manners of a high-security jail inmates on a day trip to a brewery, but they were his unit, and he'd put his life on the line for each one of them, just as surely as they would for him.

There's only one problem, he reflected, biting his lip. Just as I've never been in a battle where the stakes meant as much to me, so I've never been in one where the odds were stacked as heavily against me as they are today.

But that's the way the dice roll. When you decide to become a soldier, you don't get to choose the battles. The battles choose you. And your job is just to fight them as best you can.

'All set?' he asked Ian.

The Irishman nodded. He put his finger down on the map. 'The road leads straight down here,' he said. 'I scouted it in the dark last night, and found an old abandoned garage. The convoy should pass within fifty yards of it.'

'You've rigged the kit?'

'Yes. There's a three-foot wall in front of the garage. I've taken a set of five old oil drums, and placed them three yards apart from one another. Each one has been sawn in half, then the bottom half filled with five gallons of diesel. That was the hardest thing to find, but Neil put me in touch with a bloke who had some stashed in his garage and didn't mind being woken up in the middle of the night when I told him I'd pay him two hundred dollars for it. Next, I've slotted a small lump of plastic explosive into the base of each barrel. The old phones I gutted for some filament wire. The modern ones are just micro-chips and electronics but the old ones still have some decent wire in them. Put that to a battery and you've got a dirt-simple charger that can be safely operated from a distance. Switch on those bastards, and you're going to get more smoke than you've ever seen in your life. Great waves of the stuff will be rolling across the street.'

He chuckled to himself, the laugh of a man appreciating his own work.

'They'll think World War Three has broken out.'

'And you, Nick,' said Steve. 'All set?'

'Watch this,' said Nick seriously.

The Hyundai had been pulled up on a gravelled courtyard behind the hostel where no one could see it. Steve followed Nick out to the vehicle, then climbed on board, switching on the engine.

The HPES was a simple black box, measuring eight inches by ten, looking something like the amplifier on a small hi-fi. Inside there was a mass of wire and a charger that would create the small but powerful electronic pulse needed to knock out any other electronic device in the immediate vicinity. But on the outside, there were just a set of three dials, and a charger.

Nick glanced up at Steve, then flicked a switch.

No sooner had he done so, than the engine switched itself off. And Steve hadn't felt a thing.

'Sodding brilliant,' he said, stepping down from the vehicle. 'Just make sure it works when we need it.'

'Er – there's one more trick,' said Nick.

Steve nodded. 'Go on.'

'This works by screwing up the electronics, and that's what switches the engine off. I'll stop everything, and once the truck has halted, you can raid it. I'll switch this off for a couple of seconds, then you start the engine. As soon as it's going, shoot the ignition out. With that disabled, once I switch HPES back on again, your engine will keep running, but all the other vehicles will be disabled and you can make a clean getaway.'

'But I won't be able to start the truck again if it stalls, right?' said Steve.

'No. You get one chance at making the escape. After that, you've had it.'

'I'll take those odds.'

'Oh – and the brakes might not work either,' added Nick.

Steve grinned. 'The way I'm planning to drive out of there,' he said, 'brakes are the one thing I won't need.'

He checked his watch. Eight-fifteen. They needed to be in position in plenty of time to lose themselves in the hundreds of people expected to be lining the route. They'd have to make themselves as inconspicuous as possible. They were wearing cargo shorts, loose-fitting sweatshirts and baseball caps. There was no way they could carry AKs – the police would spot them instantly. But the Uzi machine pistols were small enough to fit snugly into the baggy shorts without creating any suspicious bulges. And they had tucked knives into their boots.

'How about you, Steve?' asked Ian. 'You ready?'

Steve drew the Uzi machine pistol from his pocket, unclipped its mag to show that it was fully loaded, then slotted it back into place. 'For a rumble?' he said. 'Of course I am. Now let's crack on.' He started to climb into the Hyundai.

'I'm coming with you,' said Sam. She was standing right behind Steve, dressed in blue jeans, a white T-shirt, and with her hair tied back behind her head.

'Don't be ridiculous,' growled Steve. 'This is no place for a woman.'

'This is my battle as well.'

Steve looked into her eyes, and knew at once that what she was saying was absolutely true. But that didn't make any difference. All she would do was get in the way.

'There's going to be big trouble brewing in this city by lunchtime.

You don't want to be anywhere near it. Get down to the Sheraton and book yourself a room. I'll call you there when it's all over.'

'I can help,' she said obstinately.

Steve pressed the Uzi into her hand. 'Show me how you fire that then.'

Holding the weapon uneasily, she began looking for the safety catch. Before she could find it, Steve had already taken the gun back from her.

'You can help best by letting us get on with the job,' he said firmly.

As he finished the sentence, he slammed the door on the Hyundai, kicked the engine into life and started to pull into the road.

Forty

THE SOLDIERS PUSHED THE FIVE men roughly up the stairs, until they emerged blinking into the sunlight. Ollie led the way, followed by Dan, Ganju, Maksim and David. The air seemed fresher this morning, decided Ollie. There were some clouds scuttling across the sky, but the sunshine was bright, and the breeze cool.

'Ready to die like a gentleman, Mr Hall?' Wallace enquired.

Ollie nodded briskly. 'I'll be happy enough to die like a soldier.'

'You gave up being a soldier the day you flunked out of the Blues,' Wallace sneered. 'You're just criminal scum. And that's how you'll die.'

'And how will *you* die, Mr Wallace?'

'In my bed, at a ripe old age, with a good book, a comfy woman and a bottle of single malt whisky,' the man said smugly.

'Don't count on that.'

One of the soldiers came out of the barracks building, a bucket in his hand. He put it down on the ground. Inside, the remains of Chris's head were clearly visible. His skin was starting to peel away, but otherwise it was the same rugged, familiar face that had fought alongside them through Afghanistan and then Batota. Ollie could feel his stomach churning: he had a strong constitution, and had needed it when he was seriously hitting the bottle, but there were some sights that were hard for even the strongest man to take.

And this was one of them.

One by one, the five soldiers guarding them dipped tin cups into the water and took a long swig of the stained liquid.

'They're going to need some courage to take your lives later this morning,' said Wallace. 'And your man was brave enough . . . some of that stuff should do the trick.'

Ollie took a step closer to the man. 'You bas—' But before he could finish the sentence a pair of soldiers grabbed his shoulders and pushed him straight back into the line. An open-topped military truck, painted camouflage green, had already reversed into position and parked right next to them. One soldier pulled its back down, while another gestured to the five men to climb on board.

Ollie led the way. He and the others stepped up onto the truck, and five soldiers followed them. They were armed with AK-47s, with knives and handguns on their belts. But the prisoners weren't bound. They intend to parade us like captives through Ancient Rome, realised Ollie. And we'll look less impressive if we have chains on us.

He fingered the knife in his pocket. They're just not counting on this, he thought with a tight smile.

Wallace bolted up the truck. 'It doesn't make any difference to us whether the crowd sees live colonialist scum or dead ones. In fact, they prefer the dead variety, although I'm sure they'd rather not pass up the opportunity of watching you be executed. So don't get any smart ideas about escaping.'

The truck roared into life, and the soldiers in the parade ground stepped aside, forming a column as they drove out towards the gates. The roads around the barracks were empty. How far it was to the stadium, Ollie wasn't sure. Probably only a few minutes' drive. He glanced into the eyes of the soldiers standing opposite him. They were expressionless, implacable, and he knew that once it came to a fight they would be formidable opponents. However, he and the others had been through the drill a hundred times back in their cell.

As soon as the attack started, they'd plunge their knives straight into their necks.

One blade for each man. That was a fair fight.

The truck lurched over a pothole, then ploughed forwards. They were approaching the centre of the city, then they would start heading west towards the stadium. Up ahead of them, the President's motorcade had joined the procession. A big black Lexus LS 460L, it was carrying President Kapembwa, and was accompanied by eight Sixth Brigade soldiers riding Honda motorbikes. Behind them was a heavily armoured Land Rover. Inside, Ollie could see Wallace, accompanied by Newton and Archie Sharratt. Briefly, his eye caught Newton's, but the man just looked away. If he was ashamed of himself, you couldn't see it in his face.

The crowds were starting to build up along the side of the road: a few people at first, then more as the line of vehicles turned into one of the big roads. As Ollie looked into the crowd, he could see only a sullen mass of faces.

We get one shot at this, he told himself.

We'll make it work, or we'll die trying.

Steve noted that he and Nick were not the only white men in the crowd. They'd taken up a position 800 yards down from the stadium. There was one other elderly white man, and a pair of youngish back-packers. But Steve was still aware that they stood out amid the men and women thronging the edge of the wide avenue.

He checked his watch. Ten-fifteen. They were already running late.

The mood was tense. Steve could see it in the eyes of the people thronging the street. They were angry, on the edge of violence, and once some trouble kicked off, there was no way of knowing which way they might turn. They didn't like Kapembwa, but that didn't mean they were ready for a bunch of white boys to start coming in and re-ordering their country. We shouldn't expect the crowd to be on our side, Steve reminded himself. We'll just grab our blokes, then get out of here as fast as we can. Treat the whole country as our enemy: that way there's a chance of staying alive.

There were street snacks on sale: fried chicken, stewed goat, and big burning racks of sweetcorn. Only a few people were buying. Up close, you could feel the poverty of the people. The kids were undernourished, most of them dressed in rags. Their parents didn't look in any better shape. Average life expectancy for men had fallen to just thirty-seven, and for women thirty-four. As you looked around, there weren't any old people. Nobody makes it that far, I guess, decided Steve.

And certainly not the foreign mercenaries.

He was standing on the edge of the road, looking down the highway waiting for the first sign of the approaching convoy. Nick was at his side, the HPES discreetly tucked away into his rucksack. Across the street, Ian was standing close to the empty garage where he'd rigged up his bombs. In his hand, he was holding the transmitter for an electric toy car: the shortwave radio signal would trigger the detonator, kick off the explosions and start the fight.

'Where the hell are they?' said Nick. You could hear the tension in his voice.

'They'll be here soon enough,' Steve replied.

As he spoke, he could hear the convoy approach. A van led the way, a loudspeaker turned up high, blaring out propaganda to the crowds along the way. 'The imperialist plotters have been foiled!' it shouted. 'The freedom of the Batotean people has once again been secured from the colonialist oppressors!'

Steve glanced across the street, and caught Ian's eye. He nodded just once, and Ian nodded back. The message they exchanged was: *Wait, hold yourself steady, but get ready to kick off the attack.*

Nick was starting to reach into his kitbag. 'Hold it,' muttered Steve.

The loudspeaker van was right alongside them now, whipping the crowd into a frenzy. Fists were being punched into the air, and a chant was rippling through the crowd. 'Death to the imperialists!' they shouted, a thousand voices strong. Steve did his best to block out the noise, willing himself to remain 100 per cent focused on the task at hand.

Policemen were walking down the street, pushing the crowd back with their batons, using force where they had to, to keep people off the main road. An occasional scuffle broke out, but was invariably settled by a brisk swipe of a truncheon.

Next, three armoured SUVs filled with troops of soldiers rolled past, the metal of their guns glistening in the early-morning sunshine. Behind that approached the Presidential limousine, its windows blackened out, edging slowly down the wide avenue.

And then came the truck.

Steve looked straight into it. You could see the five men standing in the back, their heads bowed, with their five guards standing directly opposite them. The truck was doing twenty miles an hour, making for the stadium, another pair of vehicles directly behind it. The crowd roared as they saw the men, chanting wildly and lobbing rotten fruit in their direction.

'Hold it,' Steve hissed again to Nick.

He waited. The truck was still twenty yards away.

Steve looked over at Ian. He held up five fingers, then slowly counted down the time. Five, four, three, two . . .

'*One*,' he mouthed.

Ian pulled the trigger on the toy car, then melted silently into the crowd.

It was classic IRA, he reflected to himself. Pull the trigger, then vanish into thin air. It had worked against the British, and it would work again today.

There was a split second before the plastic explosives detonated. At first, all Steve heard was a distant thump that could easily have been a truck backfiring. Then there was a sudden, violent eruption as the first of the oil drums burst into a wall of flames. The noise rocked out across the street, like a gale blowing away everything in its path. The flames spat into the air – twenty, thirty, then forty feet – kicking up into the sky like a golden fountain. Then the heat started to vaporise the air. The oxygen was sucked out of the avenue, making it hard to breathe, and creating a counter-gale. Wind seemed to be hurling from every direction. Finally, the smoke rolled out. Thick black clouds of solid tar, blasting out across the ground, it choked and suffocated everything it touched.

For a moment, the avenue was eerily still, the crowd stunned by the sudden violence of the explosion, immobilised by the shock.

That split second is our crucial advantage, Steve reminded himself. We're the only people who expected it, the only people primed to react. 'Go – sodding *go!*' he told Nick.

Nick had already pulled the HPES from his rucksack, jamming his finger into the device.

Steve looked straight at the truck. Clouds of smoke were swirling around it, and the machine had lost power. It was juddering to a halt.

'Time for a scrap,' he muttered under his breath.

And then he started to run.

Ollie felt the explosion before he even heard it: there was a flickering tremor in the air and he was primed and ready for it. Next, came the murderous roar as the diesel ignited, then the thick black cloud of smoke, descending on them like fog rolling out of the waves at sea.

'Go!' he bellowed, his lungs stretched, ignoring the fumes clogging his throat as soon as he opened his mouth.

The soldiers opposite them had been briefly disorientated by the suddenness and vigour of the attack and were now expecting a full-blown assault: the explosion sounded like the first blast of artillery, to be followed by a second wave of combat troops on the ground. But in reality, the enemy was right with them inside the truck.

Ollie leaped on the soldier directly opposite him. The man had turned to look at the source of the explosion, at the same time grabbing his AK-47. It took just a fraction of a second for Ollie to cover the two yards that separated them, flinging himself through the air like a rugby player in full flight, then crashing hard into his opponent. The man was built from solid muscle, each sinew hardened by the years of ferocious training on the Sixth Brigade's parade ground. It was like hurling yourself against a steel pylon. There wasn't an inch of give in him.

Ollie fought to ignore the pain smashing into his chest, and clung onto his opponent, kicking violently to push the AK-47 clattering to the ground. All around him, he could hear the rattle of gunfire, the screams of the crowd, and the beat of military boots against the tarmac as the soldiers rushed into position. Withdrawing his right hand from his pocket, the two-inch solid steel blade encased in his palm, with one savage movement he slammed it upwards, slicing straight into the side of the man's neck. The skin was hard, like thick leather, but the angle was a good one, and the blade arced easily enough into the flesh below.

In less than a second, however, Ollie sensed that the soldier would recover and start fighting back. The man had the strength of a bull and, should he get the chance to retaliate, it was going to turn into a brutal scrap. With a deft flick of the wrist, Ollie twisted the blade around. There was no time to fish around for the carotid artery, the main vessel for delivering oxygen from the chest to the brain, and which, once severed, would finish a man's life in seconds. Nor was there any time to punch through the windpipe: that too would kill him stone dead. Instead, Ollie just twisted and twisted the blade, opening up a bigger and bigger hole in the neck, like a drill bit punching its way through a wall.

Blood loss will have to finish the bastard, Ollie thought breathlessly as the thick crimson liquid poured over him. Empty two pints out of the sod, and he'll lose consciousness. Then I can use the blade to cut the last remnants of life out of him at my leisure.

Suddenly, the man jerked forwards, roaring with anger. A huge bucket of spit landed right in Ollie's face, mixing with the hot, sticky blood to create a thick, clingy mixture that took hold of him like seaweed. An elbow kicked into Ollie's ribs. He was struggling to hold himself steady against the force of the blow. The knife slipped a half inch, then an inch. And Ollie knew that if he allowed the blade to slip out of the man's neck, the bleeding would start to staunch, and the man would begin to recover his strength.

Thump. The man's elbow was kicking into Ollie's ribcage again, knocking the oxygen clean out of his lungs. He choked, and felt a dribble of the blood that was dripping down his face swill into his throat. He spat violently, willed himself to ignore the pain, and twisted the blade again, spinning it around and around, so that the wound it was cutting open was turning into a gaping hole. The blood was flowing more freely now, gushing out of the wound, and as Ollie clung desperately to the victim he could feel the strength slowly ebbing out of the bastard. The man was choking on his own blood, and his heart was beating furiously as the adrenaline coursed through his veins, but the effect was only to increase the amount of blood flowing out of him.

Another thump from the elbow. But it was weaker this time, noted Ollie. The power wasn't there, and the blow bounced harmlessly off his ribcage.

The soldier's legs started to buckle. And then he fell to the ground. As he dropped, Ollie drew out the knife, and slashed it once, then twice across the man's throat, neatly cutting the windpipe in two, and ending whatever slim possibility of survival remained.

Ollie glanced up.

The bottom of the truck was a pool of blood, like an abattoir with blocked drains. Dan had already slashed his soldier to ribbons in a frenzy of strong, disciplined aggression. Ganju had neatly opened up his victim's windpipe, punching a hole big enough to end his life quickly and relatively painlessly: there were no more skilful knifemen than the Gurkhas, and although his opponent was six inches taller and 100 pounds heavier, he had never stood a chance, and from the passive way his corpse had slumped to the floor, the soldier seemed to sense it from the moment the fight started.

But David was still involved in a nasty scrap. And so was Maksim.

David was being pinned back against the side of the truck by the soldier he'd been attempting to take out. The knife had gone into the man's neck, causing a nasty wound that was bubbling with blood, but the blade had slipped out, dropping to the floor, and now the two men were trading blows with their fists. Sickening sounds of bone crashing against bone echoed around the small space as the two men attacked one another like a pair of uncaged animals. Dan and Ganju had already moved swiftly to David's aid, and within a second the victim was lost in a whirl of flashing steel and flying fists.

Maksim, meanwhile, was pinned down on the floor of the truck, the swirling blood soaking into his shirt and hair. A soldier was lying on top of him, crushing his chest, a knife in his right hand, attempting to thrust it downwards straight into the Russian's heart. But Maksim was holding him off, using all his strength to keep the hand with the blade a few inches away from his body.

Ollie roared, then grabbed hold of the soldier, jerking his head back with his left hand, then using his right to stab his still-bloodied blade into the man's throat. In the same instant, Maksim bucked upwards, then kicked out with his legs, delivering a brutal blow straight into the man's chest. He whimpered with pain, like a dying animal, but within seconds, he'd been crushed to death, his heart seizing up under the violence of the sudden assault.

'I would have dealt with him,' said Maksim, pushing the corpse away from his body. The wounded pride was evident in his voice.

'Of course you would, Maksie,' said Ollie with a rough grin. 'Just wanted to save you the trouble, that's all . . .'

*

Steve was running hard towards the stalled truck, the Uzi machine pistol drawn, and his finger slotted onto the trigger.

The driver of the truck, and the soldier sitting alongside him, were looking bewildered. They were unable to understand why their vehicle had stopped working. The clouds of smoke were obscuring their vision, and the burning flames from the diesel drums had turned the sky a bright, hazy orange. A troop of soldiers were rushing to cordon off the Presidential car. All around them, the crowd was starting to panic, with men, women and children screaming wildly, then starting to run in every direction, creating a scene of chaos that paralysed the entire road.

Block it all out, Steve told himself.

Just focus on the driver.

He ran harder, but waited until he was just ten yards from the vehicle before opening up a murderous barrage of fire, using the full power of the weapon to punch a deadly blast of hot metal straight through the window and into the faces of the men sitting behind it. The glass screen shattered into a thousand fragments, but did nothing to stop the volleys of bullets that sliced into both men. Steve kept on running, slotting a fresh mag into the Uzi as he did so.

Using one hand to open the door on the driver's side of the vehicle, he used the other to rip the man clean out of his seat and cast him straight to the ground. In the same movement, he clambered up into the truck, hoisting the second corpse out into the road. He sensed there was some life left in the soldier – the bullets had peppered his chest, but not severed any major arteries – but he had lost consciousness and there was no time to double tap him now. Behind Steve, up in the main part of the truck, he could hear the noise of a fight. It was impossible to have any idea what was happening up there.

As he looked out of the window, he could see Nick approaching from one side of the road, Ian from the other. Both men were hurtling towards the vehicle at full pelt, their guns drawn, blasting their way through the crowds of terrified civilians and confused soldiers clogging the avenue. Huge fireballs were still spitting out from the row of incendiary devices, and the soldiers were rushing towards the garage, putting down barrages of fire into what they assumed was the enemy position, but the intense heat from the flames was driving them back, making it impossible for them to figure out what was happening behind the wall of fire.

Chaos we can live with, decided Steve. But in the next few seconds, they'll realise this isn't a major attack. Just three blokes, with machine pistols, and more balls than brains. And once they know they outnumber us a hundred to one, they'll crush us like maggots.

He climbed out of the cabin and peered up into the back of the truck, his gun drawn and ready to fire.

'Thanks for dropping by, old boy,' Ollie panted. 'But I think we've got the situation under control.'

Steve took a second to digest the scene. So long as you didn't count bruises, sweat, stubble, grime and hands dripping with blood, all five of them looked OK. Their knives were still in their hands, and the butchered remains of the five soldiers who had been guarding them lay on the bed of the truck.

'Then let's get the hell out of here,' he replied with a grin, and swung himself back down into the cabin of the truck.

'Christ,' he muttered under his breath, as he slotted himself behind the steering wheel, and tried to get a decent lungful of oxygen amid the smoke and fumes. *There's just a chance we're going to pull this thing off.*

Ian and Nick had already climbed, beside him.

'Turn that thing off,' he snapped, pointing towards the HPES still held between Nick's hands.

But before Nick had a chance to respond, Maksim had already bounced across the bonnet of the truck, landing on the tarmac with a thump, with one of the dead soldier's AK-47's clamped to his right fist.

And he was running towards the President's car.

'Jesus, what's that mad bastard doing now?' shouted Steve. Leaping out of the truck, he grabbed Maksim by the shoulder, yanking him backwards. 'Get the fuck back on the truck!' he yelled.

Maksim turned around. Blood was still dripping from his soaked T-shirt, and there was dirt across his face. 'I've come too far and seen too much to go home without getting paid,' he snarled.

He gestured towards Kapembwa's car. 'So long as he's dead, the money gets released into our bank accounts, remember?'

He grinned wildly. 'I'm going to finish the fucker.'

'You'll get sodding killed.'

Maksim turned around, ignoring the warning, and walked straight into the thick plumes of black smoke. 'At least I won't be the only one,' he shouted back, his tone hardening. 'There will be a whole graveyard filled up before this morning's work is finished.'

Forty-One

MAKSIM WAS MARCHING STEADILY TOWARDS the
Presidential motorcade.

The long, black limousine had been ringed by a cordon
of eight soldiers, all of them wearing the distinctive purple and gold
berets of the Sixth Brigade. The soldiers had closed into a circle, still
unsure of the nature of the threat they were facing. With the HPES
still blasting out its signal, the car was unable to move forwards, and
the sophistication of the jamming equipment had led their
Commander to assume they were facing a full-blown Special Forces
assault, possibly by the SAS, possibly by the American Delta Force.
In time, if they couldn't get the car started again, they'd bring a
helicopter in to lift the President out. But it was still only minutes
since the attack had started.

A pair of civilians had already been shot when they strayed too
close to the vehicle. Anyone else who did so was clearly going to meet
the same fate.

'What's the bastard doing?' shouted Steve up to Ollie.

Ollie just shrugged, wiping the blood out of his face. 'What the
Spetsnaz always do. Walking straight into the face of death.'

'Then give him some covering fire,' snapped Steve. 'If he wants to
die, that's up to him, but he'll have some back-up.'

This unit's got some scores to settle, he thought grimly.

And they'll be settled in blood.

On top of the truck, Ollie, Dan, Ganju and David had grabbed hold of the AK-47s carried by their dead captors. Each one had a full clip in its mag, giving them a total of 120 rounds between them. The four men lined themselves up, trying to get a fix on the car, watching and waiting as Maksim walked forwards. The moment to shoot would be when they troops guarding it noticed him – thereby taking advantage of the split second between observation and reaction.

Ten yards.

Maksim had another ten to cover before he was on top of the vehicle.

'Wait, lads . . . hold it,' Ollie told them.

Down below, both Steve and Ian had lined up their Uzi machine pistols.

Eight yards. Seven . . .

Maksim was walking steadily, without a trace of fear in his step and, not for the first time, Steve found himself admiring the suicidal valour of the man.

Just then, one of the soldiers spun around. A shout started to rise to his lips, and he made ready to aim.

'Fire!' shouted Ollie.

The sound of four AK-47s being fired in unison is a harsh one: a rapid series of deafening blows, like a hammer smashing into a steel plate. The spent shell casings spat out of the guns as the men laid down round after round in a blistering volley that put lethal quantities of hot metal straight into their opponents.

And still Maksim marched steadily forwards, emerging out of the black smoke like an immortal demon.

The first volley of fire had cut a scythe through the troops surrounding the vehicle. Three of the eight men had been killed in an instant, the bullets slicing into their heads, sending them sprawling to the ground. Two more had been hit in the body armour covering their chests: the punch of the bullets had sent them reeling backwards, and although no real harm had been done, it would take them a minute at least to steady themselves, and get themselves back into the fight.

More than enough time to kill them, decided Maksim.

Dropping his AK-47 to his hip, he slammed his finger into the trigger, and unleashed a blast into the two men staggering backwards. One was hit twice in the legs, and fell straight to the ground, using his hands to try and staunch the bleeding. Another was hit, first in the helmet, the bullet glancing harmlessly away, then in the shoulder, just above where his body armour was protecting his chest. He doubled up in pain, trying to plug the wound where the bullet had smashed through his muscle and chewed up the bone underneath.

Five men down, noted Steve from the side of the truck. Three more to go.

Ollie and the rest of the unit were putting down a steady barrage of fire, the bullets flying a foot over Maksim's head and slicing into the enemy positions. One more man had fallen, but the remaining two soldiers had thrown themselves behind the limousine, protecting themselves from the murderous assault. They were starting to return shots, spitting bullets from their AK-47s into the strange, dark figure emerging slowly from the smoke and flame all around them.

'Don't waste the ammo,' yelled Ollie. 'We can't hit them from here.'

Behind then, Wallace and Park had jumped from the two Land Rovers following the convoy. The two most experienced soldiers in the field, they had already guessed this was a dummy assault, and that behind the exploding oil drums there was no army ready to advance. They were shouting wildly, trying to get the soldiers who'd run off to deal with the mock assault to come back and round up the prisoners.

'Pin those buggers down,' yelled David.

Dan immediately ran to the back of the truck and, alongside David, started putting round after round into Wallace's position. The two men dived behind the immobilised Land Rover, dragging Archie with them.

There wasn't much chance of hitting them, realised David. Not unless they could lay their hands on some grenades or an RPG. But so long as they could stop them co-ordinating a fight back, it was worth the ammo they were using. Just until we can get the hell out of here, David told himself.

'How the fuck is he going to make it?' yelled Steve, pointing towards Maksim.

'He needs help,' confirmed Ollie.

'Sod it,' muttered Steve. The lunatic Russian was risking all of their lives. But that didn't mean they could leave him to walk straight into a hail of bullets. One man's already died on this mission, Steve thought. I'm not losing another one.

Jumping down from the truck, he started to run towards the limousine. Seems a shame to blow the bastard to hell, reflected Steve as he glanced briefly at the Lexus LS460L. *Waste of a lovely motor.*

Maksim had already thrown himself to the ground.

He'd rattled off half a dozen rounds, straight underneath the Lexus, slicing through the boots of the soldiers crouching on the other side. The bullets crashed into the mass of delicate bones threading through the ankle into the foot. Both men screamed in pain. At the same time, Steve kept running, diving along the edge of the car, pointing his Uzi towards the wounded men. He fired straight for their heads, the stream of bullets knocking them leftwards, then rightwards, then punching the life out of them.

Over by the burning oil drums, the soldiers had finally realised there that this was no major attack, merely an ambush, and were advancing back towards the centre of the avenue. There were at least fifty of them, and although they still looked confused and disorganised, in the next few seconds Steve knew they would have steadied themselves into a formidable fighting force.

One civilian was running towards Steve, shouting. Steve simply raised the Uzi and thumped a bullet straight into the man's chest. 'Get back,' he shouted. 'Put some fire into those men,' he then yelled at Ollie, pointing to the advancing troop of soldiers.

Ollie reacted instantly. While Ganju kept his AK-47 trained on Wallace and Park, keeping them pinned down, Dan and David rushed to Ollie's side of the truck and the three men laid down a volley of fire into the incoming soldiers.

They picked off one man. Enough to briefly halt their advance.

But they were running dangerously low on bullets. Of the thirty-rounds in the AK-47s they had grabbed from the dead soldiers, they each had less than ten rounds left. Dan had riffled through the uniforms of the corpses, and each man was carrying one spare mag, but that still gave them only forty rounds per man. 'Bloody move it!' he shouted towards Steve. 'We haven't the ammo to hold them.'

Maksim by now had stood up, and was grabbing hold of the back door to the Lexus. 'Right, let's finish this bastard,' he growled.

The Lexus was fitted with black tinted windows, but you could still see through it. In the back seat, Kapembwa was sitting still, his expression calm, his eyes steely and resolved, as if he expected his troops to come and rescue him within the next few minutes. At his side was a man dressed in a dark suit who looked like a security official and, up front, a driver.

'Get ready to die,' Maksim told them. Then, lifting the AK-47 to his shoulder, he pumped one, two, then three bullets straight into the window.

Sodding Spetsnaz, sighed Steve. All muscle and munitions and no subtlety.

The windows of the Lexus were constructed of bullet-resistant glass, manufactured to the highest standards. Made from a polycarbonate thermoplastic, the glass was three inches thick, and simply flattened the bullet on impact, deflecting it harmlessly away.

Maksim's bullets were leaving no more than a scratch on the surface of the Lexus. Inside, Kapembwa looked up and smiled at him condescendingly. Maksim threw the weapon down in disgust, its mag empty. Steve felt his pulse racing. There were newer types of one-way bullet-resistant glass, now regularly fitted to the armoured vehicles that carried banknotes. You couldn't fire into them, but they allowed the guards inside the vehicle to fire out at their opponents. That glass was made of two layers: one brittle, one flexible. When a bullet was fired from the outside, the first layers of glass shattered, absorbing and spreading most of the kinetic energy from the round, so that it bounced harmlessly off the inner layer. But when a bullet was fired from the inside, it penetrated the flexible layer of glass with ease, then punched its way through the brittle layer. The results could be lethal. You launched an attack on a vehicle, but your gunfire made no difference, whilst a man inside could pick you off with ease. If that type of glass had been fitted to the driver's window, then . . .

Steve could see the driver drawing a pistol.

'Get the fuck down!' he bawled at Maksim.

The driver had already twisted around, and put a bullet straight through the window. It would have hit Maksim in the throat, but he was already halfway to the ground by time the bullet was fired. The shot punched a clean hole an inch wide in the window. It was swiftly followed by another shot, then another. They too sailed harmlessly into the air.

'Recognise that gun, Maksie?' Steve asked breathlessly. Both men were crouched down below the side of the Lexus. There was smoke billowing across the street and the racket of gunfire filled the air as Ollie and his unit traded shots with the troops across the Avenue.

'Of course. It's a Skyph.'

The Skyph, or MP 448, was a Russian handgun designed in the early 1990s to replace the legendary Makarov PM Pistol. A semi-automatic gun, like its predecessor it fired 9x18mm calibre ammo, far punchier than standard, and was capable of inflicting far more damage.

'You sure?'

'In the Spetsnaz we study all the Russian guns.'

'How many rounds in a clip?'

'Twelve.'

'OK, he's got nine rounds left . . .'

Maksim knew at once what Steve was thinking. He threw a fist in the air next to the window. The driver fired, but Maksim had already flashed his fist away.

Eight rounds left.

Maksim repeated the trick, again and again, grabbing a rock to make it more effective. At his side, Steve was counting down the rounds. Three, two, one . . .

He'd have another clip, of course, Steve told himself. But even the most skilled operative needs a couple of seconds to switch magazine.

Maksim rolled his fist into the window, then flashed it away. A shot. In the same instant, Steve leaped to his feet. Pushing the barrel of the Uzi into the hole broken in the window by the driver firing outwards, he loosened off two rounds straight into the man's head. The driver slumped forwards, already dead.

At Steve's side, Maksim had ripped off half his sweatshirt, and wrapped it like a bandage around his right fist. With a savage punch, he smashed his hand right into the hole in the window, breaking the glass, then flung the door open.

Kapembwa leaned forwards. For the first time, there was a look of real fear etched into the granite lines on his face. He was not a young man, but Steve could see in his eyes that he wasn't ready to die. It had never occurred to him that his tyrannical reign might end like this, and, in the wild terror of the moment, he couldn't make any kind of peace with it.

Well, it was too late now, Steve reflected bitterly. The evil bastard had just run out of time.

'Time to meet your Maker, you son of a bitch,' Maksim informed him.

Taking the Skyph from the driver's hand, he slotted the fresh clip he'd grabbed from the man's lap into place, and slammed his finger on the trigger. One, two, three bullets, all delivered with lethal accuracy, flew straight to the head.

Kapembwa slumped forwards.

The three bullet wounds were arranged in a neat row just above the eyebrows. The man's eyes had closed. At his side, the bodyguard in the dark suit was sitting in terrified silence.

'Start brushing up your CV, mate,' said Steve tersely. 'I think you'll be looking for a new job.'

And then he started to run, Maksim following in his wake. His boots were beating against the tarmac, sweat pouring off his face, as he lunged towards the waiting truck. Some of the civilians flooding the Avenue had noticed that the Presidential limo had been attacked, and were starting to swarm towards it, creating a heaving chaotic mass of people. Across the road, a pair of soldiers had broken away from the main column and were running fast towards the car, loosening off some rounds from their AK-47s to help clear the way. Two civilians fell wounded to the ground, only increasing the chaos all around them. The screams of the crowd mixed with the rattle of gunfire to create a hellish haze of noise that only the steeliest of soldiers could fight their way through. And in that chaos, as it had done since the attack started, lay their opportunity of escape.

'Get a move on,' yelled Ollie from the truck. 'We haven't the ammo to hold them much longer.' He was holding himself steady in the back of the vehicle, using its steel panels for cover, and with his AK-47 loosening off round after round. But he was down to just five bullets left in the clip, and the rest of the boys weren't in any better shape for supplies.

Once the ammo had gone, they'd just be target practice. And Ollie hated to think what the Sixth Brigade would do to the foreign mercenaries who had just murdered their President.

I'm saving one last bullet, he thought. *And using it on myself if this all goes pear-shaped.*

'Bloody move!' he screamed again, louder this time, his face red with anger.

'Christ, mate, keep your knickers on!' shouted Steve.

He levered himself into the driver's seat, and looked straight at Nick. 'Switch that thing off,' he told him, nodding towards the HPES. Maksim was already clambering desperately into the cabin, landing on top of Nick, who'd already flicked the switch on the box. Steve turned the key in the ignition, bringing the truck shuddering to life.

On the top of the vehicle, Dan looked around at Ollie; you could tell he was worried. 'I can't hold these bastards much longer,' he admitted, nodding down towards Wallace and Park. 'We have to move out.'

Ollie could feel the truck heave and shake as the powerful diesel engine roared into life. We're off, he thought to himself. Then he saw a pair of soldiers running hard towards them, spurred on by their Commander. He used up one bullet, then another, winging one man on the shoulder, sending him tumbling to the ground, but leaving the other unharmed. 'Shit,' he muttered. The man was just yards away from the truck now. Two bullets left in the mag . . .

Ollie lined up a shot, putting it straight into the head of the advancing soldier, but it struck his helmet, glancing harmlessly away. The man was pulling a grenade from his chest webbing, raising it to his mouth to pull the pin. Grenades were the one device the unit had no defence against. It would blow the truck to smithereens, and the civilian casualties would be horrendous. Hundreds of the innocent bystanders on the Avenue would be killed. But it looked like the Sixth Brigade men didn't care any more. Kapembwa was dead – the man who had looked after them for the last twenty years, and whom they had sworn their lives to defend.

And they'd exact their revenge, no matter how high the price.

At Ollie's side, Ganju opened up with a blast of rapid fire. The soldier stopped as the bullets peppered his chest, throwing him backwards, and the grenade rolled away harmlessly into the panicking crowd, its pin still in place.

Ganju put the gun down. 'I'm not wasting any more of this ammo,' he said.

Down in the cabin, Steve blasted the ignition with the Uzi. The bullet lodged itself in the mechanics, chewing it up, but didn't totally destroy it. He fired again, the noise of the gunfire echoing viciously around the enclosed space. The ignition was turned into a mess of hot charred metal, whilst the ricochet slammed backwards, missing Nick by only millimetres. The truck kept running. Steve slammed his foot hard on the accelerator, the engine revved up furiously, and the wheels started to churn forward.

'Get it back on,' he shouted to Nick.

Nick had already slammed his finger back on the HPES, its powerful signal transmitting across the Avenue. The high-energy pulse was silent, invisible, but snaked its way out across the ground like a shadowy mist. Behind him, Steve had already heard the pair of Land Rovers commanded by Wallace spring into life but then fall silent again as the pulse killed the electronics controlling their motors. But the truck kept on running. Only one problem, Steve reminded himself grimly. If she stalls we can't start her again.

He slammed his left hand on the horn, trying to clear the mass of civilians running hysterically across the Avenue, and used his right to steer the truck forwards. Shooting out the ignition had also taken out the power steering, and the wheel was a bastard to move. Steve could feel the sweat pouring out of every inch of his body as he struggled to get the big heavy beast forwards. People were screaming, throwing themselves into the gutters to get out of the way. Steve just ignored them. Once he felt the wheels bounce across something, and he just prayed it wasn't a person. I can't worry about that now, he told himself. They've had their warning. And if they can't get out of our way, that's their problem. End of story.

'Put your foot down, man!' yelled Ollie from the back of the truck. Steve was steering the truck straight down Akwa Avenue. That would take them out of Ibera, past the National Stadium. From there, they would head due north, and keep on driving until they got back to civilisation. But there was still a long, hard journey ahead of them.

'Looks like the gallows can wait, boys,' he said, with a tight smile.

'We're not through this yet,' said David.

'I've got three bullets in my clip,' said Dan. 'How about you?'

'Two,' said David.

'Five,' said Ganju.

The Ghurkha was always the most precise marksman among them, noted Ollie. It was part of their tradition. They didn't waste any ammo.

'And you?' Ganju enquired of Ollie.

'Two,' he replied crisply. 'That gives us twelve rounds between us.'

'Great. And only a whole sodding country to get through,' said Dan.

Ollie glanced backwards. Wallace and Park were stranded in their Land Rovers, but they had made contact with the main body of troops, who were starting to co-ordinate a fight back. One squadron of five men was running hard towards them, firing on automatic, but their bullets were hitting the tarmac or pinging harmlessly off the back of the truck. They were aiming for the tyres, Ollie knew, but so far they'd missed. Another pair of men were pulling the pins on their hand grenades, then lobbing them high into the air. Ollie watched the arc of each one with mounting dread, following its trajectory, but then breathing out again as he realised they were going to land thirty yards short of the truck. The grenades exploded, the crack of the detonation whipping through the air, killing at least two civilians and injuring a dozen more. The explosions were causing yet more mayhem, but it was clear that Wallace didn't care about collateral damage.

'We need to hide,' Ollie yelled down to Steve.

Taking his left hand off the horn, Steve wiped the sweat from his face. There was dirt and blood covering the windscreen, but with the electronics all down, the wipers were no longer working. The crowds had cleared off the road now, and he could pick up speed. The truck started to climb through twenty, then thirty miles an hour.

But then he saw her. A blonde woman running along the side of the road, waving at them frantically.

Sam.

'Christ,' muttered Steve out loud. He tapped his foot on the brake, slowing the truck. His heart was thumping in his chest. If it stalled, they were done for.

'What the—' started Nick at his side.

Steve nodded towards Sam.

The truck was slowing down to fifteen then ten miles an hour. Glancing in the wing mirrors, Steve could see that the soldiers running behind them were starting to close the gap. He threw the door open.

Grabbing hold of her wrist, he hauled Sam into the cabin. In the same instant, he slammed his foot hard on the accelerator, pushed the gear up into third, and started to coax the maximum power out of the big diesel engine. Sam was lying breathless across his lap, but he pushed her towards Nick, Maksim and Ian. It was a tight squeeze in the cabin, but they could worry about that later.

For now, he told himself, we just have to escape.

He swerved violently. There was a road heading right just before the stadium. Steve had no idea where it was leading, but at least it would take them away from Wallace and the rest of the army. He kept his foot hard on the floor, pushing the truck up to fifty, then sixty miles an hour. It was literally flying across the open tarmac.

But up ahead there was a roadblock.

It was marked by a single sentry post, made from roughly painted wood, and next to it was a unit of six soldiers. They had put a wooden barrier across the road, and were pulling aside any vehicles that tried to get past them, asking the drivers for their papers.

Keeping his foot hard on the accelerator, Steve took the truck up to seventy. The roadblock was another half-mile ahead of them on a wide, open road that ran straight through the flat bushland.

'Ian – what kind of kit have they got?' he demanded.

The Irishman was leaning forward, getting as close a look as possible as the vehicle hurtled and bounced across the road.

'AKs.'

'Any RPGs?'

'Not that I can see.'

'Then I'll just swerve right past them,' said Steve.

Ian shook his head. 'You'll risk a puncture on that surface and we haven't got time to deal with that. Just drive straight through them.'

Steve gripped tighter onto the steering wheel. At his side, Sam was shaking nervously, but he ignored her. He'd already told her to tuck herself away safely in a five-star hotel: if she wasn't going to take advice, then that was her problem.

'Let's give them the good news,' he said, his tone fierce with determination.

Steadying the truck in the centre of the road, he kept the accelerator jammed to the floor. One soldier had already stepped out into the centre of the road, flagging them down with his right arm. The others were idly talking to each other by the side of their sentry post. The road block was still 300 yards away but they were closing fast. The soldier flagged again, more decisively, but Steve just ignored him, keeping the truck steady in the centre of the road. It had settled into a top speed of seventy-five miles an hour, and no matter how hard he pushed it, Steve could tell he wasn't going to drag any more power out of the engine. Doesn't matter, he told himself. We're going fast enough to break through.

The soldier started shouting at them to stop, waving his gun angrily in the air. They were 150 yards away before he realised the truck wasn't going to obey him. And 100 yards before he'd made his decision to retaliate.

'Get your heads down, boys,' yelled Ollie on the back of the truck.

Good advice, thought Steve. He nodded towards Ian. 'Cover her,' he said tersely.

Ian grabbed hold of Sam and pushed her down onto the floor of the cabin. She stifled a scream, but offered no resistance as he lay down on top of her in the cramped space.

The first round of gunfire was loud and sharp, hitting the bumpers, then the bonnet, then smashing into the windscreen. The glass fragmented into 1,000 pieces, sending a shower of shrapnel sprinkling through the cabin. Steve closed his eyes and held the wheel steady. He could feel a piece of glass nick the side of his shoulder, and some warm blood start to ooze out of the wound. He ignored the pain, and opened his eyes again.

It takes real guts to stand in front of a truck hurtling towards you at seventy-five miles an hour and still shoot straight, decided Steve, looking at the soldier now only thirty yards in front of him. And this boy doesn't have it.

Sure enough, the young man threw himself onto the side of the road, just as the truck's front bumper collided with the road block. The wood from which it was constructed was sturdy enough, but it was no match for the ton of metal barrelling into it. It crunched and splintered. The soldier diving out of the way was delivered a glancing blow, knocked senseless, and left on the side of the road. Steve could feel the vehicle shudder from the impact. He kept his fists gripped to the wheel, and eased his foot off the accelerator a touch to stop the truck from skidding as it smashed across the broken wood.

The road ahead was open, and clear, heading straight north.

At the side of the road, the remaining soldiers had opened fire with their AK-47s, but the truck was already disappearing into the distance. Dan had lined up a shot into the ranks, but as the truck disappeared into the distance, decided there was no point in wasting a bullet when ammunition was in such short supply.

Sam looked up, brushing the shards of broken glass away from her back. 'Where are we going?' she asked nervously.

'Anywhere,' said Steve. 'So long as it isn't here.'

Forty-Two

YOU COULD HEAR THE BLADES of the chopper before you could see it.

Steve took the truck down a gear. They'd covered thirty miles since the roadblock and so far, the road had mostly been clear. They'd passed a few small villages and farms, and a motorbike had scurried out of their way, but none of the people they'd passed had wanted to confront a truck full of desperate-looking soldiers.

But Wallace had a fleet of choppers at his disposal, Steve reminded himself. And there was no doubt that he'd use them to track down the men who'd just killed the President.

As the engine noise dipped, Steve heard a sound that made his nerves tighten. They were driving along a side road that led up to Hwanga, a small farming town first founded by Portuguese elephant hunters. He leaned from the window so he could hear it more clearly: the rotorblades on a big helicopter gunship. A Chinese Z-10 maybe, or a Russian Mi-24. *One thing is for certain*, he told himself. *I don't want to get close enough to find out.*

He looked up at the road ahead. A dirt track led down to an abandoned farm, and there was a small copse of woodland where he could pull the truck up and take cover from anything tracking them from the sky. Taking the truck down to second, he steered it under a canopy of trees and let the engine idle, keeping his foot lightly pressed on the accelerator to make sure there were enough revs to keep it from stalling.

Ollie had already jumped down and was leaning through the window. 'Stopping for a nice cup of tea, are we?' he asked, 'Maybe we'll get a Full English while we're at it. I'll have my eggs fried please.'

Ian and Maksim had already walked to the edge of the wood to get a clearer view. There were dark clouds across the sky: so far the rain had held off for more than a day, but it would be back soon.

'That's an Mi-24,' said Maksim, walking back to the truck. 'I'd recognise the sound of the engine anywhere. We used them in Afghanistan mainly. *Shaitan-Arba*, that's what the Mujahideen called them. Satan's Chariot. The right word for them as well. An Mi-24 can deliver death from anywhere.'

'What's its capability?' asked Ian.

'It can fly at high altitudes, just like the Alouette we used on the fort,' said Maksim. 'You can put any kit you like on it, but they usually carry rockets and Gatling guns. They can swoop down on their targets and destroy them with ease.'

Steve looked anxiously at the sky. The noise of the chopper had retreated. But there could be no question it was out on a search-and-destroy mission. And a truck wasn't hard to find.

'We've less than a dozen bullets between us,' said Ollie. 'Ian? Any bombs?'

Ian shook his head. 'Nothing.'

'We're not going to make it to the border,' said Steve. 'Not if we're using the roads.'

'Then we drive cross-country,' said Dan.

'No way,' said Steve. 'Not in this truck. We've only got a quarter tank of diesel, and if it stalls we're not going to be able to restart her. We were planning a dash for the border, making a getaway before Wallace could organise the Army's response.'

'But that's gone tits up now,' snapped Ollie. 'Like this whole sodding job.'

'I know a place we can go,' Sam said suddenly.

Ollie looked at her with dislike. 'We've had enough help from the Sharratt family.'

'I gave you the knives, didn't I?' she reminded him.

'She's been on the level so far,' said Ian. 'You boys would be hanging from the gallows by now if it wasn't for her help.'

Steve turned to look at her. 'Where?' he asked.

'Twenty miles due north-east of here,' she said.

Steve switched off the engine on the truck. The vehicle fell silent, and with no ignition, there was no way it could be started again. 'Then let's start walking,' he said. 'The first thing that Mi-24 is going to be looking for is this truck. And I don't want to be inside when they start putting some cannon and Gatling fire into the bastard.'

The march was going to be a long and hard one, and none of them had slept or eaten properly for days. Their bodies were tired, but their spirits remained strong. Ian was still hobbling slightly from the injury he'd sustained during the helicopter assault, but Dan, Nick and David were taking it in turns to prop him up, making the long march bearable. It was only Sam that Steve was worried about. They were all soldiers, toughed into blocks of human steel in some of the finest regiments in the world, but Sam was a woman, and she thought she was a lot stronger than she really was.

They kicked off due north, leaving the truck buried deep in the woodland. There was no point in torching it: the fire would just alert the chopper out searching for them. Nor could they take the main road, or even the dirt tracks that criss-crossed the farms and woodland. The chopper would be scanning those routes first, and soon Wallace would have military patrols fanning out from the capital in jeeps, intensifying the search. The further they stayed from the roads, the more chance they had of slipping through unnoticed.

Sam was guiding them. Steve had a detailed map in his kitbag, and they were using that and a compass to steer their way towards their destination. They were tramping through a part of Batota known as The Front Lands, the land north and east of the capital which, in the old colonial days, had been home to the wealthiest farms, and the gold mines that had briefly flourished in the nineteenth century. The soil was red – like most of Africa, noted Steve, as they tramped wearily forwards – but it was rich and fertile. The land was flat, between rolling hills, punctured only by forests of palms, gum trees and jacarandas – the tall, gnarled trees with the bright purple flowers that could be seen right through from the capital up to the north of the country. There were streams and small lakes dotting the landscape, all of them overflowing with water after the heavy rain of the past few weeks. More than once they had to wade across bulging streams, getting soaked to the skin.

Many of the farms had been abandoned in the past decade, and much of the land was starting to return to nature. The fields were overgrown with tall grasses and the old fences had fallen down. The forests were spreading over the landscape, turning it back into the kind of wilderness that must have existed here hundreds of years ago. It was hard walking, but at least it meant there weren't many people around. Twice they were spotted by farmers working their patch of land, but when they saw the men's guns, they scurried away, not asking any questions. Nobody up here had phones, so there wasn't any need to worry about being reported. They'd be long gone by the time the news of their tramp through this countryside got back to Ibera.

At four in the afternoon, and with another eight miles still ahead of them, the rain kicked in. It was drizzle at first, then a lashing storm, with thick, black sheets of water and a gale that whistled across the flat landscape, making the trees creak and flattening the grasses. Walking through it was like being thumped by a wet stick, but Steve kept his head down and marched steadily forwards.

'You OK?' he asked Sam.

She nodded, but remained silent, her head bent down as she forced her way through the weather.

'Living the dream, mate, living the dream,' said Nick cheerfully, clearly unaware that Steve had been addressing Sam and not him. Wiping the cold water out of his face, he concluded: 'Tramping through rough country, with twelve bullets between eight guys and a whole army on our back? What more could a bloke ask for.'

Darkness had fallen by the time they reached their destination. Clouds obscured the moon, and they were relying on the compass to steer them home. It reminded Steve of his SAS training: released onto the wild Welsh hillsides of the Brecon Beacons, usually in the driving rain as well, you had to make an RV point using only the compass. They were getting there, he felt certain of that, but at times it seemed as if they were just tramping around in a circle.

Half a mile out, they struck a metalled road, and that made the going a lot easier. A long track, wide enough to take a combine harvester, it led down to what must have once been the main house on the estate. There were brambles growing over the road surface, and at several points trees had fallen across it, and had been left where they fell, but it was still a lot less tiring than walking through muddy fields.

The house loomed up out of the darkness. Two storeys high, built from brick with white clapperboard facing, its veranda stretched the length of the building. The driveway led up to a substantial porch and, below the mass of tangled weeds, you could see the remains of the gravel that had once formed part of an impressive entrance. Around the back were stables, barns, workshops and grain stores, but the house itself was flanked by what had once been formal gardens. As you looked out from the porch, a sweeping lawn would have led down to a small river that snaked its way through the farmland. A ruin, thought Steve, squinting through the dim light. But once this must have been a prosperous estate.

'At least it's shelter,' said Ollie, looking around.

Ganju had broken up an old wooden chair, then dipped its legs into some diesel that had turned into a thick jelly in the corner of the tank of an abandoned tractor. He lit the rough torches, and the light illuminated the main building. The place had been trashed, probably years ago, judged Steve, looking at the state of the hallway. Curtains had been torn, and furniture broken into pieces. Windows were smashed, and the roof had caved in, letting rainwater stream down the main staircase. Some frogs had made their home in a corner but, surprised at being disturbed, they had hopped away. The library had been emptied of books, and the kitchen had obviously been ransacked as every last scrap of food had been cleared out of its store cupboards.

It looked as if an army had run through the place and left it for dead, Steve thought sadly. It would have been just one more of the beautifully kept farms that Kapembwa's war veterans had rampaged through as he unleashed his thugs on the white landowners.

Steve glanced across at Sam. 'I recognise this place.'

She remained silent.

'It's your parents' house, isn't it? The place we saw in the film.'

He could the sorrow in her eyes as she nodded, but she buried it somewhere deep within, and within less than a second her expression was purposeful and businesslike again. 'Come on,' she said. 'I'll show you all why I brought you here.'

Holding the torch that Ganju had given her, she stepped out of the front of the house, and down onto the lawn. Steve followed her, a foot or so behind, with the rest of the men behind him. The grass leading down to the river was tall and wiry, and you had to fight your way through it. A few of the brambles snagged on Steve's clothes, and grazed his skin. Ignoring them, he marched forward, keeping Sam close. When they hit the river, its banks were swollen from the rain, the water swirling through it in angry torrents. There was a wooden jetty, but someone had set fire to it years ago, and next to that was the sunken outline of a rowing boat. Sam turned right. Along the edge of the river was a gravelled path, overgrown with weeds, but still possible to walk on. It tracked the river up towards the hills that rose to the east of the farm.

'Where the hell is she leading us?' asked Ian.

'Wherever it is, I hope there's a hot bath and a nice cup of tea,' answered Steve. 'But somehow I doubt it.'

They walked for half an hour. As the river twisted around the edge of the farm, you could still make out the contours of the old fields, each of them fifty acres or more, designed for industrial-scale farming, but all of them long since abandoned. Finally, they reached a set of rocks, with the hills rising steeply behind them. In front of the rocks, the river opened up into a small lake, with a waterfall at the back where the river crashed out of the hills and down onto the plain.

'There,' said Sam, pointing across the lake.

'Nice one,' Steve commented, wiping rainwater from his eyes. 'I really fancied a dip.'

'Strip off, boys, we're going swimming,' said Ollie. 'Last one in's a rotten egg.'

Sam just smiled. 'Behind the waterfall, there's a secret cave,' she said. 'Nobody would ever find it unless they knew it was there. The General kept a stack of supplies inside. He prepared it after Independence, just in case the family ever had to make a run for it. It should still be there – and Archie doesn't know about it.'

Steve started to wade into the water. It was fifty feet across to the waterfall, through water that was covered with lily pads and reeds. It was bitingly cold, and the rain was still falling, creating currents that swirled around you. He waded the first twenty feet, but after that the lake became too deep. Kicking forwards, he started to swim, with Ian and Ollie right behind him. Closing his eyes and his mouth as he approached the cascading water, Steve headed into the waterfall. He could feel the spray and foam crashing over him, took a deep breath, and kicked himself right down into the water, pushing back with his legs, and not breaking up onto the surface again until he had covered a clear ten feet. As he burst upwards, he took a lungful of air and looked around. It was pitch black, but he could see the waterfall was clearly behind him now.

'There,' said Ollie at his side.

Five feet in front of him, Steve could see a rocky ledge, its surface splashed with water; behind that was a cave. He swam straight towards it and clambered upwards. The entrance measured thirty feet by ten, but narrowed sharply. Inside, it was pitch black. Behind him, Steve could hear the crashing of the waterfall, but he could see hardly anything.

'Look, at this,' said Ian.

He had found a gas lamp, attached to the wall; next to it was a lighter, wrapped in a waterproof pouch to keep it dry. The Irishman torched up the lamp, the pale light immediately bouncing across the dark rocks, revealing the extent of the cave, which stretched inside 100 feet or more. Along the side, you could see neat stacks of food and weapons, all of it carefully cratered away in wooden boxes.

'Get the others,' Steve said to Ollie. 'It looks like we're in luck. The General's stash is all intact.' He started to walk inside the cave, his eyes bouncing from one box to another. 'Christ. It looks like he put aside enough kit to take on a whole army.'

'Just as well,' said Ian. 'Because that's precisely what we're up against.'

Forty-Three

STEVE HAULED SAM OUT OF the water and up onto the ledge. Her hair was dripping wet, and her eyes were tired and strained. But you could see the hint of a smile in her eyes. The kit was still there. Just the way she had said it would be.

We've trusted her twice, thought Steve.

And both times she has come through for us.

Both Ganju and Ian had torched up gas lamps and were leading the wet and bedraggled group of men into the interior of the cave. The General had done a fine job, reflected Steve. The man was a soldier, and a good one, and he knew what you'd need if you made a run for it. It was just a shame he hadn't had a chance to use it himself.

The old guy must have been thinking about this stash as Kapembwa's thugs beat him to death on the floor of his own house.

Most of the kit had been laid down here at least twenty years ago, but it had been carefully sealed and, despite the waterfall in front of it, the interior of the cave was completely dry, and sheltered from the extremes of both summer and winter.

One row of boxes contained everything they needed for basic survival. There were two decent-sized tents, with waterproof groundsheets, and sleeping bags, as well as pots and pans to cook with. There were also knives and compasses and ropes, and ten pairs of sturdy walking boots in a variety of sizes. The tins of food contained beans, sausages and fish, canned vegetables – and more beans. It wouldn't be the best grub any of them had ever tasted but it would keep them alive. Then there was the fighting kit. Again, it had been quite old when it was laid down, and that was two decades ago. It was mostly gear used by the old Batotean Army. There was a rack of South-African-made FN-FAL assault rifles, standard issue for the Batotean infantry, and a box of Enfield .38 Revolvers, a British weapon that dated all the way back to the Second World War, but which had remained in service in Batota long after it had been replaced in the British Army. Both the Enfields and the FNs came with ten boxes of ammunition, all of it in good working order. Next to that were two cases of grenades, and two boxes of plastic explosive.

In front of the weapons were two old Land Rovers, both carefully sealed in plastic to prevent them rusting up. Steve recognised them at once: indeed, he'd thought about stocking a few in the garage, since some of the older Land Rovers were now attracting serious interest from collectors. They were rugged Series II jeeps dating back to the early 1960s, the days when a Land Rover was a fighting or a farming vehicle, not an expensive way of ferrying the kids to school. In the back were four drums of diesel. Beside them were propped wooden rafts with slots for the wheels, so the Land Rovers could be floated out beneath the waterfall and out onto the road.

Perfect, thought Steve. We've everything we need to break out of this godforsaken country.

'Right,' said Ollie. 'It's past nine, and we're all tired and hungry. I reckon we need to get some grub cooked and down our throats. In the morning, we'll start working on getting out of here.'

Dan and Ganju set to work. They opened up some cans of sausages and beans and started frying up a massive stew over the gasfire. There was plenty of tea, so they used the water from the lake to boil up a brew, served in tin mugs, with evaporated milk. There were some spare clothes as well: jeans and T-shirts and socks, along with some soap, so while Dan was cooking, the rest of the men had a wash in the lake and shaved off the stubble growing on their chins.

Within half an hour, they were sitting around the fire, washed and shaved and wearing dry clothes, and eating mounds of sausage and bean stew from tin plates.

We're feeling better already, thought Steve to himself. Like men again. Taking charge of our own destiny.

'No chance the General left a stack of rum, is there?' Maksim asked with a broad grin.

'Afraid not,' Sam told him.

'He's done us proud all the same,' said Ollie. He shovelled some more of the food into his mouth, then raised his cup of tea. 'To the General,' he said. 'He didn't leave this stash for us, but if he knew Sam was here and if he knew we had just assassinated Kapembwa – that's down to you, Maksie – then I reckon he would be glad for us to help ourselves.'

'To the General,' grunted the men in unison.

Ganju was fiddling with a shortwave radio that had been tucked into one of the boxes. It was an old Grundig model from the late 1970s, but its batteries were intact, and it worked fine. After twisting the dial, he finally managed to tune it to the BBC World Service. *There have been dramatic developments during a day of political chaos and turmoil in Batota,'* said the newsreader.

For a second, the men stopped eating and listened with rapt attention.

'President Kapembwa has been assassinated during a break-out by the foreign mercenaries who were due to stand trial in Ibera for plotting the downfall of the veteran Batotean leader. As the men were being paraded through the country's capital, a rescue was staged. During the fighting, the President was killed. His senior military adviser Esram Matola has this afternoon declared martial law in Batota. He has appointed himself President and postponed the elections until the situation has been stabilised.'

Matola's voice came on the bulletin: *'The people of Batota are united in their grief for the passing of our nation's greatest ever leader, a man who liberated us from the tyranny of the colonial oppressor. Eventually the colonialists took their vengeance upon him in the only way they know how, through murder and blood. The borders of the country have been sealed, and the Army is determined to impose discipline and order in this difficult time. The men responsible for the death of our beloved leader will be hunted down like the dogs they are and, when captured, will be made to pay the price for this terrible crime.'*

The broadcaster switched quickly to the rest of the world news: floods in Indonesia, sharp falls in share prices on Wall Street, and a suicide bomber killing thirty people in Baghdad. The men remained silent. It was clear enough that Matola had taken charge of the country, and the Army was out hunting for them.

We'll be fine in this cave, reflected Steve. It was so well hidden you might not stumble across it in 100 years.

But getting to the border? It was eighty or ninety miles north of here, and they could expected to be hunted across every inch of it.

'Any chance of getting some cricket scores out of that thing?' said Dan, nodding towards the radio. 'The first Test against you Poms will have started. I reckon your boys will have taken a pasting by now.'

'Watch it,' grumbled Ollie.

'And the Six Nations scores,' said Nick. 'Another malleting for the English at the Millennium Stadium in Cardiff.'

'Christ,' said David. 'Next time I do a job, I'm only taking blokes with the flag of Saint George tattooed on their arms.'

Ollie stood up. 'At the risk of sounding like Zebedee, boys, I reckon it's time we all got some kip. There's going to be a long hard fight to get out of this country, and the fitter we are, the more chance we've got.'

Nick and David had prepared the beds for the night while the food was being cooked. They laid out the sleeping bags on top of the groundsheets, and used some of the cardboard packaging to create a separate, screened-off area for Sam. They drained their teas, then rolled into bed one by one. Steve checked that Sam was OK, then kicked off his boots, and pulled the sleeping bag around himself.

They were taking it in turns to keep watch, with Nick taking the first shift. One of the gas burners was sitting at his side, but otherwise the cave was completely dark. As he closed his eyes, Steve could hear the beating of the waterfall behind the entrance, and the noise was comforting. He'd only just realised how tired he was. He'd been running for days now on nothing apart from pure adrenaline. And, if he was being honest with himself, there wasn't much left in the locker. A couple more days, he told himself, then we'll be out of this hell-hole.

And this time I'm out of the game for ever.

Nothing, absolutely nothing, will make me put myself through this again.

No sooner had Steve closed his eyes than he was asleep. When he woke, Ollie was shaking him vigorously. 'Your watch, mate,' he said. 'I'm getting some more kip.'

Steve wiped the sleep from his eyes, knocked back a slug of boiled water from the cup he'd stashed next to his bed, and stumbled to his feet. It was just after four in the morning. In the next bag, Maksim was snoring loudly. Steve was taking the last watch, bringing them through to dawn. Ollie put a mug of hot tea in front of him from the pot keeping warm on the burner, and Steve swilled it down his throat. 'How much longer to the wedding?' he asked softly, glancing up at Ollie.

'Ten days, I reckon, unless I've lost track.'

'We should make it.'

Ollie shrugged. 'That's the least of my worries right now.'

Steve swilled back the last of the tea and poured himself some more. 'I promised Katie I'd get you there. I don't mind taking on the rest of Batota's army, but I don't fancy telling that bird her big day with a white dress has been rained off.'

'I'll be there,' Ollie said irritably. 'It's my big payday, remember. Right – I'm off to bed. See you in the morning.'

Steve took his tea and walked towards the ledge that looked out into the waterfall. He sat down, letting the cold spray spit across his skin, and allowed himself to enjoy the peace of the moment. There would be more hard fighting ahead, he reminded himself. One of the unit had already died. And Chris might well not be the last.

He'd been sitting there for almost an hour, just watching the water swirl past him, and wondering if there were any fish he might be able to catch for breakfast, when Sam joined him. He didn't notice her at first. She slipped into the space beside him, making no more noise than a whisper of wind. Somehow, she'd managed to wash her hair using hot water and soap, and even though she was wearing a pair of men's combat trousers, along with the worst-fitting sweatshirt Steve had ever seen on a woman, she still managed to look better than anything that ever stepped across a catwalk. At least to my eyes, thought Steve to himself. He looked at her and grinned.

'It's not exactly what Bridget Jones used to call a romantic mini-break, is it?' he said. 'Eight sweaty blokes and a ferocious Army on your back.'

'Some girls might like it.'

'I've never met one.'

She dangled her toes in the water. 'I used to swim here all the time as a kid. Sometimes I'd come and hide in this cave with the General, and we'd play pirates together.'

'I bet you were his princess.'

Sam just smiled, but remained silent. 'A place like this is hard to find,' she said eventually.

'We'll go somewhere nice, once this is all over, just you and me,' said Steve. 'Find our own bit of paradise.'

'Take one of the cars from your garage, maybe.'

'The choice is yours.'

'An Aston or a Jag, I think.'

'We've got DB4s, DB5s,' said Steve. 'Or if it's a Jag you want, we've got the XK 120, the Mark III, the E-type . . .'

'Any chance of a DB5 Vantage, the one with the Weber carburettor that took it up from 282 to 314 horsepower?' Sam asked.

'Now that I don't know. It's a rare motor.'

'Only sixty-five ever built.'

'Which means they're hard to lay your hands on.'

'I'll settle for a Jag Mark II then,' said Sam. 'But has it got a 2.4, 3.4 or 3.8 engine?'

'I've got a 2.4 and a 3.4 in stock.'

'You need at least three litres under the bonnet in a car like that.'

A bird who knows the difference between a 2.4 and a 3.4, and doesn't think you're mad for caring, thought Steve with a wry smile. Perfection doesn't come much better gift-wrapped than that. He could remember something his Uncle Ken had said to him on one of the few occasions they hadn't been talking about football or cars. Once in his life, a man meets the perfect woman, but usually he walks right past her. 'Just learn how to spot it when you see it,' he'd added. Steve had meant to ask him how, but they'd been watching a Chelsea game in the pub, and Vialli had scored, and the conversation had drifted on. I wish I'd asked him how you spot it, thought Steve. Maybe then I'd know if that's what I'm looking at right now.

'What are you doing here?' he asked, looking straight into her blue eyes. 'You should be getting your nails done in Knightsbridge.'

'Kapembwa died, didn't he?' said Sam, looking down into the water, and with a hint of defiance in her tone. 'For what he did to my family, to this country, it's what he deserved.'

'Your brother didn't think so.'

'That's Archie,' she said with a sigh. 'All he cares about is money, nothing else. It's why Dad hated him. And the feeling was mutual, of course.'

'You shouldn't have come to the rescue,' said Steve, sounding annoyed. 'You should have gone to a hotel, like I told you.'

'I wanted to help you.'

'You could have been sitting on a BA flight home by now,' said Steve. He shook his head angrily. 'It's going to be sodding hard getting out of here alive, and we can't be sure we're going to make it.'

'Like I said, I wanted to help you.' Sam paused, splashing her toes in the water, then looked back at Steve. 'I think I love you.'

Steve remained silent.

He'd knocked around with a few girls in his time, but he'd never told any of them that he loved them. It didn't seem right. Maybe he loved some of them, and maybe he didn't. But he knew that he wasn't going to settle down with a girl because he couldn't even settle down with himself, and so long as that was true, there wasn't much point in trying with someone else. So he had steered clear of the 'L' word.

But this time? *Maybe.*

'I'll get us some breakfast,' said Sam, suddenly standing up.

'But . . .'

But she'd already walked back to the gas stove, and was opening up some more of the cans of beans. Over the next few minutes, she had a pan of sausages simmering up nicely, and a big fresh pot of tea brewed, and she was waking up the rest of the lads and serving the grub. Steve checked the lake to make sure there was no one out there, then walked back to get himself a plateful of food and a fresh mug of tea. It was doing the boys good to have a woman cook for them, he noticed. It made them more human. Except Maksim, of course. The Russian still ate like an animal.

'OK, lads, we need to discuss the drill,' said Ollie, pushing away an empty tin plate. 'Number one: how are we getting out of here?'

'Maybe we should stay,' said Nick.

'You mean it's better than Swansea?' Ollie shrugged. 'I can see your point.'

'I mean we stay here until the noise has calmed down,' said Nick, ignoring the jibe. 'They'll be scouring the whole country right now, but in a few weeks, things will have changed.'

'He might be right,' said Ganju. 'The next few days are going to be the most dangerous for crossing the country. We've plenty of food and drink here.'

'I've got a wedding to get to,' Ollie said moodily.

'Maybe you should have thought about that before you took the job,' said Ian sharply.

'Leave it,' growled Steve. He looked towards Sam. 'Are you sure Archie doesn't know about this place?'

'We used to play here all the time as kids but I don't think he knows about the stash of weapons the General left here.'

'But you can't be sure he won't guess?'

She shook her head. 'No.'

'Then we can't risk it,' said Steve. 'It's a good idea, Nick, but this is an obvious place for them to search, and if the Sixth Brigade descends on us then we're all dead men. So we need to get out of here by noon.'

'And go where?' Nick asked.

'There are four different borders we can go for,' said Ganju, spreading a map out on the rough, rocky floor. 'North up into Tuka, east across into Mozambique, west into Botswana, or south down to South Africa. They've all got their own challenges. But the shortest route out of here is to head straight into Tuka.'

'Which is what they're expecting,' said Ian.

'We don't know that for certain,' said Steve. 'If we try and out-think them we'll end up being too clever by half. They'll be looking for us everywhere, and every mile of country we have to cross increases the danger. So I reckon we should just get the hell out of here like a bat on roller skates. We meet any trouble, we just fight our way through it. Remember this: we're a small unit in a big country, and they don't have any idea where we are – and that means we're in with a chance.'

He glanced around the circle of men, but all of them nodded, and to Steve that meant they were all signed up to the task ahead. 'Then let's be having you,' he said. 'I want to be out on the road in a couple of hours.'

The men swiftly turned to the tasks they knew best. Ganju and David studied the map, and figured out the best possible route.

They'd head up towards Lake Hasta, because they already knew that territory, and the lake gave them the chance of slipping into Tuka unnoticed. They'd travel cross-country as far as was possible. The roads would be quicker, but two vehicles with a bunch of white men in them were going to stick out. Out in the bush, they might just be able to slip through the abandoned farms without anyone noticing them.

Dan and Maksim were getting the two Land Rovers ready. There were big plastic drums to float the rafts on, and so long as they kept those watertight, they should be strong enough to get the vehicles back across the lake onto the land. Maksim, the strongest man among them, volunteered to swim them over the water. Once they were back on dry land, Dan and then Steve, the two best mechanics on the team, would check over the engines and make sure they were in good enough shape for the journey ahead.

Nick was taking charge of the weapons. The FN-FAL rifles the General had stashed away were antique kit now but had once been among the most widely used weapons in the world. Originally designed by the Belgian manufacturer Fabrique Nationale Herstal, the gun was first introduced into service in 1953. Like the AK-47, it packed plenty of punch, fired rapidly, and was capable of bringing a man down at fifty yards.

As usual, Nick examined each weapon in turn. The rifles weren't new, but they were in good shape, and had been carefully greased and wrapped in plastic before being stored away. In total, fifteen had been packed up, along with two thousand rounds of ammunition. Nick took each one apart, re-greased all its components, cleaned it, then carefully reassembled it. That done, he zeroed the weapon, adjusting the sights as necessary to make sure it was aiming accurately. Then he set to work on the Enfields. He'd only ever seen one before, on a trip up to London to the Imperial War Museum with his mum, but he enjoyed the feel of the weapon in his hands.

Manufactured from 1932 to 1963, the Enfield had been the

standard issue service revolver for the British and Commonwealth armies for three decades – and, decided Nick, a gun didn't get much better tested than that. With its wooden stock and shiny metal barrel, it was a classic Wild West shooter, the kind of gun he'd played with as a kid. It used .38 ammo, a relatively low-calibre bullet, but even so, it had plenty of stopping power, and it was extremely fast to reload, allowing the six bullets in its chamber to be pumped out in a couple of seconds. Nick repeated the same drill: by the time he had finished, he was happy that each man would have a working rifle and revolver, and if they got into a scrap it wouldn't be their weapons that would let them down.

Ian and Ollie had headed over to the main house. Last night, Ian was certain he'd seen some old fire extinguishers up there, and that had given him a idea. A couple of the extinguishers had been let off by the robbers, but most of them were intact, and it didn't matter whether they were working or not anyway. Ollie helped him carry ten of them back to the cave on a hastily assembled raft where they carefully blasted all the foam out of them. Once empty, Ian filled them with plastic explosives, then screwed the caps back on. The General had left ten packs of sparklers, not for a celebration, but because they were among the cheapest, most effective detonators you could use: put a sparkler into a lump of plastic explosive, then light it, and you had a minute to get clear before it burned down and exploded the dynamite. They hardly ever went out either. Ian stuck one into the cap of each fire extinguisher, and loaded five onto the back of each Land Rover.

'Light these, and push them out of the back, and it's like a flying land mine,' he said as Ollie helped him complete the loading. 'It doesn't just make a big bang. The casing of the extinguisher explodes, creating hundreds of shards of red-hot shrapnel flying in each direction. Aim it right, and it can slice up a whole platoon.'

By noon, everyone was assembled, their tasks completed and their kit ready. Sam had prepared them a meal to set them up for the journey. 'More sausages and beans, I'm afraid,' she said, serving the food onto the tin plates.

'My favourite, anyway,' said Ollie, jabbing his spoon into the hot food.

'How old are these sausages exactly?' asked Nick.

'Older than you,' said Sam.

'Better-looking as well,' added Steve.

Nick scowled but said nothing. On the shortwave radio, they caught the latest news bulletin from the BBC World Service. Reports of rioting were coming in from Ibera and Akwa, Batota's two main cities, as the Army struggled to impose control following the assassination of President Kapembwa. In Akwa, at least twenty people had been reported killed after soldiers opened fire on demonstrators. The men listened in silence, finished their food, tidied away the mess so as to leave no trace of their presence in the cave, then swam ashore and climbed aboard the two Land Rovers. Steve took the wheel of one, with Nick, David and Sam as passengers. Ganju was driving the second, with Ollie, Maksim, Dan and Ian in the back.

'Next stop, Piccadilly Circus,' said Steve, slipping the Land Rover into first gear and starting the climb up the rugged track that twisted along the river. 'And let's hope to God we all make it.'

They drove the first hour mostly in silence. They were heading north-east, driving across open countryside, but keeping well away from any of the main roads, choosing instead the big, muddy lanes used by farmers – and still imprinted with the tyres of the tractors that had once worked the fields. But many of them were now over-grown, with weeds and brambles covering the route as the farms they had once served turned gradually back to wilderness. More than once, the convoy was brought to a complete stop where a track had become impassable, and Dan and Maksim had to climb out to hack a way through.

It was slow, hard driving. In total, they had to cover 100 miles to get up to the border, but they weren't making more than fifteen miles an hour. The tracks never allowed them to get up any speed, and there were constant delays. But they were making good, steady progress and, most importantly, reflected Steve, they weren't running into any trouble. They had skirted within a mile of a pair of small villages, certain that the Land Rovers had been seen, and they had three times passed small groups of women and children working on the fields, but none of them looked like they were going to confront two vehicles full of heavily armed men. And since there were no signs of any phone lines out here in the remote countryside, there wasn't much chance of anyone reporting a sighting of some suspicious white men into the capital.

By dusk, they had made their way through The Front Lands, and were driving towards the wilder north of the country that ran up to Lake Hasta. On the map, Ganju had marked out Tshaka's front line. They didn't want to go too close to that territory either, and get snarled up in the front line, but they would have to slip through if they were to make it to the lake. By eight in the evening, they had completed almost eighty miles, with only another twenty to go. But Steve insisted they should stop and kip down for the night. There was no point in trying to drive through the darkness. Going over such rough tracks, they'd only end up damaging the vehicles, and then they'd have to walk out of the country.

Steve pulled his Land Rover into a small wood, followed by Ganju's and they made a shelter as best they could. The clouds were heavy, and within an hour the rain was beating down on them. They slung up some tents, ate some dried food, and tried to get some sleep. By dawn, the Land Rovers were loaded again, and they were ready for the final leg of the journey. Ganju had mapped out a route for them that would take them up through the vast wilderness of Chikoota National Park. With any luck, they could skirt around Tshaka's forces, and come out onto the lake close to Avalanche Falls. Once there, they could rent or steal a fishing boat, and get clear away into Tuka.

By ten in the morning, they were entering the eastern edges of the national park, and the only part of its nearly 15,000 square kilometres open to the public. Originally a vast wilderness of bush and scrub, Chikoota was too dry for any form of sustained agriculture. In the 1920s, a series of big water bores had been drilled into the ground to allow animals to live there during the long dry season, and since then the park had been filled with lions, elephants, giraffes, zebra, wildebeest, waterbuck, sable, impala, kudu and buffalo. There were lodges and campsites dotted throughout the park, but Chikoota was a reserve for serious big-game spotters. It didn't have the scenery or facilities for busloads of families on safari trips. And, during the rainy season, it was all but deserted.

Which is just the way we like it, decided Steve, pushing the Land Rover up onto one of the tracks that ran north-east. The road would take them straight past the main campsites and up close to the border.

They passed one herd of elephants and, later on, a pair of lions prowled across a road they were trying to cross. 'They reckon we're lunch,' said Steve, blasting the horn to try and get them out of the way.

But as the morning pushed on towards eleven, they still hadn't encountered any resistance. And, although none of them would say it out loud, it was just starting to look as if they might break through.

It was only another five miles to the northern end of the park. Then another five miles to the lake.

Suddenly, Steve heard a noise. A sudden crack. Like a tree snapping in the wind and rain. Or like a bullet rattling from the barrel of a gun.

'Christ,' he muttered to himself.
We're under attack.

Forty-Four

IN THE FIRST LAND ROVER, Ganju was powering ahead. Its wheels were churning up mud as it slashed across the rain-sodden ground, its big engine roaring as it clawed its way forward. Glancing in the mirror, Steve could see nothing at first, and he wondered if he had imagined the noise.

Then he heard it again. The rattle of gunfire.

'It's a truck!' shouted Nick, leaning out of the back of the Land Rover.

Steve could see it in the rearview mirror now. It was a ten-man troop carrier, probably Chinese-made like most of the military kit in Batota. Two soldiers were upfront, one driving, the other protecting him with a rifle. In the back was space for another eight guys, with all the berths taken. It was at least eighty or ninety yards behind them. Two men had positioned themselves on the ledge of the truck, and were firing into the Land Rovers with their AK-47s. Fortunately, however, through the intense rain it was impossible for them to get an accurate shot. Their bullets were winging through the air, but falling short of the target.

'Can we outrun them?' yelled Steve.

'We can bloody try,' snapped Dan.

Steve slammed his foot hard on the accelerator. Up ahead, Ganju had just realised what was happening, and was pushing his own machine to the limits of its performance. The track was starting to twist through a wide plain that led up to some hills beyond, with bush to the left and a copse of woodland to the right. A herd of elephants were staring bemused at the chase unfolding before them. The Land Rover was steadily climbing up through thirty, then forty, but the road was turning treacherous, and Steve was struggling to keep the vehicle under control. Gripping the steering wheel with one hand and the gearstick with the other, he switched between second and third as he tried to hold the jeep steady on the slippery surface of the track.

He glanced anxiously in the mirror. Their pursuers were still eighty or ninety yards back, and they weren't going to be able to get a decent shot at them from there, thank God. Nick and Dan had loosened off a few rounds from their FNs, enough to give the men in the truck something to think about, but it was aimless fire. As he looked up ahead, Steve could see the track winding into the hills. There was nowhere to run, nowhere to hide. Sooner rather than later, they were going to have to stop and fight.

Up ahead, there was a crunching sound, and Steve watched helplessly as Ganju's Land Rover skidded off the muddy track. In the rainy season, the grasses grew long and thick, and the vehicle was rolling through them, cutting the grass down, but also slowing. Within seconds, it had stalled. Steve pressed hard on the brakes, bringing his Land Rover to a shuddering stop in a pool of muddy rainwater that had formed in the centre of the track.

'Unleash those bombs!' he shouted.

Nick and Dan had grabbed two of the fire extinguishers Ian had filled with explosives. With the sparklers lit, Dan hoisted them under his arms, ran twenty yards down the track, then hurled both devices towards the oncoming vehicle. Amid steady fire from the men's AK-47s, he turned and zigzagged back. The extinguisher had arced through the air, then landed in the mud, the sparklers still fizzing even with the rain lashing into them.

Thank God they are built for a British Bonfire Night, Steve

thought, grimly amused. It take will more than a bit of rain to put them out.

'Get your head down and stay down,' he told Sam. Then, grabbing his FN rifle, he threw himself down from the Land Rover, ignoring the muddy water splashing up into his boots. Ollie and the rest of the boys had taken up position behind Ganju's Land Rover. Their rifles were already raised to their shoulders. They'd wait and see if the bombs dealt with the oncoming enemy. If they didn't, their pursuers would be driving into a blistering barrage of fire.

Steve leaned his shoulder into the side of the Land Rover, craning forwards to see what was happening. The carrier was advancing steadily up the track, its driver pushing it up to thirty miles an hour, but careful of the treacherous road ahead. It was impossible to see where the bombs had landed: they must have already sunk into the mud.

There can only be a few seconds left, thought Steve. *So long as the sparklers haven't gone out.*

Nick, Dan and David had taken up position behind the Land Rover, the FNs slotted into their shoulders, ready to fire. But shooting into an armoured troop carrier was useless: their bullets were likely to bounce off it harmlessly. And if the enemy had RPGs in there, they could blast them from the safety of their cabin.

And then we're done for.

The first extinguisher exploded with a terrifying roar. It kicked up a hailstorm of mud and dirt, much of it flying into the windscreen of the oncoming vehicle. Steve could hear the screech of brakes as the driver tried desperately to bring the machine under control but, as he'd already discovered, it was hard to get much traction on the slippery surface of the track.

Another explosion. It was louder this time, right under the carrier, rolling it sideways, bursting all the tyres simultaneously. As the initial force of the explosion started to die down, the casings of the fire extinguishers fragmented into hundreds of pieces, sending a rainstorm of red-hot shrapnel flying in every direction. The temperature and sharpness of the metal made it lethal, melting skin on contact, and cutting straight into muscle and bone. The carrier wobbled again, then crashed onto its side. Three corpses fell out of the back. Two more men struggled out, but they were so badly wounded by the shrapnel, their faces shredded, and their eyes gouged out, that they only managed a couple of paces before they fell into the mud and died. The driver looked to have been crushed by the fall of the vehicle, pinned down: if he wasn't dead already, he soon would be.

But three men had walked clear of the carrier. Two were laying down round after round from their AKs, whilst the third was lining up a shot on his RPG. As he detonated the explosive, Steve could hear the familiar sound of the missile flying through the air, like a drill cutting through stone, but he could see as well that the man hadn't got his sights in yet, and the shell was going to fly harmlessly over their heads. Sure enough, it exploded twenty yards behind their position, kicking up a fresh shower of water and mud but doing no damage.

The soldier was lowering his sights.

He's finding his range, realised Steve. The next one's coming right at us.

'Finish the bastards!' yelled Steve.

He started to run. His boots were sliding across the mud, but he could feel the adrenaline pummelling inside him. His blood was up, and he started steeling himself for the ferocity of the fight ahead. At his side, Dan and Nick were running as well, whilst Ollie was leading a charge from the second vehicle. It was an old-fashioned infantry assault: there was nothing clever about it, just muscle and steel organised into a hammer blow, knocking down everything in its path.

Steve slammed his finger on the trigger of the FN, loosening off a couple of rounds, not even trying to hit anything, just getting the feel of the weapon. The two soldiers were staggering backwards, firing wildly on the AK-47s, but at the rate there were wasting ammo, their mags would soon be spent. The third man, with the RPG mounted on his shoulder, was desperately trying to resight his weapon. A single missile into the oncoming horde could blow it away. He knew that, and he knew that he had to hold himself together to have any chance of landing the punch that could yet save their lives: staying calm under fire was the first and most important lesson any soldier learned.

But he was struggling. His hands were shaking and he was flinching as the bullets ripped into his position. And when he got his shot away, it sailed harmlessly over their heads once more, and fell straight into the long grass behind. The racket of the explosion split through the air, but noise wasn't going to hurt anyone. Only gunpowder and steel would do that, Steve reflected in one of the odd moments of calm that came upon him during the heat of a battle. *Thirty more yards. We can hit them at twenty* – and with that thought he powered himself closer to the enemy.

The bullets spitting from the barrels of the FNs started to chew into their targets. One man had already fallen, his body spilling blood into the dark, reddish mud. The remaining pair were falling back, trying to take cover behind their carrier, but the volleys of fire were catching them as they ran, spinning their bodies around, and pushing them into the ground. By the time Steve was amongst them, the battle was finished, won. He looked around, searching for anyone left alive, but all the men were dead.

'Tough bastards,' said Ollie.

Steve released the pressure from the trigger of his gun. 'Think there's more of them?'

Ollie was scanning back into the scrubland, trying to see through the blankets of cloud and rain. He shook his head. 'Not yet.'

But then they heard it.

The roar of the blades filled the air then the Mi-24 dropped through the clouds, like a stone sinking through water. With its twin bubble cockpits arranged one behind the other, like a pair of insect's eyes, and with its short, stubby wings hanging underneath its vast blade, it looked more like a deadly bug than a flying machine. Under each wing, there were racks of 57mm rockets, each one capable of taking out a whole platoon by itself: above that was a nose-mounted Gatling gun, a big, lethal machine weapon that could fire up to 3,000 rounds a minute of its 25mm ammo.

'Move out, move out!' yelled Steve.

Both men started to run, followed swiftly by the rest of the unit. 'Go for the woods,' shouted Ollie. Fifty yards away, the woodland offered the best cover they were likely to find. At least they'd be invisible among the trees: the bullets and missiles could still hit them, but they'd be harder to target.

But first, Steve had to rescue Sam. She was still taking cover in the Land Rover.

There was a mechanical cough and splutter from the sky, and then the Mi-24 opened up its Gatling gun, spewing hot metal across the scrubland. Heavy bullets started to pepper the ground. Steve was running up the track, whilst the rest of the men veered right across the open ground. He lunged towards the door of the Land Rover and pulled Sam out into the mud. He suddenly noticed Maksim behind him, grabbing hold of the remaining primed fire extinguishers, but Steve had no time to pay attention to the Russian now. Taking Sam's hand, he lugged her free of the mud with one brutal movement, and started to run towards the wood. She was shaking, her face streaked with tears, but her legs and spirit were strong. Steve was running furiously, his breath ragged. Behind him, he could hear the gunship manoeuvring in the sky, its pilot battling against the wind and the rain as he turned the lumbering metal beast around for another run at his enemy.

As he ran, Steve could hear the Mi-24 unleash one of the AT-6 Spiral missiles that were its standard equipment. Originally designed as an anti-tank weapon, the Spiral had a range of up to five kilometres, and flew at 345 metres a second. Its warhead was capable of taking out a NATO armoured vehicle. A couple of Land Rovers weren't going to present any kind of opposition at all.

He heard one Spiral smash into the Land Rover Ganju had been driving. A fireball erupted into the sodden air as the huge missile punched through the vehicle then exploded into a mass of heat and fire. Within seconds, the remaining extinguishers Ian had primed detonated as well, each one splitting the air with a terrifying roar and spreading a lethal shower of shrapnel in every direction. None of it made any difference to the pilot: gunship fighter pilots were as far removed from the heat and smoke and blood of a battle as anyone playing a game on their computer.

The pilot then flicked on the Mi-24's rudder and fired a second Spiral, this one igniting the Land Rover Steve had been driving, splitting it open, and turning it within an instant into a burning mess of steel and diesel.

'Go, go, go!' yelled Ollie, as Steve dragged Sam under the canopy of branches and leaves, and the pair of them fell panting to the ground.

Steve looked around. Ollie had pulled all the men in, drawing them into a tight circle beneath a dense thicket of the teak trees that were common throughout the Chikoota National Park. The trees were thick and sturdy, growing so close to each other that they obscured all the light, and the ground beneath them was warm and dry, since even the relentless rain struggled to penetrate the deep foliage. Checking quickly, Steve could see that beyond the cuts and bruises, none of the men were injured. That in itself was a miracle.

Dan had scuttled out a few feet to the edge of the woodland to assess the damage.

'There goes our transport,' he said. 'He's taken out the two Land Rovers, and he's circling, looking for a fresh angle of attack.'

'What do we do now?' said Nick.

Steve couldn't be sure, but he suspected he heard a hint of nervousness in the boy's voice. Welcome to soldiering, mate, he thought wryly. You don't always get out of this game alive.

'Any chance of walking out of here?' Steve asked Ganju.

With thick enough cover from the trees there was just a chance that they could walk all the way to the border without getting hit. But the Gurkha was already shaking his head. 'This forest lasts another couple of miles. After that—'

The end of the sentence was cut off by a deafening explosion. A Spiral missile had landed 100 yards away, igniting as it hit the ground and knocking a huge crater in the woodland. Ten trees had been incinerated on impact, and at least fifteen had been knocked down by the aftershocks of the blast. Their branches and trunks were crashing to the ground with a thump that shook the earth all around them. If it wasn't for the relentless rain, half the forest would be on fire by now, Steve realised.

'He's going to keep firing until he gets us,' said Ollie, his voice tense.

'How many missiles does that bastard carry?' Dan asked Maksim.

'Usually twelve,' answered the Russian.

'More than enough to destroy this whole forest,' Nick commented.

'Then we fight back,' said Steve. He looked around the men for ideas.

'Lure and destroy,' said David. 'That's the technical term for how you defeat a helicopter gunship. They're deadly, but they are also vulnerable to counter strikes because they're a big bloody target.'

'With what?' Steve scoffed. 'An FN rifle and an Enfield revolver?'

'There's one RPG round left,' Nick put in. 'That soldier left it in the mud when we dropped the bastard.'

'Maksie, will that bring down an Mi-24?' asked Steve.

'If you fire it right,' the Russian said thoughtfully. 'There's no point in trying to put anything into the underbelly. Its thick steel plating is strong enough to withstand just about whatever you throw at it. But an RPG round has a range of 900 yards, and a time fuse of 4.2 seconds. Fire it so it explodes just above the rotary blade, and the shrapnel by itself should be enough to bring the bastard down. Next, the Mi-24 is packed with electronics, but most of it is 1980s-vintage Soviet kit. The shockwaves from the explosion should jam its systems. Put the machine into a tailspin, and in this weather, he's fucked.'

'Fucked?' said Ian. 'I like the sound of that.'

Steve glanced towards Nick. 'You're the best shot here,' he said. 'Reckon you're up to it?'

Nick paused. It was a brief but definite moment of hesitation, noted Steve. One that suggested he wasn't sure. And men with doubts in their mind didn't make good shots.

'There's no shame in saying no,' he told the youth. 'We've only got one RPG round and we can't afford to waste it.'

'I'll do it,' said Nick.

'Good lad.'

'Maksim and I will use these bombs to create a diversion,' said Ian, pointing to the fire extinguishers he had brought with him. 'We'll ignite them up the track, and lure the chopper into the target. Nick can blast it from behind.'

Just then, another Spiral missile crashed into the forest. It was at least 200 yards away, but the shockwaves were still brutal, making the earth shake all around them. Sam was weeping uncontrollably as the deafening noise of falling trees engulfed them.

'Come on – let's move it,' said Steve. 'We're sitting ducks here.'

Steve led the way, with Nick at his side. He'd drawn his revolver: its bullets weren't going to be any use against a heavily armed gunship, but Steve always felt better with a gun in his hand. There was something reassuring about a cold slab of steel against your skin. He looked up into the skies, but they were briefly silent. The Mi-24 had soared upwards into the clouds, was turning and coming back for another hit.

Steve ran hard and fast towards the empty troop carrier. The man had taken one bullet to the neck, another to the shoulder and, at a glance, it looked like he'd bled to death. He was lying face down in the mud, his corpse half-covering his RPG. Grabbing his shoulder, Steve rolled him away and snatched up the weapon. It was a Type 69 RPG, a knock-off of the legendary Soviet RPG-7 made by the Chinese arms manufacturer Norinco, and sold to China's allies around the world. Like the RPG-7, it was a simple and lethally effective piece of kit. It weighed just under thirteen pounds, and could be easily held by a single man.

Steve checked the one remaining grenade left in the man's ammo belt. It was an 'anti-personnel high-explosive incendiary device', or HEI. That will do us just fine, he decided. Created for use in environments such as jungles and mountains, it was no surprise that Wallace had equipped his men with HEIs. The grenade contained 900 steel balls, and up to 3,000 incendiary pellets which, on detonation, would spread over a radius of 15 yards. So long as it exploded right above the Mi-24, it would create a deadly rain of steel and fire that would literally melt the machine out of the sky.

'Sodding perfect,' Steve muttered to himself.

Success depended on just one thing: Nick firing the RPG with total accuracy.

Steve passed the launcher across. 'It's all yours,' he said.

Nick took a second to examine the weapon. It was only thirty-six inches long, and it had a set of simple iron sights at its tip. Point, aim, fire, that's all there is to it, Nick told himself. But you had to measure the trajectory of the grenade precisely, know its speed, and assess its fuse, if you wanted to make an accurate shot.

And there wasn't any time to practise.

His concentration was ripped apart by the roar of another explosion. The Mi-24 had just dropped out of the clouds directly above the forest, blasting another Spiral missile into the woods as it did so. A plume of smoke and fire was already rising into the sky and the sound of trees crashing to the ground echoed across the scrubland. Both men glanced anxiously at each other. There was no way of knowing whether it had hit their unit or not. It was close, that much was certain.

'Just crack on,' said Steve quickly. 'We've got to get that chopper out of the sky.'

Five hundred yards ahead of them, Ian and Maksim had scurried onto the track, carrying the two remaining extinguishers with them. The plan was to create a massive explosion. With any luck, the pilot would swing around, and blast his missile into the fireball, assuming there must be men there. As he flew towards it, Steve and Nick could fire the RPG into the chopper from behind.

That was the plan, reflected Steve. And they better pray to God it worked. Because they had nothing else up their sleeve.

Steve could see Ian wave towards him, then start running back towards the woods. He knew precisely what the signal meant. The fuse was lit. It would detonate in one minute.

'Ready?' he snapped at Nick.

The lad nodded.

'Remember, it explodes directly over the blade.'

Nick nodded again. His expression was concentrated, determined.

The Mi-24 was swooping across the treetops, 600 feet above the ground. The pilot was scanning the woodland, looking where to put the next missile. He swung around, heading out across the scrub, preparing to turn and put the next blast into the woods. Steve tracked every move of the machine. And he could tell at once that they'd been spotted.

The Gatling gun rattled into action, peppering the ground with its huge bullets.

'Dive, dive!' shouted Steve.

He hurled himself behind the upturned troop carrier, his face falling down into the mud and the cold, sticky rainwater. Nick was diving alongside him. As he did so, one of the bullets smashed into a grenade that must have been stored in the webbing of the dead soldiers, creating an explosion that rocked through the air. It was half-buried by the man lying on top of it. But blood, shards of bone and skin, and lethal slices of shrapnel were flying in every direction.

'I'm hit, I'm fucking hit,' screamed Nick.

Steve pulled him down behind the carrier. Five hundred yards ahead, the two extinguisher bombs ignited, sending a tower of fire and smoke into the air.

The Mi-24 turned, its movement like a lazy eagle, the pilot pointing the bug-like nose of the machine towards the explosion, ready to unleash a volley of gunfire and missiles straight into anyone who might be lurking there.

'This is our chance,' said Nick. He staggered to his feet. Blood was pouring from the gash opened up in his right thigh, and the wound was already covered in mud and rainwater. Even so, he lifted the Type 69 to his shoulder, steadying himself for the shot.

'Don't be crazy, you're wounded,' snapped Steve, pulling himself to his feet.

'I can make it,' growled Nick.

'You can hardly fucking stand.'

'Get out of the way.'

'We've only got one fucking round,' yelled Steve. 'We can't waste it.'

'And I'm the best sodding shot you ever saw.'

'Not with a bloody open wound in your leg.'

Nick's left hand lashed out, knocking Steve in the face. He stumbled backwards, surprised by both the suddenness and force of the blow. Before he had time to react, Nick had steadied himself again, raised the Type 69 to his shoulder, and squinted his right eye, making a series of minute adjustments to the barrel of the launcher.

Then: '*Kill,*' he said, his tone calm and determined. And he unleashed the single round.

As Steve recovered his balance, his first reaction had been to wrestle Nick to the ground. But then he heard the sharp retort, the drilling of the air, and he could see the grenade arching through the air on the first stage of its trajectory. He took a sharp intake of breath, aware that their last hope of survival lay within that small lump of steel. The chopper had turned, flying fast towards the explosion, gunfire still rattling from its cannons. The round was disappearing into the sky, impossible to track through the cloud and smoke. Steve counted down the seconds. It was a virtually impossible shot, he realised as he watched and waited. The RPG round had to be fired to detonate precisely over a fast-moving target. Impossible, he repeated grimly to himself.

The HEI round exploded with a sudden crack, like a flash of thunder. Instantly, the Mi-24 started to wobble in the sky, as if it had just been slapped around the face. The 900 steel balls blasting from the grenade were jamming up its blades, cutting the power, and it was losing altitude. The incendiary devices were popping all around it, creating little balls of fire, and flames were starting to lick all around its hull. And the shockwave had jammed the electronics, making it impossible for the pilot to respond to the assault.

It was spinning and stalling.

Steve watched closely, his breath still held. A helicopter was one of the most deadly pieces of equipment on a battlefield. But once it got into trouble, it was also one of the most useless, since it had no ability to respond or retaliate. The flames were starting to rise all around it, sending fumes of black smoke upwards. Suddenly, the blades jammed completely. The loss of power was total. The Mi-24 dropped from the sky colliding with the ground and exploding with a deafening fireball. Even 500 yards away, the ground beneath their feet shook violently, as if they were standing on the edge of an earthquake. A wall of flame ignited, the smell of burning diesel filled the air, and a shower of debris flew in every direction.

Nick dropped the Type 69 and thumped his fists together. He glanced across at Steve, a grin on his face. 'Just like I told you, the best shot you ever saw.'

Forty-Five

S AM WAS BUSY DRESSING NICK'S wound. She'd ripped the trousers open with a knife, and pulled his Medipack out of his webbing. The wound was a nasty one. A shard of shrapnel had cut a gash four inches long in the thigh. It had bled heavily, and mud and water – and possibly the blood from one of the corpses – had already splashed up into it, increasing the risk of infection. Sam had done nursing training as a teenager growing up on the farm, and insisted on taking charge, cleaning out the wound, and applying a bandage across it.

'How bad is it?' asked Ollie anxiously.

'It's a flesh wound, he should be fine. Unless . . .'

Steve fell silent for a minute. On their last job, Jeff had taken a wound to the leg. He'd have been fine as well if they'd managed to get him to a hospital. Instead, he'd lost more and more blood, until he'd died in the remote mountain ranges between Pakistan and Afghanistan. They couldn't let the same thing happen to Nick.

'We'll get him to a hospital,' said Ollie, and he meant it.

After the Mi-24 had crashed into the ground, Steve had carried Nick straight back into the forest. He'd said he could walk, but Steve had told him not to be stupid. He shouldn't be putting any weight onto the leg until they'd had a chance to look at it properly. The rest of the unit was cheering them back. The final Spiral missile had landed just fifty yards away, forcing them to dive for cover to avoid being flattened by the falling trees, or burned by the shockwave rippling through the forest. Now they were safe enough, reckoned Steve. The troop carrier was destroyed and so was the chopper.

'The Land Rovers are buggered,' said Ollie. 'So how are we getting out of here, Ganju?'

'Two more miles of forest,' said the Gurkha. 'Then it's another four miles across open country down to the shore of the lake.'

'Is Nick going to be able to make it?' Ollie asked Sam.

She finished dressing the wound. 'It'll be OK,' she said. 'There's no shrapnel in there that I can see. He needs a hospital to clean it out properly, and make sure nothing gets infected, but he can walk on it.'

'Bloody hell, I thought I was getting a stretcher,' said Nick. 'A chance to put my feet up.'

Steve laughed. He checked his watch. It was just after noon. With any luck, they should make it to the lake in a couple of hours, so long as they didn't encounter any more opposition. 'Let's make a move,' he said tersely. 'We've all spent enough time in this sodding country.'

Using his knife, Dan cut a rough staff for Nick. Within minutes, he'd made what looked like a crutch from a branch of teak, and Nick was able to prop himself up on it and swing forwards, keeping as much weight off his right foot as possible. Ganju was leading the way, having figured out the best route on the map. They'd walk through the forest as far as they could: there was less chance of being spotted that way. Then they'd cut through four miles of open scrub and savannah which should bring them out onto the lake a couple of miles down from Avalanche Falls. They walked nervously at first, still wary of the possibility that there might be more attack helicopters out searching for them, but as they drew closer to their destination, their confidence grew.

'I'll tell you what Nick, I'm going to buy you a bloody big slap-up meal when we get home,' said Ollie. 'No expense spared. That was a damned fine shot you put into that chopper.'

'What's the free toy at McDonald's this month?' said Ian. 'Make sure he gets two of them.'

'Leave it out, mate,' snapped Nick. 'I'm off to . . .' He paused.

'What's it to be then, maestro?' said Ollie.

'TGI Friday's, I reckon,' said Nick. 'Maybe the Skins to the Brim to start with. Potato skins topped with cheese and crispy bacon, with a layer of sour cream on top. Followed by a full rack of Jack Daniel's ribs, the pork ribs coated with the bourbon glaze. With Cajun-battered onion rigs and chips as well. Maybe double chips.'

'I'd start with the Jack Daniel's chicken wings,' said Steve. 'Followed by the American grill.'

'I'll just stick with the Jack Daniel's,' said Maksim. 'And maybe the phone number of the waitress. Or her sister. I'm not fussy.'

'Stop it, boys,' said Dan. 'I'm bloody starving already.'

'Of course, I'd have to finish with the Dirt Cake,' Nick said dreamily. 'You know, the brownie cake topped with clotted cream, marshmallows, and finished off with an Oreo cookie.'

'And I'd finish it with a Silver Mercedes,' said Maksim. 'Smirnoff vodka, cranberry juice and orange sherbet, all poured over some sparkling white wine.'

'Enough,' joked Sam. 'I'm putting on weight just listening to this.'

By one o'clock, they were out of the woodland and into the open ground again. The thunderstorm had moved on and been replaced with brilliant sunshine. Steve could feel steam sweating off his clothes, and after ten minutes, walking across the open bushland, he was dry again. A rainbow was arcing across the plain, beckoning them forwards. Even though mud from the battle was still caked to his skin, Steve could feel his mood improving. The journey had been a long and hard one, but for the first time he could feel it was nearing its end.

At two, they stopped at one of the water bores. Some lions were drinking there, but the group laid up in some of the long grass for twenty minutes, waiting for them to move on before approaching the water. Steve reckoned they'd been in enough scraps already without taking on any wild animals. When the lions had retreated to a safe distance, they moved up close to the pool of fresh water, its level swelled by the heavy rains of the past few days, and washed some of the dirt away from their skin, refilling their water canisters before resuming their march north.

Over the next hour, they crossed through the northern boundary of the National Park, its border marked by nothing more than posts strung out every few hundred yards, and walked across the last couple of miles that should take them to the shore of the lake. To the west, there was a road that led up towards Avalanche Falls, and they could hear the occasional rumble of a truck or a car rolling across it. But they kept well away, pushing on through the open grassland, making sure they couldn't be seen or heard by anybody.

They were a mile from the lake when Ganju called a halt. He directed them towards a small copse of big mopane trees and told everyone to rest. Spreading out the map, he pointed to their position. 'We're still a mile from the lake, but we should lay up here,' he said. 'I reckon I should go ahead and scout out the situation on the lake. We don't want to walk into an ambush.'

'Good plan,' said Ollie. 'But you need some protection.'

'I'll go,' said Maksim, drawing his revolver.

Ganju shook his head. 'Two men are conspicuous, one man can slip through easily,' he said. 'I'll go alone.'

'It's . . .' started Ollie.

'Let him go – he's right,' snapped Steve.

'Give me two hours,' said Ganju. 'If I'm not back by then, assume I've been captured.'

They wished him luck, then settled back to wait. The ground was dry enough under the cover of the mopane trees. Maksim collected a few handfuls of the bugs and offered to cook them up something to eat but no one was in the mood. 'I'm just waiting for those Jack

Daniel's ribs you keep talking about, mate,' said Dan. 'Somehow the worms aren't in the same league.'

Steve put his head back and tried to close his eyes. The big branches of the trees provided cover from the afternoon sunshine, just as earlier they shaded the ground from the rain, and the spot was both dry and cool. He glanced across at Sam, smiled, then shut his eyes. There was still plenty he meant to say to her. Back at the pool she'd said she loved him. Only a few hours after that, Steve had been certain he was about to die, and certain as well that he didn't want to go without telling her that he felt the same way about her.

There will be time, he told himself.

As soon as we get out of this hell-hole.

He woke with a start. Dan was leaning into his face, and the smell of the Australian after a day in rough country was enough to wake the devil himself. 'Christ, mate, we can all have a kip when we get back home,' he said. 'Right now, we've got a country to escape from.'

Steve washed some water down his throat, and pulled himself up off the ground. Ganju was back with them, surrounded by the rest of the unit. Just one look at the Gurkha told you all you needed to know, however.

The news wasn't good.

'The place is swarming with soldiers,' said Ganju tersely.

'On the lake itself?' questioned Ollie.

Ganju nodded. 'Patrol boats, with searchlights.'

'And the shore?'

'There are foot patrols along the pathways.'

'Some of the shoreline is just wilderness,' said Ian. 'We might be able to slip through.'

'There's still the boats,' said Ganju. 'And I saw two choppers. There may be more.'

'But if we break through?'

'Forget it,' Ollie said immediately. 'We can't risk being seen. If that

391

happens, we'll bring a whole army down on our heads, and then we've no chance of getting away.'

'I'm not going back to that jail,' said Maksim. He was toying with the mag of his FN. 'I'd rather make a fight of it, and die with my boots on like a soldier.'

'We know you can't wait to get to that great vodka distillery in the sky, Maksie,' said Steve, 'but the rest of us aren't quite ready yet.' He paused, swiping a blade of grass from the ground. 'Ollie's right. We can't risk breaking through the lines. Maybe we should take a different route out of here . . .'

He looked towards Ganju, asking, 'Is that an option?'

'We could head towards Mozambique,' said Ganju. 'But it's a walk of at least two hundred miles across hostile country.'

Steve played with the grass in his hand. That didn't sound right either.

'Or down towards Botswana? We could cover a hundred miles in three or four days.'

'We can't guarantee that border isn't swarming with soldiers as well,' Ian warned.

'They can't seal the whole bloody country,' said David. 'They haven't got enough men.'

'But we can't walk around indefinitely, searching for a weak spot,' said Steve. 'We'll be caught long before then.'

'I know a way,' said Sam.

Forty-Six

SAM TOOK A COUPLE OF steps forward, so she was standing in the centre of the group.

'Dad used to help journalists get in and out of the country sometimes, after they were all banned by President Kapembwa,' she stated. 'They would fly to Tuka, then approach the bridge that crosses Avalanche Falls. They'd mingle with a group of tourists making the crossing, then slip away on the other side.'

'And the soldiers don't check?' said Ollie.

Sam shook her head. 'Tourism at the Falls is one of the very few sources of foreign currency the country has left. They don't dare do anything that would put it at risk, and the soldiers are under strict orders not to harass the tour groups in any way. If there's any trouble, they get shot.'

'I like it,' said Steve.

'Even if we're spotted, we can make a run for it,' said Ollie. 'I don't think the soldiers are going to open fire on a bridge full of tourists.'

'Aren't we putting innocent people at risk?' asked Dan.

Steve glanced at the Australian. He'd served time in a military jail after two children got killed on a mission in Afghanistan back in the Special Air Services Regiment. It wasn't Dan's fault. Just crossfire, the kind of tragedy that occurs every day in every war that ever got started. But it had made a big impression on Dan, and Steve was aware of it. The bloke didn't mind risking his own life, and he certainly had no qualms about malleting the enemy. But civilians? That was different. He didn't want to see them get hurt.

'It's our only chance,' said Ollie.

'There's no way we're walking a hundred miles, mate,' said Ian tersely. 'We haven't got it in us.'

Dan nodded, but his expression was serious. 'OK,' he grunted. 'But make sure there aren't any kids around. If there are, we're not crossing.'

'We'll need some tourist clothes,' said Sam. 'Ganju, take me close to the Falls. There will be some stalls selling T-shirts. I'll get us some kit, and then we can make a move.'

'I'll go,' said Steve. 'It's too dangerous.'

'Right,' said Sam. 'And in combat gear, and covered in mud and blood, you're really going to blend in.'

Steve fell silent. He knew she was right. 'Be careful,' he said.

'I'll have a black T-shirt and some jeans,' said Nick with a rough grin. 'And a baseball cap, if you've got one.'

'Drainpipes, though,' said Steve. 'This unit's not going to be seen dead in flares.'

'And some shades,' said Nick. 'Police or Boss. Fakes, of course. No point in wasting money on the real thing.'

'And some Armani boxer shorts for Maksie,' said David. 'He only wears designer, as I'm sure you can tell.'

'And none of that fake Lacoste rubbish,' said Ollie. 'This unit has its standards. We're not going into battle with a stupid grinning crocodile on our chests.'

Sam smiled. 'I'll see what we can do,' she said.

Steve sat back under the tree. There was nothing to be done now except wait. He felt bad about letting her go, but Ganju would protect her if there was any trouble. The unit had been to hell and back twice now. He'd trust each man with his life. And with Sam's as well.

Dan was checking Nick's dressing, cleaning the wound again and applying a fresh bandage, not because he really needed it, but because it gave them a way of passing the time. Maksim and David were carving out a fresh staff. Ollie was kicking around suggestions for the stag night, along with Dan and Ian. The wedding was just a week away now, and for the first time in days, it looked like they might actually make it.

Steve lay back against the tree. He didn't feel like talking, but wasn't able to get back to sleep. Instead, he just looked out into the wilderness; the view stretched for at least a couple of miles. In the distance, he saw first a herd of elephants, and then giraffes, ambling through the empty land in search of fresh pastures. Deep within the interior of the wood, he could hear the yapping of the green monkeys that were common throughout this part of Africa.

Beautiful country, he thought again to himself. He knew Regiment boys who'd settled in Africa. One guy, Mick, was running tour boats, taking bankers out deep-sea fishing in Kenya. Another, Rick, was training the Nigerian Special Forces. And he could see the attraction. A man could lose himself in this kind of space. Find peace.

Maybe I should join them. *Take Sam with me.*

It was five in the afternoon by the time Sam and Ganju returned. Steve was just starting to get worried about her. They'd been gone almost two hours in total, more than enough time to get to the lake and back. They were carrying six bags, three each. She started to unpack. They'd bought ten pairs of fake Levis in a variety of different sizes, and a selection of T-shirts and sweatshirts in a range of colours. Some had logos on, and some didn't. 'And here's a Liverpool shirt for you, Nick,' said Sam, tossing it across.

'What number?'

'Eight, of course,' said Sam. 'You look like a Steve Gerrard fan to me.'

'Bloody fantastic,' said Nick, pulling the shirt on. 'I'm taking this one home with me.'

Within minutes, the unit had changed into their new kit. The trousers were all baggy, and the shirts were all large, and by swapping them around, they managed to find outfits that fitted them well enough. They washed their faces, scraped some of the stubble from their chins using their knives, and slotted their dark glasses over their faces. They'd replaced their military boots with open-topped sandals, and Sam had bought a selection of guidebooks and plastic water bottles for them to carry in their hands. *We look the part,* thought Steve. *All we need to do now is act it.*

'No rifles,' said Ganju seriously. 'We can hide the Enfields inside our trousers, but we can't try and slip across the bridge with assault rifles under our arms.'

'I'm not going anywhere without my weapon,' growled Maksim.

'Drop it, Maksie,' snapped Steve. 'If you want to fight your way out of here, you're welcome to. But if we're going through as tourists, we shouldn't be carrying any obvious weapons.'

Each man checked that the chamber on his Enfield was fully loaded, then slipped the weapon inside his waistband. If they wore their sweatshirts loose, it wouldn't create any noticeable bulge. They collected together some piles of leaves and broken branches, and hid the FNs underneath. If it turned into a scrap, they'd need them again., and they wanted to be able to find them.

'Otherwise, one of the monkeys can find them,' said Ian. 'And turn himself into the king of the sodding jungle.'

'Not with an FN,' said David. 'He'd need an AK for that.'

They started to walk towards the lake, with Sam and Ganju leading the way, and with Steve just behind them. There was only just over a mile to cover. As you got closer, the vegetation changed dramatically. There was so much spray from the massive waterfall that for a half-mile radius it created a mini-rainforest, with thick, dark vegetation, through which you'd need a machete to cut a proper path.

Ganju slipped onto one of the trails cut into the landscape for the tourists, then motioned to the rest of the unit to follow. They were close enough to hear the Falls now: a massive tumult of water crashing through the air in a churning riot of noise. Spray was flicking through the air, flashing across all their faces, which, combined with the cool early-evening breeze, made for a relaxing walk. But Steve was still on edge, and, as he glanced around at the rest of the men, he could tell that he wasn't alone.

They were about to walk straight through the enemy.

And a few revolvers aside, they had already laid down their arms.

They came out onto a dirt track, and as they looked east, they could see the bridge clearly enough. A wrought-iron structure, it had been built in 1905 under the orders of Fitzpatrick, who wanted a direct rail link between Batota and Tuka. It was constructed across the second gorge, 500 yards down from the main waterfalls, and taking advantage of a peninsula that rose up out of the river. Fitzpatrick wanted it built close enough to the Falls themselves so that train passengers could feel the spray on the windows as they crossed. In total, the bridge ran for over 250 yards, and provided the best views of the main Falls. There was a rail, road and foot crossing, all within the same structure. But the bridge was no longer judged safe for trains, and trucks were rare. It was mostly a footbridge, and, although there were border posts at both sides, a longstanding agreement between Batota and Tuka meant that tourists were allowed to pass freely from one side to the other without being stopped or asked for visas.

Escape, thought Steve, as he looked up at the bridge, and at the massive cascade of water that lay directly behind it.

There was a string of stalls on the track leading up to the bridge, selling clothes, drinks, souvenirs and food. Dozens of hawkers were touting their wares, and plenty of tourists were milling amongst them. It wasn't the height of the travel season, and the chaos within Batota wasn't helping either, but Tuka was peaceful enough, and Avalanche Falls was still one of the greatest tourist attractions in the world, and that meant there were always plenty of people around.

There were soldiers among them, however, and more standing over the entrance to the bridge, all of them armed, even if they were trying not to frighten anyone by acting too aggressively. They'll have seen our pictures, Steve reminded himself. And if they spot us, we're in big trouble.

'We'll go in three batches,' said Ganju. 'Wait for my signal.'

Steve started to browse amongst some of the souvenirs. He picked up one piece of African carving after another, using the big blocks of wood to help disguise his face. The stallholders were pestering him to buy one. 'Twenty dollars, twenty dollars,' one of them kept saying. 'This is the finest you can buy in the whole of Africa.'

The tourists were a mix of South Africans, Arabs, Americans, Japanese, British and Australians, a few Dutch, and some Germans. Ganju had chosen David, Nick and Sam to go first. He waited until a group of Dutch went past, then nodded towards David. Together with Nick, they stepped casually into a group of twelve people. Nick had left his staff behind: it would only draw attention to himself. David had bought himself a disposable camera, and was holding it up, pretending to take pictures of everything, so that if you glanced towards him, all you could see was a Fuji logo.

Good trick, thought Steve. He grabbed a camera from the stand and handed across twenty of the Tukan kwachas he had left for it. Then he went back to studying the artefacts.

'I make you the best price in the whole of Africa,' said the stallholder.

'How about twenty, then,' said Steve, holding up a carving of an elephant made from Batotean teak.

'American?' said the man.

They didn't even bother pricing things in Batotean money, noted Steve. 'No, Tukan.'

'It's worth fifty kwachas.'

Steve couldn't be bothered to argue. He fished the note out of his pocket, and could see at once that he'd paid far more than it was worth.

'It'll look lovely on your mantelpiece, mate,' said Ollie, grinning. 'Make sure you get some matching cushions.'

'It'll make me look more like a bloody tourist,' complained Steve. 'Anyway, I can always give it to you and Katie as a wedding present.'

'Not unless you can get him to stamp "The White Company" underneath it you can't,' said Ollie. 'Katie won't just take any old rubbish.'

Ganju signalled. A group of Americans were going past. Quietly, Ollie, Dan and Maksim slipped into the group. Steve watched them, and they fitted in snugly enough to the party. Dan with his huge build, barrel of a chest, and big hands, could have been a Californian, whilst Maksie, dark, short and swarthy, could have been one of the Poles from the Midwest. Looking further up ahead, Steve could see that Sam, Nick and David were already halfway across the bridge. They were walking slowly, taking it easy, stopping to admire the spectacular views. Just the way real tourists would, Steve reminded himself. *So far, so good.*

He moved onto the next stall. This time, the wood carvings were mostly of tribal faces. The man in charge had seen Steve buy something from his neighbour, at a good price as well, and reckoned he was an easy mark. He wasn't going to take no for an answer. 'Listen, mate, I've already bought enough crap for one day, I'm just looking, right?' growled Steve eventually. But it made no difference. For fifty Tukan kwacha, nothing short of the Enfield was going to shut the bloke up. And Steve wasn't about to go that far.

Ganju nodded towards both men.

A group of South Africans was walking past, and had stopped to look at the carvings. Steve and Ian stepped amongst them. One man in his forties was haggling over the price of a carved lion, and got it down to fifteen rand. That completed, they started to walk back towards the bridge. There were eight of them in total, five men and three women, all in their forties and fifties, casually dressed, and visibly tired after a long day of sight-seeing. They didn't pay any attention as Steve, Ian and Ganju walked alongside them: even if they did, they were hardly likely to object to three harmless-looking tourists amongst them. They started to walk. It was 500 yards to the bridge, and there was a sentry post right next to it. Five armed soldiers stood grouped around a wooden barrier, but the gate wasn't down, and so long as you looked like a tourist, the soldiers weren't checking any papers. Another dozen soldiers were patrolling the path that ran down the side of the lake. They were scanning the lake on one side, and checking the paths cut into the rainforest on the other. They weren't looking closely at the tourists, noted Steve with relief. They were looking for soldiers.

His carving under one arm and his disposable camera in the other hand he kept up a steady pace every movement calculated to draw as little attention to himself as possible. As they got closer, he could hear the roar of the water, the noise gradually growing in intensity until it drowned out everything around them. And he could feel the spray on his face: a few spits at first, but then a steady, fine mist that left his face damp.

'Bloody amazing views,' said one of the South African guys at his side.

Steve grinned. Conversation was good, he reckoned. It made you look like part of the group. 'Fantastic,' he replied. 'Best thing I've seen since the Pyramids.'

'Where you from?' asked the South African.

'London,' said Steve. 'Well, Bromley.'

'My cousin lives in Chislehurst. You know it?'

Chislehurst? Christ, thought Steve. About the most boring commuter town on the whole of Network South-East. 'Lovely spot.'

'Just had another kid.'

'Boy or girl?'

'Boy. Got three of them now.' The man chuckled. 'Not much peace in his house, I reckon.'

Steve glanced to the left. They were walking right past the soldiers. A pair of them were scanning faces but they weren't stopping anyone. There must be twenty or thirty people walking past each minute, judged Steve, and that was a lot of faces to look into. He could see one of the soldiers looking straight at him, and for a second he half-caught the man's eyes.

'Girls are less trouble,' he said to the man next to him.

'Not my two.'

Steve laughed.

They were ten yards clear of the sentry post now, and walking over the bridge. People were slowing down, taking a last admiring look at the panorama stretching out in either direction. To the left, you could see the deep gorges cut into the ground, then the twist as the Zambezi River continued its course, and then Lake Hasta stretching far out into the distance, like a massive inland sea. To the right, Avalanche Falls. From the bridge, you could look straight into the walls of white water, cascading over the rock. The water swirled and eddied, kicking up foam and spray in every direction. For a moment, Steve just stood and watched, awestruck by the power of the scene. Then he snapped himself back to attention: there were five Zambian soldiers manning a checkpoint on their side of the bridge, and they weren't safe until they were past them.

'How about a picture of me and the wife?' said the South African, handing Steve a Sony digital camera.

Steve looked nervously back towards the soldiers. None of them were paying much attention to the bridge. In fact, they looked like they were about to knock off for the day. Glancing ahead, he could see that the rest of the unit was already safely across into Tuka, waiting for them amid the tour buses pulled up in the car park opposite.

'Sure, mate,' He took the camera, waited for the man to put a protective arm around his wife, pointed and clicked.

'You want a picture with your pals?'

Steve shook his head, jerking a thumb towards Ian. 'Have you seen the guy's face? I'll buy a postcard.'

Ian and Ganju were already walking alongside the rest of the party towards the Tukan border. Steve took one last look at the cascading wall of water. The early-evening sunset was streaking the sky a golden orange behind it, and he promised himself that one day, he'd come and take a proper look. Then he quickened his pace. A hundred yards turned into twenty. He heard some shouting back on the Batotean side of the bridge, and allowed himself to steal a quick glance: a tourist had just got into a shouting match with a stallholder about their change and one of the soldiers had intervened. Still holding his camera and his carving, Steve walked casually past the checkpoint. The Tukan soldiers didn't look at him, nor did Steve look at them. As he stepped off the last metal girder, and onto Tukan soil, he could feel the air emptying out of his chest.

We've made it, he told himself.

'Have a good trip,' said the South African.

Steve nodded curtly. 'You too.'

The man walked towards the waiting bus, while Steve strode across the bustling car park towards the taxi rank. Nearly all the visitors to the Falls these days stayed in Tuka and, with the day drawing to a close, the place was thronging with people getting back into the tour buses that had brought them down from the safari lodges and the hotels.

'Keep it calm,' hissed Ollie to everyone as they started to regroup. 'No celebrations, and don't do anything to draw attention to ourselves. We can have a few beers when we get back to London.'

He'd already organised a taxi. There was a line of cars waiting to take the few tourists who hadn't come in an organised party back to their hotels: Mercedes and Toyota people-carriers, all of them with plenty of years on them, but all kept in immaculate condition by the drivers. The driver slid open the doors to his Toyota. Nine people was a squeeze – the vehicle wasn't built for any more than six – but Ollie had already paid him twice the going rate and the man seemed pleased enough with that. He told the driver to take them to Ramsey. Ten kilometres from the Falls, and named after the Victorian explorer Heathfield Ramsey, the first European to explore this part of the Zambezi River, it was an old colonial town, with some light industry, but which mostly served the tourist traffic. From Ramsey's Hakata Airport, there was one flight a day to Johannesburg, and from there they could get any one of a dozen different connections back to Europe.

Home, Steve told himself. Safety . . .

The driver pulled away from the kerb, honked his way through the parking lot, and steered up onto the road. There was still a mass of stalls up on the highway, selling fruit and soft drinks, but after half a mile they disappeared, and they were driving through the dusty, flat scrub that would take them up to the airport. Steve closed his eyes, paying no attention to the view. South African, BA and Tukan Airways all operated flights out of Hakata to Johannesburg, but Steve had no idea of the schedules. They'd get on any plane they could blag a ticket for: if there were no flights tonight, they could find somewhere quiet to stay, sink a few well-earned beers, then get on the first flight they could buy a ticket for in the morning.

'Where the fuck are we going?' Ian said suddenly.

Steve opened his eyes again.

They were driving down a dirt track, travelling far too fast. The driver had pushed the Toyota up to sixty, and it was skidding over rocks and slamming into the holes which pitted the surface of the track. The clouds had darkened, and rain was starting to spit down on them. On both sides of the track were thick trees. Through a gap, Steve could see a flash of water. The rain was increasing in intensity, coming down in thick waves, reducing visibility. But the driver didn't seem to care.

'I said, where the fuck are we going?' shouted Ian, louder this time.

The driver remained silent, his hands gripping the wheel.

Where the hell *are* we going? Steve asked himself. Because it sure as hell isn't Hakata Airport.

Ollie had already pulled his gun. 'Answer the question, man,' he growled.

The driver jammed his foot even harder on the accelerator. There was sweat pouring off the back of his neck but he didn't turn around.

'Answer, or I'll shoot.'

'You'll bloody kill us all,' shouted Ian.

The Toyota swerved suddenly, as the driver jammed his foot on the brakes, pulling simultaneously on the handbrake. The Toyota started to skid, sliding across the surface of the track like a puck sliding over ice. It began to spin, then one of the wheels hit a rock. The Toyota shuddered, then stalled. The window smashed, the glass splintering over the men inside as the barrel of an AK-47 was thrust through the window, pointing straight at Ollie.

'Get the fuck out of the car.'

Ollie started to draw the Enfield from inside his trousers.

'Bloody move it,' barked Wallace. 'Or I'll spray this vehicle with bullets, then put a bomb under it, and you bastards will be fried to death.'

Forty-Seven

OLLIE'S HAND WAS STILL HOVERING close to where the Enfield was hidden. Straight ahead of them, through the driving rain, he could see a jeep. Out of it stepped a tall, strong soldier, gripping an AK-47, and with the distinctive purple and gold beret of the Sixth Brigade slotted onto his head.

Steve recognised him at once.

Yohane.

The bastard who murdered Chris.

Behind him were another two soldiers, their guns pointing straight at the Toyota.

'Move it, boys,' snarled Wallace. 'Just take a look in the mirror.'

The image was quite clear in the rearview mirror. Newton was standing at the back of the Toyota with a flaming torch in his hand. He'd already taken the petrol cap off, and was poised to plunge the torch straight into the tank. The vehicle would explode instantly.

'If you don't get the fuck out now, you'll all die.'

'Do as he says,' said Steve.

'We'll bloody die with our boots on,' snapped Ollie.

'Then you'll die thinking with your arse rather than your brain,' hissed Steve. 'Do what the fucker says.'

'He's right,' said David. 'We've got no chance.'

Slowly, Ollie started to climb out of the Toyota, followed by Ian,

Maksim, Nick and Steve. Only Dan remained in the Toyota, dropping down below the back seat of the people-carrier.

'Put your hands in the air,' ordered Wallace. He was armed with an AK-47; so was Newton. The barrels of the two guns were pointed straight at them. Reluctantly, Steve folded his palms behind his neck. He could feel the cold steel of the Enfield pressing against his skin inside his waistband, but he knew there was no time to draw and get a shot away without getting mown down by the assault rifle pointing straight at him.

Wait and watch, he told himself. Our chance will come.

'This way,' Wallace said roughly.

He was pointing towards a track that led down to the lake. Steve started to walk, followed by the rest of the men. Behind them, Yohane kept his own gun trained on them. Ahead, Steve could just make out a jetty and, alongside it, a motor boat tethered to the mooring.

'Sod it,' he muttered to himself.

We were so close, so bloody close.

Archie stepped out of the boat and walked to the head of the jetty, with the waves whipped up by the storm swirling behind him. He was wearing a dark-green anorak to protect him from the rain, and there was a thin smile on his face.

'How did you find us?' Steve asked steadily.

'It was her,' Ian said viciously, nodding towards Sam.

'No!' cried Sam. She'd run forward and was now standing between Archie and the rest of the men grouped around the head of the pier. Behind them, the boat was bobbing around in the rough water slapping at the jetty.

'Don't lie, you bitch,' said Ian. 'We get delivered straight into the hands of your brother. It's obvious, isn't it?'

'Christ,' muttered Steve to himself. That can't be true, can it?

Sam wouldn't betray me.

'It wasn't that hard to track you,' said Archie. 'Our father used to pull that trick of bringing journalists in and out of the country by mingling with the tourists on the bridge. I was certain Sam would suggest it. We didn't want to create any trouble at the bridge. Bad PR for what remains of the tourist industry and, as you know, I'm not a man who ever lets anything stand in the way of business. We just paid the taxi drivers on the other side a few hundred dollars, and told them that as soon as eight ugly-looking guys got into one of the cabs, they were to drive them straight to us.'

He flashed a grin. 'Went like clockwork – just like this whole operation.'

'It was nothing to do with me, Steve,' said Sam. She was looking towards him, her eyes desperate. 'You have to believe me.'

Steve remained silent, his expression as implacable as a lump of granite.

'What's going to happen to us now?' Ollie demanded.

'We're taking you back to Ibera,' said Wallace, jabbing at Ollie with the barrel of his AK-47. 'And this time, we're going to make bloody sure we execute you.'

'It will solidify the new regime of President Matola, with our friend Newton here as the man running the armed forces,' said Archie. 'And, of course, the whole of the country, and all its mineral wealth, will be a subsidiary of my fund.'

'So get on the boat,' barked Wallace.

Nobody moved.

'I've already executed one of you bastards,' he spat. 'If I need to kill another of you, right here and now, then I will.'

Suddenly, Maksim grabbed hold of Sam. He yanked her head back hard and, in the same instant, whipped the Enfield from his belt, jabbing the cold barrel of the gun straight into the side of her head.

There was sweat pouring off him.

'The bitch dies – right here, right now,' he threatened.

Wallace had already raised his weapon and was pointing it straight at him. 'Drop the fucking gun,' he commanded.

'The bitch dies,' repeated Maksim. 'We're getting on the boat, and getting the fuck out of here, and if anyone tries to stop us – she gets it.'

Steve could hear something wild in his voice. A note he'd heard before, usually just before the Russian was about to shoot someone. He looked straight into Sam's eyes, and he could see the panic welling up inside her. The Russian was crazy enough to kill his own mother when his blood was up. He'd snuff out Sam's life the same way most men would crush an insect crawling across their skin.

'Drop it, Maksie,' Steve told him, trying to stay calm.

'She's fucking dying!' shouted Maksim.

'She's on our side,' Steve told him.

'I don't care what you think, man, they're not taking us without a fight.' He looked towards Archie. 'Now, you – move. We're going to climb on board, and we're going to sail out of here, and if any of your men try to stop us, then your sister dies.'

Wallace nodded towards Yohane. Together with the other soldiers, he'd stepped forward five paces. Their rifles were raised, and they were standing in a neat semi-circle, like a firing squad.

'Let her go,' said Wallace coldly.

Maksim ignored him, looking straight at Archie. 'I'm giving you one last warning, *mudak*,' he spat. 'Your sister dies in the next minute.'

'We'll drop you,' warned Wallace.

'No,' started Archie.

Let them fight, thought Steve. That's our opportunity.

'He doesn't have the balls,' sneered Wallace.

From the corner of his eye, Steve could see the Toyota start to move. He glanced furtively towards it. Wallace hadn't counted them out, he realised. Sloppy. Dan had remained hidden inside it all along, and now he was at the wheel, the driver pushed out, but in the stand-off over Sam, no one had noticed. Its engine was inaudible through the swirling wind and rain.

And it was advancing towards the backs of Yohane and the two other men.

Steve gripped tight on his Enfield, and nodded to Ollie and Ian. There was an unspoken acknowledgement between them. *This scrap is about to kick off. And once the bullets start flying, we'll all just have to take our chances.*

Archie was starting to walk towards Sam and Maksim. The latter was backing away, tugging hard on her hair, but she was too terrified to even scream. Wallace was shouting at Yohane to line up the shot. They are distracted, noted Steve. They can't hear the car . . .

The Toyota slammed into the man's back with a sickening thud.

There was a crunch of bone and metal. It was a big, powerful machine, but the man with whom it had just collided was built from steel just as much as the vehicle crashing into him. He shuddered, then creaked, the way a lamp-post might, and a single round was loosened off from his AK-47, the bullet flying harmlessly into the air. Dan was revving the engine furiously, swinging on the wheel at the same time. Yohane's belt had caught on the bumper, and the Toyota was pushing him down into the mud. Two of his comrades had already leaped aside, turning their guns onto the vehicle, unleashing a murderous barrage of fire. The glass shattered, and smoke started to rise from the bonnet, as bullets peppered the engine. The wheels were spitting up mud, sending it flying straight into the faces of the men, making it impossible for them to direct their fire. In the next second, there was a piercing grunt, like a pig being slaughtered, as the damaged front of the Toyota collided hard with a man's stomach.

In the same instant, Steve, Ollie and the rest of the unit had drawn their Enfields and released a terrifying blast of ammunition. The air was thick with hot, deadly lumps of metal. Steve was firing straight into the soldiers, whilst Ian and Ollie had turned their fire onto Newton and Wallace. The Enfield was a light weapon, easy to fire, without much accuracy, but at this range it didn't matter very much. The targets were easy enough to hit. By the time he'd emptied half its chamber, it was clear they wouldn't be having any more trouble from the Sixth Brigade.

'Drop your weapons or she dies,' Masksim was shouting wildly. He was still dragging Sam backwards.

Wallace was running towards him, his weapon ready to explode into life.

But Ian and Ollie had started to punch bullets into the man's back, whilst Ganju had run to the side, slotting one then two bullets into the man's ribcage. He wobbled first under the impact, then lost his grip as his boots slid on the mud, and crashed painfully onto the ground. Blood was flowing from his wounds, the life draining out of him.

The gunfire stopped as suddenly as it had started, the silence broken only by the relentless rain.

Steve glanced anxiously around. The Toyota had stalled, steam rising from the broken bonnet, and its wheels caught up in the tangled and crushed remains of the soldier.

Maksim was still holding onto Sam, but had put the gun down. Wallace and Newton were dead, and Archie was backing nervously towards the jetty. None of the men had been hurt.

Steve ran towards the Toyota.

Dan was crouching under the steering wheel. His back was covered in shattered glass, and there was a streak of blood where a shard from the windscreen had sliced through his shirt. Steve reached down for his hand. 'You can come out now, mate,' he said. 'Looks like you missed out on the fun.'

Dan climbed from the vehicle. He could see at once that Yohane had been crushed by the wheels. Bullets had entered his body at three different points, but he was already dead by the time the munitions struck. Leaning over the man, Dan pushed his face down into the mud. Pulling the knife from Yohane's belt, he allowed the blade to glisten in the rain for a brief second, then lunged forward with it. 'That's for Chris, you bastard,' he almost sobbed as he stuck the knife hard into the man's neck.

Steve waited for a second. Dan was twisting the knife, cutting the corpse open, the way a butcher might fillet the carcass of a bullock. It was a brutal sight, cold and cruel, but Steve waited a moment. That's soldiering, he reflected sombrely. Each man takes vengeance in his own way.

Slowly, Dan stood up, his hands dripping with blood. He threw the knife away in disgust: the anger had drained out of him, and he was embarrassed by the ferocity of his rage.

Steve ran towards Maksim. He had let go of Sam, and was walking briskly towards Wallace. The Russian's anger was raised – and like a tiger with blood on its lips, once the killing had begun, nothing could save the prey. Maksim dropped down onto Wallace's body, and from the way the old mercenary's legs twitched, it was clear there were still a few embers of life left in him. Maksim began to throw punch after punch into the man, until his knuckles were stained crimson with blood. He kept on, even after Wallace had lost consciousness, unable to stop himself, until finally he paused for breath. With sweat pouring off his face, and with his lungs gasping for oxygen, he took the knife he'd hidden inside his trousers and, holding the blade in the air, he leaned in close to Wallace's face.

'Let's see how you die, *mudak*,' he said quietly and, the sentence completed, he cut a surgically precise hole in the man's throat through which blood started to foam and bubble.

Steve didn't know much Russian, but he knew *mudak* meant bastard – and it was a fitting-enough epitaph for Wallace. Even he was taken aback by the savagery of Maksim's attack, but the dead man had fought for the scum of the planet. Steve had watched plenty of men die on the battlefield: he'd never seen a man who deserved his fate as completely as Wallace did.

He checked on Sam: she was shaken, and there were tears smudging her face, but she was OK. Steve then looked towards Archie.

Sam's brother was standing on the edge of the pier. The anorak was still pulled up around his neck, protecting him from the rain lashing in from the lake, but you could see the fear in his eyes. He had been looking feverishly at Wallace, soaking up each blow as if it had landed on his own skin. He'd pulled a pistol from his jacket pocket. A Swiss-made Sphinx 3000, noted Steve. At more than $2,000 a time, it was one of the most expensive firearms in the world.

But it doesn't matter how much a gun costs, Steve reminded himself. It is the man firing it that counts.

'Stop, or I'll fucking shoot you,' said Archie. His voice had gone up a pitch, so that it was practically a squeal. Nerves, Steve decided. Never a good thing to take into a scrap.

'Just stand back,' said Archie, even louder this time. 'You can keep the bloody money I promised you. I'll leave on this boat, and we'll forget about the whole thing.'

Steve took another step towards him, so that he was standing just five yards away from the man. He looked towards his right hand. The Sphinx was shaking.

'Another step, and I'll shoot.'

'As the gun lobby likes to say, it's not guns that kill people, it's people that kill people,' interrupted Steve. His tone was low and menacing. 'And since you don't have the fucking guts to shoot a man, that weapon's no bloody use to you.'

Moving with the suddenness and agility of a cobra, in a flash, Steve had covered the space that separated them, and put a brutal punch straight into the wrist of Archie's right hand. The man's finger brushed the trigger, but without the force needed to release the bullet, and the Sphinx tumbled harmlessly to the ground. Steve smashed straight into him, using the weight of his body like a hammer, winding the man and sending him staggering back along the pier. Steve grabbed hold of him, then jerked his right arm up hard behind his back. Archie screamed in pain as the muscles and bone were twisted out of shape. With his left hand, Steve put a punch straight into his face, cutting open his lip. Then, releasing his arm,

Steve pushed him down onto the jetty. Stooping, he picked up the Sphinx and held it rock steady into the side of Archie's head.

'I'll show you how this fancy bit of kit works, mate,' he said thickly.

Archie was kneeling. Tears were streaming down his face, mixing with the blood and rain.

'I can pay you . . .'

Steve gave a disgusted shake of the head.

'Millions . . .'

Steve remained silent, the wind howling around him, and the rain lashing into his face.

'Please,' wept Archie.

'Stand up and take your bullet like a man.'

Sam was rushing towards him, approaching the edge of the jetty.

'No!' she screamed.

Steve paused. His finger was half-squeezing the trigger. Another milligram of pressure, and the 9mm bullet would already have chewed up Archie's brain.

'He set us up from the start,' he said, his tone harsh and uncompromising. 'He's been working alongside one of the most brutal dictators in the world and he's about to install another one in his place. He's inflicted misery on millions – all just to make his company a bit richer. He's scum.'

'He's still my brother. He's the only family I have,' she sobbed.

Rain and tears were washing across her face.

'He's a bloody criminal.'

She took a step closer, holding out her hand a few inches. 'If you love me, Steve, don't do it,' she pleaded.

Steve held himself steady. If he shot Archie, it would be all over with Sam. He could see that clearly. He weighed the verdict in his mind.

The bastard deserves to die.

But I don't want to lose her.

He started to put the gun down. And as he looked into her eyes, and saw the relief flooding through her, he knew he had made the right decision.

Ollie picked up the gun Newton had dropped: the chamber of his own Enfield was empty. It was nothing like as sophisticated as the Sphinx. A Chinese-made Type 77 pistol, in clean black, it was among the cheapest handguns in the world, but it would do the job effectively enough. Unnoticed by the others, he stepped forward, pace after pace, and grabbed Archie roughly by the hair. A single image was playing through his mind: Chris's baby son, sitting on his lap back on the farm in South Africa, and the look of pride on the big man's face as he cradled his boy in his arms.

'There's a kid who's never going to know who his dad was because of you,' he said hoarsely. 'And that's a fucking shame, because he was a bloody good bloke, and he was a mate of mine.'

'No!' shouted Archie.

'And now it's you who's knocking on heaven's door.'

Ollie squeezed the trigger – once, then twice.

The first bullet blew a hole in the side of Archie's head, and the second split open half his brain and emptied it onto the side of the pier. The man jerked violently in one last spasm of life, then slumped forward onto the decking.

Grim-faced, Ollie tucked the pistol back into his belt and stepped back onto dry land.

Sam started to walk towards the boat. She stepped right past Steve, not even looking at him, and there was not a trace of fear on her face. Carefully, she untethered its mooring, and stood behind the wheel.

'Sam!' cried Steve. 'What are you doing?'

'I'm going home,' she said simply. She fired up the engine.

'Sam!' shouted Steve again.

'Just leave me alone.'

The engine kicked into life, and she started to steer the boat into the rough, stormy waters that would take her back to Batota.

Steve was about to speak. But his voice died on the wind swirling in across the water.

Ian had already put his hand on his shoulder 'Leave it, mate,' he said. 'We're out of here.'

Epilogue

SANDRA THOMAS BUSTLED BETWEEN THEM like a mother hen who'd been turbo-charged. Nick's mum was a fine-looking woman, there was no question about that, reflected Steve. Nick's dad, whoever he was, must have been uglier than a rusty JCB, since you certainly couldn't blame Sandra for the way her son looked. She had platinum-blond hair, long and silky, and so natural and fresh, you might almost believe it hadn't come from a bottle. She was small, no more than five feet two, but with a slender figure, sharp green eyes that had an easygoing warmth to them, and full, ruby-red lips that had no doubt been breaking men's hearts, or at least their wallets, since she'd first learned to pout.

'I've got one special dance lined up for you, Steve, and one of our VIP dances for you, Ollie,' she said, casually flicking away a lock of blond hair from her perfectly tanned and sculpted breasts. 'Nick's told me so much about you boys. I'm really pleased to finally have the chance to meet you.'

She cast a knowing look at Ollie. 'We might even line up one of the stag-night specials,' she said, and chuckled earthily. 'Not many marriages survive one of those.'

'Bloody hell,' spluttered Ollie. 'If I'd known the stag night was going to be this much fun, I might have given into Katie a bit earlier.'

'Leave it, Mum,' snapped Nick.

Sandra ruffled his hair. 'Now, now, lovely boy, don't speak like that in front of our guests.'

Steve took another swig on his beer. They'd opened a bottle of champagne, but the Sensations lapdancing club where Sandra worked was more of a beer hall than a champagne bar, and all the better for it. It was classier than Steve had expected. Close to the castle in the centre of Cardiff, it occupied the whole of a large basement underneath a row of shops. There were twenty alcoves in black leather, a long, brightly lit cocktail bar, and two separate poles with non-stop dances. If there was a better place for a stag night, Steve couldn't think of it right now.

From Ramsey, they'd picked up a flight to Johannesburg, then caught a connection to London from there. Nick's leg had been patched up at the medical centre at the South African airport. Now, a week later, he was walking fine again, and although he was still bandaged, the wound should have fully healed in a few more weeks. It was Friday night, five days after they'd all arrived back at Heathrow, completely exhausted after the mission they had been through. Bruce Dudley had met them at the airport, and congratulated them on a job well done. Since President Kapembwa had died, and Archie Sharratt had mysteriously disappeared, the money he'd placed in the escrow account for them in Malta had been released and $500,000 had been transferred to each of the Dubai accounts he'd already established for each man. The wedding was planned for lunchtime tomorrow, at Katie's parents' village in Dorset. A taxi had been booked for three in the morning, to take Steve and Ollie down to the B&B where they would crash for the night.

Whether Bruce had known that Archie was planning to double-cross them from the start, Steve had no way of knowing. He denied it – but there was one thing Steve knew for certain. He wasn't working for Bruce again. And he wasn't going on any more missions. This time, he was out of the game for good.

'More drinks,' yelled Maksim. 'More vodka, and more dancers.'

There were twenty girls working in the club tonight. Brunettes, blondes, even one slinky redhead. They were all lookers. Steve hadn't seen so many naked women since . . . well, since the last time he'd had a few beers at a lapdancing club. A brunette called Ariel had writhed all over him and, if she didn't genuinely fancy him, then she was a fine actress – which, now Steve came to think about it, she probably was, since the fat car dealer a few booths away was getting exactly the same treatment.

Sandra had sent over a blonde called Alycia, and the woman had a body that would make the whole of Girls Aloud feel they'd been shortchanged in the looks department. But it made no difference to Steve's mood. The rest of the boys were well into the swing of the evening, knocking back beer after beer, and flirting with the girls. They'd all had a couple of dances already, except for Nick: by some strange twist of lapdancing morality, which Steve couldn't quite figure out, Sandra wouldn't allow Nick to get a dance from any of the girls. But, as much as the rest of the boys were enjoying themselves, tonight Steve was finding the 'no touching' rule a lot easier to stick to than he usually did.

It doesn't matter how stunning the girls are, Steve reflected. If they aren't Sam, I can't get interested.

Sandra and a girl called Romaine dragged Ollie away to the VIP room for what they called their 'stag-night special'. When he re-emerged, ten minutes later, he looked ruffled and bemused.

'Bloody hell, Nick, I wish that was my mum,' said Ian, sitting Ollie back on his chair, and breaking open a fresh bottle of beer to put in his hand. 'I don't know what they did to him in there, but this man needs medical attention. Any chance of a swap?'

'What's your mum like then?' said Nick.

Ian chuckled. 'Nothing like this, I can tell you that much.'

While Ollie had been away, Bruce Dudley had rolled up into the club. He'd pulled a wad of fifties from his pocket, paid for another few rounds of drinks, and told everyone to have another dance. 'It's on Death Inc., boys,' he'd announced with a broad grin. Maksim had disappeared with two girls from Swansea, insisting that since Nick wasn't getting any dances, he should have both. Dan had declared his undying love for a brunette from Newport, telling her again and again that since he was from New South Wales, they were practically made for each other. From the look on her face, Steve reckoned she'd heard that line before, and it didn't get any more impressive for being repeated. Ian was being entertained by a blonde from Barry, whilst Ganju was deep in conversation with a half-Chinese girl from Bristol, and David was trying to explain about the twins to the redhead.

As Ollie returned, Bruce ordered a bottle of vintage single malt whisky from the barman, and raised his glass. 'I've got two toasts to make,' he said.

He looked at each man in turn. 'To Chris,' he said, his tone solemn. 'He was a bloody good soldier. And a good man as well.'

Chris, thought Steve to himself. Poor sod. I left behind a mate and a woman in Batota, and that's not something I'd planned on. I'm not getting the mate back. Nor the woman either, I reckon.

Knocking back the whisky in a single gulp, he let it scour the back of his throat, but no matter how strong the liquor, it wasn't going to clean away any of the regrets. 'To Jeff as well,' he said.

'Aye, to Jeff,' said Bruce, raising his glass a second time. He grabbed hold of the bottle and refilled each glass. 'And to a job well done,' he said. 'You gave a bad bastard a malleting, and nobody can ever take that away from you. Now, if anyone is interested, there's a job in Cuba. The old dictator is about to die, and some gentlemen I know want a few things sorted out before the whole place falls apart.'

'Cuba?' Ollie knocked back the rest of the Scotch, and refilled both his and Maksim's glasses. 'Sounds like a riot.'

'Jesus, mate, you never give up, do you?' said Steve. 'You're getting married in the morning. If Katie doesn't mean enough to you to stop risking your bloody neck, then what the sodding hell are you doing.'

There was a silence around the booths, punctured only by the opening chords of 'Walk This Way' that greeted Alycia striding up to the main pole in a pair of thigh-high leather boots.

'You're right,' said Ollie flatly. 'I'm not going.'

'To Cuba? Good.'

'To the wedding.'

'You can't be serious?'

Ollie looked straight at Steve. 'You're going to drive down there and you're going to tell her the wedding's cancelled. It's true. If we really loved each other, I wouldn't keep running away.'

'You're drunk.'

Ollie chuckled, holding up the empty shot glass. 'I've seen the bottom of too many glasses, I'll admit that much. But I've never seen anything this clearly.'

'You can't do that to the woman . . . she's stood by you.'

Ollie poured a fresh glass of whisky. 'OK – I'll play a round of poker for it. I win, the wedding's cancelled, and the pair of us are off to Cuba. You win, I'll get in the cab, and you can walk me down the aisle.'

'That's the stupidest sodding thing I've ever heard.'

'What's the matter, Steve – you scared?'

Steve remained silent.

There was a drunken taunt to Ollie's voice when he said to the others, 'Looks like Stevie boy here is scared of a pack of cards.'

The blonde on Maksim's lap laughed, then slapped the Russian's hand away from her left breast.

'I'm—' started Steve.

But Bruce had already slammed a pack of playing cards down on the table. 'Deal,' he said curtly.

'It's—'

'There are worse ways for a man to make a decision, Steve,' Bruce said patiently. 'Now deal!'

'Five-card stud, one hand,' said Ollie. There was a manic grin on his face. Behind them came some wild cheering from the group of car dealers as a local black girl called Pearl approached the second pole, miming to Shirley Bassey's 'Goldfinger'.

Steve looked down at the cards.

Five of them were spread out in a fan.

He picked them up.

'Christ,' he muttered under his breath.

Two eights.

It's always two sodding eights.

'What have you got?' he asked, glancing up at Ollie.

'Two Jacks.'

Steve shook his head. Then he looked across at Bruce. 'You'd better book the flights to Havana,' he said. 'I don't even want to be on the same continent when Katie finds out about this. And may God have mercy on all our souls.'

Appendix:
The Weapons

The weapons described in this book are all in common use by military forces around the world.

AK-47: The AK-47 is probably the most famous weapon in the world. It was designed by Mikhail Kalashnikov, who fought in a tank division in the Soviet Army in the Second World War. Whilst wounded in hospital, he started playing around with designs for a new assault rifle. It needed to be simple to maintain and simple to fire: Red Army troops had very little training. The result was the Avtomat Kalashnikova of 1947, better known as the AK-47. Its standardised 7.62mm cartridges can hit targets at up to 200 to 300 metres. It was easy to maintain, carried on operating even when it was covered in grease and mud, and was always very cheap to manufacture. The Soviets licensed the technology to the Chinese – Kalashnikovs were used by the Vietcong in Vietnam – and throughout Eastern Europe. The result: there are now an estimated 100 million AK-47s in circulation around the world. There have been better assault rifles built since then, but mercenaries still favour the AK-47 because it is practical, rugged, and so common that you can always find fresh supplies of ammunition. The only fault ever identified with an AK-47 is that its safety-catch is on the right-hand side of the weapon, making it tricky to release it and fire at the same time.

AK 630 Naval Cannon: The AK 360 is a fully automatic, six-barrelled 30mm cannon first designed in the early 1960s for the Russian Navy. It was mainly designed for use against other ships, but can be used just as effectively against aircraft and helicopters, against coastal targets, and against floating mines. It can be controlled by radar, or manually, and has an effective range of 4,000 metres. It has a 2,000 round magazine which, combined with its six barrels, allows it to unleash an awesome barrage of fire.

Alouette III helicopter: The Alouette III was one of the most successful military helicopters ever built. A successor to the Alouette II, it was both larger and was specifically designed to operate at high-altitude. The key to its capabilities was the work of the engineer Joseph Szydlowski, who was born in Russia, but moved first to Germany, and then to France to escape the Nazis. He founded the helicopter engine company Turbomeca, and developed the first small gas-turbine engines for use on helicopters, replacing the far heavier piston engines then in use. The gas-turbine engine allowed the Alouette to operate at far higher altitudes than the machines it replaced. The Alouette III first flew in 1959 and was manufactured by Sud Aviation, later by Aerospatiale. It was an instant hit. In 1960, it took off successfully from Mount Blanc at an altitude of more than 15,000 feet – an unprecedented feat for a helicopter at the time. Over the next two decades, more than 2,000 would be built and sold to countries around the world, including Australia, Iraq and South Africa. An Alouette could carry a pilot plus six men, and could be fitted with a machine gun. It had a maximum speed of 124 mph, and a cruising speed of 113 mph.

Enfield .38 Revolvers: These days, the Enfield .38 looks like a museum piece, but in its day it was one of the most effective handguns in the world. After the First World War, the British Government decided it needed a smaller, lighter revolver than the side arms that had been used during the 1914-18 conflict. Conscription armies with troops that had often been rushed into service needed weapons that were far easier to use than those given to the professional, long-service colonial armies of the pre-First World War era. The result was the Enfield .38, named after the Royal Small Arms Factory in the North London suburb of Enfield. A double action revolver, it had a range of 200 yards, but an effective range of only 15 yards. It was designed for close quarters combat and trench clearing – tasks at which it excelled. Between 1932 and 1957, 270,000 Enfields were produced, both for the British Army and for colonial armies around the British Empire.

FN-FAL Assault rifles: The Fusil Automatique Léger was designed and manufactured by the Belgian arms company Fabrique National – hence the name FN-FAL – and quickly became one of the most widely used assault rifles in the world. It was designed by Dieudonné Saive and Ernest Vervier, and has since been described as the classic battle rifle of the Cold War era. It was so widely adopted by NATO countries that it became known as 'the right-arm of the Free World', and, if the Cold War had ever turned hot, it would have been a contest between the AK-47 and the FN-FAL. It is a light weapon, weighing only slightly over four kilogrammes, and its barrel is just twenty-one inches. Its magazine varies from five to thirty rounds, but in standard configurations contains twenty bullets. It fires a 7.62 NATO standard round. It has light recoil, making it simple to operate, even by troops who have received very little firearms training. Like the AK-47, it was designed for use by mass conscription armies, and that meant it had to be practical, easy to maintain, and simple to use.

Holland & Holland .375 Magnum: The British manufacturer Holland & Holland is the world's most respected designer of big-game hunting rifles. The firm was started by a tobacco wholesaler called Harris Holland, who was also an accomplished sportsman. After starting his own gun manufacturer, he opened a factory in Birmingham, then moved it to London. Holland & Holland still has a factory near Paddington today. Its speciality has always been big-game rifles, of which the .375 Magnum is the most famous. The principle of game rifles is very simple. You need a much larger bullet to bring down a rhino or an elephant than you do to stop a man, and the H&H delivers a far harder punch than any conventional weapon. The .375 was introduced in 1912, during the golden age of African big-game hunting, and was specifically designed to bring down the big beasts of the jungle. Even a century later, the basic design is considered unimproved among hunters, and the H&H is still the Rolls-Royce of the big-game weapons industry.

HPEMS: The high-power electromagnetic system, or HPEMS, is a device that uses microwave energy to disable or damage a vehicle's electronic microprocessors which control the engine. It takes advantage of the fact that most vehicles built in the last ten years have so much electronics on board that they can be disabled simply by taking out the computer chips. The device takes a high-voltage electrical current – more than 600 volts – and converts it into a microwave pulse using an oscillator. In turn, that will disable any vehicle within a radius of up to fifty metres. The device has mainly been developed by police force for use in car chases, but the military applications are just starting to be explored.

KPV Machine Gun: The Krupnokaliberniy Pulemyot Vladimorova, or KPV, is a heavy-duty Soviet-designed machine gun, which first entered service in 1949. It was designed by Semjon Vladimirow primarily as an anti-tank weapon for the Soviet infantry and remains to this day one of the biggest, most powerful machine guns ever built. It fires 14.5mm rounds, the world's largest non-explosive munitions. A KPV round can pass through just about any obstacle it encounters. The KPV was widely used by the Soviet Army in Afghanistan, and later sold around the world. Many of them were shipped to Saddam Hussein's Iraqi Army, which is how they later ended up being used by insurgents in Iraq to attack American armoured vehicles – with devastating effect.

The L118 or 'Light Gun': First produced for the British Army in the early 1970s, the L118 or 'Light Gun' has become one of the most widely used field artillery weapons in the world. A howitzer weapon, it can be towed easily by a Land Rover and is light enough to be dropped into position by a medium-sized helicopter such as a Puma or a Westland Sea King. It can even be dropped by parachute. The L118 can fire between six and eight rounds a minute at a distance of up to 17,000 metres. After coming into service in 1976, the 'Light Gun' proved itself during the Falklands War. During the final battle for Port Stanley, five batteries of L118s, a total of 30 guns, hammered the town into submission. It has since been used in the Balkans, Iraq and Afghanistan, and has been sold to armies around the world. An adaptation of the L118, called the M119 A1 Howitzer, is used by the US Army.

M-40 Sniper Rifle: The M-40 is a bolt-action sniper rifle originally designed for the US Marines. It is based on the Model 700 hunting rifle made by Remington Arms but heavily modified by the Marines' own specialists. It fires a NATO-standard 7.62 round, while its 61-centimetre barrel gives the shot the stability and accuracy that a sniper rifle needs. It has an effective range of 1,000 metres. There are longer-range rifles available which pack a heavier punch, but they are inevitably more complex, and a kilometre is enough range for most military situations.

MAG Machine Gun: The MAG 7.52mm general purpose machine gun was manufactured by the Belgian arms company Fabrique Nationale (usually known as FN). Its name is a shortening of *Mitrailleuse d'Appui Général* (general purpose machine gun), and it was first designed in the 1950s. It uses a standard 7.62mm NATO cartridge, and can fire between 650 and 1,000 rounds a minute, over a range of 200 to 1,000 metres. It was designed as a universal machine gun that could be used in any military situation: a MAG is just as effective equipped to a helicopter or a boat as it is manned by a gun crew on a battlefield. Its versatility and reliability is demonstrated by the fact that it is used by armies in Belgium, Britain, Canada, Australia and the US.

Mi-24 helicopter gunship: The Mi-24 is a large helicopter gunship manufactured by the Mil Moscow Helicopter Plant. It was first put into service in 1972, and has been sold to more than thirty countries. Soviet pilots immediately called it the 'flying tank', and that was an accurate description of its ferocious firepower. It has a big 17.3 m five-blade main rotor, and a three-blade tail rotor but, unlike traditional helicopters, the gunship also has two short, stubby wings, both to give it additional lift and also to mount rockets on to. It was most extensively used by the Soviet Army during the war in Afghanistan, where its ability to put heavy fire into ground positions, plus to drop infantry troops into battle, made it a versatile and effective weapon. But it also proved its vulnerability. Despite its heavy armour, the Mi-24 was vulnerable to surface-to-air missiles supplied to the Afghan fighters by the CIA.

P4 Explosive: A variant of the mostly commonly used plastic explosive, C4, P4 is used both by armies and terrorist groups around the world. Like every plastic explosive, it takes a mix of chemicals then binds them together in a plastic slurry to make a substance that is light, and can be easily turned into any shape required, and yet will still carry an explosive force capable of inflicting widespread devastation. For mercenaries, one advantage of P4 is that it is widely used by mining companies, meaning there is usually plenty of the stuff available even when you don't have access to any traditional military suppliers.

Raven-25: In 1968, the US Government passed a law restricting the import of cheap handguns into the country. In response, George Jennings, who ran a small factory in California making parts for the aerospace industry, designed a small, dirt-cheap handgun and started a company called Raven Arms to manufacture it. The Raven 25 was no bigger than the palm of your hand, and came in either a black or chrome finish, with a wood or mother-of-pearl handle. Its chamber held six .25 calibre rounds. With a retail price of just $60, the Raven was so small and cheap, it became known as the 'Saturday Night Special': these guns were regularly used in bar-room brawls. The weapon acquired a notorious reputation in the US, and was fiercely attacked by the gun-control lobby, which saw it as a contributor to rampant gun violence. Production was stopped in 1991. However, there were still millions of Raven 25s in circulation around the world and, among professionals, it still has a following. If you need a weapon you can hide easily, and which will work reliably, there are few better choices, and although it doesn't pack much punch, it has more than enough stopping power for close-quarters combat.

Thunder-flash stun grenades: When the SAS set up its counter-terrorism unit in response to the IRA in the early 1970s, it asked the Royal Ordnance researchers in Enfield to come up with a weapon that would confuse the enemy. The result was the G60, otherwise known as the 'flash-bang'. It mixed mercury and magnesium to produce a blinding flash – the equivalent of 300,000 candlepower – as well as a deafening noise. The idea was that the enemy would be confused and disorientated, allowing the SAS men wearing protective gear to gain the upper hand. The G60 was first used when the Regiment helped German Special Forces overpower terrorists holding an aircraft in Mogadishu in 1977, but was mostly famously used in the storming of the Iranian Embassy in London in 1980. Since then, variants of stun grenades have been developed by Special Forces and police units around the world, growing in technical sophistication all the time.

TWS Gun: TWS or 'Through the Wall Surveillance' is one of the hottest areas of military technology. A wall is one of the oldest forms of military defence: it is hard to shoot through it, and impossible to see your target through it. That's where TWS, or STW for 'Shoot Through Wall', technologies come in. The US Defence Department has developed Radar Scope devices that use miniature radars to look through walls up to twelve-feet thick, and create a computer image of the room to be fitted to the scope of a rifle. Combined with a concrete-piercing bullet, it gives an experienced marksman the ability to hit a target through the wall. The image isn't perfect: it looks something like the scan taken of a baby during pregnancy. But it is good enough to get an accurate shot away. Soldiers using TWS technologies are trained to recognise different gun types on the imaging software, since it is regularly used on hostage rescue missions, where the greatest risk is that you will shoot one of the hostages rather than their captors. Existing TWS technology works best with brick or concrete walls, and can be blocked by solid metal walls or by foil-backed insulation. In response, magnetic sensors are being developed to look through metal walls.

Uzi Machine Pistol: Uziel Gal, who gave his name to the machine pistol he designed, was born in Weimar Germany. After the Nazis came to power, he moved first to Britain, then, in 1936, to what would later become Israel, where he was briefly imprisoned by the British for carrying a gun. In 1946, shortly after the Israeli War of

Independence, he started to design the weapon that was soon to be adopted by the new Israeli Army. He was creating a machine pistol, sometimes known as a sub-machine gun, a category of weapon that combined the rapid rate of fire of a machine gun with the compactness and flexibility of a pistol. Made from stamped sheet metal, the Uzi was cheap to manufacture and simple to maintain, making it a natural choice for the newly-created and cash-strapped Israeli Defence Force. The Uzi was capable of firing up to 600 rounds a minute, and its sophisticated safety catch meant it rarely went off accidentally (a common and lethal problem with machine pistols). It was to prove itself deadly in close-quarters combat, and became the weapon of choice for Israel's elite light infantry assault troops. It acquired its reputation clearing out Syrian and Jordanian bunkers during the Six Day War of 1967. Over the next three decades, the Uzi was to prove a mainstay of the Israeli economy as well as its army. The weapon was sold to more than 90 countries around the word, including the German Army, and Rhodesian Army, and netted more than $2 billion in export sales. The Uzi was used by the US Secret Service men deployed to protect the President: if you look at pictures of the shooting of Ronald Reagan in 1981, you'll see Secret Service men pulling out their Uzis in the background.